Praises for S.C. Eston's other novels

"If you love the fantasy genre, revel in stories of mystic deeds and enjoy the verbal sparring of well-crafted characters, you will like reading The Conclave..."
Jane Tims, Author
on *The Conclave*

"Great characters, terrific writing. This novel keeps you up until you're finished."
Allan Hudson, Author
on *The Conclave*

"It's a captivating story of a life's journey that transfers the characters emotion right to the reader."
Rosario Martinez-Rosales, Freelance Writer
on *The Burden of the Protector*

"More than an adventure story, an existential philosophy... This book is well worth reading at any one of the multiple levels that are presented by the author. It will disturb you and it will make you think."
Roger Moore, Poet
on *The Burden of the Protector*

"... I consider Eston a great teller of tales, indeed."
Glen Christie, Glam Adelaide

Also by S.C. Eston

Novellas
+
THE CONCLAVE
THE BURDEN OF THE PROTECTOR

Short Stories
(available on www.SCEston.ca)
+
EMPTINESS
FOG
A FRIEND
LAKE
LOGBOX
THE MATRIARCH'S REMEDY
ZANATHU

Deficiency

S.C. Eston

Thank you for reading my story.

- Steve

This is a work of fiction. All the characters, organizations, and events portrayed in this novel are either products
of the author's imagination or are used fictitiously.

DEFICIENCY

Copyright © 2020 S.C. Eston
All rights reserved.
ISBN: 978-1-7771789-3-2
v1.17.2

Edited by Amanda Sumner
(www.engagededitor.com/)
and
Forrest Orser
(www.thodestool.com)

Cover by James T. Egan
(www.bookflydesign.com/)

Inside map and illustrations by Kirk Shannon
(www.kirkshannon.com)

Dedication

*To the greatest person I know:
my wife and life companion,*

Leigh

Thank you

*This book would not be here
if it was not for you.*

Content

Characters 1
Map of Prominence City 3
Induction 7
Segment A 9
  . Missing Imagram 11
  . . Meeting Call 19
  Code 00.000.0001 27
  . . . Transit 28
  . . . . Profile Failure 35
Segment B 43
  - Management 45
  - . Wave 1 and Wave 2 53
  Code 00.000.0012 60
  Code Output 00.000.0012 61
  - . . Laboratory 62
  - . . . Traitor 71
  - . . . . Gone 79
Segment C 89
  - - Rift 91
  - - . In the Cafe 98
  - - . . Back to the Workshop 104
  Code 00.000.0044 111
  Code Output 00.000.0044 113
  - - . . . Fugue 115
  - - . . . . Lodges 121
  - - - Emergency Link 130
  - - - . At the Gate 137
  Mission 001201 146
Segment D 149
  - - - . . The Reporter 151
  - - - . . . Torture 159
  - - - . . . . Authentic Banner 168

- - - - I Bot Shop 173
Mission 001202 A 184
- - - - . Passageways 188
Mission 001202 B 193
- - - - . . Breach 198
Code 00.002.0065 213
- - - - . . . Underground 215
- - - - . . . . Disoriented 227
I Hideout Plaza 244
I . Friends 254
I . . Connections 265
I . . . Help 276
I . . . . In The Dark 289
I - To the Pillar 298
I - . Virtual 303
I - . . Renunciation 307
I - . . . Insurgence 317
I - . . . . To the Pillar 323
I - - Caged 331

Segment E 337

I - - . Deficiency 339
I - - . . Virus 354
Code 01.003.0083 364
I - - . . . Distribution 366
I - - . . . . The Low Lands 376

Epilogue 385

. Retrieval 387
. . Lift 391
. . . Goodbyes 395
. . . . Report 399
Mission 000000 404
- Ascension 407
- . Artificial Life 409
- . . Signal 412

Appendices and Glossaries 419

Acknowledgements 429

Characters

Detel Scherzel, biologist and researcher at Thrium Laboratories.
Keidi Rysinger, master pad technician. Detel's best friend.
Artenz Scherzel, team lead and coder for BlueTech Data. Detel's younger brother. Keidi's husband.
Marti "Red Dragon" Zehron, coder for BlueTech Data and Artenz's friend.
Zofia Rikili, biologist at Thrium Laboratories.

Drayfus Arlsberg, manager at BlueTech Data and Artenz's supervisor.
Irek Elson, Drayfus's assistant.
Mysa Lamond, executive for Crystal Globe Conglomerate.
Okran Delaro, lead enforcer.
Irbela Zuttar, master enforcer.

The Authentic Banner
Aana Figuera, retired reporter and sleuth. Founder of the Banner.
Xavi Olton, leader of the Banner and bodyguard.
Eltaya Ark, reporter.
Ged Briell, doctor.
Styl Starner, transporter.
Kazor Deltaros, former enforcer.
Praka Orensen, transporter.

Arnol Dessol, artificer for New Design Inc. and partner of the Banner.

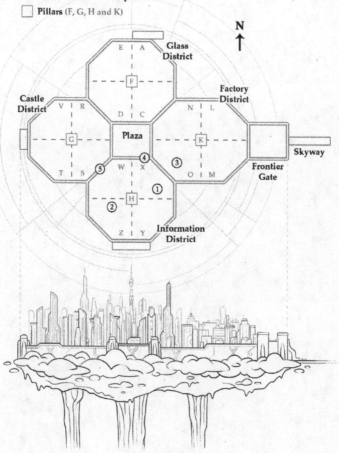

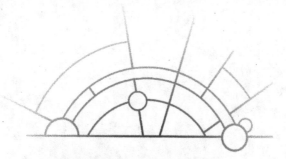

Deficiency

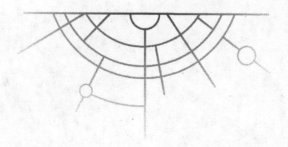

Induction

White walls and a white ceiling. Blinding white lights and a strong smell of disinfectants.

In the center of a silver table rested three small bundles.

"What's wrong with it?" the inspector asked, pointing at the second bundle.

"The eyes, they don't focus. One goes to the left, and the other—"

"I see the obvious. I asked, what's *wrong* with it?"

The three birth-engineers exchanged a brief look. One nodded and one looked away. The third swallowed and answered. "It originates from the brain."

"Explain."

A brief cry escaped the third bundle.

"Some nerve cells are damaged. Some connections are not happening."

"How's that possible? Aren't these a few days old?"

From the first bundle, small feet pushed out of the blanket and kicked twice.

"They are three weeks and a day old, but yes, they are part of the latest batch."

"Will it heal?"

"I'm afraid not."

The inspector sighed. "Disappointing."

The birth-engineers waited.

The eyes of the second bundle searched randomly and independently, but it did not otherwise move. "It seems you have little information about the deficiency."

"It is recent."

Deficiency

"But prevalent."

"Increasing, yes. This is the fourth anomaly in the last three batches."

"Then you do not know what is wrong."

The birth-engineers looked at each other. "We could speculate," one offered.

"No, you cannot, and you will not speculate. If anyone—*anyone*—asks, your answer is that *you do not know*." The inspector paused and took a step closer to the table, but never reached out. "Understood?"

The three engineers nodded.

"We do not know," they said as one.

Satisfied, the inspector turned and walked away from the table. Midway to the door, she paused but did not look back. "Get rid of it," she said and left.

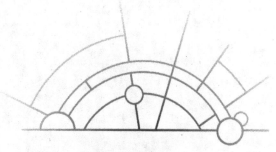

Segment A

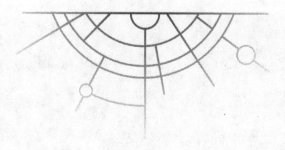

"An apprentice coder is 2 times more efficient than a novice coder."

- Marti Zehron

. Missing Imagram

Artenz first awoke in the bio-sphere. As he surfaced from the depths of sleep, words appeared in the bottom right corner of his vision:

```
Brought to you by InfoSoft Corporation, a division of CGC.
Year 3.4k60 Season 05 Day 11 Hour 0600.
Welcome to the bio-sphere, Artenz Scherzel.
```

Everything was gray, with the type being a shade darker than the surroundings. Artenz wondered if anyone noticed the printed words anymore. Probably not—not consciously, anyway.

The words disappeared and blended into the background as the profile room built itself. This early in the morning, it loaded quickly.

The floor emerged first, covered with flashing panels: products on sale, deals on services, gadgets free to try, trials of a day. Each just a touch away, accessible before anything else appeared. All in black and white; the colors would load later.

The walls filled in next, forming an elongated rectangle, a simple reproduction of the relaxing room in their lodge. A blank elliptical window appeared on one of the walls. Shelves expanded from another surface, 10 centimeters wide, stacked from floor to ceiling. On a third wall, a large screen slid down from the ceiling.

In front of Artenz, a pole popped out of the floor, with a keyboard and a monitor hanging from it. The screen was an inert black.

A low chair materialized under Artenz. He enjoyed the momentary confusion as his brain tried to reconcile the fact that until now, he had been sitting on empty air.

Imagrams appeared on the shelves, one by one: silhouettes of friends and acquaintances, some asleep and lying down, others awake and moving around their allocated cells.

The large screen presented news of Prominence City and updates from the bio-sphere. This friend did this. That friend did that. A sunny day with passing clouds. Sections of the Plaza closed for the day due to construction. Tram 336 is 15 minutes late. The number of Promients reached 45 million. The visage of Rakkah, master manipulator of the Low Lands, large and scary. The old woman had finally been caught and was on trial.

A calendar emerged on the remaining wall, completely covering its surface. A circle for each day and in each circle, reminders in different shapes and colors.

All around, hue and tint bled across everything. The walls painted themselves a metallic blue, and the ceiling turned beige.

The elliptical window opened and showed the streets of Prominence City, the same view as the one from their lodge. It annoyed Artenz. His setting indicated that the window should present a clear blue sky, no buildings or tram-rail, no streets floating over streets and no walk-way. Yet every morning, the setting was ignored, as if it had never been changed, as if the program could not keep it in memory. This was one of the many unresolved issues of the bio-sphere, which would never be able to replace the real world, no matter how much some believed it eventually would.

Finally, on the monitor in front of Artenz, an action prompt appeared.

+

Artenz sat forward and looked at the monitor.

```
Welcome to the Data-sphere.
Load time 0.007012 seconds.
Year 3.4k60 Season 05 Day 11 Hour 0600.

Action>
```

The load had been extremely fast. As Artenz had observed before, the early hour helped. He looked around and noticed that his mind had once more missed a few elements. Even with the enhancements of his b-pad, his brain had not been quick enough to follow everything.

Today, he had missed the appearance of the rug. It covered most of the floor and hid the constant flux of publicity. Artenz had written the snippet of code a few months ago. Proud of himself, he had inserted it in Keidi's profile room and shared it with Marti to do with as he pleased. The last time Artenz had visited Marti's room, it had covered all of the floor area.

Artenz typed a command on the keyboard, and the window's content transformed from the view of Prominence City into the blue sky he preferred.

That done, Artenz entered a second command, one he had entered almost daily for the past month.

His medical chart appeared, followed by Keidi's.

He inhaled deeply to fight his growing anxiety, but it did not work. In the bio-sphere, there was no need to breathe.

+

The medical charts predicted that they had between 17.50 and 20.00 percent chance of a successful natural pregnancy during any given month. Keidi's personal success percentage was at 30.00, excessively high.

Deficiency

She was 33 and Artenz was 37. Although this was not an excessive difference in age, his average was significantly lower. Between 5.00 and 10.00 percent only.

Had this information been true, their chances would have been good.

His sister had insisted on doing her own calculations. "The charts' numbers are much too simple," Detel said. "On top of being pure nonsense."

Her calculations put their success rate closer to 2.13 percent, with Keidi at 3.00 percent and Artenz at 1.25. These numbers were even harder to believe. Yet Detel insisted 2.13 was extremely positive.

"What is the general average?" he had asked.

"My latest analysis put it around 0.34, but who can really say?"

Detel attributed Artenz's low percentage to the presence of the tiny pad in his brain. The chip had been installed when he was 10 years of age, to the great displeasure of his parents.

"Pads are installed at birth," Artenz had argued with Detel.

"Exactly," she replied. "Which is why the two of you have better than average chances. No thanks to you, I have to say."

Keidi had her pad inserted when she was 22. She regretted it and seldom used it. She preferred the first model, the wrist-pad, which was an actual flat screen worn on the forearm. The second model, the palm-pad, had nested in the inside of the hand and had constantly broken. The third model was a chip on the side of the neck.

Its name was terrible, but Artenz had to admit that it was an impressive device and that he was, for lack of a better word, addicted to it.

2.13 percent.

Despite Detel's confidence, it did not seem promising.

"Better than the alternative," said Keidi.

So, by pooling her technical skills with his coding abilities—and Marti's—they had modified Keidi's brain-pad to hide her health information—not hide, not exactly. The b-pad constantly monitored health signs, so it needed to receive something. The modifications meant that Keidi's b-pad read falsified information.

If they were going to try natural birth, there was no reason to alarm the authorities.

For a year, they had monitored Keidi's health signs, storing the information and using it to create new outputs mirroring the data collected.

2.13.

It was like playing the lottery, which Artenz had never won. Almost everyone he knew had won a few credits here and there, but not him. He had not been optimistic that the natural birth could even be done. After all, they had been trying for close to two years now.

Artenz had not mentioned anything to Keidi, but in truth he'd felt relieved. He wanted a family but had not felt ready yet.

But three days ago, when he had gotten back to the lodge after his day at the office, Keidi had been sitting on the relaxing room floor with a picnic set up: red wool blanket, candles, a little feast, and the widest of smiles on her face...

+

Keidi was everything to him, and when she had proposed trying for a natural birth, Artenz had indulged her, never thinking it would work.

After all, it never did.

Or, now that he thought about it with a clear mind, it was not that natural birth never worked—it was that people never tried. The law was clear on the matter. By going this route, Keidi was declining medical assistance and support for both pregnancy and birth. On top of this, many organizations had policies of their own, stating they would not keep employees who selected natural birth. Some went as far as calling it immoral.

Deficiency

Given that Keidi was unmovable on the matter, the birth would have to be done in secret, with the help of a hired medic. Trust Detel to know someone who was willing to help in secrecy. Still, there was no doubt in Artenz's mind that if the matter became known, he would lose his job.

The law did not discourage natural birth without cause. There was another number, another percentage, that was extremely important and that scared Artenz greatly.

This number had plagued him for the past three days. The number was 67.80 percent.

Out of any 10 newborns arriving via natural birth, seven were blanks.

The terrible number was imprinted in Artenz mind, especially now that he knew that Keidi was pregnant.

A blank baby would change everything. It meant that the secret birth would turn into a secret life.

If they decided to keep the baby.

Artenz hated thinking this way, but what kind of life could a blank baby have? And what about the parents? Still, even with all his doubts about being ready for fatherhood, a part of him could not help being excited.

A baby. A little boy.

His growing excitement was overshadowed by the thought that the baby could be blank. The possibility terrified him, which was why he needed to talk to Detel. The sooner, the better. This morning, to be exact.

His sister had said once that some numbers could be altered. He needed to know if that number—the 67.80—could be changed. He wanted it to go down, way down.

+

The fake blue sky danced in the elliptical window. It felt as if Artenz had been sitting for hours. He asked the monitor for the time.

```
Year 3.4k60 Season 05 Day 11 Hour 0601.
```

The number represented the actual time in the real world. Time passed more slowly in the bio-sphere due to the processing speed of the technological environment. You could spend 10 minutes in the bio-sphere with only a single minute expiring in Prominence City. Artenz believed the disparity could potentially be changed, as it was a property of the bio-sphere. Because the disparity was deeply ingrained in the environment, major reprogramming would most likely be required to make an adjustment. That was his hypothesis on the matter.

Artenz turned toward his friends-panel. It covered a full wall, the largest of his profile room. Not his choice. He didn't even need half of the shelves available. Most were empty. The others had figurines, some transparent and dormant and others active and moving around in their cubicles.

On the center shelf was Keidi, her silhouette bundled on the floor in a cute curled-up position, sleeping.

Artenz closed his eyes while staying in the bio-sphere. He smiled as he felt the warmth of Keidi's naked body cuddled against his in their bed, the sensation transcending from reality to his artificial room. He enjoyed the intimacy for a brief moment, then reopened his eyes, staying in the bio-sphere.

He looked at the shelf to Keidi's right and was surprised to find it empty.

No imagram.

No Detel.

Quickly, Artenz looked up and down, browsing through the panel, making certain it had not been rearranged. That happened more often than it should, and certainly more often than Artenz would have liked.

Deficiency

The moderators simply chose to rearrange things now and then, maybe to force people to interact with their panel and their room. If only they would concentrate mainly on keeping an eye out for anomalies, instead of interfering. To Artenz, the whole thing was an idiosyncrasy more frustrating than anything else. He had tried to write a snippet of code to block updates to his wall. So far, all his attempts had failed, but it was only a question of time before he succeeded.

In this case, though, the order hadn't changed.

Detel's shelf was where it should be.

"Reload," Artenz said.

The walls around blurred and crashed down, leaving an open-ended gray space. Artenz closed his eyes to dodge the dizziness. Even with his eyes closed, he saw the print.

```
Brought to you by InfoSoft Corporation, a division of CGC.
Year 3.4k60 Season 05 Day 11 Hour 0602.
Welcome to the bio-sphere, Artenz Scherzel.
```

He waited another moment, keeping his eyes closed while the load completed. When he finally opened them, the room was ready.

Only, this time, Detel's shelf was not empty.

It was completely gone.

.. Meeting Call

An alarm rang. Still uncertain what had happened to his sister's imagram, Artenz turned toward the wall calendar. A bold, fat, and bright-red exclamation mark blinked crazily in today's circle. Artenz fumed at the invasion of his work into his personal life.

The message came from the managers at BlueTech Data. It always did. His employer had access to his calendar and did not hesitate to take advantage of it.

Today was the launch of the Falcon Flight Project. It was not a good time to panic and ask for a status report. Yet as usual, the managers would do exactly that.

Artenz typed a request for the time on his terminal. Some commands could be worded. Others could not. This one could, but Artenz preferred using the keyboard.

```
Year 3.4k60 Season 05 Day 11 Hour 0603.
```

Which manager was up this early, anyway?

Artenz stood, reached out, and touched the notice on the wall. It opened into a floating note. The name at the bottom was Drayfus. No surprise there. The man was infuriating. He was so reactive, so

Deficiency

impulsive. Unprepared while being controlling. One of the worst supervisors Artenz had ever had.

The note said:

```
We need a status on Falcon and a detailed action plan for
the day.
Drayfus

Location: Conference Room 98.202 Hour 0715
```

0715! Who in the world scheduled a meeting for 0715? The tram to the Blue Tower took 40 minutes!

What if Artenz ignored the invitation and showed up at 0800, the normal beginning of a working day, the time at which they had agreed he would start his day? The launch of the project was scheduled for 0900. A project team meeting was in place for 0815. Everything was in motion, in logical order, steps that should be followed—steps that Drayfus risked interrupting.

The thought of his supervisor going into a frenzy because Artenz was late was satisfying, but it would not happen. Not today. Artenz did not have it in him to be that insubordinate. On top of that, he liked his team and would not let them down.

Artenz closed his eyes and withdrew from the bio-sphere.

+

The first thing Artenz noticed as he awoke in his real bed was that he was terribly tired. His body was heavy, and his eyes didn't want to open. An annoying sound was also ringing.

"What is that?" asked Keidi, lying beside him. She flipped her pillow over her head.

Keidi's pained question awoke him further. The alarm was coming from his b-pad. He found it on the left side of his neck and pushed a button. The meeting invitation that had appeared on the wall of his profile room now floated in front of his eyes, on his eye-veil.

```
We need a status on Falcon and a detailed action plan for
the day.
Drayfus

Location: Conference Room 98.202 Hour 0715
```

"A meeting call," said Artenz.

He ordered the message to be hidden.

"This early?" Keidi asked, her voice muffled by the pillow.

"Yes, this early." Artenz looked for Keidi's face but couldn't find it. He settled for a kiss on her forearm, which was holding the pillow tight. "Try to get some more sleep," he said.

She sighed loudly, as he had known she would. It made him smile.

Their morning alarm had started illuminating the walls. Forest noises would follow, including a flowing river and chirping birds. Then the plate covering the small window of their room would open. Artenz rarely got to rest through the full experience.

He slipped out of bed and tucked the covers around Keidi before ordering his b-pad to turn on the shower.

"Isn't this your big day?" asked Keidi, still muffled by the pillow. "The Falcon leaving the nest or something?"

"It is," said Artenz, now getting his clothes ready. "Falcon Flight," he corrected.

"Weird name," muttered Keidi. "I've never seen a falcon."

Neither had Artenz. Keidi's comment made him smile nonetheless. He kissed her arm again.

"Get some sleep," he repeated. "Shower time for me."

He stopped just as he was about to enter the next room.

"Actually," he said, "when you get up, can you check for Detel? Her profile was gone from my wall. Can you check yours?"

He saw her hand turn his way and give him a thumbs-up.

Deficiency

+

Thanks to Artenz's oh-so-thoughtful supervisor, there was no going back to sleep now.

Again!

Keidi pushed the pillow aside and sat up. She could have slept longer, but admitted that it had been a restful night. She remembered getting in bed and being awoken by the alarm of Artenz's b-pad. Nothing in between.

A good feeling. She had needed the rest.

She heard the shower, and the walls around were half aglow. Artenz had set the alarm for 0615, so she estimated the time at 0610.

With her left hand, she activated her b-pad. Since they had falsified her health signs, the chip in her neck had felt out of place. It took a few moments before the brain-pad booted. Keidi looked at the ornate vid-disk on her night table. On its round, flat surface, she saw the familiar infinite spiral of Telecore Enterprises rotating slowly, showing that her pad was starting.

Sometimes, Keidi wondered why she was so hard-headed. She did not have an eye-veil, which would be easier than relying on a portable mini-vid or the vid-disk on her night table. Even without the veil, the b-pad could show small icons, as well as the time, in the bottom corner of her left eye. If she wanted it to... which she did not.

Actually, what she really wanted was to have no b-pad at all. She was not certain how that would work, but it would make it easier for her to hide her pregnancy.

She sighed. Too late for that.

On the vid-disk, Telecore's spiral faded and was replaced by the time: 0608. Keidi put her head back, closed her eyes, and relaxed.

"Join," she said.

As the b-pad pulled her brain in, the smiley face representing the bio-sphere appeared. She ordered yes and was sucked in.

Her profile room appeared, from left to right, completely round. Keidi ignored the marketing stunts on the floor and waited. Artenz's rug would appear shortly and cover the gibberish.

Keidi had to admit she liked her room. Unlike Artenz, whose employer demanded he use a predefined room template, she had a customized room. She had it located on the top of a high hill, surrounded by rows of mountains, all of which were visible through transparent walls. Her friends-panel, also transparent, was located directly in the middle of the small space. Her terminal was on the side. She had three chairs for visitors and a hammock, where she now appeared. Her screen floated in midair.

She stood and walked to her friends-panel and touched it. It became opaque. She looked quickly to the spot where Detel's imagram usually was.

It was not there.

She scanned the shelves but didn't find Detel. This was not necessarily unusual. Each person's profile information originated from the data-sphere, not the bio-sphere. Sometimes, the connection between the two failed, with strange results.

Keidi grabbed a chair and set it in front of her terminal and floating monitor.

```
Welcome to the Data-sphere.
Load time 0.099914 seconds.
Year 3.4k60 Season 05 Day 11 Hour 0611.

Action>
```

The terminal allowed direct access to the data-sphere. Keidi typed a search.

```
Action> Search Detel Scherzel, sister of Artenz
```

She could have used Detel's name alone, but the extra details helped get the result faster. Usually.

```
Searching . . .
```

As the request was executed, periods appeared one at a time, as if to show that the computer was working hard. Keidi knew better. She counted the dots as they popped up.

One, two, three.

The dots kept appearing.

Six.

Eight.

Eleven.

The delay was surprising.

Finally, a single result appeared: a profile card with a static imagraph of Detel's stern face on the left and her information on the right. The face mirrored Artenz's. The eyes were the most striking feature. They both had deep-brown eyes, shining with intelligence and a touch of mischief.

Keidi noticed that the imagraph was new. Great! Detel was not one to update her profile, room, or card. Keidi had been on her case for a while. Maybe this was a sign that Detel was ready to socialize.

Satisfied that everything was in order, Keidi withdrew.

+

"It's unnecessary pressure," Artenz was saying, "as if he's deliberately sowing stress."

He stood at the door of their lodge, almost out. Keidi picked a few snacks and packed them in his backpack. She sidestepped as the maid-bot made its way back toward its wall hole beside the entrance, done with the morning cleaning.

"0715, really?" Artenz continued. "Like, you know, really? They could not have waited a bit? Scheduled the meeting in the normal working hours that the rest of us—you know, all of us—live by... Or maybe join us at 0815. Which, although logical, is a bad idea, now that I think about it. Having the managers at the preparation meeting would make everything worse. One of the basic laws of business: you don't put management and operations at the same table, not on a launch day. Very bad idea."

Keidi passed the backpack onto Artenz's shoulder and adjusted the collar of his overcoat and shirt.

"I went over all of this with Drayfus just yesterday," Artenz continued without missing a beat, "and two days before that! He has the deployment plan. He has like 10 copies of it. And nothing has changed since—well, since like three weeks ago. It's a good plan. There's no need to change it."

Keidi looked at the vid-disk, which she could see through the opening to their bedroom. It showed 0622. She kissed Artenz on the lips, stopping his words.

"I love you," she said.

He smiled, out of breath. How charming he was.

"I'm sorry," he said. "It's just—"

"It'll be over today." Keidi pushed Artenz out the door.

"Over until the next project," he said.

"Go," she said. "You'll be late."

"I love you." He smiled sheepishly. "Sorry again for the tantrum."

He stepped out, and the door slid. At the last minute, his foot stopped it from closing, and Artenz's face reappeared in the narrow opening.

"You checked for Detel?" he asked.

Deficiency

Keidi had hoped he would mention something else.

"Yes, yes," she assured him. "Well, she was not on my wall, but I found her in Data. Probably a glitch with the Bio again. Did you know she updated her imagraph?"

"Did she?" said Artenz. "I wonder what happened there. I'll have to ask her."

He kissed his index finger and sent it toward her. Then he stepped away and let the door close. Keidi turned away, walked to their bedroom, and sat on the bed.

Again, there had been no mention of the baby.

Code 00.000.0001

```
// Program Information
// Version: 00.000.0001
// Program Name: secret
// Coder Name: secret
// Date Created: Year 3.4k60 Season 05 Day 11 Hour 1808
// Date Updated: Year 3.4k60 Season 05 Day 11 Hour 1808

function main ()
[
  // Here we go!
]
```

... Transit

The lights in the hallway barely illuminated the posters on the wall. A few of the room numbers above the doors flickered on and off. The hallway was narrow, and Artenz could touch both walls at once.

He reached the air-tube. The plastic number 32 above the sliding doors was cracked. Artenz's destination was already programmed in his b-pad, so he simply waited.

It took a moment before the doors slid open. Artenz stepped in and let himself fall to the 15th floor. It was a short fall, and the brief rush always helped him get ready for his day, clearing his mind, refocusing it. Falls were so much better than climbs. And air-tubes were so much better than air-saucers. One individual at a time, no stop, no platform to step on, direct transportation to the desired level.

Artenz's fall came to an abrupt end. The air-tube was old and not as smooth as the newer models. Artenz stepped out, his thoughts focusing on his project, the upcoming meeting, and the launch of the day.

The project's scope was small but its complexity high. His team was developing a better algorithm to transmit information through the data-sphere so it would be available in more places, faster. It was all about marketing, and changing the billboards throughout the city depended on a series of complex criteria, including the surrounding crowds.

Artenz knew the advancements made during the project could and should be used in other fields, such as improving communications with other cities as well as with space explorers and possibly other civilizations. The algorithm was to be deployed today through the data-sphere. BlueTech Data stood to gain much in popularity if it succeeded. Targos Information could gain even more. They had invested a lot in the project and would come out as the uncontested leading marketing agency.

There was no doubt in Artenz's mind that the project would succeed. He had a darn good team, and the people reporting to him were the main reason he enjoyed BlueTech so much.

He crossed the building's lobby and exited on the street. His b-pad now showed 0627. The tram was leaving at 0630. Artenz started running. If he caught the tram, he would be at the Blue Tower on time. If not, he would miss the meeting completely.

Even at this early time, there was some life on the streets. A pair of uni-racers passed to his left. Above, a tram flew by, momentarily hiding the flat gray sky. Tram 343—the same one Keidi would take later to get to her work. There were a few people walking to and fro, most of them lost in their b-pads. Artenz made his way between people, sprinting now, and jumped on the fast-walk. The moving belt helped him gain speed, so much so that he almost lost his footing. He could see the station ahead and tram 2-blue entering. He put his head down and ran some more.

The jump off the fast-walk was tricky, and once again, Artenz almost fell. He caught himself at the last moment, using one hand on the ground to push himself up. He stormed into Trinity station. Three people stood in line in front of the closest air-tube, so Artenz dashed toward the air-saucer, the door of which was open. Two people waited on the platform, holding onto the post in the middle. As he stepped in, Artenz ordered the door closed through his b-pad. It shut behind him,

Deficiency

and the platform started up. It reached platform 17 a moment later, and Artenz was the first out, apologizing as he exited. It took him four long steps to enter the tram. He barely made it, the door sliding shut behind him.

Sweat trickled down his forehead as he grinned. He would be on time.

+

Artenz sat in a back corner of the compartment. The few people on board all acted like sleepwalkers; none looked at Artenz, all lost in their b-pads. Artenz thought about going into the bio-sphere but decided against it. It had caused him to miss his stop once before.

Instead, he ordered the eye-veil to be turned on. It showed the time (0631), his number of unread messages (97), his last two callers (Keidi and Detel), a few icons predicting the weather (a small sun hidden behind clouds), and the current temperature and humidity (27 degrees and 55%). The information was equally spaced around the periphery of his vision.

"Link Detel," said Artenz, his voice low.

Not everyone was this respectful when using their pad. A woman of about 18 was sitting at the other end of the compartment, and Artenz could clearly hear every word she was saying.

In front of Artenz's eyes, the b-pad was trying to link with his sister.

```
Linking Detel Scherzel . . .
```

A dot appeared every few seconds, until there were five. Then it started at one again.

Still, the link did not connect.

"Link Marti," said Artenz.

The charade repeated itself, but after two dots, he heard Marti's voice.

"Hi, boss," Marti said, sounding tired, as he always did.

"Hey Marti," said Artenz. "Are you on your way to the office?"

"You bet. What about you?"

"I am."

"Isn't it a bit early for you? I thought you liked your morning cuddles."

"Oh, I do. Got a meeting call for 0715. Can you put the project plan on my tablet and have it ready for when I get there?"

There was a brief pause.

"Seems like you'll make it, if you go up quickly. I'll have it ready."

Artenz had to admit he was impressed.

"How do you know where I am?" he asked, thinking Marti had either hacked into a video-cam or into one of the local networks.

"Better you don't know," said Marti. "I'm about to enter the tower, but one thing, boss."

"Yes?"

"Did you talk to your sister this morning?"

Although it was no secret that Artenz and Detel often linked in the morning—most mornings, to be accurate—the question had an odd feel to it.

"No," said Artenz. "Why do you ask?"

"No reason," said Marti. "See you when you get here."

"Okay," said Artenz, pausing. He let the question go, making a mental note to ask Marti about it later. "Have my tablet ready."

"Will do."

Marti unlinked.

+

The slow-tram was ascending. This particular model could speed up to 150 km per hour but would only reach that speed once it entered

Deficiency

Quadrant X. In Quadrant Z, it stopped every few minutes, picking up mainly employees of BlueTech and surrounding businesses, which explained why it took 40 minutes to reach the Blue Tower. There was no direct tram to the Blue Tower from Artenz's lodge.

Buildings flew by on each side, mostly metal and brick surfaces, often covered with huge billboards. On most, the aged face of Rakkah appeared.

Artenz's thoughts turned to the project launch and the upcoming meeting. He knew the managers would ask him to go over the plan one more time. They would ask about the risks, the worst-case scenario, the best-case scenario. Then they would ask him to deliver sooner than what the plan said. It did not matter if he explained his approach or the rationale behind a launch spread over 25 waves. If he said the deployment was to take two weeks, they would ask for it in one week. If he said two minutes, they would demand one. There was no logic to it. It was just how management worked. And everything had to be done without a single glitch.

Still, the launch would go well. Artenz knew it would, if only because of Marti. The man must be close to 60, but he looked 80. Marti's official title was apprentice coder, but Artenz knew him for what he really was: simply the best, one in a million.

He should know his age, though. Artenz ordered his b-pad to show him Marti's profile card. It appeared in front of his eyes almost instantly. That was the data-sphere for you.

"Damn you, Marti," exclaimed Artenz with a smile.

The profile card was there all right; the imagraph showed a mad red dragon, breathing fire through both nostrils. For each field of information on the card, including surname, first name, date of birth, address, title and ethnicity, it simply said "secret."

As much as Artenz liked Marti's daring nature, he also worried. One of these days, Marti would get a visit from the enforcers.

Which reminded Artenz of Marti's last question before they had unlinked. Marti knew Detel, but Artenz couldn't remember the last time he had seen the two together.

"Link Detel," he ordered.

Again, there was a delay and the link failed. It was now 0651.

Glass buildings from Quadrant X sped by outside the window, some as tall as 200 levels. Most days, the sight was impressive. This morning, though, Artenz was not able to enjoy the view.

He tried the link once more. It didn't work. He ordered Detel's profile card, and it appeared instantly. That was good, but not a surprise.

Artenz debated whether he wanted to enter the bio-sphere. He disliked connecting while on the move. It always left him disoriented and nauseous. Not the case for most of the other passengers. The new generation, especially, was immune to these side effects.

"Where are you?" asked Artenz, looking at his sister's imagraph. "Link Keidi," he ordered.

It took a moment.

"Hi, love," said Keidi. She seemed in good humor, as always. After all, she was the one with the good attitude.

"Were you able to reach Detel?" he asked.

"I didn't try again, why?"

"I can't link with her," he said.

"She could be at the lab. She probably spent the night there, doing some experiment or other, and crashed."

Detel didn't sleep enough.

"Maybe," Artenz said.

"What is it?" asked Keidi. "Are you all right?"

"Yes, yes, I am. It's just... It's probably nothing, but Marti asked about Detel earlier. He asked me if I had talked to her."

The Blue Tower appeared ahead. The tram only needed to maneuver through a final curve before reaching the tower's station. Then access to the bio-sphere would be lost for the day. Another

Deficiency

restriction implemented by BlueTech, something about negative impacts on the employees' productivity.

"I'm almost there," said Artenz.

"I'll check on her," said Keidi. "Don't worry, and concentrate on your day. Want to link during morning pause?"

"I'll try, but don't wait on me. At lunch for sure. I'll be at the usual spot."

"Perfect. Talk then. Good luck and love you."

"Thanks. Love you too. Have a good morning."

They unlinked.

As the tram entered under the Blue Tower and the sun disappeared to be replaced by artificial cyan lights, Artenz realized what was bothering him.

Detel would not have forgotten about the launch. She would have linked and wished him good luck.

.... Profile Failure

Keidi sat on her bed, leaned her head against the wall, and closed her eyes. The sickness was something she would be happy to do without. She had eaten a piece of toast, but it had not helped.

She knew the nausea was not going to be the last thing about this natural pregnancy that could make her regret her decision. At least, for now, it came only in the mornings. Detel had taken a perverted pleasure in listing some of the effects the pregnancy might have on Keidi: swelling, numbness and cramps, itching, fatigue and long nights, aches and changes in her body. Or worse: constipation... and a few other things Keidi preferred not to think about.

She studied her stomach. It looked normal, the same as always, except it hid one of the greatest miracles of the universe: a growing life. A tiny organism that sprouted from Artenz and herself. It was hard to believe.

And it felt normal, natural.

Cell-birth was the only legal option, but Keidi had a few issues with it, issues that she was not ready to ignore.

She hated the idea of her baby growing in an egg-cell in a laboratory somewhere in Prominence City, where she would not have access to it. If something went wrong, she and Artenz would not know about it. She assumed that if something happened, the fetus would be discarded, and another growth would be started. If that was the case, there was no way for her to know how often this would be done.

Also, they would receive the baby when it was a year of age. That first year seemed important to Keidi. She did not understand why it was necessary to keep the baby away from its parents that long. Was it to hide the many attempts that went wrong? Or was it something even worse, experiments no one knew about?

Detel shared most of Keidi's concerns. Artenz's sister had spent her whole life studying biology and birth. So when she said the problem was probably worse than they imagined, Keidi believed her.

And there was the b-pad... the brain tempering and alterations. It was possible Keidi was alarmist. Maybe nothing really happened. Nothing more than the implantation of the brain-pad, that is. Twenty years had passed since the law was put in place that b-pads be installed at birth in Quadrant Z. Five years later, the law had been extended to all of the Information district. It seemed logical to assume the plan was to distribute b-pads to every inhabitant of Prominence City.

Detel had explained that the first few years were critical in brain development and that the b-pad should not be implanted until 18 or even 20 years of age. This seemed extreme to Keidi, but Detel had been adamant on the subject.

"We're not ready to tamper with the development of the brain," she insisted. "We don't know enough yet. Some parts of the brain grow even in the twenties and thirties. The b-pad law should never have passed. The consequences, the long-term ramifications, are completely unknown."

There had been a vote, a public vote. Over 95% of the voters had said yes to the b-pads. How could they not? It was provided at no cost and included a permanent and direct link into the bio-sphere, which meant each baby received a profile room.

It meant no implantation or installation costs. No yearly subscription and maintenance fees. No renewals. No time wasted trying to figure out which provider offered the best deal.

On top of this, certain add-ons could be purchased later at lower costs; the eye-veil and the sound-inc being the most popular. Both were exclusive to the b-pad.

From the beginning, Keidi had not liked the idea. Neither had Detel.

Artenz was getting there, but he had received his b-pad at 10, and the subject was a delicate one for him. Only Detel seemed to be able to talk to him about it. And her message scared him.

Hell, Keidi was scared, and she had only gotten hers at 22.

She wished she hadn't.

She didn't regret much in her life, but switching from her wrist-pad to the brain-pad was one thing she wished she could change. She had refused to return her w-pad and now kept it with her at all times. A lucky charm, or nostalgia of the worst kind, at the bottom of her backpack.

Obviously, had she not switched to the b-pad, she would not have been able to move to Quadrant Z, would not have worked as a technician, would not have married Artenz. So it was not all bad.

Yet her work was now falling apart, fast. Her days as a master technician were numbered. Already, her work consisted mostly of dismantling old w-pads and p-pads. She specialized in the palm-pads, while favoring the older wrist-pads. There was a simplicity and a style to the first generation of pads that Keidi liked. She loved looking at her wrist and seeing the small round screen. It probably stemmed from old action movies, with the heroine looking up some last-minute information on her w-pad, saving the day at the last possible moment.

Also, the fact that the wrist-pad was not directly connected to the brain was something she liked. Especially when listening to all the warnings Detel shared on the subject.

Despite all her gloomy words, even Detel had a b-pad. It was mandatory, had become so two years ago. Detel had been one of a few hundred, a small contingent really, who had protested against the motion. The government had sent enforcers and silenced the resistance

Deficiency

quickly. P-pads and w-pads became illegal, which Keidi still could not understand.

This fact, by itself, was one of the main reasons why she had such a problem with the authorities, with the government, and especially with the corporations. There had been no valid rationale to discontinue the older generations of pads. The b-pads were hailed as the hope of the future, but the device was mostly untested... It did not make sense.

These were things she did not like to ponder, but there was no escape. She worried for herself and Artenz... for everyone, really. And now, she worried for their baby.

Keidi opened her eyes. The nausea had passed, and she felt better.

She looked at the vid-disk, and it showed a time of 0721. She didn't have to be at the workshop until 0830.

She remembered her promise to Artenz. With the sickness, she had almost forgotten about it. She pushed herself farther on the bed, placed her head back on the pillow, put a finger on her b-pad and joined the bio-sphere.

+

The load was slower than it had been earlier, significantly slower. Keidi kept her eyes closed during the load, trying to minimize the dizziness. Every few moments, she opened her eyes to see if the room was ready. It took almost a full minute for the hammock to appear.

Clouds floated outside her room, accompanied by a light rain. The weather was too random. It would make more sense if it stayed consistent for the day or for a few hours. Sometimes, it changed in a matter of seconds.

Keidi stood and walked to her friends-panel. She scanned it and didn't find Detel. Artenz's imagram was transparent. He was standing and frozen in mid-stride because his connection with the bio-sphere was interrupted when he entered one of the outside elevators of the Blue Tower.

"Link Detel," Keidi said as she took a seat in front of her terminal. It read:

```
Welcome to the Data-sphere.
Load time 55.486634 seconds.
Year 3.4k60 Season 05 Day 11 Hour 0722.

Action> Link "DETEL" [Detel Scherzel]

Linking . . . .
```

Keidi waited.

And got a strange message.

```
Link unsuccessful. Recipient nonexistent.
```

It was a message Keidi had never seen before.

Nonexistent?

Even here, in the bio-sphere, a knot formed at the bottom of Keidi's stomach.

"Link Detel," she tried again.

And a minute later, got the same result.

She didn't know how the links worked, where the recipients' information was kept. It could be in the data-sphere. Keidi believed it was entirely done in the bio-sphere, for a better connection speed. The raw data was in the data-sphere, probably synchronized now and then with the bio-sphere. If she was correct, then this message could be another glitch.

She wished she could talk to Artenz. He would know.

Keidi tried a search instead, which looked directly in the data-sphere.

```
Action> Search Detel Scherzel, sister of Artenz
```

Deficiency

The search started.

One dot. Two dots. And another. It took forever.

At least three minutes went by and still, the search went on. There were too many users on the bio-sphere nowadays. Keidi remembered the announcement when it became mandatory in their district: access to all, stay connected at all times.

Artenz had laughed, saying the network would not be able to support the volume of users. He had been right. The whole Sphere had slowed down to a crawl for weeks on end.

Even the data-sphere had been impacted. All users were assigned a priority level. Corporations, special government agencies, and some city services had precedence. General users like Keidi were at the bottom of the list.

And then there was the expansion of the holo-sphere. It was not yet what it promised to be, but it gained more users every day. If the bio-sphere was taxing on the network, the holo-sphere was impossible. People joined it at night to relax and decompress and in the morning because they were addicted. They traveled to exotic places, played the heroine in a role-playing game, or immersed themselves in any other sensory experience to forget about their daily reality.

Keidi had tried it only once and had been impressed. She had also had a headache for two days after the experience. It was extremely addictive and highly stimulating.

Finally, a message appeared.

```
Search failed. Timeout. Try again.
```

This was not a complicated search, and Keidi tried again.

This time she walked around her profile room while waiting. She went in circle and ignored the news coming on the screen. Nothing there interested her, although she remembered that Artenz had been excited about a story a few days before. What had it been about?

It came back to her: space exploration. A mission on a planet, or was it a moon? They were looking for traces of civilization. If they found evidence that someone had been there, it could change everything.

The sound was on, albeit low. It provided some background noise—nothing Keidi could make out. She looked at the screen and saw an old woman's face, but nothing about space.

She returned to the terminal and was even more perplexed by what she now saw.

```
PROFILE FAILURE.
```

First, *recipient nonexistent*. And now, *profile failure*. What was happening?

Nothing was ever deleted from the data-sphere. Artenz's parents, who fled the city 20 years ago, still had detailed profile files stored in the data-sphere. Anything ever recorded since the creation of the Sphere was still there.

Keidi tried the search again.

This time, she stood in place, steeling herself for the result, hoping the profile card would appear, as it had earlier that day.

She imagined two possibilities: the Sphere was falling apart, or something had happened to Detel.

Unable to wait longer, Keidi turned away from the screen and starting pacing, a hand on her head, trying to stop her swirling thoughts. When she came back to the monitor, a new message had been written.

Its significance was undeniable.

```
No match found. Try again.
```

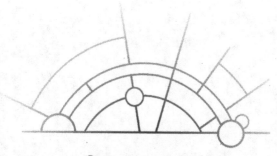

Segment B

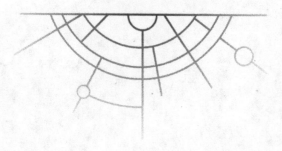

"An adept coder is 5 times more efficient than an apprentice coder."

- *Marti Zehron*

- Management

The office door closed behind Drayfus. He shook his head. He hated the words he had had to say during the meeting. Certainly, the meeting had gone well. He had never really doubted it. Artenz was reliable. Artenz always delivered.

They had worked together for more than two years now. Drayfus got Artenz from the 67th floor. He had wanted him bad, which was why he had accepted when Artenz had said he wanted his whole team with him, including that old geezer Marti. Drayfus had needed to pull some major strings to make the move happen, but it had been worth it.

Still, one would not have believed it the way he had spoken at the meeting.

There had been no other way than to pound on Artenz, challenge every facet of his plan, question his methods, reinforce the priorities.

It had been unfair.

Four managers against one chief.

Artenz had kept his composure, but barely. As competent as he was, he did not comprehend management's reality.

Sometimes, Drayfus thought Artenz did not want to understand, was making an effort not to understand. Drayfus did not consider himself overly intelligent, yet he could play the game required to be a

Deficiency

manager. If Artenz would do his part and help placate those above, they could be on the same team.

That was not quite true.

There was a clear demarcation between operations and management, one that could not be crossed. Artenz was not management material. As much as Drayfus disliked being this hard on his project chief, he understood why it was important.

Looking at the big picture, he admitted it had gone well so far. Next, it would be his turn to be on the defensive and face the executives. He wondered how demanding they would be.

He walked toward his glass desk, locking the door with an order to his b-pad. One could never be too careful. He needed to sit down, relax and rest a bit.

Drayfus dropped in his leather chair and made it spin away from his large desk until he was facing out the windows. The view always helped. It made him feel like he was floating. The wall was glass, from floor to ceiling.

What a sight it was, all those buildings, as far as the eyes could see.

Ahead, Drayfus could make out the Plaza; a patch of greenery located in the exact centre of Prominence. It was surrounded by four districts.

The Glass district, the most impressive, was straight ahead, to the north. The Factory district appeared to the right; residues of smoke still visible even with all the effort put into trying to make it go away, even with moving some of the biggest factories out of Prominence. To the left and west stretched the Castle district, with its turrets and rock buildings. It was in fact metal masquerading as stone. And here, the Blue Tower was the tallest of many towers forming the Information district.

Each district was in turn divided into quadrants, and Drayfus agreed with those who claimed that each quadrant was a small city in itself. Prominence was not a city, but a world. The whole world, really.

Sure, there were other cities on Garadia, but they could not compete. Drayfus never even bothered learning their names. There was no need. There never would be.

Prominence was the center of it all and would remain so.

The Blue Tower was the tallest building in Quadrant X and its 98th floor offered a spectacular view. In the Glass District, some buildings had over 300 levels. Even from this great distance, it was humbling. Prominence was humbling.

The time in his vision said 0759. Unlike the other employees, Drayfus's eye-veil was not blocked in the tower. He could use it as he would at home, with complete access to the Sphere. One of the perks of being part of management. His meeting with the executives was at 0830.

His messages indicator was at 33 new. Drayfus should be reading these, would regret not doing so. Would be told he needed to read and reply inside an hour or something just as unreasonable. But he didn't have the strength.

He had not slept well, if at all. At 2130 the night before, he had received additional instructions for the project launch that were to be shared with the project chief first thing this morning.

Drayfus had debated for most of the night whether he would schedule the extra meeting or not. He had known that Artenz already had a planning session scheduled for 0830 with his team. His project chief had a plan and although Drayfus didn't know all the details, he trusted Artenz. In the end, he requested the meeting anyway.

The executives didn't trust anyone. Which was why they continually asked him to hammer on his team. Something about getting the most out of every employee. Now and then, Drayfus pushed back. Most of the time, he didn't. It wasn't worth it. The executives always got what they wanted. Either you helped or you did not, in which case your career in management would be short-lived.

His eyes were closing of their own accord. He could fall asleep right now.

Deficiency

He linked his assistant.

"No disruptions for the next 20 minutes," he said.

"Noted, sir," came the reply.

Drayfus unlinked.

Good. That was good.

A thought came to him, one that surfaced too often lately. It was not even noon, and his wife would be unhappy to know he had fallen prey to his old habit. But it was the only thing that helped these days.

Drayfus got up, opened the cabinet, took out a bottle, and poured himself a glass of bourbon. He did it quickly, before guilt took over. He then returned to his seat, put his feet on his desk, and drank a sip. Then another.

And another. Not sips anymore.

It took only a few moments before he put the empty glass on his desk and drowsed off.

+

The melody awoke him slowly. It came from afar. Sleep was heavy and would not let Drayfus open his eyes. As his b-pad realized he was awake, the icons and information came into focus, brighter, eyes closed or not. His assistant was trying to link with him.

Time was 0827.

0827!

As he jumped out of his chair, Drayfus linked to his assistant.

"Miss Lamond just entered the building," his assistant announced instantly.

This woke him completely. The accursed executive from CGC! He hated no one more than Mysa Lamond. She came from nowhere, had no management experience that he knew off, and yet she was right up there at the top.

"Is the conference room ready?" he asked.

"It is."

"Good. Great. Who else has arrived?"

"They are all there, waiting."

Drayfus was instantly infuriated.

"Why didn't you wake me up?" he yelled.

There was a brief silence, then:

"I didn't know you were asleep, sir."

Indeed. Good point, but there was no need to acknowledge the fact.

"Next time, do better," he said.

"I understand, sir. They are waiting, sir."

Another good point.

"Tell them I'm on my way," he said.

A glass logo of BlueTech Data rested on his desk. Drayfus grabbed the T of BTD, shaped as a tower, and lifted, opening the container. He took out a mint, threw it in his mouth, closed the logo, and exited his office.

✢

There was no better way to make a bad impression than to arrive late at an executives' meeting. It could cost a manager his job. *At least*, thought Drayfus, half running through the halls of the Blue Tower, *I will be there before Mysa Lamond.*

Actually, that gave Drayfus an idea. Instead of going to the meeting room, he made his way to the elevator, where he waited. The mint in his mouth was so strong it almost brought tears to his eyes.

The elevator, designed around an old and archaic model, arrived, and a small metal bell hanging outside its doors rang. Drayfus put on his best smile.

As the door slid open, he said, "Welcome to the Blue Tower, Miss Lamond."

✢

Deficiency

Arriving at the conference room with Mysa Lamond had the desired effect. No one minded Drayfus's lateness. Most probably didn't see him at all. Mysa Lamond was the center of everything.

She had come alone, sole representative of the Crystal Globe Conglomerate. She wore a crisp white suit with no buttons, just a few folds. It adhered to her skin like a swimsuit. Drayfus had no idea what the suit was made of. It was never dirty, and the folds never moved.

Her pristine face, her small, bright red lips, her even smaller eyes, and her blond hair made Mysa Lamond stand out. And her posture. She always stood erect, never flinching. Her neck was long and her skin smooth and perfect. Drayfus didn't know how much of her was real. Some said she was part cyborg. Her lack of emotion certainly supported the theory. She didn't have a b-pad on her neck, so she had other augments. Of that, there was no doubt.

She walked to the head of the table and sat down.

"Have a seat, gentlemen," she invited.

The table was oblong, with 11 chairs around it, including the head seat. All were taken.

There were three directors from BlueTech Data, Drayfus's supervisors. Only one of them was his direct supervisor on paper, but the project seemed to have blurred the usual hierarchy. Drayfus reported to all three these days.

Four directors represented Targos Information, their main client for the project. Drayfus thought that one or two would have been enough, but there was strength in numbers. Targos Information planned to use the solution to expand their marketing services.

And because Telecore Enterprises were everywhere since the expansion of the b-pads, they had sent one of their directors. It was unclear to Drayfus how the brain-pads could benefit from the project. He remembered a meeting he'd attended a few seasons ago, where the idea was thrown out that ads should be sent directly to the b-pad screens, where it would be impossible to miss them. With the growing popularity of the eye-veils, the idea had potential. Drayfus guessed this was why Telecore Enterprises was interested.

Finally, Universal Communications had a representative. Someone to take notes, if nothing else. Observe. Their interests lay with the potential of the solution. Drayfus remembered Artenz talking about using the propagation component to reach farther into space. He had not really paid much attention and couldn't see any corporation having any interest in the idea. There was no profit in it.

"Please proceed," said Mysa Lamond as soon as everyone was seated. It was impressive to see the ease with which she took control of the whole room. She was not from BlueTech, nor from Targos, and so very new. And yet...

The four directors from Targos Information turned their heads toward Drayfus. He looked back, and the interrogation began.

+

He did well, Drayfus did. He thought so, anyway.

Still, as he walked out of the conference room, he was sweating profusely. The hour had been endless and the many questions grueling. Drayfus had answered each concern one by one, reassuring the directors over and over. He had gone through the project plan twice. It didn't matter that the deployment had already begun and that it was too late to change the plan. The directors made recommendations, as if they knew better, as if they knew everything.

Drayfus took notes and promised to bring the ideas to his team. The directors seemed pleased, although the next meeting would be the important one. By that time, they would know how the deployment had gone. The initial results would be in.

"Mr. Arlsberg, can I have a word please?"

The voice belonged to Mysa Lamond and made Drayfus jump. Even though he was in the corridor, out of the room and on his way

Deficiency

back to his office, the words sounded as if Mysa Lamond was standing beside him.

Voice projection, most likely. Disturbing augment, that one.

He turned around and went back in the conference room. He supposed he should have offered to escort Mysa Lamond out of the building.

During the meeting, Mysa Lamond had only said a few words, yet every time she had spoken, everything had come to a halt. Her presence was disrupting and confusing. Drayfus didn't understand why she was here. The CGC didn't have any direct stake in the project, other than through a pledge with BlueTech Data, four directors of which were already present.

Indirectly... it was possible.

Indirectly, the CGC might own Targos Information. It was impossible to know what they owned and what they didn't. Drayfus only knew that on the most recent corporate census, the Crystal Globe Conglomerate was ranked second in value, behind Priam Corporation. Maybe they were interested in acquiring a new division: Targos. Drayfus suspected they already owned Telecore.

Now the woman came around the table. They were alone in the room, a fact that Drayfus did not like. He admitted she was attractive, in a cold, inhuman way. She was also untouchable.

And she was partly robot, a notion that was not a problem when they were in a room full of people, but one that disturbed Drayfus now that they were alone.

Mysa Lamond stopped beside him, her eyes locking with his. Drayfus tried to hold the gaze, but couldn't. He looked around, came back, looked away again.

"May I utilize your office for the day?" she asked.

Drayfus's spirit fell...

"Certainly," he said.

-. Wave 1 and Wave 2

Wave 1 of the deployment went as planned. That is to say, without a single glitch.

The program was sent to 10 distribution points in total, all in Quadrant X. There had been two sub-waves. Wave 1.1 had deployed the program inside the Blue Tower. Wave 1.2 had sent the program to five trial sites, preselected by management.

In those initial 30 minutes of the deployment, more than 500 screens and billboards were upgraded. At 0920, all the billboards in the Blue Tower showed a commercial about the project itself, presenting it as a new era in communications.

Wave 2 was now underway, and after a minor glitch, quickly fixed by Artenz himself, things seemed to be going fluidly.

This wave targeted the four key sites, one in each district. Wave 2.1 sent the program to the Information district and Wave 2.2 to the Castle district. Wave 2.3 would upgrade the Glass district and 2.4, the Factory district.

Artenz was mostly worried about the deployments to the Information and Factory districts, where he thought the impacts of a faulty deployment could be graver. Management, on the other hand, was more worried about the Castle and Glass districts, where most of the investors and the most powerful people of Prominence City lived.

Deficiency

Management wanted to make a good impression and demonstrate that the investment would lead to profits. A flawless launch would go a long way in securing funding for future endeavors.

Artenz moved his weight from one foot to the other. He was at his desk, standing, looking around, supervising, ready to react to any surprise. He had not sat since the beginning of the deployment, not even when he had quickly fixed the only issue they'd had so far. He had coded the solution standing and, once done, had received a shy round of applause from his team.

The clock on his monitor now showed 1002. His team had just released Wave 2.3. Another 13 minutes to 2.4, and then on to Wave 3, which was substantially larger.

The approach of going with small waves and expanding the deployment had always provided the best results, allowing for more flexibility. It was an approach Artenz and his team had used before. Five waves in total, usually distributed one per day over five days.

This time around, everything had to be completed in two days. Waves 1 to 4 would be done today, with Wave 5 tomorrow. Hundreds of thousands of monitors, screens, terminals, and billboards would receive the program and install it to upgrade their system. Waves 1 to 3 targeted the major distribution points, Wave 4 the secondary sites, which would be accessed through the main sites. Then Wave 5 was for the remote and isolated sites located outside of Prominence City, in faraway cities and facilities, most on Garadia, but some out in space, in satellites and roaming stations.

The propagation could take several days to spread over Prominence, several weeks to reach all the remote sites. That was where Artenz's responsibility stopped, but not the deployment. It would continue to expand for seasons, maybe even years, until it reached faraway stations and traveling spacecrafts.

The project was already in its 11th month. It had gone through initiation, analysis, approval, and design. The deployment was the last step in the implementation. Then would come the project closure, follow-up, and evaluation.

All in all, Artenz was proud of himself. This was by far the biggest project he had led and his biggest success. Looking around, he was proud of his team.

It was not a large group. He had 12 members, seven of whom were on location in the Blue Tower. Their office space, including his own, was open and formed a circle. Thus, they faced each other and could easily exchange ideas and instructions, keep each other apprised of what they were doing, step by step. Marti was seated to Artenz's right.

His other five members were located in small offices, isolated, in other districts. Their faces appeared on his monitor.

Artenz would have to make a speech tomorrow, at the end of the day, as he usually did at the completion of a project. It was important to him to take the time to thank each and every one of his employees, make them understand how much he appreciated them. After all, the success was not his alone.

"Boss?"

Artenz looked at Marti. The old man was deep in his chair, his feet far under his desk. It was hard to believe he didn't just slide to the floor. At first, Artenz thought there was a problem, but he noticed that Marti was not even following the progress of the deployment. His monitor showed a black screen. The data-sphere.

Quickly, Artenz took two steps and bent over Marti's shoulder.

"What are you up to?" he asked, not hiding the annoyance from his voice.

He knew Marti could easily hide his tracks, but today was not the day to take chances.

"Can you spare a minute?" asked Marti. "In the boardroom."

"Not really," said Artenz, "we're in the middle of something here."

"It's important," said Marti, hiding the data-sphere and bringing the tracking of the project on his monitor. Everything was going well. Yet,

Deficiency

as Marti talked, he never once looked up at Artenz, and he kept his voice low.

"What is this about?" asked Artenz.

"In the boardroom, in five minutes," said Marti. "It's about your sister."

+

The boardroom door slid open, let Artenz in, and slid closed. His team was monitoring the deployment. The next wave was already scheduled. Everything should be good.

Artenz's full attention was on Marti.

"What about Detel?" he asked.

"Sit," said Marti, bringing two chairs close to each other.

The boardroom was located between the large open room that was his team's office space and the corridor leading to his manager's office. On both sides, the walls were made of glass. Marti put his chair with his back to the team's room and Artenz with his back to the management's offices.

As Artenz sat down, Marti took a device out of a hidden pocket. He put it on his knee and pushed a button. Instantly, Artenz heard a buzzing coming out of his b-pad.

The small object was a scrambler.

"Sorry, boss," said Marti, "it'll only be a minute."

Suddenly, Artenz had many questions, one of which was about the need for a scrambler. His b-pad was limited to the Blue Tower when in the building, so was Marti worried about someone internally?

"Did you talk to your sister today?"

It was the second time Marti had asked that question.

"No, I haven't. Why? What is going on? Did something happen to her?"

"I don't know. Maybe—"

"What do you mean, maybe? Marti—"

"Boss, listen, we don't have much time," said Marti, now crouched forward.

Artenz did the same, worried now. For his sister, but also for himself and Marti. Maybe even his team. His hands shook. The whole thing was crazy.

He stole a glance toward the corridor behind him. In the middle of the hallway, he saw Drayfus talking with a woman completely in white. If Drayfus saw him, he would automatically storm this way, asking why he was not supervising the project.

"Artenz!"

It was rare that Marti used his name. Artenz whipped his head back to his friend.

"I'm listening," he said.

Marti hesitated, swallowed and then said:

"Your sister is gone from the Sphere—"

"I know," said Artenz, "this morning—"

"Completely."

This stopped Artenz cold.

"Her profile room is gone; her profile card is gone. All the information on her is completely gone. She's been flushed from the data-sphere."

This didn't make sense.

Flushed?

All her information gone from the data-sphere?

Marti was still talking, but Artenz was not listening.

"You must be mistaken," he cut in.

Marti took a deep breath. This seemed painful for him.

"I don't think so," he said. "I've been trying to find her for the past hour."

This probably explained why there had been a glitch in Wave 2. Marti had not been paying attention, or he would have caught it before it happened. That was what Marti did best, monitoring and catching

Deficiency

issues before they became visible. Marti never said when he caught any problem, but more often than not, Artenz knew when it happened.

"I've dug deep," said Marti, "probably too deep."

"What do you mean?" asked Artenz. "Too deep?"

"I've gone to tier 0," said Marti.

Privileges in the data-sphere were granted by tiers and zones. There were 10 tiers. General information was stored in tiers 8, 9 and 10. Tier 10 was open to all, including kids. Tier 8 and 9 contained a wide variety of information, all of which was deemed acceptable for general viewing.

Tiers 5, 6 and 7 contained protected information, which included sensitive information, private and personal. Tier 4 contained sensitive business information. Tiers 3, 2 and 1 were confidential, secret and top-secret information, said to be related to the defense and the maintenance of social, political and economic stability.

Each tier was divided by zones, and each individual had access to different zones. As a coder and employee of BlueTech Data, Artenz had tier 4 when in Quadrant X and tier 8 when outside.

Marti's level of access was lower than Artenz's, but he didn't follow the rules. Marti had ways.

"What is tier 0?" asked Artenz. "Is there a tier 0?"

"Forbidden," said Marti. "Information deleted over the years. History changed, possibly. It is an endless pit, of which I've only scratched the surface."

"Are you certain?"

Artenz was trying to wrap his head around what Marti was saying. Marti only looked at him.

"Of course you are," said Artenz.

The risks were now evident. It was one thing to navigate tier 7 and look up somebody's financial or medical history. It was something else entirely to dig into the state's and corporations' secrets.

Changed history. Deleted facts. This was serious stuff.

"Were you found?" asked Artenz.

"Maybe."

"Why did you go that deep?" he asked.

"For you, boss," said Marti. "I thought you would want me to be thorough."

The words were spoken softly, with affection. The severity of the situation was starting to sink in for Artenz, to take over his composure. Slowly and painfully.

"You believe Detel is gone," said Artenz.

"I just can't find her," Marti replied.

Deficiency

Code 00.000.0012

```
// Program Information
// Version: 00.000.0012
// Program Name: secret
// Coder Name: secret
// Date Created: Year 3.4k60 Season 05 Day 11 Hour 1808
// Date Updated: Year 3.4k60 Season 05 Day 11 Hour 1809

// data-sphere module
include global: data
// marti custom module
include district/3:quadrant/z:user/marti424:_marti

function main ()
[
  var dataNodes as _data_coordinates
  var DSinfo as _info
  var X as integer

  // Retrieve data coordinate
  dataNodes = _data_convert ( _marti_DScoordinates(),
NODES )

  // Concatenate all data into a single block
  loop X from 1 to dataNodes( _count )
  [
  DSinfo = _data_append( _data_get( dataNodes( X ) ) )
  ]

  // Output data, 1 line only, testing
  _data_print ( DSinfo )
]
```

S.C. Eston

Code Output 00.000.0012

```
Welcome to the Data-sphere.
Load time 0.026012 seconds.
Year 3.4k60 Season 05 Day 11 Hour 1810.

Action> run secret
Packaging secret . . .

Paused
Password required (_marti):

Action> encrypt(Red!Dragon?232)

Unpaused
Packaging secret . . .

Running secret:

===================================================
K0pnYh7OyEzFrSWsprC5TAi4aHx6ccSxPNG5Daub
```

- . . . Laboratory

The deadline was unreasonable and incomprehensible. The last shipment had contained over 500 palm-pads. They had to be dismantled in 10 days. Each p-pad needed to be opened, the memory chips extracted and filed with the pad's serial number and the user's identifier. Then the pad itself had to be taken apart, each piece categorized and re-boxed and sent back to warehouses, where it would eventually be reused.

The workshop had four massive metal tables in its center. Keidi was standing at one of them, working on one of the devices. It was only two centimeters wide. A lamp hung over her head, and she had a magnifying glass over one eye. Using small pliers and screwdrivers, she was taking the gadget apart. It was no more than three millimeters thick. This p-pad had belonged to a child and was caked in dry blood.

It was gruesome, and Keidi tried not to think of the trauma the child would have had to endure while it was pulled out of his or her hand.

"We've been set for failure," said Tarana, working from the station on Keidi's right. They were alone. Ronin was coming in at 1100, and Keidi had already alerted Tarana that she was leaving then. She wanted to look for Detel.

She didn't comment on Tarana's jab. She had heard it before.

"Seriously," continued Tarana, "this is crazy. These pads are not used, nope. There's absolutely no reason to rush. None."

"Except the quicker we do it, the fewer hours they need to pay us."

"There is that," said Tarana. "Any idea what you're going to do next?"

They had not been told they would be dismissed, but it was only a question of time. Both of them were pad-2 technicians. Except Keidi was also well versed with the wrist-pad, or pad-1, and the brain-pad, pad-3. When Telecore had purchased PadTech, it would have been logical for her to move with Telecore. Minimum training and she would have been ready to work on the b-pads. That had not happened.

"Not really," said Keidi. At least she had options. "What about you?"

"Nope. Nothing."

Things looked bleak for Tarana. And Ronin. If they couldn't find other work, their lives could take a turn for the worse. They might have to leave Prominence. And that meant one thing, one destination where no one wanted to go.

The Low Lands.

It still didn't make sense to Keidi. When things had been prosperous, there had been proficient technicians in this workshop, 20 at one time. Most of them would have adapted well to the b-pads. Instead, PadTech Enterprises was renamed Alloy Recycling, and one by one, the technicians were let go.

Until there were three.

Obviously, Telecore had their own technicians. Training was never going to be offered. After the extreme success of the b-pads, the new mega corporation simply bought the competition and dismantled the older products and the companies.

The first generation of pads had been completely wiped out a year ago. Except for the wrist-pad she currently kept in her backpack, hidden. Illegal, yes, but she had not been able to part with it, even when Artenz had warned her he didn't want it in the lodge. Her lucky charm,

Deficiency

although Artenz believed she kept it because of some nostalgia she couldn't get over. He was probably right.

Since he had agreed to modify her b-pad and go with natural birth, having a wrist-pad did not seem like such a big deal. Keidi knew Artenz would agree to almost anything she asked. As much as he had accepted the idea of natural birth for love, she hoped a part of him was excited about the prospect of adding a new member to their family.

"I'm telling you," said Tarana, "these pads will be the death of us. Yup."

The dismantling of one p-pad took anywhere between 20 and 80 minutes, depending on its condition. By that simple calculation, there was absolutely no way they would meet their quota on time.

"Why do you have to leave anyway?" asked Tarana. "Not feeling good? You do look pale, yes. We'd have more chance to finish everything if you and Ronin worked full days, you know."

"I know, and I'm sorry," said Keidi, not for the first time. "It is important, or I'd not leave you. You know that."

"I know. Yes. Whatever it is, let me know if I can help."

"Thanks, but no. I'm meeting with Detel."

"What for? Another surprise for Artenz?"

"Not this time."

"Seriously? Another surprise? I can't believe this. Does he know how lucky he is to have you?"

Tarana smiled. Keidi faked a chuckle. Her colleague liked drama a bit too much. Keidi already regretted mentioning Detel. If she were to tell Tarana that Detel had disappeared, there would be no end to the questions. Tarana was a good friend but could not control her tongue. She would repeat the story to whoever wanted to hear it, and probably to some who didn't.

"Right," said Tarana. "Well, you're not looking so sharp. Smile a little. We're not dead yet."

Keidi did smile then, albeit briefly.

+

She walked out on the open street and checked to see whether Artenz had replied to her messages. He hadn't.

The street was mostly empty, with a few preoccupied people on the walk-ways. A tram passed overhead. Closer, a woman was pushing a one-wheeled stroller. Keidi tried to catch a glimpse of the baby inside, but did not have any luck. Since learning she was pregnant, she could not help looking at every baby she came across.

The baby in this stroller would be a cell-birth. They all were, which made Keidi proud to have taken a different path, not because it was rebellious, but because she was doing the right thing despite all the opposition. She wondered how many out there had considered natural birth. Probably not a lot.

One of the reasons Keidi told Tarana she did not know what she would do if they were dismissed was that she was hoping to quit work. Her pregnancy was not far along; only two weeks and a few days. Detel had been monitoring her closely to capture the change in her body early. The best scenario for Keidi would be for her to be dismissed before the pregnancy showed.

Keidi pulled her eyes away from the mother and her stroller and walked in the opposite direction. The stagnant air and a thick smell stayed lodged in the nostrils. Pollution, which many would not believe was present in Prominence. During her university years, Keidi had written a paper on waste. Most of the toxic fumes were evacuated outside the city by large pipes. The remainder stayed and polluted, sometimes causing smog. But only in the Factory district.

She walked fast, trying to make up for the fact that Ronin had arrived late, as he always did. It was hard to blame him. They were obsolete, the three of them. They had been made to be obsolete.

Their manager had only visited them once in the past year. The visit had lasted less than 30 minutes, during which he sat with each for about five minutes. Then he wandered around, a constant expression of distaste on his face due to the condition of the workshop. The facility was falling to pieces. Half the light bulbs had been removed. The clean-bots were taken out for upgrade and never seen again. Every corner that could be cut to save a few credits was cut.

Keidi stepped on a walk-way and continued walking, gaining speed. On her left was a small restaurant, Alice's Snacks, where she often met Detel for lunch. It was the one thing she liked about the workshop, its closeness to Thrium Laboratories, where Detel did her research.

A loud voice overhead was enthusiastically talking about the upcoming Athletics at the Plaza. In 19 days. Races, jumps and acrobatics, with the best athletes of Prominence, over the course of 31 days. The festivities would flood out of the Plaza and reach every corner of the city. It was a fun time. Keidi liked to follow the competitions and watch the shows. She even wished she could see it in person. Maybe one day. The Plaza was the Plaza. Keidi could make out its high walls ahead, in between buildings. She didn't even know what you had to do to be allowed inside.

Keidi looked up as the billboard flashed and illuminated. It was a full level in height, and its image was pale and fading. The screen shifted to show the face of Rakkah. The verdict of her trial would be announced today, although Keidi knew it would be guilty. It just could not end any other way.

Rakkah was the face of the Low Lands, and she had been vilified over and over. A message was passed here.

The billboard made her think of Artenz, who did not share her views. Not yet, anyway. Keidi was working on it. She looked away from the news, hoping Artenz's launch was going well.

The Thrium Laboratories sign appeared down a street to her left. The sign was immense, presenting a picture of three researchers dressed in white coats, smiling broadly. The building matched the sign in size with 40 levels up, 60 in total. The laboratories were located on the top 15 floors.

Keidi stepped off the walk-way, crossed a platform, and jumped on a perpendicular walk-way, moving her toward the Thrium building.

She had never liked the place. There were stories of atrocities once performed in the lower rooms of the building. Detel had dismissed most of them, but not all.

Once, Artenz's sister had taken Keidi down to level 18. Detel liked the solitude down there. Keidi had hated it, especially the smell of decay, faint yet unmistakable.

"Chemicals from the lower laboratories," Detel had said.

Most likely dead animals, had thought Keidi. *Or worse, corpses.*

+

The entrance room of Thrium Laboratories was a large atrium with a glass ceiling. Once, it had probably been a magnificent sight, but practicality had long ago taken over presentation. One didn't feel welcome when entering Thrium Laboratories.

A hallway made of fake plasti-metal walls forced visitors toward a large reception desk. No one was seated behind it. As she stepped forward, a message appeared on a display and welcomed Keidi. Her b-pad had already connected with the building's virtual intelligence.

```
You have entered Thrium Laboratories.
Year 3.4k60 Season 05 Day 11 Hour 1120.
You are now interacting with a virtual intelligence (VI)

VI: Welcome, Keidi Rysinjer.
VI: What is the reason of your visit?

Action>
```

It was such a rudimentary program, sharing many similarities with the data-sphere interface. The goal was obvious: discourage visitors.

Keidi's distaste for the place resurfaced. She didn't know how Detel could come here every day and not be depressed. Keidi swore she could smell the putrefaction from the levels below. She ordered her b-pad to transmit the reason of her coming.

```
Action> Visiting Detel Scherzel
VI: Please be patient while I review your request.
Validating . . .
VI: You have been cleared Keidi Rysinjer.
VI: Please proceed through the scanner.
```

Most VI could talk, using a mechanical voice. They sounded quite unnatural, which was why Keidi didn't mind the simple black screen. Sometimes, simple was better. In some ways, it was the same with the p-pads versus the b-pads.

Keidi went around the desk and stepped toward the scanner. She felt a prickle around her b-pad as she passed through the arch. She looked back to see a green light appear on top of the machine.

She proceeded forward. There was nowhere else to go. The air-saucer was preprogrammed with Keidi's destination. The doors opened and she stepped inside, grabbed the circular railing in the center of the platform, and waited as the disk climbed.

It had been a while since her last visit, but she remembered that Detel's lab was located somewhere in the back of the building. The corridors were long, straight and bare. Sliding glass doors restricted access to some areas. Three corridors went out from the air-saucer, yet only one was available to Keidi.

She started moving. The place felt deserted. She didn't come across anyone, no geeky scientist or researcher walking around, lost in thought. As she turned a corner, she noticed why.

There was a lounge area to the left and it was crammed with workers, researchers of all types.

Keidi hesitated until a familiar face appeared.

It was Zofia, Detel's colleague and friend. Long blond hair, charming eyes, with a smile Keidi always found forced. The only person in the whole building making her white coat look sexy. She was a leech when it came to friends. She had the annoying habit of forcing herself into friendships that were not hers. Like Detel and Keidi's.

But if someone knew where to find Detel, it would be her.

Yet something felt wrong.

Zofia's skin was pale, and she seemed distraught. Her eyes were red from shedding tears. When she saw Keidi, her skin turned paler. She put a hand on the wall and took a long breath. Then she came to meet Keidi.

Keidi didn't know what to do or what to think. Since the morning, she had been able to push aside the eerie fact that Detel's profile was gone. She had concentrated on going to work, and had almost convinced herself that she would find Detel here.

Zofia, whom Keidi had once jokingly called a bitter enemy, opened her arms and hugged her. The gesture only added to Keidi's concerns.

"Where's Detel?" she asked, disengaging herself from Zofia.

"Gone," said Zofia in a cracked voice.

For an instant, Keidi hoped the woman was playing with her. She wanted this to be a charade of some sort. But Zofia was not acting. Keidi felt tears coming. The terrible truth was sinking its claws into her.

Detel's imagram, gone.

Detel's profile card, gone.

And now...

There were rumors of such things. People disappearing. People gone. Most people discarded such stories. Not Keidi. When rumors became numerous, it was extremely difficult not to think they held some truth.

"Come, I need to show you something," said Zofia, pulling her by the hand.

As they passed before the lounge area, all eyes turned their way. Everyone was whispering. Everyone was scared.

Deficiency

What had happened here?

+

"There's her laboratory," said Zofia, pointing to the door at the end of the hallway. Keidi knew this, but didn't say so. "See what they've done."

The door opened. Keidi took a step and looked inside.

The sight weakened her knees.

She remembered the room, with its long island in the center. Apparatus of all shapes and types covering all surfaces. Six monitors on the far wall. Six! She remembered the exact number, because she had asked Detel why she needed so many. Detel had laughed and said what she really needed was 12! And the microscopes, showing wonders. And the refrigerators, with tubes and bottles filled with liquid of magnificent colors and strange consistencies. And the preserved organs... Atrocious, certainly, but Detel's pride.

Keidi remembered Detel explaining some of what she was doing, trying to make it simple, to make it fun and interesting. She had been standing at the end of the island.

Keidi remembered Detel's face the most, her easy smile and the crooked tooth, only one.

As Keidi took a step inside, stunned, she could not push Detel's image away. They had met on Keidi's first day at university. Detel had already been a student. She was four years older than Keidi. Still, they had instantly become friends. Later, Detel had introduced Keidi to her brother.

Always, they had stayed friends.

Could Detel be permanently gone?

The laboratory seemed to say she was.

- . . . Traitor

Wave 3 was proceeding flawlessly. The script had successfully propagated to 10 of the 16 primary sites, and the network held strong. Given that they had been promised priority bandwidth for the duration of the launch, it was not surprising. The big corporations, and not only those directly involved, wanted the project to succeeded so much that they had even convinced the government to reduce its low-priority communications temporarily.

It should have been a good moment for Artenz. His employees all wore larger-than-life smiles. He also smiled, a smile that did not extend farther than the surface of his face. Marti's words still resonated in his head.

"I just can't find her." he had said with such desperation.

Marti Zehron rarely put his feelings on display, and the fact that he had done so showed how much he cared. Although the two had been friends for years, Artenz was touched by the man's dedication.

Surrounded by his team, by success, by people who believed in him, Artenz still felt alone. Marti had stepped up and answered a few questions. His team had accepted Marti's answers, probably because they were so inebriated by how well everything was going.

For all of them, the worst was over.

Artenz took three steps and crouched over Marti's shoulder.

Deficiency

"I can't wait any longer," he said. "I have to talk to Keidi."

Marti nodded. "Go. Everything is under control."

On Marti's monitor, several layers of panels showed the status of the launch with growing progress bars. One of the panels, barely visible in a corner, was black.

The data-sphere.

"You're still trying to find her?" asked Artenz, hopeful.

Marti's silence was hurtful.

"You are not?"

"I'm trying to find clues," said Marti.

"You don't think she can be found," accused Artenz, whispering each word. "You've given up already."

Marti turned his head and looked directly at Artenz. Struggle was visible on his face.

"Go talk to Keidi," he said. "I'll keep trying. I promise I won't stop until I find her."

There was something more there, on Marti's face. Culpability?

"What aren't you telling me?" asked Artenz, his voice louder.

"Not here… " warned Marti. "Not now. Go talk to Keidi. When you return, I'll tell you what I know. I promise."

Two promises, too close to each other.

A figure appeared on Artenz's right. The damn manager, always looking over his shoulder, never satisfied.

"Keep looking," said Artenz between tight teeth.

Marti didn't say a thing. He simply turned back toward his workstation.

Artenz told his team he was going out for lunch and would be back in 30 minutes. As expected, Drayfus stopped him.

"The launch is not over," the manager said. "We need you here."

"I need to eat," said Artenz.

"15 minutes," said Drayfus. "Not a minute more."

There was no point in arguing. Artenz nodded and left the room.

+

As he watched Artenz leave, head down, Drayfus worried.

Had he pushed Artenz too far? Had Artenz reached his breaking point? The project seemed on track, but that was sometimes how it happened. The stress built up, little by little, growing, until it exploded. It would have seemed normal that the success would have freed Artenz. It might just have been too little, too late.

Sadly, today, it didn't really matter.

With the presence of the directors and the CGC, Drayfus could not take any chances. He needed Artenz on the floor. Everything had gone well so far, and Drayfus planned to do anything in his power to keep it that way.

Suddenly, a flashing exclamation mark appeared in the bottom right corner of his vision. The warning indicated that Drayfus's b-pad had lost its connection to the BlueTech Data internal network. A brief moment passed before it reconnected.

When it did, his agenda for the day was not present. A pivoting thunderbolt icon showed that the b-pad was looking for the information. With the connection to his office's workstation, the information should have been instantly available.

Drayfus entered the adjacent meeting room. There, he ordered his b-pad to connect directly to his office workstation.

He received a message saying he had insufficient privileges. He knew instantly what had happened.

The CGC bitch had taken over his workstation.

+

Drayfus left the meeting room and entered the management hallway. Protocol said he needed to make sure that the door was completely closed before proceeding, but he didn't. A small rebellious act.

Deficiency

He turned a corner, and there was his assistant, standing in the middle of the corridor, instead of being seated behind his desk.

"What is going on?" Drayfus asked.

"I don't know," said the assistant. He seemed at a complete loss. "I've lost all my accesses and been kicked out of my system. I checked your office door, and it's locked and won't respond to my b-pad. It seems we've been hacked. Do you think the CGC executive is in any danger?"

Drayfus stopped by his door.

"No," he said. "Quite the opposite. She took over my system."

This shocked the assistant.

"Can she really do that?" he asked.

"What do you think?" said Drayfus, knocking on the door of his own office.

Mysa Lamond was from the Conglomerate. There was almost no limit to what she could do. "Miss Lamond, this is Drayfus Arlsberg. I'd like a word with you."

"But... why?" murmured his assistant in his ear.

"That is what I want to know," said Drayfus.

He would have cooperated. No matter what this was, he would have cooperated with the Conglomerate. He did not really have a choice.

There was no sound coming from his office. He knocked again, harder.

His assistant suddenly grabbed him by the shoulder. Drayfus turned around to see enforcers coming down the hall toward him. Six in total, dressed in navy and black, rifles in hand, faces hidden behind helmets and goggles. His assistant moved rapidly behind his desk, located in an open space on the side of the hallway.

Drayfus felt a moment of raw fear, as if these people would shoot him if he did not step out of their way. They certainly moved with a purpose.

"Come in, Mr. Arlsberg."

The voice came from behind him. Drayfus turned and found the door to his office open. He stepped in, moving sideways, keeping an eye on the enforcers. He saw them stop outside the office and take position, as if this maneuver had been rehearsed.

One of the enforcers did not stop, though. He kept moving and followed Drayfus into the office. A heavy gray cape fluttered behind him with each of his long steps. His helmet was a sphere of dark reflective glass. His armor black and gray.

"Take a seat," said Mysa Lamond.

Drayfus was sweating as he backed toward the settee located on the side of his office, just by the cabinet. The door to the office closed. The sight of the enforcers on the other side disturbed him.

The enforcer in the room had stopped in front of the main desk, erect, rifle in one hand. The weapon was bulky, of a shape Drayfus had never seen before; its design slick, with two golden lights pulsing atop the trigger.

Mysa Lamond had been standing and now took a seat, behind his desk, in his chair.

"Sit!" she ordered, looking at Drayfus.

He realized he was frozen in place, on his feet. He forced himself down, dropped on the settee.

"At ease," Mysa Lamond said to the enforcer.

In response, the individual pushed a button behind the glass helmet. It became loose with a brief whoosh. Drayfus noticed that cracks appeared on the face of the helmet; not cracks but lines, as if the surface was made of several pieces of glass fused together. Along the bottom, there was something that could have been a respiratory opening or a microphone. Cables like veins connected to the earpieces, devices to enhance hearing maybe. Here was technology like nothing Drayfus had seen before.

With one hand, the enforcer removed the helmet and deposited it on the corner of the desk. He was a man with short and precise white hair. No mustache. A strange square face, terribly severe. Almost inhuman…

This *thing* was not a normal enforcer, it was a bionic!

Drayfus was instantly disgusted and frightened. Bionics were enforcers, specifically selected to become super soldiers, most of their body replaced with mechanical parts. More cyborg than human. Unnatural. Drayfus had never seen one before.

And then Mysa Lamond looked directly at the enforcer. Her eyes became completely blank. Something was happening. An exchange. Between eyes, between pads, maybe, or machines. Half-machines.

Surreal.

Drayfus felt out of place.

It dawned on him then that Mysa Lamond could not be an executive. She was something different, something more. What, he did not know. His dislike for the woman turned to raw fear.

The exchange between Mysa Lamond and the bionic was brief, yet millions of bytes of data were probably exchanged in those few moments.

Next, Mysa Lamond turned to Drayfus. The crispness of her bright lips and the perfection of her blond hair bothered him. A single long black pin that reminded Drayfus of a dagger kept the hair flat on her head.

"What… what's going on?" he asked. "Why did you take over? I'd have cooperated."

"What is happening is not good for you," said Mysa Lamond. "It is not good for BlueTech Data. Your cooperation is not optional. It is expected."

Drayfus nodded violently.

"You have my cooperation," he said, trying to figure out what was going on. "What happened?" he tried again. "What can I do to help?"

"We have locked down the building," said Mysa Lamond. "No one is to enter or exit until we have what we came for. We are monitoring the tower's network in its totality." She pointed at Drayfus's workstation. "I needed an entry point."

No apologies would be forthcoming, Drayfus knew. He didn't really care anymore. Obviously, something big was going on. The directors would not be happy. What if... what if the project was in jeopardy? What then? What about the Blue Tower? What would Mr. Blue say? This whole matter could quickly bring Drayfus's career to an end.

And who or what was Mysa Lamond?

If she was not an executive and not an enforcer, then what? If she could take over his workstation that easily, that quickly, what could she be? She needed special privileges to perform such a takeover.

A sleuth?

"We know the importance of the project you are launching today," said Mysa Lamond, as if she had been reading his thoughts. Accessing his b-pad? "That is why we waited until now. Can you confirm that the project is proceeding as planned and that it will continue to do so henceforth?"

"I... I suppose so," said Drayfus. "Wave 1 and 2 were the critical ones, and Wave 3 is almost done and going well so far."

"You do not foresee any problem if we were to interrogate a member of the project team?"

"I guess not. I mean, it depends who you want to talk to."

"We only want one individual," said Mysa Lamond. "Certainly, at this point, one person can't make a difference."

To be honest, Drayfus didn't really know if one person would make a difference. Artenz had been adamant that he needed his whole team for the success of the project.

And if Mysa Lamond was a sleuth, she probably knew more than he did about the project—its progress, who was working on it, who was doing what, and who was dispensable.

Drayfus pushed his fears aside, although he could not bring himself to feel at ease with these two individuals. It seemed Mysa Lamond

Deficiency

would not interfere with the project. Not too much, anyway. Drayfus was worried though, worried they wanted Artenz. Why bring it up otherwise? Mysa Lamond would know he was their best asset, the lead on the project.

Enforcers were present, meaning... well, meaning they might lose someone for good. Drayfus had high hopes for the future, and that future included Artenz.

"I asked a question," said Mysa Lamond. "A single individual, no more."

"I... suppose so," Drayfus answered.

He had no other choice but to comply.

"We will set up an interrogation room in your office. We are allowing you to keep this operation's impact to a minimum. No one has to know what is happening. I assume you can handle and explain a lockdown of a few dozen minutes?"

"Yes," said Drayfus. "It shouldn't be a problem."

He could pass it off as a security test, as a possible network threat, anything really.

"Continue to cooperate, Mr. Arlsberg, and we will be out of here inside the hour."

Drayfus found himself nodding again.

Mysa Lamond told him who she wanted.

- . . . . Gone

Thrium Laboratories was a subdued place that morning. Keidi stood in the hallway, her back against the wall, Zofia on her right. She felt emotionally empty and physically exhausted.

She had heard stories, as had anyone else, of people disappearing. *It never happens to you, does it?* she thought. *Never anyone you actually know.*

Of all the researchers, it was evident that Zofia struggled the most with Detel's disappearance. The others worried, but it seemed mostly out of fear and confusion, not because Detel was gone. Not surprising, as Artenz's sister was not much liked. Detel never hid the fact that she thought little of most of her colleagues.

"They abandoned the scientific approach," she once said to Keidi. "They forge results, for credits."

It was a dangerous accusation, and Keidi had warned Detel more than once to be careful about what she said.

"What is Detel researching?" Keidi asked.

Zofia turned her way. She looked awful.

"Everything Detel does is related to the body," she answered. "She has so many paths on the go, so many different things she's involved with. She wants to understand it all, you know. No one here can follow her. I tried. But she stays here crazy hours. I can't keep up. But you know all that."

"Yes, Detel was dedicated," said Keidi, regretting instantly that she'd used the past tense. "But, I mean, what is she working on these days? Surely you'd know something, as her partner."

At this, Zofia did a double take, looking directly at Keidi.

And there it was, in her eyes, the reason for such pain.

"You were actual partners?" murmured Keidi. "I mean, more than work colleagues… "

She had not known, had not even suspected. Instead, she had been jealous—a vain jealousy, as it turned out. Battling over friendship, while…

Fear flooded Zofia's eyes now. Keidi reached out and hugged Zofia.

"I did not know," she whispered in the woman's ear. "I truly did not know. Your secret is safe with me."

+

They walked to the small cafeteria at the end of the hall. The place was empty. They picked a table by a window, although it offered a view of a gray brick wall. Keidi held Zofia's hands. They were linked now, the two of them. They finally understood each other. Detel's best friend and Detel's lover.

"This isn't your fault," said Keidi.

"How do you know?"

"Because they would have fired one of you, or both. Or moved you to another lab, something like that."

It happened often enough. The slightest suspicion, and the employer took quick and strict action. Relationships at work brought too many problems. Keidi could not say she agreed. She liked the idea of working with Artenz, spending her days with him. They would work well together.

Zofia did not look convinced.

"This is extreme," added Keidi. "There must be something else for them to take such drastic measures. You know I'm right."

Finally, the other woman nodded.

"It has to be related to her research," said Keidi.

"I don't know exactly where her research was taking her," said Zofia, her eyes dry and red. "The details, I mean. She wouldn't tell me, but she was onto something. She spent many nights here over the past month."

"Could it be related to newborns?" asked Keidi. After all, Detel had helped her and Artenz with the pregnancy. She wondered if Zofia knew about their natural birth. Would Detel have told her?

"I don't think so, but it's hard to say. Lately, she was especially interested in the mind, its working, and the brain. I would never peek, you know. I respected her too much for that."

Keidi did understand. She was not certain she would call it respect, though. Politeness maybe? With a smudge of fear, both for the nature of the research and the chance of upsetting Detel?

Artenz and Keidi never challenged Detel about her research. Sometimes, Keidi felt that Detel was into something she shouldn't be, exploring avenues that some might not want explored. Instead of asking about it, Keidi would brush it aside, telling herself that Detel knew what she was doing, convincing herself it was so. She knew Artenz did the same.

Why hadn't she asked? She now felt it had been lazy somehow, a way to avoid worrying, to avoid responsibility. Or to avoid Detel's temper and strong opinions. No one wanted to argue with Detel. She knew the facts, more than anyone, and always won.

"Has anything like this ever happened before?" Keidi asked.

"No. Projects come and go. We get our instructions. Inspectors visit every few months and review the progress, look at the potential. They choose which research paths to abandon, which ones to explore further. That is the way of things."

"But Detel has her own goals," said Keidi.

Deficiency

"She does. The inspectors don't like her, which means no one here likes her. Her defiance makes everything harder for the rest of us. It is no secret that she's doing her own things. I think the inspectors know. After a while, there's no way to hide it. So they must be allowing it, you know. If they didn't, they would have ordered her to stop, would they not?"

A shape appeared in the doorway. One of the researchers.

"We should get back to the lab," he said.

"Give me a minute," Zofia said. "I'll be right there."

He made a face and left. Keidi wondered if Zofia's relationship with Detel was impacting how the others perceived her.

Zofia turned to Keidi. "To get back to your question, we've had computers and equipment taken away before. It's normal and part of the research. They only provide what we need for what we work on. Some of the things we discover have major impacts, so the work is transferred to more capable hands. But there's never been anything like this. Never this exhaustive. There's nothing left. Not even... her."

Zofia trembled, while keeping the tears away. They stood and hugged briefly. *She's a good match for Detel*, thought Keidi, now seeing the woman in a different light.

"You'll let me know if you hear anything, won't you?" Zofia asked.

"I will," said Keidi. "Please do the same."

Zofia nodded and left. At that moment, an incoming link beeped on Keidi's b-pad.

+

Artenz stepped out of the Blue Tower on level 40. The floor was mostly made of transparent glass, allowing the light to reach the levels below. Artenz walked away from the tower and stepped onto an arched bridge.

There was an opaque street 10 levels below. Artenz could see individuals going and coming, some on the walk-ways, some not. A transporter riding a uni-racer sped along a belt. The tram appeared from under the Blue Tower and sped toward the west.

A long fall. It happened more than the news let on. People jumping from high streets to lower streets.

"But why?" he had debated with Keidi.

"Possibly because they decide not to accept this life anymore," she had said.

"Such a waste," he had replied.

"True, but you're missing my point. You don't understand them because you just do what everybody does, never asking any questions."

And maybe that was a good thing. His parents had not accepted much about Prominence. They had strongly opposed the b-pads, and that had forced them out of the city. Artenz, then 17, had moved in with Detel, who was attending university. He had enrolled the next year.

Now Detel was gone.

And Keidi... as much as he loved her, he could not help thinking about their predicament. Without Detel, how could they hope to safely give birth to this baby? Detel had been the one monitoring Keidi and the one with the knowledge of how the whole thing would happen.

What now?

Artenz had always liked the rebellious side of Keidi, its unpredictability. He wondered if he had chosen her, subconsciously, because she reminded him of his parents. An interesting twist, now that he thought about it, as he resented his parents for that exact quality.

But he loved Keidi. How he loved her... He could not imagine life without her.

Prominence was as it always had been. Large, shiny. Immense and powerful. With its beautiful, healthy and law-abiding citizens.

Yet in Artenz's tumultuous head, the city did not look so perfect anymore. It felt like a scam, a falsity. The words spoken by Marti seemed to have changed everything for him. Like a switch. All his doubts, which he had dismissed easily before, were now in his face, undeniable.

His sister, his older sister, who had always been there for him since their parents had left... gone.

It did not register.

It could not be real.

The feeling of betrayal was suddenly very much like the one Artenz had felt when his parents had moved. He was mad—at life, at Keidi, and especially at Detel.

Like their parents, Detel had dabbled in things better left alone. She...

He stopped his thoughts and put a hand on the railing of the bridge—too late. The traitorous thought that Detel had gotten what she deserved had come, unwittingly. Artenz hated himself for it.

He... could not believe she was gone.

Trying to calm the chaos in his head, he started walking again.

Detel must have done or said something that had angered someone powerful. A corporation, most likely. It was the only possibility. Anything else, and Detel would have warned him, left him a note. Something.

He thought about the note left by his parents. It had been vague. No destination had been mentioned. Still, over the years, they had often talked about the Dara Gulch, providing hints they would go there if the day came when they had to leave. Artenz had no idea where the gulch was. Possibly, one had to go down to the Low Lands and find a way from there. His parents had mentioned beaches and green patches along a river's edge, a small, isolated paradise hidden deep in some ravine.

Artenz was mad at his parents too. If they had stayed, maybe Detel would not have been so obsessed with finding problems with the world.

As he reached the entrance to Ilda's Cafe, on the other side of the bridge, Artenz forced a stop to his thoughts. He never liked thinking about his parents. He missed them, true, but he was also mad at them; the anger stayed fresh even after 20 years.

He entered the cafe, a small place attached to the side of a wall that Artenz visited often. He found his round table and sat down heavily. Two seats. Often, Marti came with him.

He did not know what to think or what to do next. There was a void inside him, growing, hurting. He linked Keidi.

+

"Love?"

Artenz could not stop his voice from breaking.

"I am here," uttered Keidi.

They said nothing more for a few long moments.

+

Finally, Artenz asked, "Where are you?"

"At Thrium," Keidi answered.

"And?"

"Well… " The defeat in her voice told him what he had feared.

"She's gone," he said. He felt like his words were accusatory, even though he knew it was not her fault. "Marti told me," he added quickly. "Remember, this morning, he was asking about her?"

"I do. Did he know already?"

"He suspected. I still don't know why. He's been searching for her all morning."

"Was he able to find anything? Surely there must be something in the data-sphere."

"You'd think, but no, there's nothing, and Marti went deep. From what he said, too deep maybe, whatever that means. He's still looking, but I don't know, I don't… He knows something. Something about what Detel was doing, I think. With the project, we haven't had time to

Deficiency

talk yet. And I had to come out, to let you know... to hear your voice." Artenz stopped, feeling the truth behind his last words. He liked talking with Keidi. Her voice alone gave him strength. And right now, she was the only remaining constant in his life. "How are you doing? You know, the sickness."

"I'm good, on that front," said Keidi.

The small cafe was quickly filling up. Most tables were occupied. Lunch hour.

"Did you find any clue as to what is happening at Thrium?" he asked.

"Nothing," answered Keidi. There was a strange tone in her voice.

"What is it?" asked Artenz.

"It... they took everything. Absolutely everything. There's not one trace that she was ever here. I went to her lab, and it's empty. It's the same in the Sphere. Her room is gone and her profile is gone."

The words were not easy to hear, even though Artenz had suspected.

"Did you ask about her research?"

"Yes. Zofia knows nothing. Detel kept everything to herself. You know how she can be. No one knows exactly what she's been working on."

There was a pause, then:

"You'll have to talk to Marti," said Keidi. "I'll go to her lodge, but I think I know what I'm going to find there. Or not find."

"Maybe you should go back home," said Artenz, "and I can go to her lodge on my way home."

"Don't be ridiculous, it's only a few blocks away. It'd take you forever. And I'm not going back to the workshop. I took the rest of the day off. Do you think you can leave early?"

"I doubt it, but you can be certain I'll try. Really, there's not much more for me to do. The team can handle the remaining waves. They don't really need me, whatever the managers may think. They gave me 15 minutes for lunch."

"Ridiculous," said Keidi. "Go, see what you can find out from Marti and let me know."

Artenz still didn't feel good about Keidi going to Detel's lodge.

"We don't know what happened," he said. "You don't know what you'll find over there. Be careful, please. I'm serious. Do not enter if you feel anything is wrong."

"Something will be wrong," Keidi said, "but yes, I'll be careful. Try not to worry."

But he knew he would. She knew he would.

And she worried for him just as much.

"Love?" said Artenz.

"Yes?"

"I… " Artenz hesitated. "I love you," he said finally.

"I love you too," said Keidi. "Talk soon."

"Soon," he said.

✢

Artenz stood and offered his table to an older couple that had just entered. As he made his way out, he thought about Keidi, about how important she was to him. He needed her in his life, now more than ever. On the other hand, without Detel, maybe they should think about aborting the baby. Early on, Detel had mentioned it as a valid exit option, if they ever changed their minds. It seemed like the logical step, now that Detel…

Artenz took a deep breath. The fear was muddling his thoughts, making him panic. At least he had a plan. He must stick to the plan: talk to Marti.

As if on cue, his b-pad flashed.

A new message, flagged as urgent. It was from Marti.

Artenz stepped to the side, face to a wall, and put his head down and opened the message. It appeared in front of him, shining words on the flat surface of the eye-veil.

Deficiency

```
Bio-sphere e-mail service

From:          Red Dragon M
Sent:          Year 3.4k60 Season 05 Day 11 Hour 1201.
Subject:       [n/a]

The fuckin sleuths found me. It's the corporations. Do not
come back inside. Get a scrambler, then run and hide!
Keidi too.
This is VERY serious shit. Remember your parents.
I'll get in touch when I can.
M.
```

Segment C

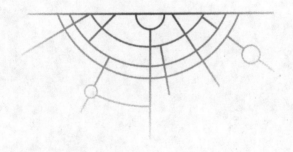

"A master coder is 20 times more efficient than an adept coder."

- Marti Zehron

- - Rift

Marti would never again work for BlueTech Data. Drayfus, seated on his assistant's desk, knew it. As a matter of fact, he doubted Marti would ever again work for anyone.

The old man had always seemed shady to Drayfus. It was probably prejudice on his part, but he couldn't help it.

The gray thinning hair, always oily, and his fat and bloated body, stuck to his chair; Marti had never fit the mold of a good corporate employee. An adept coder at best, even after all those years in the development world. The man had barely passed the adept aptitude test. Paying his salary was a waste of money.

Drayfus did not understand why Artenz had kept Marti on his team. He was slow, and his social skills where poor. He was a team demoralizer if ever there was one. Drayfus had thought that maybe he was some kind of relative of Artenz's. An uncle maybe. It was not the case.

In all honesty, Drayfus had not really cared. He had wanted Artenz, and if it took Marti to have him, so be it. He had not cared, while suspecting that Marti was involved in some kind of scam.

And it was bad.

Deficiency

Drayfus had done what Mysa Lamond had asked. He had fetched Marti. When he reached the team's room, the old man looked as if he had been expecting the summon.

"About time," the old arrogant geezer said.

He had no idea what he was in for, and that Mysa Lamond was the one asking for him.

Marti followed Drayfus through the boardroom, then the hallway, and as he turned the corner, the enforcers were on him.

No one from Artenz's team saw the enforcers. At worst, they might think Marti's job was in jeopardy. They would never guess the extent of the trouble he was in.

The enforcers had not been gentle, grabbing the old coder by the arms and the neck, pulling him, pushing him. He bounced off a wall and fell to the floor. Before he could even try to get up, the enforcers were on him again, dragging him. He was big, but some of these enforcers were half-machines, powered by augments. Marti was hauled all the way to the office, where the door closed behind him.

Not once did he resist. Too lazy even for that.

Still, looking at the closed door of his office, Drayfus felt bad for the old man. How could he not?

He had gone back and informed the team of the temporary lockdown. As expected, they had taken it calmly, professionally. After all, it was temporary. There had been a few murmurs, but nothing to worry about. He had reassured them that the lockdown would not impact the launch and that everything would shortly be back to normal.

Those were his expectations as well.

"Can I get you another coffee?" asked his assistant.

"No, but I'd take a glass of..." Drayfus stopped as he looked toward his office. "Never mind."

He had heard rumors, bad rumors, about the Crystal Globe Conglomerate. It was one of those things you ignored as a manager, if you wanted to keep your job. It was there if you dared to look; most did not.

People disappearing, some in high places.

Such rumors sometimes kept Drayfus awake at night, knowing a bad move on his part could result in him being sent away.

Away...

Profit was what mattered. To do what you were told and do it well.

The competition between corporations was fierce and terribly complex. Cartels formed and broke apart, replaced by others instantly. The launch of the Targos module was most likely part of another partnership that would provide a temporary advantage to the CGC and its affiliates. It was a good move for BlueTech and all its directors and managers, including Drayfus. It was not bad for Artenz and his team, even though they were operations. They would never climb much higher in the hierarchy, but a good reputation always helped. Directors did not care much about them, but Drayfus did. He knew their worth. He would keep them with him as long as he could. As long as they provided value.

Although the economy of Prominence was mostly self-sufficient, the games played by the corporations extended beyond its borders, far beyond.

There were outside resources, outside players, other locations. Probably a lot more than even Drayfus could guess.

Maybe he did care. He had thought about it during those sleepless nights.

The corporations never wasted anything, including human labor.

They didn't dispose of.

They recycled.

Drayfus knew the asteroid mines were real. It was a known fact in the management circle. Known, yet never discussed. Never spoken out loud.

The asteroids were an endless source of rare gems and metals. Drayfus was fairly certain he had worked out where the unlimited

Deficiency

number of miners and laborers came from. The Low Lands, certainly, but also from Prominence City itself. Individuals like Marti here, who did not fit, who were causing problems. Criminals, mostly, but also anyone who did not meet the Prominence standard: unkempt or ragged, independent or disobedient employees, some colored skin, deformed and handicapped, probably even blank babies. Yes, even babies.

Drayfus admitted he wasn't certain about that last one. It would make sense, though. Value anywhere it could be found. As disturbing as the thought was, it just might be true.

Marti would be shipped out, most likely off the surface of Garadia, all the way to the asteroids, where he would work for the rest of his days in dark tunnels.

+

The door to his office opened, and the bionic exited the office. He was most likely the leader of this squadron. His glass mask was back on, covering his face. His massive rifle was in his left hand, snug between his arm and chest.

Drayfus was taken aback as the bionic came directly at him. Drayfus jumped off the desk and backed away. His assistant tried to put himself between Drayfus and the bionic. A bad decision.

Without hesitation, the bionic lashed out with the butt of his rifle. It caught the assistant in the stomach, forcing him to the floor, where he curled up in a ball.

Drayfus was still looking at his assistant when the bionic's right hand grabbed him by the neck. The touch was cold. Drayfus's feet left the floor as he was pushed hard against the wall. Then the bionic sat him on a table and pointed his rifle's nozzle at Drayfus's mouth.

"Tell me and tell me quick," ordered the bionic with a steady voice. No intonation, no exertion. "Tell me about the rift in your building's security. Tell me who stepped out of the tower. You might yet make it out of this unhurt."

"I… have no idea what you're talking about."

Drayfus's thoughts were scattered, unordered. The only things he could see were the rifle pointed at him, and behind it, the reflective mask of the bionic.

"Let me tell you the details." The rifle's barrel touched Drayfus's lips lightly, sending a shiver of terror down his spine. "1145, the building is locked down. 1150, someone walks out. Right out, on floor 40. Do you have any idea who that was?"

Drayfus shook his head.

"I am not convinced." The fingers squeezed, and Drayfus choked. The pain around his neck brought tears to his eyes. "You are the chief manager here. You control security. You would have ordered the rift. No one else could."

Drayfus tried to talk but could not. The bionic pulled back the rifle and slightly loosened his grip.

"I swear," Drayfus said. "There's no rift."

"There is a rift." It was Mysa Lamond, who appeared behind the bionic. "Release him, Okran. He is not lying."

The bionic stepped back, letting Drayfus crumple on the table, head low, gasping for air.

Mysa Lamond stepped in front of him, tall in her high heels. She was immaculate. Not a crease in her clothes. Not a hair out of place. She was as calm and composed as when she had arrived in the morning. For his part, Drayfus bathed in his own sweat, his suit wrinkled. His hate for her grew.

"Pull yourself together, Mr. Arlsberg," said Mysa Lamond. "I still need you. The person gone is your chief programmer, Artenz Scherzel. Any idea where he might have gone?"

Artenz?

Deficiency

For the first time, Drayfus thought about rebelling, about not cooperating. Artenz was one of the best assets of this company. He had just completed, almost completed, another successful major project.

BlueTech could certainly do without Marti. But Artenz?

Maybe BlueTech could do without Artenz, and it was Drayfus who couldn't. Or didn't want to. He had found someone he could count on. Employees like Artenz were hard to come by. Artenz meant bonuses for Drayfus, and possibly a promotion or two.

Drayfus began to wonder about Mysa Lamond's motives. It was his job to worry about the competition. And although BlueTech currently had a pledge with the CGC, partnerships—especially hidden agreements like this one—were known to change quickly and without notice.

Had he made a mistake by allowing Mysa Lamond in the building?

He looked at his assistant, now seated on the floor behind the desk, hidden and looking back at Drayfus. Terror on his face.

Then Drayfus noticed the bionic called Okran standing to the left of Mysa Lamond, his rifle still pointing right at him. Two more enforcers were standing by the door to his office.

This was not the place for heroics.

"He goes out to lunch, across the bridge. There's a cafe there," he said.

Mysa Lamond looked at Okran.

"Go," she said simply.

Okran pointed to the two enforcers by the door, one after the other, and ordered them to follow with a movement of the head.

+

With no enforcer in the hallway, alone with his assistant and Mysa Lamond, Drayfus thought he should try one more time.

"What is this about?" he asked. "You come here, infiltrate our network, lock down the building, abduct one of my employees, and now go hunting one of my best assets. This isn't part of the pledge."

Mysa Lamond had already turned toward his office. She stopped and looked at him with a single eye.

"You have no idea what is part of the pledge and what is not," she said. "This investigation is not over. Until it is, you will know nothing. Once it is done, it will be for others to decide what they want to tell you."

With that, Mysa Lamond disappeared in his office. Drayfus quickly stepped forward and looked inside. Before the door closed, before an enforcer from inside stepped in front of him, Drayfus got a glimpse of Marti.

The old man was on his knees in the center of the room. His back was to Drayfus, his head bent forward. On the floor, Drayfus noticed the clean-bot hard at work, washing away what looked like a puddle of blood.

- - . In the Cafe

The cafe seemed to shrink as Artenz re-read Marti's message. The walls were too close, space nonexistent. There was nowhere to go or hide. It didn't really matter anyway. His b-pad was buzzing, or so it seemed, in his neck. The b-pad would give away his position.

Artenz moved to the cafe's front window and looked at the Blue Tower, thinking he might see something different.

He did not.

It was the same building, tall and blue, a giant structure in the middle of Quadrant X. Over 110 levels tall. This was level 40.

Artenz looked toward the entrance from which he had exited. He saw no one.

He moved back to the far corner of the store, looking around, looking for an alternate exit. Surely he had a few minutes. Surely he could link Keidi.

He did.

"Love, listen," he began, before he even heard her voice. "Marti was taken. I don't know why, or how. He said to run. He said to hide. Can you get a scrambler?"

No reply came. "Love?"

"I'm here," she said. "I'm thinking." Then: "Who took him?"

"Not sure. He mentioned the sleuths and the corporations. Maybe both."

"And they want us? Why?"

"He didn't say, but my guess is that it's because we know Detel. I trust Marti on this. And he said to remember my parents."

"All right, all right... We have some at the workshop."

"What?"

"Scramblers. We have some."

"Good, perfect. Get one. Use it."

"What about you?"

"I don't know. I can't, no. Not quickly anyway."

"What year did you get your pad?"

"What... year? What are you talking about?"

"The year, Artenz. 3.4k34? How old were you?"

"I was 10. Year 33."

"Good, good. Try a dual-reset."

"A what?"

"Dual-reset. Just reset your b-pad, and while it is resetting, reset it again. Yours is an older model. The dual-reset was put in place to flush out issues and start the pad again."

Artenz had never heard of such a thing. Keidi would know. Pads were her expertise, not his.

"How much time does it give me?" he asked.

"About a minute, completely offline."

"And when can I repeat again?"

"As soon as it starts. It'll destabilize your pad, give you headaches."

"Any data loss?"

"Local only, no worry."

Everything was synchronized to the Sphere, so there should have been no worry. Except Artenz used his local storage. With Marti, it was something he had been working on expanding. It was a risk he would have to take.

Deficiency

"All right," Artenz said, amazed at how clearly Keidi seemed to think. "We need a meeting place, or a time to relink."

There was a moment of silence.

"Time won't work. Your pad will be all over the place. The Cable Den?"

It was a small bar where they used to hang out, with Detel. Quadrant Z.

"No, some new place, where we've never been. The bot shop on Business Street."

He couldn't remember the name of the place. They used to make fun of it. It was squeezed between two lodge complexes, in Quadrant O. It meant Artenz would have to cross borders, but it was closer than going all the way back to Quadrant Z. He might have to cross on foot. Also, that shop might have scramblers for sale. If he could get there, then he would be able to hide.

"Good idea, what level?"

"33."

"Right."

"All right." Artenz didn't want to unlink.

It seemed Keidi didn't want to either. There was a prolonged silence.

"You be careful," he said.

"You too," she said.

Another silence. They needed to unlink.

"Is this real?" Keidi asked.

And for a moment, Artenz felt time stop.

Was this real?

Everything around him was so normal, so ordinary. It was his routine. Lunch at Ilda's. Sometimes with Marti. Sometimes with Keidi, when she was able to get away from the workshop. Sometimes on his own, like today, talking to Keidi.

Usually, he would be seated, not standing in a corner.

Normally, he would be relaxed, not sweating.

"It is," he said finally.

"Talk soon," Keidi said. "Be careful. I love you."

"Love you," said Artenz and unlinked.

Artenz had always been proactive when it came to technology. He liked innovations; he craved them. The minute one became available, he wanted it and would even wait in line at the store if that meant he would be one of the first to get it. It happened that way when he turned 10 and the b-pad became available for everyone.

No parents' consent required.

"Isn't that worrisome?" Keidi had asked much later, throwing ideas around. "The fact that no parent needed to approve the implant should have worried many."

At 10, it had not worried Artenz. His parents had not been able to hide their disappointment when he got home with the brain-pad stuck in his neck. Artenz remembered their reaction still and how bad he had felt at the time.

He had not understood his parents' reaction. How could he? At 10? It took him a long time to understand. Even when Detel and Keidi had shared their concerns about the b-pads, he had not bitten.

It took until today.

He now saw the full range of its problems, the extent to which it infiltrated a person's life. As he stood in Ilda's Cafe, Artenz had no illusion about his chances to meet up with Keidi.

They were extremely low.

He could do the dual-reset. That would hide him, certainly, but also cripple him. His credits were available through his b-pad. No b-pad, no purchase of any kind. He would not be able to take the tram. Even some walk-ways and speed-walks would be inaccessible to him. No air-tubes. He had a long way to go to reach Quadrant O.

Deficiency

The b-pad was also his only mean of communication. No pad, no link. No pad, no information. The device was his single point of access to the Sphere. No pad, no time of day, no map.

It was an impressive device, almost an extension of himself. The eye-veil put everything right in front of his eyes. The ear-sound sent audio to his ears. And these were only two of the many augments available for the b-pad.

The device was meant to be permanent. Artenz could not pull it out or remove it. Even without augments, it was connected to the eyes, ears and brain. On top of this, it was attached to the left carotid artery, something Detel had said did not make sense. Why the artery? Some speculated the b-pad used the blood flow to power up, to keep working.

It was not the case. Most people simply did not know the b-pad was attached to the carotid.

So, why implement it in such a crippling way?

When his parents left, they had been strongly opposed to the mandatory implantation of the b-pads in every infant. Artenz had not understood their position or their decision. His parents had always been vocal about their opposition to the corporations, saying a neutral government would be a better ruling body. The government existed, but all knew true power resided with the corporations. Phasing the government out completely would not change a thing. It was surprising it had not been done already.

As much as Artenz had pretended that his parents' departure did not bother him any longer, deep down it still did. They had continued to categorically refuse to get a b-pad, which they would have had to do if they had wanted to stay. Artenz had always struggled to understand their view.

Until this very moment, the hate had never left him.

Now, finally, he understood. He got it.

He felt utterly trapped.

He needed the b-pad, even though the device was continuously broadcasting his location to whoever wanted it, sending it to the Sphere.

And the sleuths were after him. They... had unlimited access to everything.

A chair had become available, and Artenz dropped into it. If Marti had not been able to hide, how was he supposed to?

"One thing at a time," he said.

Using a single finger, he found the button on his b-pad and pushed. He waited and felt it reboot. The information in front of his eyes disappeared. He was so used to the thing that doing a simple reset gave him a brief moment of vertigo. As it started again, the weak vibrations noticeable on his finger, he pushed once more. The simple reset did not disconnect or shut down the b-pad. Not really. Refresh might have been a better term for it.

After a few seconds, Artenz felt the pad power down. Completely.

He was not ready for it.

As the device died, a powerful sensation pulled on his mind and brain. His vision turned blurry. The sounds around, voices and music and everything, became muffled.

Artenz closed his eyes and put his head in his hands, trying to stop the nausea and vertigo.

And then it passed.

Sounds returned, as if his ears had popped. His vision came back and with it, clarity.

Now, it was time to move.

Now...There was a commotion at the front of the cafe. People had gathered, exclamations sounding, fingers pointing, pointing outside, pointing toward the Blue Tower.

Artenz stood, looked through the front glass and saw three enforcers coming out of the Blue Tower.

He had waited too long.

- - . . Back to the Workshop

After unlinking with Artenz, Keidi made her way back toward the lounge. She was glad to find that Zofia was still there and signaled to her. The biologist finished her exchange with one of her colleagues and came to Keidi, who pulled her farther down the corridor.

"First," murmured Keidi, "I didn't know. About you and Detel. I promise I won't tell. In truth, I'm glad that Detel had someone." Zofia smiled briefly. "Second, this is bad. I got news, and it's not good at all."

Zofia flinched at the words but got her composure back quickly. Maybe she had already come to the same conclusion. Either way, Keidi believed she deserved to know.

"It's not just Detel. Now they're after Artenz," Keidi hated the tremors in her voice.

"I'm sorry," said Zofia, putting a hand on Keidi's shoulder. "Can I help?"

"No, not really," said Keidi. "Just be careful. And third, did you go to Detel's lodge today?"

"No, I didn't. I never saw her lodge."

They probably did not want someone seeing them together at Detel's place. Or maybe it was just another of Detel's quirks.

"Thank you, Zofia. And I'm sorry as well."

The two hugged.

"Be careful," said Zofia, sincere.

Keidi couldn't help being sad that it had taken such extreme events to bring them together. She liked this woman.

Without another word, Keidi turned around and made her way out of Thrium Laboratories.

+

She stopped outside the workshop, hesitating. If she went back inside and Tarana was there, she would not hear the end of it. On the street, life was going on as usual. Overhead, a tram flew by against a steel gray sky. Keidi ordered the time and her b-pad showed 1228.

Ah! Lunch time.

Tarana and Ronin could just be out. If not, they would be out soon. It was their way to rebel against the deadlines, making a point of not missing a meal and taking the full 30 minutes allotted to them. Keidi was not sure why their employer had not yet taken that away as well, forcing lunch in the workshop or something. Efficiency being so important, it would not have been surprising. It was probably an oversight.

Keidi approached the door to the workshop, and it recognized her b-pad and slid open. The entrance was a small room where two security guards had once been stationed. It was empty, and Keidi could hear her colleagues' voices coming from the workshop doors as they dismantled pads.

She decided to wait. If they didn't come out soon, she would go in. But she'd try not to involve them, if at all possible.

Keidi backed away and looked around for a hiding spot. The street was wide and open. Then Keidi saw the walk-way on the opposite side of the street, with its three-foot-high railings. She went toward it at a steady pace, although she wanted to run.

She took her coat and backpack off. Then she quickly pulled the hood of her long-sleeved sweatshirt over her head. She didn't take the walk-way but instead made her way to the other side. There, she sat down, her back to the railing. She rapidly opened her backpack, took out her mini-vid, and pretended to read.

A few minutes later, to her relief, she heard Ronin's and Tarana's voices. She put her head down even more as they chatted on the walk-way behind her.

They passed and went on.

Keidi waited a few minutes longer, then stood and walked quickly toward the workshop. She stored away the mini-vid and put back her coat.

So far, so good.

+

She left the workshop a few minutes later, a scrambler in the hood of her sweater and a few more gadgets in her bag.

There had never been any doubt in Keidi's mind that she would check Detel's lodge, despite the warning from Marti. Artenz would not approve, but someone had to do it.

She took to the street in the opposite direction taken by Tarana and Ronin. She jumped on a walk-way, then switched to a speed-belt, holding on to the railway as it sped quickly toward the east.

Going to the lodge was only a brief detour on her way to the I Bot store. Artenz had noticed the shop during a night stroll following a visit at Detel's. It was only a few minutes away from her lodge.

The scrambler's vibrations tickled through the b-pad on her neck. It was bothersome. But not as much as it would be for Artenz, who had lived with the b-pad for years and who slept logged in to the bio-sphere. The dependence was real, although Artenz kept denying it. Which he did only to make himself feel better. He knew she was right.

Keidi wondered if the speed-belts and walk-ways logged who stepped on them. And what about air-tubes? She would have to take at least one tube to climb up to level 30. Most air-tubes connected to the b-pads directly. She could possibly use stairs, but there weren't many of them, and they would take longer. Some buildings didn't even have them anymore. She had to climb 15 levels to reach the street on which Detel's entrance was located. It was a lot.

Ahead, through the speed-belt glass tube, Keidi could see the streets floating above. The air on her face was cool and whipped her hair left and right. She sat down and took an elastic from a side pouch on her bag. She tied her hair and stood back up, losing her balance momentarily on the fast-moving floor.

The end of the belt came, and Keidi switched to a slower walk-way and, a few moments later, to the street. She kept a fast pace. She could feel the cold sweat accumulating on her back.

As she reached a street corner, she grabbed the scrambler and turned it off. She waited for the interference to disappear, instructed level 30 to her b-pad and jumped in the air-tube.

The tube was weak and the push up slow, to the point that Keidi wondered for a moment if it would be able to get her to her destination. It did.

She stepped out on level 30 and turned the scrambler back on. This was Dorion Street. The Actus Dorion Complex, where Detel rented a lodge, was at the end of the street.

+

The building had once been grandiose. Its gigantic facade climbed all the way to level 65. Located at the end of the street, its marble courtyard was now empty. Ten large steps led to the large statue of Actus Dorion himself. A figure forgotten.

Keidi and Detel had looked him up in the data-sphere one night. He had lived more than 300 years ago, and the statue had been erected shortly after his death, which explained its faded features. He had been the executive of a construction enterprise—successful, it seemed, based on this building and others he had owned.

Deficiency

The fortune was long gone, as was the prestige. The lodge complex now looked poor and unmaintained. It was the story of many buildings in the Factory district, where production was more important than the comfort of the workers.

Keidi stopped by the two heavy doors forming the entrance. One of the panels was permanently secured while the other was locked, as she had known it would be. That was why she had packed extra tools from the workshop.

She located the entrance recognition box on the side of the door. Depositing her backpack on the floor, Keidi took out a small case, a positive demagnetizer, and a flat screwdriver. Holding the demagnetizer in one hand, she moved it close to the box. Using the screwdriver, she forced the box open. It took a few moments for the demagnetizer to weaken the box and have it pop open.

Then Keidi connected a cable directly from her b-pad to the box. The scrambler in her hood stopped the b-pad's emission, but had no effect on the direct connection through a cable.

Next, she took out her mini-vid so she could see the command prompt and information from the system she was hacking. She connected it to her b-pad and powered it. Instantly, she could see the welcome message from the system.

```
FrontShield Security System 2.7K

Actus Dorion Complex
1 Dorion Street, Xarlington, D3QO
Initial Contract Y2702-11-01-000001-L10-65
Active Contract Nil

Latest Contract Y2852-11-01-004230-L15-65 Expired

Do>
```

Old buildings had old security systems. It was impressive that the third generation of pads could interact with systems spanning centuries. The b-pad had no problem.

Keidi entered a few commands, easily bypassing several layers of security. Her training in action. Her final command was:

```
Do> Set Admin KeidiRysinjer
Admin user confirmed.
```

Keidi unplugged her b-pad and put her tools away.

She moved to the door and took the scrambler out of her hood, turned it off, and waited. Her b-pad talked with the system.

It only took a few seconds for the system to recognize her as an administrator.

The door clicked and opened. Keidi went in.

+

Inside the building, the marks of time were visible at the bottom of the walls and in ceiling corners, where the surfaces were darkened, possibly moldy. The clean-bots still did their job, but poorly. Their cycle had been brought to a crawl. As she had gone through the system earlier, Keidi had noted that the cleaning routine in this building was a whole season, rather than 30 days.

Since she only had two levels to climb, Keidi decided to use the staircase. She found it not far from the entrance.

It was quickly obvious that this had been a bad decision. The metal steps were slanted, and the whole structure swung from left to right as Keidi climbed. She was afraid it would not hold long enough for her to reach Detel's floor. Still, the scrambler was back on, and Keidi didn't want to use her b-pad if she didn't need to.

Deficiency

She reached level 32 and stepped into the corridor. The building was a large rectangle, the main hallway going around the structure with lodges on both sides. As she turned a corner, approaching Detel's door, excited, Keidi stopped abruptly.

Two enforcers were standing in front of Detel's door.

One was looking directly at her.

Code 00.000.0044

```
// Program Information
// Version: 00.000.0044
// Program Name: secret
// Coder Name: secret
// Date Updated: Year 3.4k60 Season 05 Day 11 Hour 1808
// Date Updated: Year 3.4k60 Season 05 Day 11 Hour 1810

// data-sphere module
include global:_data
// marti custom module
include district/3:quadrant/z:user/marti424:_marti
// marti hidden module
include district/3:quadrant/z:user/reddgn:_reddgn

function main ()
[
  var dataNodes as _data_coordinates
  var DSinfo as _info
  var X as integer

  // Retrieve data coordinate
  dataNodes = _data_convert ( _marti_DScoordinates(),
NODES )

  // Concatenate all data into a single block
  loop X from 1 to dataNodes( _count )
  [
  DSinfo = _data_append( _data_get( dataNodes( X ) ) )
  ]
```

Deficiency

```
  // Decrypt data
  var key as _reddgn_key
  key = L3zr3hsL3t3D
  DSinfo = _reddgn_decrypt_AM( DSinfo, key )

  // Output data, 10 first lines of data, testing decryption
  Loop X from 1 to 10
  [
  _data_print ( DSinfo )
  ]
]
```

Code Output 00.000.0044

```
Welcome to the Data-sphere.
Load time 0.004113 seconds.
Year 3.4k60 Season 05 Day 05 Hour 1811.

Action> run secret

Packaging secret . . .

Paused
Password required (_marti):

Action> encrypt(Red!Dragon?232)

Unpaused
Packaging secret . . .

Paused
Password required (_reddgn):

Action> encrypt(current_user)

Unpaused
Packaging secret . . .

Running secret:
==================================================

[empty]
[empty]
[[Data-Title]] The Root Causes of the Neonates' Deficiency
```

Deficiency

```
[empty]
[empty]
[empty]
[[Author-Information]] Detel Scherzel
[[Title-/-Occupation]] Master Biologist
[[Corporation]] Thrium Laboratories
[[Data-Creation-Date]] Day 13, Season 3, Year 3.4k60
```

‐ ‐ . . . Fugue

The cafe had one exit. It stood directly across from the Blue Tower, opening on the street, for everyone to see. Artenz's thoughts were in disarray. He needed Keidi's self-control.

"Think," he said, looking down and trying to push everything else away, including the pounding of his heart.

The enforcers were coming. He had less than a minute, after which his b-pad would start once again. A minute!

"Damn!" exclaimed Artenz, moving across the cafe now, toward the exit, as fast as he could.

If he was right... He came out and yes, indeed, from where he was standing, it was impossible to see the entrance to the Blue Tower because of the arched bridge. The elevation of the bridge created a barrier and blocked the view to the other side.

Artenz was also hopeful that the enforcers did not know where he was. His b-pad was dead, at least for another 30 seconds.

Artenz turned left, his steps rapid. Ahead was a speed-belt. He needed to reach it. It was a major artery and would take him all the way down to level 30, more than 15 kilometers away.

True, the belt went in the opposite direction of the meeting place with Keidi. Artenz would deal with that later.

Deficiency

He dared a brief look toward the Blue Tower. At this angle, the cover offered by the bridge was gone, and Artenz could see the entrance. He was relieved to notice his pursuers were still in front of the entrance, standing, hesitating.

They didn't know where to go. It was working.

But the small vibrations on the b-pad told him it was about to turn back on!

There was no option left. Artenz dashed forward, jumping on the walk-way, which increased his speed. Then he jumped onto the speed-belt, which was going much faster. He lost his footing. He crashed down and stayed there, lying on his side, using the railing as cover. His elbow had taken the brunt of the fall, and the pain stung.

Artenz pushed on his b-pad, wanting another reset. He didn't know if it would work this quickly. Maybe it needed to power up before a dual-reset.

The speed-belt moved at more than 40 km/h. In his current position, on his side, Artenz was in major discomfort. He pushed himself up, trying to sit. As he did, his finger slipped off the pad.

The reset cancelled. The b-pad came on.

"Shit!" He pushed once more on the pad, although not before noticing that his headache had already started to go away. He was surprised by his dependence on the device.

He peeked over the railing. The enforcers were on the bridge! Moving quickly, in a line, with discipline. Their leader was looking his way. From this distance, his head looked like a dark sphere on which light danced. Artenz had never seen an enforcer wearing a gray armor before, or such a helmet.

It was obvious the leader knew where Artenz was. His pad had been on for only a few seconds, but it had been enough for them to locate him.

Artenz ducked back down, certain he had been seen, sweating profusely, trembling.

The b-pad powered down. Artenz removed his finger and then pushed again.

Second reset.

"Go, go, go," he said.

Hiding the b-pad would not be enough. Artenz looked around, noticed people ahead and behind looking at him. No one moved on a speed-belt. They just stood, holding the railing, waiting for a walk-way exit. Because he was lying down, he stood out.

At least no one was pointing, only staring.

He stretched his neck, looked back, and realized that the belt's downward trajectory was providing him some cover. He could not see the street on level 40, where the cafe was. It meant his pursuers couldn't see him either.

He stood and saw a platform ahead. There was another speed-belt parallel to the one he was on, going back the other way, toward the cafe.

He ran. It was challenging with a finger on his neck and the speed of the belt under his feet.

The b-pad reset.

The shock was twice as powerful as the previous time and crashed into Artenz's mind with a vengeance. His vision went awry. His ears stopped functioning. There was a humming, maybe the belt, maybe not. And there was pain.

He realized the pain came from a fall. He was down on the belt again, had lost his footing. He had collided with a woman. She was saying something. So was another man who was helping her stand.

"Sorry," he apologized, getting up again.

He reached the platform. There, he switched to the slower walkway, then to the stable floor. Running now, he crossed the platform in three steps and jumped on the walk-way going in the opposite direction and finally the speed-belt.

There, once more, he crumbled to the belt, behind the railing.

"Shit, shit," he exclaimed under his breath.

Deficiency

His damn hands were shaking with adrenaline. He had created quite a commotion. He knew someone would point him out to the enforcers. He couldn't rest, not yet.

He crawled up the belt.

"Stupid," he said.

The enforcers knew where he was, or had a good idea. There was no point resetting the b-pad until he could hide. He had missed his chance when exiting the cafe. He needed to create another opportunity.

An air-tube!

He needed an air-tube. He peeked over the railing, saw the enforcers going down the other speed-way. Artenz smiled. He had a good lead.

This was when the leader stopped. Looking directly at Artenz, he crouched and jumped, up toward the side glass of the speed-way. The protective wall was curved, slippery and six meters high. Yet with one extended gloved hand, the leader of the enforcers grabbed the top of the glass and pulled himself on top of the wall. From there, he jumped again. Artenz saw the glass crack under his armored boot.

The distance between the speed-ways was great, but the leader would make it, he would...

Artenz needed to risk it all. There was no other option.

He stood and dashed up the belt.

+

As he reached the top, Artenz was still wobbling. He wanted nothing more than for his b-pad to turn back on. How was it possible that his eyes, ears, and brain relied so heavily on this little device?

The sensation of pulling was the worst. It felt as if strings were attached to his eyeballs and someone was pulling on them from somewhere in his brain. It made his eyes water.

On top of this, Artenz was shaken by the power demonstrated by the enforcer. He looked back quickly, saw the leader closing in rapidly. He would be on him in an instant.

Back on the street, Artenz made his way toward the corner of the building where the cafe was. A public air-tube was on the parallel street, close by. Around, people were stopped. More stares directed at him. He wished he could ask for help, but knew no one would dare interfere.

Why would they?

Turning the corner, Artenz saw the air-tube. There was a line of people waiting to use it. He would not be able to wait. Also, he needed to use his b-pad to set a destination. The tube would not open without it.

Pacing and massaging his head, he waited until his b-pad came back on. When it did, the relief was like a warm and soothing balm.

Now, timing was everything.

He looked at the tube and slowly made his way forward. On this street, no one was paying much attention to him. Other than the fact that he was sweating and heaving, he was just one of them. When the tube signaled it was ready, Artenz stepped forward. He was about to apologize and provide a brief explanation when he saw the shiny black sphere appear on the street corner. For a brief moment, he had the distinct impression that this enforcer was more machine than human.

Artenz rushed past the person at the beginning of the line, a man of small build who was caught by surprise and fell on the floor. While keeping his eyes on the tube, Artenz apologized and ordered level 20 with his b-pad. It was the lowest level he knew would work as a destination. Below that level, well, Prominence was dead.

From the corner of his eye, Artenz saw that the man he had pushed was back on his feet and approaching. It seemed as if he was coming to wrestle Artenz for the tube.

A muted thunderclap reverberated.

Deficiency

The man, and four other people around, shook and crumbled to the floor. The other enforcers had appeared, rifles up.

The tube opened. Artenz jumped into it as he heard the zap of another rifle.

Next, he was falling, the tube taking him rapidly to the lower levels. His heart was pounding against his rib cage. His breathing coming with difficulty.

He had made it.

.... Lodges

The enforcer looked directly at Keidi. Keidi looked directly back, weighing options rapidly. He was tall, standing straight. He had short-trimmed black hair and thin lips that formed a straight horizontal line. He was holding a pistol in each hand, one of which he pointed at her. The blue of his suit looked almost black due to the poor lighting of the hallway.

Keidi took one step, then another. She looked at the guard a bit longer, didn't hide her surprise, then turned toward the door in front of her. She ordered the door to open, and it did.

Administrative privileges could do that, open any door.

Keidi entered casually.

Behind her, the door closed.

Keidi put her back against it, taking a long breath. Hopefully, the enforcer would think she was a resident. It had been a reflex to enter the first room available. Keidi was proud of how quickly she had reacted.

She looked around and was relieved to see it was empty. Or close to empty.

In a far corner, a clean-bot was doing its work, vacuuming the floor. Some shoes on the floor provided a hint that there were at least two lodgers, an adult woman and a child. The lodge was a long rectangular space, not unlike Detel's. The main space had the kitchen, dining table and resting area, with a large screen mounted on a wall.

At the end of the room, a floor-to-ceiling glass provided a view outside. It was not much, as it showed the windowless wall of the Mollo factory. Detel had often complained about the building and the odors it produced. It had been built after the lodge complex. Obviously, the residents did not have a say and lost the sights they'd had, which Keidi could not remember. Detel insisted it had been a pleasing view.

To the side, there were two small bedrooms and a bathroom. Keidi looked inside each.

She was alone.

Returning to the main room, she sat at the table and thought about what she could do next.

+

The situation was utterly frustrating. She was so close, and yet Keidi could not get into Detel's lodge. The presence of the enforcers did not tell her much. Detel could be already gone or kept hostage inside. Keidi did not hold any high hopes. Most likely, Detel was already gone, in which case, she wanted to go through her lodge for clues.

There might be a way, she realized.

The building was old, with a surveillance system that was even older.

Keidi turned off the scrambler and accessed the security system through her b-pad. From her brief hack earlier, she knew the system had been developed by FrontShield. Keidi didn't really know what had happened to FrontShield, the main provider of security systems a century earlier. What she knew was that once the company had dissolved, no one had taken the time to go back and replace their systems, with the result that older buildings, such as this one, still used the outdated software. It was good news, as Keidi had studied the old system during her university years and knew its flaws.

Setting her mini-vid on the table in front of her, Keidi browsed the system, in search of video-recorders. She found them quickly. There were four on each level. The devices were on railings, located at the top of the walls, along the ceiling.

Two of the cameras were on the outside of the corridor, while two were on the inside. They should even be able to move, if Keidi remembered correctly.

Optimistic now, Keidi checked the status of the devices on her floor.

```
Do> show vidcorders status -level#32

Device-ID/Device-Type/Device-Status
01/Sphere2 Vidcorder/Offline
02/Sphere2 Vidcorder/Offline
03/Sphere2 Vidcorder/Offline
04/Sphere2 Vidcorder/Offline
```

Not good. She should have expected it.

Keidi tried to activate the first video-recorder. It was a simple command line.

```
Insufficient energy
```

She tried the other three and got the same message. These older models tended to have batteries, which needed to be recharged regularly. There was a slight chance, though, that they would be directly connected to the power grid. Keidi browsed through the system and found a chart of the electricity distribution in the building.

"There it is!" she exclaimed.

The video-recorders had simply been severed from the building's circuit. It was probably another way for the proprietors to save costs. They would promise security to the tenants, even provide a demonstration of the devices, but then turn them off, saving energy.

Keidi reopened the circuit and checked the status again.

Deficiency

```
Device-ID/Device-Type/Device-Status
01/Sphere2 Vidcorder/Online
02/Sphere2 Vidcorder/Online
03/Sphere2 Vidcorder/Offline
04/Sphere2 Vidcorder/Offline
```

Maybe the circuit needed more time to power up all cameras. Keidi waited a few seconds and checked a second time. She was happy to note that all four devices were now online.

Not that it mattered. Keidi only needed one. Well, at least, if one didn't work, she had options.

It took some manipulation, but Keidi eventually figured out how to forward the video-recorder's feed directly to her b-pad.

She connected her pad with video-recorder 01 and was excited to instantly see an image appear on her mini-vid. It showed an empty corridor, the camera pointing at the floor.

Another search revealed a guide on how to operate the video-recorders. It was possible to pan left or right, up or down, and move forward or backward on the rail. It also had settings for the panning speed and the moving speed. There were also a few pre-set scans.

Next, Keidi went on to perform a few extra tests, checking the options and possibilities. These devices only transmitted videographs, two-dimensional images with low resolution. She switched between 01 and 02, then went to 03 and 04. Video-recorder 02 was close to Detel's room and already had a view of the lodge's doorway. 04's feed was poor, washed out by static. It was a pleasant surprise that three out of four video-recorders provided decent images.

Keidi came back to 02. The two enforcers were standing on each side of Detel's door. As unmoving as statues, weapons at the ready. The door between them was open.

Perfect!

02 was located on the inside wall of the corridor, opposite Detel's room, and if Keidi could move it down the hall, it would eventually provide a view of the inside of the lodge.

Perfect indeed.

Keidi set everything in motion.

The four video-recorders started their normal daily scan, the pattern they would have followed when the system was up and active. Keidi was happy to see video-recorder 02 making its way toward Detel's lodge.

The guards would notice the movement, but hopefully wouldn't think anything abnormal was happening. The risk that they would connect the video-recorders with the woman they had just seen was minimal.

Someone came out of a lodge two doors from Detel's. A man, young, covered by a long gray lab coat. Detel had mentioned that most of the renters in this building were researchers, the same as she.

Good. This was good!

Other people walking around meant Keidi's arrival would seem less suspicious and that the movement of the video-recorders would be less likely to be noticed.

On the feed, Keidi saw one of the enforcers take one step toward the man, lift his rifle, shout a few words. The feed didn't have sound, but Keidi heard muffled words through the door. The man lifted his two hands, showing them to be empty. Then he moved rapidly away, down the corridor, and Keidi lost sight of him.

At that moment, a flash perturbed the screen on Keidi's mini-vid.

Could it be that the enforcer had used his rifle? She did not hear anything through the wall, and it was too risky to pan the video-recorder to look back.

Video-recorder 02 was approaching Detel's lodge. Keidi adjusted the angle slightly, slowly, and continuously as it approached Detel's room. It would probably look quite suspicious if the video-recorder

Deficiency

stayed aimed at the lodge, so Keidi randomized the movements a bit until she could look into the room.

+

What she saw bothered Keidi immensely. It was intrusion to the highest degree. A desecration of Detel's possessions.

The lodge was ransacked, destroyed. Keidi noticed an imagraph on the floor. It was large. It had hung on the wall and depicted Artenz and Detel. It was not possible to see the details on the feed, but Keidi remembered it. It was from four years ago, during the Athletics. Together, the three of them had camped on the street to watch the competitions on the big screen.

Keidi wondered how long the door would stay open. Maybe they were almost done, which might explain why it was open. She saw four more enforcers in the lodge, each going around, throwing things on the floor, using force to open anything and everything. One had a lacerated fist-knife, which he used to open up the couch and look inside. This one's armor seemed to be a lighter color than the others, either white or a pale gray. His helmet, on the other hand, was a dark sphere.

A man suddenly appeared in her view. He didn't have any rifle or armor. He was slim and tall and wore a black suit. He was obviously in charge and seemed to be conversing on his b-pad. Then something got the man's attention.

He shook his head, tried to concentrate on his pad, but was interrupted again. He made his way to the lodge's entrance. One of the enforcers there had called him, it seemed.

He came closer and spoke with one of the guards. Keidi could hear their voices from the hallway. And other noises. There seemed to be a lot of people out there.

Then the guard pointed... directly at the video-recorder!

As the tall man turned his gaze her way, Keidi felt a chill go down her back.

+

Instantly, Keidi stopped the feed and disconnected her mini-vid and closed her link with the security system's interface. She stood and paced back and forth.

It occurred to her that it was possible the video-recorders had only been powered down today, while the lodge was raided.

If that was the case...

"Oh my," thought Keidi, seriously afraid now, desperately grabbing for the scrambler. Turning it on.

If that was the case, there was also a possibility that the security had been monitored. And if it had been monitored, then they would see that someone had hacked in and taken over.

Not someone.

They would see who it was: Keidi Rysinjer.

+

There was no way she could simply walk out now.

No way.

She went to the door and put her ear against it. She heard words exchanged and heavy footsteps right in front of her hideout's doorway. They came and went.

Keidi moved to one of the bedrooms, the one farther back, the one with a window on the outside.

The scrambler was on. It was not an agreeable feeling, but it was good. It provided cover.

Was it enough?

Artenz had mentioned the sleuths. If the man in black was one of them, she would not be able to hide for long. They had the best technologies available. Not only the best—they had technologies no one else had access to.

Deficiency

One day, while dismantling devices at the workshop, Keidi had come upon a palm-pad that was different from the others. She remembered how she had debated with her colleagues about what it was, where it could possibly have come from. They had joked, nervously. Nervously because they had never seen such a device. It was old, but advanced, far superior to any of the newest mainstream b-pads.

It had been plain scary.

Keidi had surmised it had once belonged to a sleuth. That had been enough for Tarana and Ronin to never touch the thing again. Keidi had studied it as she pulled it apart. She had not been able to understand its design.

Also, the sleuths didn't have any affiliation or loyalty. They worked for the highest bidder. Period. Their services were extremely expensive. Evidently, the large corporations made good use of them. The government, rarely.

It was not possible to know who this one worked for, if indeed he was a sleuth. It made the whole matter a lot more real to Keidi. She thought of Artenz. Was he, too, running from sleuths?

She hoped not.

There was a commotion in the hallway. Loud words and then heavy pounding. A muffled cry?

She had to get out of here.

There was the window.

Did she dare? Did she have any other option?

Swearing under her breath, Keidi moved to the window and scanned it quickly. Blunt force would not work. These old buildings overused tempered glass, and here it was. Keidi rummaged through her backpack and produced one of three sparking plugs. This scenario was not the reason she had brought the gadgets, but it would do.

She dropped it on the floor and, using a small hammer, smashed it to pieces. She put all of her things away, made sure the scrambler was secured in her hood.

Then she took a piece of the broken ceramic and threw it at the window. It was not a powerful impact, but where the piece of ceramic hit, the glass shattered. Cracks formed up and down around the small opening. Using the sole of her foot, Keidi widened the opening until the bottom frame was clear.

She looked outside.

Two levels up. The wall of the Mollo factory was not as close as she had hoped. It offered no help. Down below, there were piles of debris and detritus, garbage, hidden from the main streets. The sight was shocking. For all its beauty, it seemed Prominence was rotting in the crevices between buildings.

Keidi took her backpack in one hand and let it fall. Then, facing the room, she knelt and backed out, letting her feet slide down the wall, her stomach against the bottom window frame. It was high. She did not know what waited for her below.

It had to be done.

Her hands ached where they gripped the inside of the window, and her feet scraped against the outside wall. She looked one more time below, was not able to find any comfort in the distance of the fall.

This was her only way out.

Taking a breath as if plunging into water, Keidi pushed from the wall and jumped.

- - - Emergency Link

The managers and directors left the conference room. The meeting had gone well. Management's appetite had been satiated. The first numbers from the launch were promising. The deployment to the 16 primary sites, one per district, had gone smoothly. A few tests had been performed, and indeed, the reaction time of the billboards was impressive, almost without any delay. This meant that displayed ads could now be updated more quickly, for example to target a particular crowd using an on-site or live scan.

Wave 4 was underway and targeted another 70 secondary sites. No complication was expected.

Drayfus took a seat at the end of the table and waited. Despite how well the project was going, he could not relax.

Blood had soaked the floor of his office. How could he go back and work in that place? The sight of the stooped shape of Marti also haunted him. As much as Drayfus disliked the man, the scene had been too much. It made him seriously wonder who Mysa Lamond was.

She was not a manager or director, not a sleuth either. Sleuths did not use that kind of… method. What then? An intimidator? A coercer? The blood certainly pointed toward the latter. Yet it did not feel right. There was more to Mysa Lamond than that.

On top of this, Artenz had not returned. It had been more than one hour and a half since she had sent the enforcers after Artenz. It was surprising that Artenz had been able to elude them this long. Or maybe he had been caught and…

Drayfus's assistant came into the conference room and closed the door behind him.

"You have the necessary?" asked Drayfus.

"I do."

The assistant took a small safe from his pocket. It was the size of the palm of his hand. He put it on the table in front of Drayfus. The device was only to be used in extreme situations. Drayfus did not hesitate and put his thumb on a plate attached to the side of the box. A click resonated.

Drayfus opened the safe and took out a small device. He brought it close to his b-pad, and it attached automatically.

The emergency channel was open.

Drayfus linked.

+

"Mr. Blue," said the voice at the end of the link. It was smooth and matter-of-fact. Drayfus knew the appellation was a pseudonym. No one in this tower knew who the owner of BlueTech Corporation really was.

"Yes, sir, this is manager Drayfus Arlsberg, from the Blue Tower. I apologize for disturbing you, but I have a situation on which I'd like to consult."

There were a few words exchanged on the other end, muffled, brief. It seemed Mr. Blue was already engaged, which made Drayfus bite his lip.

"Arlsberg, yes," acknowledged Mr. Blue a few moments later. "This is a first." There was reproach in the tone. It was never a good thing for a manager to reach out to an owner. The managers were expected to engage with the directors or to solve problems on their own. "I hope this is not related to the Targos deal?"

"No, sir, not really. The launch is going as planned."

"You previously mentioned the new module would be launched in waves. When is the last one to be completed?"

This was not what Drayfus wanted to talk about, but he knew he had to humor the owner.

"Wave 4 is in progress. Secondary sites. Wave 5 is scheduled for tomorrow morning."

"Wave 5 includes the remote sites, doesn't it?"

"It does." Drayfus was surprised that such details were of import to the owner.

"Why not complete the launch today?"

"Time will not permit it."

"Time—how long is Wave 4 going to take?"

"A few hours, sir."

"That is what I thought."

Silence followed, and Drayfus almost missed the cue.

"It'll be done as you say, sir," he replied.

To his assistant, Drayfus mouthed the new order. *He wants Wave 5 to be completed today*.

The assistant nodded, unsurprised.

It meant extra hours of work for all, all the way to midnight, possibly overnight. Artenz had planned the last wave in the morning, explaining it was the trickiest. Reaching the remote sites, especially those located outside of Prominence, would be the hardest to track. Artenz had wanted his team rested. There was nothing Drayfus could do. When the owner asked for something, he got it.

"What did you want to consult on?" asked Mr. Blue.

"We're the center of an investigation, here, of sorts," said Drayfus.

"Yes, I see," said Mr. Blue, seemingly distracted. Again, he exchanged a few words with someone outside the link. Drayfus could not make out what was said. Mr. Blue's initial reaction had not been one of surprise, though.

"I've lost control of the tower," continued Drayfus, unable to restrain himself. He realized he needed Mr. Blue's support on this. He wanted to regain control of his tower.

"I know," said Mr. Blue, surprising Drayfus. "I asked Miss Lamond to take over."

"But—"

"I am talking, Arlsberg," Mr. Blue cut in. He waited a second for the reprimand to sink in. Drayfus swallowed. The warning had been clear. He shut his mouth, tight.

His assistant passed him a tissue. Drayfus took it and dried the sweat from his forehead.

"As I was saying," continued Mr. Blue, a hint of impatience in his voice now, "I asked Miss Lamond to take charge. How else do you think she could have done so? This is a matter in which you must assist. I do not think I need to say more."

Drayfus swallowed again.

"No, sir," he answered.

"Good. Is that all, Arlsberg?"

"It is. I thank you, sir, for your time."

Mr. Blue had already unlinked.

+

"It didn't go as planned, I take it," said his assistant.

Drayfus shook his head. He removed the device from his b-pad and deposited it back in the safe. He closed the box and locked it again, using his thumb.

"This was a bad move," he said, fixating on the box. He felt weak.

"Surely he understood your position and why you felt the need to contact him."

"I don't know. Maybe."

Deficiency

Drayfus didn't know if there would be repercussions because he'd used the emergency link. It had been the first time for him. It would forever be a blemish on his career record. A reminder that he had cracked under the pressure, had possibly panicked, had not been able to sort through priorities.

He should have known Mysa Lamond would not have been able to take control of the Blue Tower without approval from higher up. He did know, but something was not right.

About the situation, and about the woman.

She was so cold, so focused. A cyborg, some said. Maybe she was something else, even less human. Who knew?

He did not trust her. But then, was it even his place to decide to trust her or not? He felt responsible for the Blue Tower, even if he was not the owner. Mr. Blue was, and it was clear what Mr. Blue wanted.

Drayfus made up his mind.

If that was the only thing to come out of the link, then so be it. From now on, he would be what he was asked to be. He would not doubt. He would not ask questions. He would not fear.

Harder to control, that last one.

Part of Drayfus's success so far had been his willingness to support those working under him. Such support was rarely understood by management, never requested, always risky.

Now the time had come to work solely for those above, for management. Drayfus felt his career depended on it.

"Let's see how we can best assist Miss Lamond," he told his assistant.

He gave the safe back and walked out of the conference room.

+

When he got to his office, the door stood open. Drayfus entered and was surprised that Marti was nowhere to be seen. He scanned the room and saw no trace of the old coder. The clean-bot had done a good job. No blood anywhere.

"You are with us now?" asked Mysa Lamond, looking directly at him, lifting an eyebrow.

Drayfus froze.

She knew.

She already knew about his exchange with the owner. How was this possible?

A moment ago, Drayfus had felt reassured that Mysa Lamond was also employed by Mr. Blue. But the fact that she knew about his discussion told a different story. The emergency link was completely shielded, independent in every way.

Either she was playing a dangerous game indeed, spying on things she should not, or she was in direct contact with Mr. Blue.

Again, Drayfus forced himself to weigh whether it mattered. Both scenarios put Drayfus in a dangerous predicament. Both scenarios hinted that Mysa Lamond knew much more than he did, that she was much more powerful than he was, and much more important.

Just as he had somehow initially guessed.

"So?" she asked again.

What could he do but obey? He was a simple manager, at the bottom of the management chain. Cooperation had to be the best, and possibly only, approach.

"I am," he said. "May I?"

He was pointing to a chair on the side.

Mysa Lamond nodded.

Drayfus made his way to the chair, looking directly at the two enforcers in the room, one after the other. He kept his head high, showing them that even though Mysa Lamond was in charge, he was just below her.

"What can I do to help?" he asked.

Deficiency

"Nothing for the moment," answered Mysa Lamond, turning the monitor on the desk his way. "Soon enough, though. Watch. We are closing in on the defector."

136

- - - . At the Gate

A dark gray mass of cloud hung over Prominence. The tallest buildings disappeared in the folds of the gathering rain. Artenz rested his back against a metallic wall. One meter in front of him stood another wall. The narrow space was his latest hiding spot.

Once more, he reset his b-pad. He had found the perfect timing so that the device never turned back on. He suspected he had given up his position a few times before getting the timing right. He had been resetting his pad for at least an hour, maybe longer. As a result, most of his fingers were hurting.

He didn't know the time and felt completely lost without his pad. He thought of Keidi, again, for the 100th time. She would be standing at the small shop, waiting. Irrationally, a part of him wanted to be mad at her, for the baby and for indirectly encouraging Detel in her research, whatever that research was. Mostly, though, he worried about her and wanted to hug her, make this bad dream go away.

His progress through the streets toward Quadrant O had been slower than he had anticipated. He had not been able to take the tram, which would have taken him directly to his destination. Had he done so, enforcers would surely have been waiting for him at the end of the line, detecting him the moment he stepped on the tram.

Deficiency

He had not dared take any other air-tube and so had stayed on level 20.

The buildings on the street outside the alley where he was resting were old factories that had once belonged to Quadrant O. They were being renovated, large scaffoldings decorating each building. The faces were hidden behind thick plastic tarps. Two giant cranes lifted heavy pieces, moving them around in a strange improvised play.

Artenz had crawled under the tarps and found a niche between two buildings. Luckily, from where he was standing, he could see the street ahead and the gate to Quadrant O.

From here, he could quickly plan his crossing.

He was tired.

His brain screamed in pain, as if split in the middle. A few times, he had almost linked with Keidi, or Marti. Or even Detel. Keidi, to make sure she was safe, as he himself felt more and more powerless to find his way to her. Marti, just in case the devil could think of any brilliant move that Artenz could try. Detel, because he could not believe she was gone.

He was also hungry. He ate one of the crackers Keidi had packed for him. The thought that these were from Keidi increased his desire to reach her. How he missed her now. Guilt ate at him as he nibbled at the cracker. He had not been as supportive as he should have, especially during that last exchange they'd had. Maybe she had not noticed his mood...

Who was he trying to convince? Keidi could read him better than he could read himself.

There was nothing he wanted more than to reach the little store. Its name came back to him as he took another bite: I Bot.

His legs were tired and his knees burned from the pounding of his recent running. He had once wanted to get an endurance augment, but Keidi had been against it. She was against anything modifying the body, including hair dye or skin preservative. As much as her values could be infuriating sometimes, Artenz now found himself loving her for sticking with what she believed.

He imagined Keidi standing at the little shop, waiting, regret eating at her for not letting him get the augments. He saw himself offering comfort by saying it would not have changed a damn thing and that it was not her fault.

He sighed.

These out-of-control thoughts had to be desperation. He did not know if he would make it, and his brain seemed to be retaliating.

With his next cracker, he thought of Detel. Where could she be? He wondered if she was thinking of him, right this instant. He missed her tremendously. They had always been close, even before their parents had left.

Artenz liked Detel, as a sister, as a friend, as a person. She was eccentric, many of her ideas wild. She was also rebellious, a trait coming directly from their parents.

Thinking of it all morning, he had come to the conclusion that Detel must have stumbled on something big, something the corporations did not want anyone to know. It was the explanation that made the most sense. The government did not make people disappear. Corporations did.

This would not be the first time someone had disappeared. Nobody wanted to believe it or admit it. Nobody wanted to talk about it. Including him... until now.

He wondered what Marti had to do with what was happening, what they wanted with him, and why Marti had told him to flee. He wondered how far they would go.

He wondered who *they* were, exactly.

Was BlueTech involved?

He swallowed the last of the crackers and tried to order his thoughts. He wanted answers, but what he needed was to reach Keidi.

And he possibly even wanted a natural baby after all. Maybe it was to retaliate against the world around, against the rules, the limitations, against what was happening to his sister. It was probably all that, and also because he loved Keidi and wanted a family with her.

He... he wanted to leave Prominence!

"I want to leave Prominence," he said.

There.

He had said it.

The admission freed something in him, made him lighter somehow.

Why had he fought the idea for so long? Maybe to prove that his parents had been wrong in leaving? Maybe because he hated them for going away and did not want to admit he longed to follow?

Artenz looked toward Quadrant O and realized that he hated Prominence City. Until now, he had accepted the place and had stopped himself from thinking about it. It was outside of his control, wasn't it? Or maybe it was just easier to accept.

He had been born here. He had followed the flow, accepted what was given to him. He had diligently stayed the course.

Prominence, the Floating City.

The gray fog above seemed to push down. Did the clouds feel the same way? Was Prominence City an abomination on the world? Was it a cancer against which Garadia was constantly fighting? What did the other cities think? What did they know about Prominence?

Artenz's knowledge of the outside world was surprisingly scarce.

Could it be that the ignorance was planned? Certainly, the rulers of Prominence never hid their opinion of the outside world. They wanted nothing of it.

Garadia was a barren world and did not have much to offer. That was why the city had been built. That was why it was self-sufficient. A closed ecosystem, independent, self-sufficient. Beautiful.

How beautiful was it now, from this hiding place? Artenz chuckled—a brazen sound, difficult for him to hear.

They were told that Prominence had everything, and that its inhabitants were never left wanting. Was it true? Was Prominence really the paradise they were told it was?

Once, Artenz had seen beyond the city. His parents had taken him and Detel to the edge of Quadrant W, where they had lived at the time. Beyond Prominence, he had seen clouds, hugging the perimeter of the city, cuddling it warmly in huge arms. Or so it had looked. Far away, there had been the peaks of high mountains, some covered in snow, some dark brown and threatening.

That was how it had seemed to him at the time.

His parents had told him that below the clouds, there was another world, an old city. Garadia, the name of their planet, had once been the name of that city. It was now known as the Low Lands, the world of primitives and savages.

Prominence was built on a plateau balanced on four huge pillars. It was built on top of the Low Lands, where many still lived. Maybe millions. Who could say? If you searched the data-sphere for information on the Low Lands, you found nothing—at least not in the tiers and zones to which Artenz had access.

Why?

The idea that Prominence City was floating was a nice image, certainly, but a lie.

Another lie.

Artenz had had enough of Prominence.

He wanted out.

He wanted to find the Dara Gulch, look for his parents and… start a family of his own!

There were many unknowns, too many to think about now. Still, Artenz made his decision. He was excited, even, to tell Keidi. She would be happy. She had been ready for a while, probably ever since her parents had disowned her.

"I don't have any family," she had told him, early on. It had started when she'd enrolled in a different university than they'd anticipated, in a course they disapproved of. They saw her decision as a betrayal. Artenz guessed that things worsened from there, as Keidi developed views that even he had a hard time understanding. Over time, she had

Deficiency

tried to contact them but had stopped a year after her graduation, on the day two enforcers had knocked at their door.

"Stalking is the complaint," one of the enforcers had announced.

When Keidi challenged that she was their daughter, the enforcers had accessed the sphere. "There's no relationship between you and the claimants," was their finding.

That night, with Artenz standing close by, Keidi searched the sphere herself. Somehow, the fact that she had parents had been erased. Based on the information available, she was an orphan. The discovery, and the betrayal, could have sent her into a depression, but it did not. Not to say it was easy, but Keidi kept her head high and focused her energy on pursuing her own goals.

So she had been ready to leave for a while. He was the one who had hesitated.

Not anymore.

He looked at the street, at the gate into Quadrant O. It stood high, a stone archway with two massive metal doors, open wide. People walked between the quadrants freely. From Quadrant X to O; from Quadrant O to X.

Artenz knew the passage of every person from one side to the other was tracked. There was no walk-way or fast-way or speed-belt crossing over. One had to walk between quadrants. Or use a tram.

Artenz's passing would not be tracked. His b-pad would not emit anything.

He smiled and adjusted his backpack.

It was time to go. He had another hour of walking once he crossed into Quadrant O. He knew Keidi was worried, would worry until he reached her.

He also knew she would wait for him.

+

After resetting his b-pad, Artenz made his way along the large tarp and the face of the building. He stayed close to the wall, in the shadows, as long as he could, then crossed the street, moving toward the gate with assurance.

He was focused, had a clear plan. He knew that the streets of Quadrant O would provide easy cover for him. They were narrower, more numerous, and there were fewer enforcers.

His thoughts were on Keidi, on the baby, on a new life, on new horizons outside of Prominence.

The streets were alive, and he joined the crowd. Billboards' announcements battled with the voices of pedestrians. So many people, coming and going. Certainly he could pass unnoticed.

A couple walked hand in hand, pushing a stroller with their other hands, in concert, maybe in love. A blanket covered the stroller, but the face of a child appeared in a small opening. A girl, possibly, with long curly hair. She looked directly at Artenz and smiled and pointed. Artenz put his head down and pushed forward. He did not know how to guess the age of the girl. Two, three? He had never paid much attention to children. That would have to change.

He could not help thinking that the girl had been born in a laboratory, as had everyone else, as he himself had been. Artenz felt suddenly empowered by the fact that his and Keidi's child would not be. He or she would be born from Keidi, from their mother. That had to be a good thing.

He was getting closer to the gate and Quadrant O.

Artenz felt the danger before seeing it. It was in how the voices diminished around him, in how he could clearly hear the billboards. He looked around and noticed that people were moving away from him. He accelerated his pace, scanning the surroundings.

An enforcer appeared to his left, coming his way, pushing between the pedestrians. Another appeared on his right.

How had they found him?

Deficiency

Artenz started jogging, then sprinting. As he did, movement exploded all around.

He was running now, running as fast as he could toward the gate, seeing more enforcers appear in his peripheral vision.

On the other side of the gate, the street continued straight before branching out in several directions. One of these streets was dark, and Artenz headed toward it.

He was almost at the gate. His pursuers would not reach him before he went through it. He had expected shots, attempts to stop him with stun guns.

He realized too late why that was not necessary.

As he was about to enter the gate, a large net fell in front, from the top of the gate, blocking access to Quadrant O. It was too late to swerve away, and Artenz rammed into the net.

The electric shocks were instantaneous, pulsating through his clothing, making his muscles jump. Yet Artenz continued to push forward. The weight of the net was pulling him down. It was large, spreading around and away from Artenz, several meters in each direction.

There was no one close, no enforcers yet. So Artenz continued.

He had to put a hand on the ground and saw that he had made progress. If he pushed a bit more, he would be able to crawl out from under the net.

In random spots, his skin felt as if it were burning. Some parts of his body were completely numb—his right ear, his left elbow, portions of his back and his nape.

But Artenz did not stop. While his strength drained, he kept his thoughts on Keidi.

He would get to her.

His head popped out from under the net. Feeling a surge of renewed energy and hope, Artenz pushed the thing aside.

And he was through!

He had made it. Putting his head down, Artenz sprinted through the gate.

Deficiency

Mission 001201

The invisible carrier floats down toward the gate's rooftop. The low rumble of its engine fades away in the ambient sounds of Prominence. On board, a computer captures the view on one side and projects it on the other side, producing a quasi-flawless chameleon-like camouflage effect. As it descends, chances of detection are 0.14%.

Two invisible carriers exist in Prominence, and at any given time, one is always airborne over the city. The second is used for special missions. This one was transferred under the responsibility of Okran for 24 hours. Okran now stands in the open side door, ready.

It is a useful vehicle. Manufacture cost is 1.2 billion credits. Only one factory on Garadia can build the carriers, and it is located at an undisclosed location, more than 1,000 kilometers out of Prominence. Okran notes that the details of the factory are not available to him, which is of no importance. It has no impact on the current mission.

The carrier is still high above the surface when Okran jumps out. The air on his face is inconsequential. The distance of the fall is manageable. The augments in his legs and knees compress to absorb the impact of the jump.

The visor of his helmet displays information about the surroundings, including the position of the carrier and his own squad, the location of soldiers in the vicinity, the number and placement of civilians, and an approximation of the target's location.

Okran stands and walks to the edge of the platform. There, he kneels and looks at the street below. It is one of the five main arteries of Quadrant O. Down on the pavement, a man cuts a path through the civilians.

The target.

Okran follows the man with his eyes. His speed is calculated at 25 km/h. The fastest sprinter at the Athletics of year 3.4k55 clocked a speed of 44.25 km/h. With his current augments, Okran can reach a maximum speed of 60 km/h. Normal limits of leg strength and heart resistance do not apply to him.

He orders his squad to stay in the carrier. He does not need help for this mission. He prepares to move. The force of his jump and the trajectory are computed, as well as the roll required to reach the street with the most efficiency.

Okran takes a step back, pushes forward and leaps. The maneuver is executed with perfection. His upgraded knees and legs absorb the impact. Okran follows through with the roll and comes up smoothly, transitioning into a run.

Panic and screams from the civilians are ignored.

The speed of 48.8 km/h required to catch the target is easily attained. Once the man is in reach, several harmless actions are available. Okran ignores them and, using an open hand, pushes the man in the back.

The target is momentarily propelled in the air. When his feet touch the ground, he tips forward and falls, rolls and hits his forehead on the pavement. Instantly, a red alarm rings in Okran's helmet. The parameters of the mission appear in his field of vision, impossible to ignore.

Deficiency

```
Mission No: #001201 - Target: Artenz Scherzel
Parameters:
Target must be apprehended with minimal injuries.
Target must be able to talk.
Target will be interrogated.
```

Okran acknowledges receipt of the parameters, and they disappear. He looks at the target as the man tries to get up. A quick scan confirms that none of the parameters have been violated.

"Artenz Scherzel, stop where you are," he says.

The target gets up, looks at his pursuer, and starts running again. Okran takes a few steps and grabs the target's elbow. The man twists around and tries to break free. He launches a punch, which Okran stops with his metallic forearm.

"Do not make this harder than it has to be," he warns.

The target tries another punch, which is easily blocked. Okran lifts a fist to strike, then stops. As the man wiggles in his grip, hesitation assails Okran. A part of him, buried deep down, resurfaces, the part of him that is still human.

The Okran-that-was reminds the Okran-that-is of the mission's parameters.

A closed fist comes toward his face. Okran lets the punch hit, and it causes no damage to the dark glass of his helmet. The target is desperate and rapidly tiring.

Once again, Okran closes his fist and readies to strike.

The Okran-that-was once again reminds the Okran-that-is of the mission's parameters. This time, a consensus is achieved: respecting the mission's parameters represents the best action for the near future.

Okran pulls the target closer and places his open hand on the man's chest. From his palm, he discharges a stun beam and the target is projected into the air, falling in a bundle 10 meters down the street, inert.

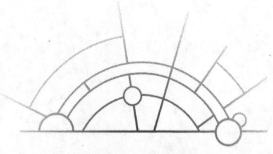

Segment D

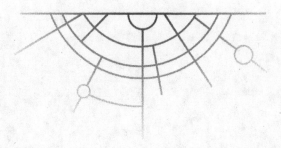

"A genus coder is 100 times more efficient than a master coder."

- Marti Zehron

- - - . . The Reporter

The 11 members of the Authentic Banner were all looking at Eltaya. Some were seated at the elongated table in the middle of the newsroom, while others simply stood around, leaning on the wall, on a table, or on the back of a chair.

All the members of the organization were present, and Eltaya did not have much support. Aana, founder of the Banner, kept her head down. In her day, she had attempted quests much more dangerous than the one Eltaya was now proposing.

"Why not?" Eltaya asked, legs crossed, seated on the chair at the head of the table. The others formed a half circle, all facing her.

In the background, monitors and computers were dormant. It had been a while since they had transmitted any news. It was not that nothing was worth reporting. It was simply that the type of news they transmitted needed to be planned, as it usually attracted much attention from the authorities, especially the corporations.

The hideout was located along the border of Quadrant W and Quadrant S, in a space between the Information district and the Castle district. Although the Banner owned the entire 60th floor, the organization met and operated in a collection of small rooms on level 18, under the bottom floor of Prominence. It was risky to inhabit a room in the Underground, but the group was also less likely to be discovered.

Deficiency

Signals and connections were weaker down here. The Dominance was located three levels below, and although some streets on that level had once been cleared to allow quick movement for the enforcers, it was not so any longer. Something was stirring down there, had been for many years.

On level 18, the building selected by the Authentic Banner for its hideout was surrounded by the rubble of decaying rocks. It could only be reached by foot. Some believed the debris of rocks was the result of deliberate actions, not the erosion of time.

Either way, it remained a good hiding spot. Eltaya had found it, and Xavi, their leader, had approved.

"Someone has to try something," insisted Eltaya. "People are disappearing out there between the stars. They're taken and forgotten. Surely you all understand that."

On the table, an imagram of the Arkos system floated, with all its planets and their orbits. A lone tube on the ceiling provided the only other source of light in the room. The imagram showed the Arkos star off-center, with its 13 planets orbiting it, pulling toward the left. There was an asteroid belt between the planets Dalileah and Tryon, while another larger field appeared farther away, at the fringe of the system.

"There has to be another way," said Ged, looking directly at Eltaya. If she knew his heart, this was a plea for her to find something better, some solution that did not involve her leaving, or involve her at all. Most days, Eltaya liked Ged more than she wanted, but it was hard to like him now.

"No one is disputing what you're saying," said Xavi. His black face was almost invisible in the dark room. He sat on the opposite side of the table, facing Eltaya. "We're just not ready to let you go. You've only been back for a year and are doing a lot of good work around here. Let's just wait a bit, see if we can find other leads, other ways."

Eltaya sighed loudly.

"We've done that already," she said, "with absolutely no result. How much longer can we wait? How much longer are we ready to wait? I, for one, say we've waited long enough."

In the farthest corner of the room, Kazor moved slightly. The light danced on the shotgun lying across his knees. A former enforcer, Kazor did not use many words.

"I agree," he said now, to Eltaya's relief.

Many around the table looked toward Kazor, which he did not seem to appreciate. He pulled his beret forward and looked down.

"Why do you care so much about what happens between the stars?" interjected Ulie. She was their youngest and newest member. She was a good addition, a coder with some moderator experience. Eltaya had recruited her, and although Ulie wanted to become a reporter, Eltaya found she was too young, too inexperienced, to be taken as an apprentice. Ulie's day would come, but for now, she was trying too hard to impress. And she talked too much. Eltaya ignored her.

"We need more stability," Xavi added. "If you leave now, we may just lose all the progress made over the past few seasons."

The old excuse.

It infuriated Eltaya. Were they really that incompetent?

Obviously not. She knew that. They were the best. She had already delayed her departure longer than she wanted.

"I will not always be here," she said, more directly than she had intended. "You all know this."

Sorrow appeared on some of the faces around the table.

"You are an important member of this band," put in Styl. He was seated on the side, legs stretched and hands behind his head. He was using his goggles, even when not needed—a bad habit, but understandable in his case. She raised an eyebrow at him. "But, I say we let her do what she wants," he added.

No one else said anything.

Damn you all, thought Eltaya, looking around and fighting the affection she felt for these people. Such a good group, all here looking for some truth. So selfless, all of them. They were the reason she had not left already, and when they talked like this, it made her want to stay. She loved them because they were the only family she had. The others—her brother, her mother—gone so long ago. Eltaya did not even remember how many years.

Lost between the stars.

Such a dark past, one she hated to remember, but one she could not stop pursuing. And it was not just about finding her lost family. Dark things were taking place out there. Someone needed to investigate and report on it.

It was not these people's story, though. It was her own, and Eltaya knew she was being selfish about her quest, to a certain extent. These people, they deserved better from her, and what they fought for was certainly important.

Eltaya had decided to apologize to the group when Xavi stood.

"That'll be enough for today," the leader said. "Eltaya, I only ask that you think about it some more. We know the role you played in the asteroids." Two years ago, and nothing since then. "They want you up there. We want you down here. We know we'll have to broadcast soon, but not yet. Some facts are still unconfirmed, and we need you to help us get to where we need to be. Then we move up to the 60th and broadcast. If by then you still want to leave, no one will stop you, although we'll miss you."

Eltaya acquiesced. "I'll think on it," she said. "But even though I don't know when I'll leave, remember that I *will* leave. Soon."

+

The members left the room with an air of defeat. Eltaya stayed where she was, unmoving. Ged put a supporting hand on her shoulder as he walked away. The touch was reassuring, telling her everything was good between them.

Xavi stayed behind, probably wanting a word with her. It had become a ritual of late. She felt he depended on her too much.

A monitor came to life on her left; a pale silhouette of a face appeared, feminine, not unlike her own.

Her ghost: Ayatle.

"I have a link on hold," she said in a weak parody of Eltaya's own voice. "I believe you'll want to answer."

"Who is it?" asked Eltaya.

"Keidi Rysinjer," replied the ghost.

+

"I'll take this," Eltaya said to Xavi.

"Will you come to my office after?" he said.

"I will."

As the leader left, Eltaya's feelings jumped from incomprehension to surprise to utter curiosity.

Keidi Rysinjer?

The name awoke buried emotions, most of which were related to Keidi's husband: Artenz.

Eltaya had fond memories of their university days. Their relationship had only lasted two years, but it had been difficult to let him go. He had taken it even harder than she had. Trying to spare him had been the hardest part of their separation: how she had tried to be patient, to stay friends, to give him the time he needed to detach himself. A full year.

Artenz had not wanted to move on. Friendship had not really been an option for him. In the end, Eltaya had decided to simply cut all ties. It was not something she had enjoyed.

All direct ties, that is. She had kept track of his life from afar, and had been happy for him when finally he had met someone else.

And here was that someone else, on a link, asking for her.

Intriguing indeed.

Deficiency

Eltaya put the head-chip around her right ear and rested it on her cheek. She pushed a button; it connected instantly.

"Open the link," she told Ayatle, whose blurry face was still looking at her from the monitor.

"Linking," answered the ghost. "Complete."

"This is Eltaya," Eltaya said.

"Eltaya Ark? Is this really Eltaya Ark?"

"It is I," said Eltaya. "How did you find me?"

"I... from Artenz's contacts list. He... I didn't know who to call."

"Just a sec," said Eltaya, turning toward her ghost and muting her head-chip.

"What link did she use?" she asked.

"A very old one," said the ghost. "Year 3.4k42."

University years.

"You monitor incoming links that far back?" Eltaya asked.

"Farther. The net I use is very large."

"Good."

"Most links are telemarketers. This one was different, and I thought you should be notified. She sounds in distress."

"You did good," said Eltaya, reactivating the head-chip.

"... and he told me to—" Keidi had not stopped talking, and panic was now rampant in her voice.

"Are you all right?" interrupted Eltaya.

There were sounds in the background. Keidi was in the city, on a busy street, although not directly on the street, in a side alley maybe. Eltaya couldn't be certain. B-pads automatically reduced background noise, but it was a technology with limitations. Eltaya's ghost was in Keidi's b-pad, enhancing the sound, getting what information she could. It was an invasion of privacy and, with the type of individuals Eltaya usually dealt with, risky. But Ayalte was good at remaining undetected, and the danger worth the benefits.

"I... yes, no," said Keidi. Her voice was shaking, and Eltaya thought it had a trace of pain. Maybe injured? "I'm safe, and all right, but

Artenz... They got him, I think. He never came. We were to meet, and I've been waiting for hours now. I didn't know who to turn to. I remembered him telling me about you. About your... connections."

It was obvious from Keidi's intonation that she knew about Eltaya's past relationship with Artenz.

As to the connections she was referring to, Artenz would not know much, so Eltaya could only speculate about what he would have told Keidi.

Eltaya muted her chip.

"Call Xavi," she said to the face on the screen. Then, reactivating her chip: "I might be able to help, but I can't make any promises. When was the last time you heard from him? Who are *they*? And what would *they* want from him?"

This was exactly Eltaya's biggest fear.

Someone she knew disappearing.

Again.

It was too early to say if Artenz would be sent away, but it did not sound good.

"I linked with Artenz at lunch," said Keidi, her voice growing stronger, calmer. Eltaya was liking her already. "We unlinked at 1211. The sleuths caught him, I think. I don't know really, but Artenz told me the sleuths got Marti. Or the corporations. Marti is Artenz's friend and employee. Artenz works at the Blue Tower..."

"I know," interrupted Eltaya.

There was a brief pause, "You know?" asked Keidi.

"It's my business to know," said Eltaya, although it was not, not really. She was interested in the truth. The Banner was interested in the truth. Still, Eltaya had kept an eye on Artenz over the years, in part because of their brief relationship, in part because of his parents and their resistance and the danger they'd put everyone they knew in. "Why do you think they're after Artenz?"

Xavi was back in the room. Eltaya muted her chip again.

Deficiency

"The corporations got a friend of mine," she told him. The sleuths worked for hire, and only the corporations could afford their services. "He needs our help."

Xavi nodded and left to reassemble the team. Eltaya returned to the link.

"I don't know why," Keidi was saying, "not really. But this morning, his sister disappeared. His older sister... sorry, I assume you know Detel, from before? Anyway, she's completely gone. From the bio and data. Her laboratory's empty, and enforcers were in her lodge, going through her stuff."

It was not the parents then.

Eltaya did know about Detel, about her research, although she did not know any specifics. She watched Artenz from afar, but it was not so with Detel. Detel's research was something worth monitoring, although Eltaya had not done so in a while now.

"Do you know where Artenz is now?" Eltaya asked. "Or where he was when they caught him?"

"No, I have no idea," said Keidi.

"Where are you?"

"At a small shop called I Bot."

"I know the place," said Eltaya. "You were to meet there?"

"Yes, and then, I don't know, we planned to run. Hide. I don't know."

They would never have made it. It was almost a good thing they had caught Artenz before he had met up with Keidi, because they would have taken her too.

"Go inside the shop," said Eltaya. "Stay there. We'll come for you."

"And Artenz?"

"We'll try to find him."

"Is it too late?"

"I hope not" was the best answer she could give.

- - - . . . Torture

Enforcers entered the office, pulling a blindfolded and gagged Artenz between them, pushing him forward. Drayfus's chief coder took a few steps before falling forward, hitting the floor hard. He moaned through the gag—a low lamentation. Drayfus noticed his arms were covered in fresh bruises. One side of his face was dark and covered in long scratches, as if it had been dragged against a rough surface. Drayfus shivered, trying not to think about the encounter between Artenz and Okran's party.

"Get him ready," said Mysa Lamond, moving through the room to meet with the lead enforcer.

She stopped midway and looked at Drayfus.

"Get him ready," she repeated, her words steady and chilling.

Drayfus jumped up and went to Artenz and knelt beside him, not knowing what he was supposed to do or say.

He looked toward Mysa Lamond. She was exiting the office, followed by the bionic. Two guards stood by the door as it closed.

Drayfus turned back to Artenz. Drops of blood appeared from some of the cuts on the man's face and rolled as ruby pearls, falling and pooling on the floor.

Time seemed to have stopped. Drayfus could not believe what was happening. Once again, he looked toward the door, toward the guards standing there—their masks blocked him from seeing if they were looking at him. For all he knew, they might be enjoying his discomfiture. Were they even human? Did they care?

He turned away, hid his face. He didn't want them to see how distraught he was.

The blindfold on Artenz's eyes was made of a leathery material Drayfus could not identify. It seemed tight, the skin around it bluish. The lips were also pulled back by the gag. Drayfus wondered if he should try to loosen the blindfold and gag, decided against it.

He was scared.

Many times, he had been scared. His job demanded that he be fearful of those above him. Of Mr. Blue, of people like Mysa Lamond, whatever she was. He could handle that type of intimidation, understood where it came from, used it himself on his subordinates from time to time. To get results. To get value.

But this violence was new.

He passed a hand in his hair, realized he was actually pulling at the hair. Stopped.

He had to get Artenz ready—ready for what? He didn't know, didn't want to think about it.

What he knew was that Artenz was in a poor state. He had not moved since his fall on the floor. At least he was breathing. Drayfus could see the chest going up and down, hear the air pushing through the man's throat and nose.

The droplets of blood were accumulating on the side of his face, a timer of sorts. One more drop appearing, one more minute slipping by.

Not looking at the door or the enforcers, Drayfus stood and went to his desk. He opened a drawer and took out a tissue, beige, from a pile within. The softness of the tissue contrasted gravely with the events happening. A gift from his wife, each tissue had the logo of BlueTech Data on it, the letters BTD, a tower standing representing the T, all in a bright blue.

Drayfus kept his head low and returned to Artenz. He grabbed a chair on the way and positioned it beside his chief coder.

Putting the tissue in his pocket, Drayfus put his hands under Artenz's shoulders and tried to help him up. He was shocked when Artenz did not respond in any way.

On his knees again, Drayfus checked for a pulse. It was there. He let out a long sigh of relief.

He almost asked Artenz if he could hear him but restrained himself. He did not want Artenz to know he was here, that he was part of this.

Drayfus used the tissue to dry the blood on Artenz's face. The beige tissue quickly absorbed the crimson liquid.

This tissue is not meant to come in contact with blood, thought Drayfus.

This was all wrong. So very wrong.

+

An hour or so later, Drayfus was back in his chair, frozen in place, feeling sick. He struggled to understand what he had just witnessed.

It had been torture.

In the middle of the room, his best employee sagged in the chair, the chair in which Drayfus had placed him once he had come back to his senses.

In front of Artenz stood Mysa Lamond and the bionic, Okran. Both looked inhuman in the late afternoon light, and Drayfus did not know which one he feared the most.

Artenz's head rested on the back of the chair, at a sharp angle. His breathing was slow and harsh. The blindfold was still on, but the gag was off. More droplets of blood. Not on his face, where Drayfus had dried them with the tissue, a tissue now in his pocket and of which Drayfus was terribly aware. No, the drops of blood had resurfaced around the b-pad on Artenz's neck.

That blood was one of the most disturbing sights Drayfus had ever seen. He just didn't know what it meant when... when a b-pad bled.

Deficiency

"What next?" asked Okran, the harsh voice making Drayfus jump.

In the bionic's hands was the little box they had used to torment Artenz. It was hard to guess what it did or what it was. Some type of mental agony, using the device to get to Artenz via his b-pad. It had turned physical quickly enough. Drayfus could still see it, how Artenz had grabbed at his ears, then his eyes, then his skull. Images that could never ever be erased from his mind.

Images he knew he would see again in nightmares.

Drayfus realized he had been scratching at his own b-pad. He forced himself to stop, but he could not help the feeling that he wanted the device out.

Until today, Drayfus had been unaware of how vulnerable the device made him, made all of them. An image of his daughter appeared. She was six, and he was so proud of her. He loved her, and that love had been a surprise, something he had not thought himself capable of. She had softened him, his daughter had. She was the most beautiful little girl he knew. He was biased, certainly... And now, as he thought of her, he saw the little round device implanted in the side of her neck.

"Find his wife," commanded Mysa Lamond.

Drayfus could not help wondering again what she was. Not a sleuth after all. The way she inflicted pain did not align with the little he knew of their operations. They got paid to find individuals, find information, investigate. They had access to some of the deepest tiers of the datasphere, and their activities were outside the realm of the corporations and the government. Their secrets were their own.

Over a century ago, the corporations had tried to put a stop to the sleuths, seeing them as the enemy. The silent war between the two groups had raged for decades and left a long trail of crippled and ruined companies. It seemed the sleuths had not lost much during the conflict. Rumors suggested many lives were lost during those long years, although there was no record of such casualties.

It was not secret, though, that the corporations were at a disadvantage. The knowledge of the sleuths was too extensive. They could see any attack before it happened. They could turn corporations against each other.

Which is why the corporations had decided to work out an agreement. If they couldn't defeat the organization, they would make use of it. Thus, the corporations decided to hire the sleuths, the details of the pact kept hidden.

It had been this way since Drayfus could remember.

That said, the sleuths operated under very strict rules that prohibited this kind of activity. Whatever *this* was.

If Mysa Lamond was not a sleuth, then what? She did not fit the mold, and much in Prominence was about fitting in and playing a predefined role. Maybe that was why she was here, because this was nothing normal.

Drayfus could not conceive of what was going on in his building, in his company. What he had noticed, though, during the past hour, was that things were not exactly going the way Mysa Lamond wanted.

She had just given the order to go after Artenz's wife. Between spasms of pain, Artenz had rasped where he had planned on meeting with her. It had not really mattered, as his b-pad would most likely had given it away anyway. A recorded conversation, easily tracked by the likes of Mysa Lamond.

The only thing Drayfus knew about Artenz's wife was that she was a technician with outdated skills. He didn't think they would find more from that lead. What could a technician know, anyway? They were extremely low in the hierarchy, at the bottom of the operations layer.

Following the command, the bionic left the room, once again on a mission. The man's excitement about being back on the hunt did not sit well with Drayfus.

+

Deficiency

"What do you know of Marti Zehron?" asked Mysa Lamond suddenly.

"The old coder?" he asked.

"Yes, the old coder."

Mysa Lamond was standing straight again, and he could feel her eyes on him. Her suit was as white as it had been that morning, as perfect, as expensive.

"Not much," said Drayfus. "I was never able to tell why Artenz kept dragging the guy along. He's slow, not quick or bright. He certainly doesn't fit with the rest of the team. Most people dislike him. I didn't really care, as long as the work got done. Maybe he's a good friend to Artenz. Maybe a distant relative?"

The woman smirked at Drayfus, mocking him. Drayfus was instantly enraged and finally looked at her.

"This could be costly for you," she said.

"How so?" he challenged.

"Marti is a genus coder," she said.

The title did not make any sense. A level 5 coder?

"What? No, no, no," Drayfus said, half laughing now. "He's a level 2, at best. Possibly an adept. I never saw anything come out of him. Maybe in his younger days, but I really don't think so. I can't see it at all. He never did anything worth much since he joined BlueTech."

"No, he did not do much you would have seen," said Mysa Lamond, without providing any details. She sat on top of his desk. Drayfus did not like that, how she seemed to own his office. "Did you figure out how Artenz was able to escape the building, walk right through our net?"

Drayfus had not.

"It could not have been the old coder," he said, weakly.

Mysa Lamond produced a chilling smile.

"The old coder, as you like to call him, opened a hole in your building's defenses and let his chief out."

"That's not possible."

"It is, and the old coder did it easily, inside a few minutes. He was monitoring your defenses, was probably monitoring your whole building, for years."

Drayfus wanted to laugh the accusations away; instead, he felt sweat trickle down his forehead. Did Mr. Blue know about this?

"So, let me ask again, what do you know about of him?"

"I... you'd have to check the data-sphere," said Drayfus truthfully. He did not know much. Why would he? Coders worked in operations. He was careful about his chiefs, about who he selected for those positions, but why waste energy on those below?

"We looked," said Mysa Lamond. "And there is nothing there. I repeat: nothing. So think, will you, and tell me what you remember."

Artenz unexpectedly took a long breath. His head lolled to one side, then the other. Drayfus almost wished he would come to and take the attention of the woman away from him.

"What do you mean, nothing?" he said, not hiding his surprise. "Surely, one like you can find more information than I could ever provide."

Mysa Lamond pouted, once, twice. She seemed unhappy, yet Drayfus was not certain if it was at him or the whole situation. Most likely both.

"You do not seem to understand the gravity of the situation," she noted calmly but with a threat in her voice. "This situation, if not resolved in the next few hours, will have a wide blast radius. Let me put it this way, so you understand where you stand. Marti is already gone, if you have not noticed. Artenz here will also be gone shortly. His wife, who you will agree with me knows nothing, will go too." Could she read his thoughts? Was she monitoring his b-pad? "Some of the relatives will follow, some friends, some colleagues... and some..."

"I get it," said Drayfus, standing now. He paced for a moment before making his way toward the window, realizing too late that he was now in Artenz's line of sight. He looked back, and thankfully saw that his chief coder's eyes were still covered by the bandanna.

Deficiency

Thinking of it, if Artenz was awake, he would have heard Drayfus's voice by now and be aware of his role in the matter. Drayfus was not certain why he cared whether Artenz knew he was implicated. He just did.

Would they really dare make him disappear?

Drayfus thought of his daughter, and his anxiety increased. "It's like I said," he muttered. "About the old man, I know almost nothing. He came with Artenz, who came from Surface Designs. Both came from Surface Designs. A small firm of interface coders. Negligible. There, Artenz did some good work, becoming chief of an impressive team. The firm presented some of their work at a conference here at the tower. I recruited Artenz then and there. He asked if he could bring his team."

"You did not interview any of them?"

"We, a board of five managers, interviewed Artenz. BlueTech also performed an extensive background check on each member of the team, obviously. Including the old man."

"What did you find?"

"I don't remember, but nothing out of the ordinary or we'd not have hired him. He had a profile, believe me, in the bio and the data. He checked out."

Drayfus wondered if any of Artenz's success was the old coder's doing? The thought was brief. Artenz was charismatic, a good leader. There was no denying his abilities on that front. If anything, a resource like the old coder, a genus, was a powerful asset for a leader as good as Artenz.

A genus coder was one in a million. Most coders were level 2 apprentices. Level 3 adepts were rare. Artenz could possibly had become a master coder, but he had stepped into a lead role. Level 4 master coders—now those provided an advantage over the competition.

A genus coder's salary was easily in the seven figures. Marti had been paid a five-figure salary.

A thought occurred to Drayfus.

"But you have him," he observed. "So what is the problem?"

Mysa Lamond did not answer right away.

"You have him, right?" he asked again.

"We do," she finally answered. Yet nothing about her words was convincing.

- - - - . . . . Authentic Banner

There was no plan. Nothing firm, nothing they could pull together quickly. And even though the rescue was not typical of the organization's activities, they had to act.

Aana Figuera established the Authentic Banner in the year 3.4k20. At the time, she was a sleuth, a fact that surprised Eltaya every time she thought about it. Sleuths were an exceptionally tight and elite group. Committed and loyal. Eltaya knew of no one other than Aana who had left their ranks.

By leaving, Aana forsook all her privileges, including most of her accesses to the Sphere. She also underwent a memory-wipe, although it was known that the procedure did not always work 100%. Aana, for example, had retained some of her memories.

The woman had been 45 when she'd left the organization and begun a crusade to unearth the truth behind Prominence City and Garadia. The old woman rarely talked about her reasons for splitting from the sleuths. Eltaya herself didn't know what the woman's motives could be. She had never asked.

In any case, Aana had left, with some type of agreement with her former employer: *Let's stay away from each other*. Something to that effect.

The Banner was formed, and the first true reporters were born. True reporters, because the Authentic Banner was only interested in reporting on facts, on reality, on what was really happening, every statement accompanied by a series of proofs, some of which were painstakingly obtained. Mainstream reporters, newscasters by title, were more interested in shock value than in reality.

Eltaya joined the Banner on her 30th birthday. It was the minimum age to join, the only exception being Ulie, who was 29 and had joined at 28. Her experience as a coder and moderator of the bio-sphere filled a most needed role on their team. Although she was certainly young, all knew she would rapidly become the best of them.

The newsroom was again filled with the members, 10 in all. Ged and Styl had gone to collect Keidi. The focus of the group was now solely on Artenz.

"He's in the Blue Tower," said Ulie, seated in the middle of the table. She had a tablet that showed search results from the data-sphere.

"How can you tell?" asked Xavi, crouched over her shoulder, staring at the screen. "Did you follow his location trail?"

"I did," answered Ulie. "He used a scrambler or something like it while on the run. During that time, he popped in and out. Then he was caught at the gate between Quadrant X and Quadrant O. He was brought back to the tower, as you can see here. Then the trail disappears."

The coordinates of all inhabitants of Prominence City were easily accessed by those who knew where to find them. Much information was available in the data-sphere that most people did not even know existed.

"They froze his pad," Xavi.

Or something worse, thought Eltaya.

"It'll be tricky," she said. "The tower is locked down."

"Do we know who ordered the lockdown?" asked Xavi.

Eltaya was at the end of the room, in her usual spot, seated crossed-legged on her chair.

Deficiency

"It was approved by Mr. Blue, and activated by someone named Mysa Lamond."

There was a sigh from Aana. The woman, 85 now, was nodding slowly.

"You know the name?" asked Xavi.

"I do," said Aana. "She's dangerous."

Eltaya did not know the name.

"Who is she loyal to?" asked Xavi. "Who does she work for?"

The old woman shook her head.

"No one," Aana said. "She's a rogue, she's cyborg."

Ulie whistled.

Xavi tapped his fingers on the table. "You are telling me this woman is half-machine and outlawed? What are her roots? How old is she?"

"She must be over 130," said Aana, "and her resume is substantive. She tried to join the Agency when I was there." A sleuth wannabe. Interesting. "She was rejected and swore vengeance. We kept an eye on her. The Agency did. She became a newscaster, then an impersonator, although no one knows how that transition happened. She mimicked being an enforcer before becoming an assassin, although it is not believed that the Guild ever accepted her." It was an impressive resume, and Aana was not done. "She later came back and tried to infiltrate the Agency, and failed. She was severely injured during the capture. The Agency does not kill, so we let her go. She disappeared, and it was believed she had learned her lesson. Some, myself included, thought she had left Prominence. It seems she has not."

"Cyborg, how?" asked Kator.

"She excels at whatever she does and gets paid accordingly. She paid for the augments one by one."

The group, including Eltaya, was silent for a few moments, taking the information in. Eltaya felt as if she was missing something, but had no idea what.

Then, as usual, Xavi spoke, his voice calm and confident.

"Do we know if she's still in the Blue Tower?" he asked.

"I'll check," said Ulie.

"Can we find out if there was a contract?" added Xavi.

"Good idea," said Ulie. "I'll add a search."

Xavi would lead the rescue. He had been a bodyguard before joining the Banner. He knew how to secure a person and make an escape. That said, the Blue Tower was not an easy place to breach. The more they knew about the situation, the better the chances of success.

Still, Eltaya was becoming impatient. She had her own tablet and called her ghost.

The figure appeared.

"How can I help?" it asked.

"Scan the Blue Tower network for a weakness, anything that could allow us to enter and escape."

Aana was shaking her head again.

"I know," said Eltaya, "but she's good and can help."

"You use her too much," said Xavi. "It will cost you, eventually."

"Maybe, maybe not," said Eltaya. "Let's stay focused here. She can help."

In reality, no one knew the long-term effects of using a ghost. They were not widespread, and where they had been used, it had been with mixed results. The ghost was an entity on its own, a type of virtual intelligence. It was connected directly to the subconscious of the host. Its initial use had been to perform tasks in the electronic world while its host slept. Synchronization happened before awakening. It was a way to expand one's knowledge, learn, clear out unwanted memories, and so on.

It had cost Eltaya a small fortune to acquire the extension, but she felt it had been worth the price. She had been experimenting and was now using her ghost while awake. It was another area where many members disagreed with her. It provided an advantage that Eltaya found she could not ignore.

"I cannot find anything," said Ulie. "No contract. No profile. Nothing on this Mysa lady."

Deficiency

"That is hard to believe," said Xavi. "Continue looking."

"This could take a while," said Ulie.

"We don't have a while," put in Eltaya. "We should already have left."

She was part of the deployment team. There was no way she would not be.

Praka would be their transporter. Like Eltaya, she was close to 40. Unlike Eltaya, she had two daughters, who she raised on her own when not with the Banner.

Kazor would come for additional protection. The big man was already equipped and ready, standing by the door, stunner shotgun in hand. Looking at him, it was hard to imagine that he was the loving father of an 18-year-old daughter. The others, including Ulie and Aana, would supervise from here.

They had a blueprint of the tower, including the floors in the Underground, 01 to 20.

"Eltaya is right," said Xavi, "if we wait any longer, we could very well be too late."

Earlier, Ulie had confirmed the disappearance of Artenz's sister. Detel's vanishing had all the marks of a flush, with no data left in the data-sphere. Ulie was continuing to perform side searches on Detel, just in case.

"Eltaya, someone wants to talk to you."

The voice had come from her ghost. The room became silent.

"You found someone that can help?" Eltaya asked.

"Possibly."

"Who?" Eltaya asked.

"He calls himself Red Dragon," said the ghost.

172

- - - - I Bot Shop

I Bot was not a large place. Wedged between two buildings on level 33, three levels over the level 30 street, it was hard to miss with its twin flashing signs, one on each side, embossed in the adjoining building's surface. The signs were identical and bold in their simplicity. They showed the shop's name, with the round head of a gigantic smiling bot forming the O. Each large letter changed colors like a rainbow. The signs encouraged mockery.

A single mini air-tube took the customers from the street to the shop's level. A small platform bridged the tube and the store entrance.

And from this platform, Keidi scanned the streets in the hope of seeing Artenz. She had watched the streets for so long now that she did not even know if she would see him if he appeared. She had a hard time focusing.

She had unlinked with Eltaya a few minutes ago and was still shaken by the exchange. She had hoped the woman would reassure her, tell her she was mistaken, something of that nature.

Instead, Eltaya had been cold, firm, decisive and terribly intimidating. It was not a good time to worry about such details, but Keidi did. It was almost as if Eltaya had expected something like this to happen, almost as if she had been ready for it.

Deficiency

Keidi decided she had waited long enough. She felt exposed on the platform, in plain view of anyone looking its way. Eltaya had asked her to go wait in the store, and that is what she would do.

She turned toward the shop and cringed as pain shot from her ankle, up through her leg. Since her jump from Detel's window, her ankle had protested, made worse by the rapid walk from the apartment to this place.

She entered the shop.

Inside, space was at a premium. An alley led to a counter in the back. On each side, rows of parallel high shelves displayed the wares, which varied from bot parts to strange gadgets, some new, most ancient and nonfunctional. There was barely enough space for visitors to walk. In the front, two windows covered in painted markings offered a partial view outside.

Almost instantly, Keidi found the scramblers. Artenz would need one, and she wanted a backup. She picked three, went all the way to the back of the shop, and transferred the credits. The owner was short, with a mechanic arm, and distracted, probably keeping an eye on the bio-sphere via his eye-veil.

Next, Keidi made her way to the front of the store where she could look out through the glass. She reactivated her scrambler, although she doubted it would help now, after the call, after the purchase.

She waited.

+

The owner showed no sign of caring that Keidi stayed in his store. For all she knew, he traveled the bio-sphere, not even aware she was there.

A customer appeared at the top of the air-tube. An imposing man, tall, wide, and bald. Keidi pulled away from the windows, trying to hide in the shadows.

The man entered the store and didn't seem to notice her, went on to browse through the items.

Keidi closed her eyes, trying to ignore the pain in her ankle, trying hard not to worry about Artenz. Failing miserably.

+

A bit later, she opened her eyes. The big man was still there, possibly in the same spot as before. She was not sure. The owner had not moved either, seated at the counter, in the back. Keidi could see him through the shelves.

She turned toward the streets, which she could partially see over the edge of the platform. She reflexively pulled back when she saw two enforcers walking in her direction. As they crossed the street, Keidi held her breath and lost sight of them momentarily.

To her shock, they appeared at the top of the air-tube, rifles in hand, visages hidden behind inhuman masks.

Keidi could not move farther back. She hoped it was enough, she hoped…

One of the enforcers stopped by the entrance. She could see him through the storefront glass. It could not be a coincidence. The other opened the door and entered, barrel first.

This was when Keidi noticed that the customer had positioned himself in her aisle, directly in front of her.

The enforcer was inside the store now. His metallic boots resonated on the floor with each step. Keidi could not see him—the big man in front of her blocked her view. The enforcer made his way to the back of the store before returning to the entrance.

"Anyone else in here?" he asked, authority in his voice.

"Just what you see," said the big man standing in front of Keidi.

The enforcer didn't say another word. He exited, and Keidi saw through the window that he rejoined his partner, both now guarding the store.

Deficiency

They knew she was here, or close by. Were they waiting? If so, for what? Reinforcement?

Keidi wished she could just walk out and trust the enforcers would do what they could to protect her. After all, that is what the government promised. And maybe that is what they thought they were doing. The problem might not be with them, but with the rules and laws they were told people broke. Corporations wrote most of those.

Without saying a word, the big man left her aisle and walked toward the back of the store. Keidi was perplexed. He had moved in front of her on purpose. Who was this man?

She heard him move something in the back of the shop, dragging it on the floor. Then he stopped where she could see him, but facing the other way. Behind his back, he waved, invited her to move. Keidi hesitated.

"There's a better place in the back," he said, not looking at her. "Better for your ankle. On the left, a stool. Go to it now—they're not looking."

Not saying a word, Keidi obeyed.

Was it possible this man had been sent by Eltaya?

"Thank you," she whispered, as she passed by him. She made her way to the back of the shop, keeping to the shadows.

The owner was behind the counter, his head low, lost in the biosphere.

The stool was where the man had said it would be. She went to it and sat and was instantly grateful. The pain fled from her ankle.

Reflexively, Keidi put a hand on her stomach. She could barely feel any change inside her body. Her belly was the same, although something was growing inside. Keidi couldn't stop her hand from shaking.

As much as she worried about Artenz, and Detel, her thoughts were now on the baby. She wondered if this whole thing was somehow related to them hiding her pregnancy, trying to have a natural birth. The measures taken so far seemed extreme, but she was breaking the law. Artenz was as well, and Detel had helped… It made some sense, but it did not sit well with Keidi. There had to be more.

The big man had hidden her, but she was still a prisoner, incapable of escaping. Looking around, it was obvious there was only one exit, and it was guarded.

The enforcers were here for her. The more she thought about it, the more she was convinced of it. They were waiting for something or someone, and once whatever they were waiting for arrived, they would come for her.

And once they had her, a simple check would reveal her deception and the baby growing inside of her.

Keidi did not know where Detel was or what had happened to her. She did not know where Artenz was or what had happened to him.

What she knew was that if she was caught, the baby would be aborted.

+

Styl stepped onto the level 20 of Quadrant O, followed closely by Ged. The sun forced its brightness down through level 30 above. Quadrant O was not kept as clean as other places in Prominence, and it left level 20 in a perpetual haziness. Styl found it depressing.

His goggles adjusted automatically to provide him with a crisp view of his surroundings. Around and above, numerous billboards flashed and changed and screamed and tried to get attention. Styl ignored it all.

"Only 10 more levels to go," he said.

Standing beside him, Ged nodded. "You're on your own for the rest of the way."

"You're the young one. Why am I doing most of the work here?"

"You're the stealthy one, remember."

"True," said Styl.

"Let's keep walking," Ged said.

Deficiency

Styl pressed on the fake b-pad on his neck, making sure it stuck. This quadrant had mandatory b-pads. Was only a question of time before the device became mandatory everywhere in Prominence. Maybe a year. It would happen. People were too ignorant to care, and the corporations, the damn corporations, wanted it badly.

He did not have a b-pad, had never needed one and would never get one. Just thinking about it brought back painful memories of his sister. Even wearing the fake device was like a thorn in his neck.

She had been 12!

Ged had a b-pad, but since joining the Banner, he wanted to get rid of it. He rarely used it anymore. Styl was on his case to make the change happen sooner than later.

They both wore g-tools, although the device was new to Ged. Not so with Styl. He loved the gauntlet and had used one model or another for years. Could not understand why one would need a pad if one had a g-tool. It was the perfect extension to his goggles; he could not do without. Part computer system, part weapon, Styl's gauntlet also bore a few interesting upgrades.

It all came down to profits. Profits that only benefited an elite few. There was only so far you could push a society while neglecting its basic needs. Or taking advantage of its populace. An uprising would come. Not fast enough, though.

Out loud, he said: "If the corporate world does not change—"

"I know, it'll be the end of Prominence," finished Ged.

"Or maybe the whole of Garadia."

"Maybe." Ged was distracted, listening to final instructions from the base. "It'll be a few minutes before we get what we need."

Styl knew he had to stop repeating the same things over and over. Must have talked about this with Ged 100 times. Time to change the subject.

"How are things?" he asked.

"Things?"

"With you-know-who."

Ged shrugged.

"You'll get burned," said Styl.

"I already have," admitted Ged. "She's not interested in me."

"She said so?"

"Not in so many words."

"I think she is. But has bigger things to do first. She's a complicated one." And someone for whom Styl had deep respect. Not an easy life she had, and yet she was the best of them. "One day, maybe soon, if you are patient."

"Maybe."

"Don't be like that. You knew from the start what you were getting yourself into."

"True."

Ged received a communication.

"The escape route?" Styl asked. Ged nodded. "All set?" Ged nodded again. "Should we expect action?"

"It's possible," said Ged. "Two enforcers at the I Bot entrance."

"Will they be a problem?"

"Shouldn't, not the way you're coming in."

No easy way to know who the enforcers worked for these days. Government kept their accounts full of credits, but somehow, corporations seemed to dictate more and more what they did to earn those credits.

"One entrance, one escape route?" Styl asked.

"Correct."

Ged had a map of the area on his eye-veil. Styl knew it showed stairs, air-tubes, elevators, building entrances, and enforcers in the area. He would be Styl's eyes during the brief operation and share only pertinent information. He would also monitor the mission, keep in touch with the base, and modify the plan if required. Ged was good at that kind of stuff.

Deficiency

The chip hidden under their right ears provided a closed network for the two of them to communicate. Styl pressed the chip and activated it.

"One-opportunity operation," he said, his voice echoing through the air and the chip. "I like it."

"I knew you would," said Ged. "Don't go fancy on me."

"I'm never fancy," said Styl. "Remember, I'm the definition of stealth."

"You are good," said Ged, who chose a bench at the corner of a street and sat down.

"But?"

"But something here is not what it seems."

Taking a few steps farther, not looking at Ged, Styl agreed. The whole thing had come out of nowhere. There was never any doubt they would help; after all, these people were Eltaya's friends. But something stunk.

"This could be big," he said.

"Agreed. Just get out as fast as you can."

"Any worry about the racer?"

"Not for the amount of time we'll be here."

The tri-racer was on level 15, hidden, ready for escape. On the Dominance, the enforcers' floor. A risk, but a calculated one. Since the disappearances had started 90 years ago, most enforcers preferred not using the Underground. Logical. Still, the events were not well documented, and most continued to believe the floor was used by enforcers. The Banner knew better, and this was one of the rare cases where they left the truth unexposed. Eltaya had disagreed, which made Styl wonder.

In response, he had performed his own investigation.

Conclusion: danger lurked below, although he still had to figure out its exact nature. He went down only a few times, found bodies, some in a disturbing state. Did not touch anything, left right away in each case. Not a good idea to go down on his own, but worth the disobedience if it eventually determined what was happening down there.

The enforcers who still used the floor did so in emergency cases only, without lingering, in and out. The main arteries remained clear and fairly safe, if one did not linger.

The Banner usually used level 10, deeper, but leaving the tri-racer there would have lengthened the escape route significantly. The vehicle was prohibited in Prominence, so bringing it to level 20 would have attracted too much attention.

It was not the first time Styl and Ged had performed this type of operation together.

"Time for you to go," announced Ged.

Styl nodded and walked away, hands in his pockets.

"Upload the route, will you," he whispered, now communicating through the chips.

Instantly, a faded map appeared on the inside of his goggles, and a pale yellow arrow popped up on the screen of his g-tool.

"Here we go," he said, and quickened his pace.

+

The shop owner's head fell forward some more, coming to rest on the counter. Either he was deep in the bio-sphere or truly asleep.

The other customer, the big man, paced back and forth, from the entrance to the counter, every few minutes. In wait of something, it seemed.

As he came back, this time, he stopped and looked at her. The particularities of his face were lost in the shadows of the shop.

"Are you all right?" he asked in a surprisingly soft voice, different from the one he had used earlier.

"Yes," lied Keidi. "Thank you."

"All right," said the man. "I have water here, if you want some. You don't look so good."

Deficiency

Keidi smiled.

"No, really, I'm fine."

"All right," repeated the man. His voice and demeanor were awkward, but there was a genuine generosity about him. "Here it is," he said, depositing a bright yellow thermos on the end of the counter, close to her.

He walked back toward the entrance.

"Damn," said Keidi under her breath.

She was thirsty.

She grabbed the thermos, opened the cap and took a sip. The water was icy cold and refreshing. The most surprising thing was its lack of taste. The liquid didn't have the usual heavy leaden taste of Prominence. Keidi drank more than was polite before putting the thermos back.

"Go on," said the big man, now standing on the other side of the shelf to her left, as if he were browsing. "Don't stop. I have another."

Keidi drank some more.

"Thank you," she said, when she was done. "That was very good water."

She did not hide her suspicion. The man didn't bite.

"Arnol," he said, extending a puffed-up hand through the shelves. It was accompanied by a warm smile.

"Keidi," she said, taking his hand.

His grip was nothing special and did not give anything away.

"Here," he said, passing another thermos through the shelf. "Keep this one."

"I don't... " started Keidi, and stopped. There was no point refusing. The thermos was given out of necessity, not generosity.

There was something in his eyes, a message, an understanding. It had not been there before.

She put the thermos in her bag.

"Thank you," she said.

He smiled briefly, then looked over his shoulder.

"Here it comes," he said, and made his way toward the front of the store.

From where she was, Keidi could not see well outside the shop. Still, it was enough to see an enforcer step out of the air-tube.

This one was different. He looked dangerous. He was shorter, wore heavy gray armor, with pistol and rifle on his belt. His face was completely hidden under a black opaque sphere. There was a purpose to the way he walked, an unnaturalness to his movement.

Keidi stood and took a step back, placing herself against the wall, as far as she could from the entrance. Her ankle screamed in protest.

"Keidi." It was Arnol. He was standing by the door, blocking it. "Stay put, stay on the stool."

He was going to interfere.

He opened the door.

Mission 001202 A

The invisible carrier floats down toward the building's rooftop. Chances of detection are 0.02%.

Okran jumps while the carrier is still high above the surface. The augments in his legs absorb the impact. Without waiting for those he leads, Okran stands and walks to the edge of the roof. There, he kneels and looks at the streets below.

The visor of his helmet provides detailed information of the scene. Level is 36. 124 civilians in the current block. 102 adults, 15 children and seven babies, all in good health, all with active and fully trackable brain-pads.

Of the 102 adults, 12 are enforcers working undercover. Four more enforcers are in uniform, two of whom are guarding the destination shop. Of the other 90 adults, 10 are classified as important and should not be harmed. The others are inconsequential.

The destination is on level 33. Three air-tubes are quickly accessible, one in the building under Okran, one to reach the shop itself and another, hidden and only accessible to soldiers, can be used to reach the roof of the building located to the right of the shop.

His visor also shows the position of his squad and the carrier on which they are being transported. It is now floating on level 36, at a distance of 0.75 meters from the floor. At 0.50 meters, the squad, formed of seven soldiers, three apprentices, and four adepts, will debark and follow him in tight formation. This will happen in 12 seconds.

Okran stands and jumps. Six levels, 36 to 30, are manageable for a master soldier. The augments in his legs can sustain a fall of up to 10 levels. 11 or 12 levels are achievable, but minor impairments will happen 90% of the time. At 13 or 14 levels, major impairments are expected. 15 or more levels can be attempted, but major reconstruction will most likely be required.

The fall's trajectory was calculated before Okran left the roof. As he falls, he orders one of his soldiers to stay on the roof with the carrier. He orders another to take position on the roof across the street, on the building to the right of the shop. Two more, he orders to stay on the street. The others are to follow him.

Okran touches down between walking pedestrians, their reactions not registering, as they are deemed unimportant to the mission. The augments absorb the impact of the jump easily.

Using the velocity of the fall, Okran stands and jogs toward the air-tube. His squad will require a minimum of 35 seconds to reach him. His augments are far superior to those of his squad. For that reason, they will use the air-tube to reach the street instead of jumping.

Okran knows the target is trapped in the shop. Current parameters dictate that one soldier is enough to secure the woman. Chances of success are higher if he goes himself, ahead of the others.

He reaches the air-tube and waits while it propels him three stories higher.

Okran steps out and makes his way toward the shop's entrance. There is no need to exchange with the soldiers on guard. They know why he is here and they will not interfere.

The door opens before Okran reaches it. A man appears; he is one of the three civilians identified as being in the shop. He is blocking the way.

Information instantly appears inside Okran's visor.

Deficiency

Arnol Dessol is his name. 48 years of age. 187.8 centimeters in height. Weight of 136.9 kilograms. Adept artificer for Innovative Designs Inc. Married to Ezmine Regalia, 42 years of age. One daughter: Tria Regalia, 12 years old. Current residence is at 1026-34-125 Delgarde Street, Quadrant M, Factory district. Classification: Dispensable.

"Move aside," says Okran.

"I do not think so," is the reply.

The man dives at Okran. He is slow. Heavy, but no threat to Okran's armor.

Okran pushes aside the man's fist and counters with a punch of his own. Ribs crack; internal bleeding is expected. The man stands his ground and locks one of his arms around Okran's helmet.

Okran punches a second time. More ribs crack.

The Okran-that-was surfaces and brings hesitation. The interruption is fleeting, momentary. The cyborg regains control—unfeeling, uncaring, utterly focused on the mission. True artificial intelligence is illegal, thus the human part remains. Fear of death cannot be programmed, thus the human part remains.

The human part once lived for battles and fights, for power and superiority. It led him to accept the transformation, to accept sharing his being with the machine.

The Okran-that-was now follows, and feels old, and feels weak. He has seen too much violence, too much unnecessary violence. The Okran-that-was feels compassion for the man standing in the door of the shop. He knows his attacks are against protocol. But his feelings do not matter.

The cyborg punches a third time. More cracking. Bleeding is guaranteed. The man growls in pain and grabs the door frame, staying up, still not moving aside.

Okran frees his head from the man's arm, takes a step closer, and using his elbow, strikes the man on the side of the head.

The neck snaps.

Okran holds the man up in front of him and ignores the shock plastered on the faces of the soldiers standing by the door.

Instead of instantly pursuing the woman inside the shop, Okran hesitates.

The Okran-that-was resurfaces, torn by painful remorse, momentarily freezing his cyborg counterpart. When he was human, he had never once taken a life. His name had been Okran Delaro, then enforcer Delaro. Not soldier. Employee of the government and protector of the people.

He acknowledges this is not the first life he has taken since being a bionic. He does not have a precise count. The cyborg part of him is programmed not to keep track of that information. It is unwillingly and in shame that the Okran-that-was steps aside, retreats and lets the cyborg continue with the mission.

Okran drops the body of Arnol and enters the shop.

- - - - - . Passageways

A dull detonation reverberated and muffled the fight between Arnol and the enforcer. It came from the wall on which Keidi was leaning. Reflexively, she turned toward the sound. A portion of the wall crumbled, forming a hole from her waist to the floor.

A man appeared in front of her, kneeling, his face covered by dark goggles, his long brown hair streaked with white flattened backward. Keidi noticed he was holding a crumbler, a small device that produced shock waves and vibrations. It was usually used to weaken stone structures, to eventually bring them down. This one had been modified. The device didn't normally make walls fall to pieces.

"What have you done?" exclaimed the store owner. His voice was shrill.

"Keidi?" asked the man protruding from the hole in the wall. "Come," he added without waiting for an answer. "We have to move, quick."

Keidi stole a glance toward the entrance. The shelves were obstructing most of her view. She had been able to see Arnol in the entrance before. Not anymore. A shape moved in, accompanied by the sound of metal against the floor.

What had happened to Arnol?

It did not change anything. Keidi knew there was nothing she could do to help. She suddenly feared never seeing Artenz again. She thought of Detel, her best friend, who was gone. And she thought of her baby.

In that brief moment between uncertainties and fear, the baby seemed the only important thing.

Keidi closed her eyes, shutting Arnol out, and turned away. She took a deep breath and opened her eyes. Her first step was a stumble. She gasped with pain and forced herself forward. As she entered the dark hole, Keidi felt as if she was leaving her life behind.

"Quick now," said the man with the dark goggles, appearing at her side. "Lean on me."

She did, and together, they left I Bot.

+

They ran into the adjacent building, through a storage room, then a long hallway, until they reached an air-saucer.

"Jump on," said the man.

Keidi did. The man followed and grabbed the stability bar in the middle. The saucer moved down. In the light emitted by the tube, Keidi looked more closely at the shades on the man's face. They were like nothing she had seen before, similar to sunshades, yet glued to his skin.

"Will they follow?" she asked.

"Most certainly," said the man.

The saucer stopped on level 20. Keidi stepped out, and without hesitation, she turned off her scrambler and knelt on the floor. From her backpack, she took out a tech-cable and her mini-vid, connected both to her b-pad. The man looked at her, surprised, but did not stop her.

Keidi scanned the frame of the tube, looking for a small plate. She found it quickly and connected the other end of the cable to it.

Her b-pad connected to the system.

Deficiency

```
Welcome to the Valda Complex.
Year 3.4k60 Season 05 Day 11 Hour 1644.

Sol Development Inc.
Air-saucer Model B11.V103.Range120

Valda Complex
30-2050 Gage Street, Rozanburg, D3QO
Initial Contract Y2922-01-01-000091-L20-30
Active Contract Y3400-01-01-001023-L20-40

Action>
```

Keidi had worked with this model of air-saucer before. She knew her tech-cable would do the trick. The man stood beside her, looking at what she was doing.

"Locking it down?" he asked.

Keidi nodded.

"Good idea." He stepped away. "We're on level 20," he said, not to her. "We're locking the saucer."

Keidi continued.

```
Action> Grant Admin -KeidiRysinjer
Enter Password
```

This is where the tech-cable came in handy. As a technician, Keidi used to do repairs on a series of different machinery, including tubes and saucers. Usually, a tech-cable only worked with a specific device and model. Tarana was the one who'd first created her own cables. She called them passe-partout, and a single cable could be used for many devices. The cable provided full access for quick repair.

Keidi left the password blank, letting the cable bypass the request. After a few moments, it did.

```
Admin access has been granted.
```

Keidi took over, entering command after command.

```
Action> Lock -all
Air-saucer locked down.

Action> Stop
Air-saucer powered down.

Action> Protect -password "0uRB4bY"
Temporary protection added.
```

Keidi exited the system and put her equipment away.

"Done," she said as she turned on the scrambler.

"Good and efficient work," said the man. "I'm impressed." Yet something was different about him, in his voice, in the way his head was tilted to the side.

"What is it?" she asked. "What happened up there?"

He instantly regained his composure and was about to say something when he stopped and put a hand over his right ear. He was communicating again, listening to instructions maybe? Keidi found it strange that he was not using his b-pad. Although, thinking of it, it was a good thing.

"Noted," he said before looking directly at Keidi. "Name is Styl, by the way, your guide to safety."

They exchanged a quick smile. Once more, he gave her his shoulder. Keidi leaned on it, and they were on the move.

Surprisingly, Styl did not lead her toward the main lobby. He turned into a side corridor and through a door. It slid shut behind them.

"I know this'll be difficult," he said, looking at her ankle, "but we have to go down."

Deficiency

He left her side and knelt a few paces ahead. On his right, stairs were going up. On his left, there was a wall. This is when Keidi noticed the g-tool on Styl's right forearm. It was an impressive piece of equipment, slick, small. It covered only part of his forearm, light, yet made of plasti-steel, a quasi-indestructible alloy.

A moving arrow appeared on its screen, possibly showing the way.

Using his left hand, Styl entered a few commands on the g-tool. To Keidi's surprise, the wall opened and a descending staircase appeared.

Keidi thought about the lower levels of Detel's laboratory. She shivered, uncertain she liked the idea. No one went down there.

Her concerns did not matter, though. She needed to trust this man.

"Ready?" asked Styl.

"Yes," she said.

They climbed down. As soon as their heads were low enough, the wall closed behind them.

Mission 001202 B

A steel blade springs out of Okran's right wrist. He inserts it between the sliding doors and forces them open by twisting the blade. The two soldiers behind him step forward to provide assistance. He orders them back. Using his elbow, Okran pushes one door to the left while sliding the other to the right. The doors open.

On the other side, instead of the usual disk of the air-saucer, emptiness appears. Okran's brain-pad tries to connect to the system to call the platform back to his level.

The connection fails.

Okran's visor tells him no air-saucer is ready. Either it is broken, without any platform, or powered down.

Okran sends a command to power up the air-saucer.

Nothing happens.

His visor notifies him that a password is required. He is not surprised or annoyed. He simply notes the resourcefulness of his target.

Jumping is not an option. The platform's depth is unknown. It may be missing or, if it is there, it may not hold under the impact of his descent. He requests an override and waits.

It is estimated that the request will reach the enforcers' main station in less than a quarter of a second. There, it will be received by a

Deficiency

powerful virtual intelligence known as ECI, which will instantly pass it through a complex validation logic. The mission code 001202 will provide all the necessary background information and will associate a priority one to the request. The fact that the sender is a bionic will push the request ahead of regular enforcers' submissions. The request will be approved in less than one second, and the override will arrive a quarter of a second later.

These details are known to Okran—they were part of his training. The estimated time of implementation of the override is thus 1.5 seconds, yet Okran receives it 4.72 seconds later. The delay is unusual and he takes note of it; he will report it later.

With the override, Okran powers up the air-saucer and probes the system. He instantly learns the destination level of the air-saucer's previous drop.

Level 20.

He also receives information about the previous users of the air-saucer. There were two.

The first is Keidi Rysinjer. The second is asset 11 of body 36211. The first is the target of the mission. The second is a member of rebel group number 36211.

When the saucer arrives, the two enforcers step forward. Okran follows and orders it to drop to level 20. As it falls, Okran performs a search in the data-sphere on the rebel group number 36211. His credentials allow him access to tiers 10 to 3 of the data-sphere.

The following information is displayed on Okran's visor.

```
Search Result for Rebel Body 36211

Body ID:
36211
Body Name:
The Authentic Banner
Current Body Leader:
Unknown
Current Headquarter Location:
Unknown
```

```
Current Number of Members:
Between 15 and 30
Inception Date:
Between year 3.4k15 and 3.4k25
Previous Headquarters Location:
Sun Tower, 50-125 Crystal St, Arkanton, D2QA
Known activities:
None found
```

The saucer stops, and the two enforcers step off.

Okran does not move.

He ponders the data. The objective of mission 001198 and mission 001191 was the dismantling of a rebel body. In both cases, Okran completed the mission successfully and efficiently. Such a success will not be possible with this organization. The data available is scarce and most likely falsified. Okran has seen this before.

Most believe that the information in the data-sphere is 100% accurate. Based on his knowledge and the 42,567 searches he has performed over the past 10 years, Okran estimates the accuracy of the data-sphere at 72.24%.

In many cases, when information is lacking, false information is inputted. The information about the Authentic Banner most likely fell in that category. The vagueness of the date of creation and the number of members says as much.

Okran performs a search on asset 11. The information appears instantly.

```
Asset ID:
36211-11
Asset Name:
Unknown
Asset Body Name:
Unknown
Asset Birth Date:
Unknown
Asset Home Address:
Unknown
Asset Known activities:
None found
```

Deficiency

The search is a waste.

Okran steps out of the air-saucer and orders the enforcers to scan the surroundings. Jogging and running, aware that only a small window of opportunity is available, Okran explores. He knows that his hesitation to step off the air-saucer might allow the fugitives to flee.

Coordinating his squad's movement, Okran terminates the search after exactly 240.00 seconds, which allows them to cover most of the building's level 20. Their presence is disrupting to those they encounter.

Once, the human part of the bionic would have enjoyed being feared this way. Now, the Okran-that-was feels sadness and cannot comprehend why he once had such a need for superiority. He can only wait as the cyborg completes what he came to do.

No sign of the target is found in the building.

Okran takes 30 seconds to scan the street outside.

Nothing is found.

The Okran-that-was feels relief. The cyborg takes over and ignores the feeling.

+

Soldiers by his side, Okran returns to the shop.

The soldier he left behind is questioning the owner. The body of the big man is in a heap in a corner. The two soldiers that accompanied him take position by the hole in the wall, awaiting orders.

The time on Okran's visor is 1700. An alert notifies him to report on the mission's parameters. Without hesitation, Okran links his direct supervisor: the woman known as Mysa Lamond.

The link does not connect.

Okran tries again, as he was programmed to do.

The link once again does not connect. Assumption by default is that the mission's parameters remain the same.

"Provide analysis of the subject's pad," he orders to one of the soldiers standing by the hole in the wall.

Okran waits while the action is performed.

"He communicated with a man named Ged Briell exactly four minutes before you got here," answers the soldier a few moments later.

Ged Briell automatically becomes the mission's next objective. His last known position appears on Okran's visor. Precise coordinates are available, although the man tried to hide his location. The target is stationary.

Without a word, Okran walks out of the shop. His visor shows his soldiers converging to meet him on the street below.

The last soldier to leave the shop transferred the owner to the two local enforcers. The man will be sent away. He was dealing in illegal merchandise. None of this has any significance for Okran, but it is recorded in his memory.

------ .. Breach

The jet-car raced through the darkness of the Underground at incredible speed. Safety belt tightly fastened, Eltaya was nestled in the front seat beside Praka. She tried to keep track of where they were, of what street, quadrant, or district was above them in Prominence City. She couldn't. Praka's mouth was set in a concentrated line. Her eyes were hidden behind impenetrable goggles that allowed her to see through the darkness and avoid obstacles.

Praka was exceptionally good at what she did.

"Oh-five minutes to destination," Praka said.

The jet-car had been purchased nine years previous by the Banner from a seller in the Underground. It was black-market merchandise, but then, much of what the Authentic Banner did was already considered illegal. Eltaya had recommended the purchase. Xavi approved it.

The logical step after acquiring a vehicle was to find a transporter to drive it. They hired Praka. Styl could have driven it, but he specialized in smaller vehicles. Praka was 30 and had instantly bonded with the vehicle, almost more than she had with the team. The thing became her third child.

Jet-cars had been banned from the streets of Prominence City almost four centuries ago, a few years before access to the levels 15 to 19 was closed off. The opposition to both changes had been significant.

Many inhabitants had lived in levels 15 to 19. They'd had to be relocated. Eltaya had read in the data-sphere that the transition had been disastrous, with enforcers sent to force out the inhabitants. Civil war was the closest term to describe the one-year transition. Hundreds of dead, thousands of disappearances. Riots, exiles. Tumultuous years.

On the other hand, those living in the Underground welcomed the additional protection, and possibly a significant number of immigrants. Five more levels between their world and Prominence could only be a good thing.

Praka's personal touch was all over the vehicle. It belonged to the Banner, but Praka was both its driver and its caretaker. She had to keep it clean; it was spotless. *In better condition than when it was purchased*, Eltaya thought.

The front cabin had a comforting smell of sweet flowers. Pictures covered the dashboard—Praka's two daughters, from when they were young to today. One picture was of the whole family: Praka, her two daughters, and her husband. His death had been the trigger that had pushed Praka to join their organization.

"Oh-two minutes to destination," said Praka.

The vehicle swerved to the left and shot up one of the rare ascending ramps still intact. As it reached the top, it maneuvered a difficult curve, and Eltaya saw the corner of a building pass by. Had she been able to extend her hand, she could have touched it. At this speed, she would have lost her hand.

She looked over her shoulder. Xavi and Kazor sat in the back seats. Kazor had the stunner shotgun on his knees. It had been altered by their artificer, Viline, who was also Ulie's aunt. Viline had insisted that the modifications would work, while making it clear that they had not been tested. But Kazor would not part with the weapon. He volunteered to test it in the field.

Deficiency

Eltaya touched the stunner pistol on her belt. She was not a good shot, but the weapon was forgiving, and all of them wore one. Eltaya's was unique; like Kazor's shotgun, her pistol was modified, making it more powerful than the regular model.

Xavi wore his guardian bracelet—a device that was smaller than a g-tool, while much more potent and much more complicated to operate. Only bodyguards had the training and knowledge to operate one. Eltaya wished she did. Maybe one day. The bracelet on Xavi's wrist, like most of the other pieces of equipment they had, would quickly be confiscated if discovered.

Xavi looked back at her, and they shared a nod.

The Authentic Banner's main goal was to discover the truth, but when a friend fell victim to the corporations, they were ready to help, accepting the risks.

No one had asked Eltaya how close a friend Artenz was. No one would. They trusted her. They all trusted each other.

Besides, the friendship between Eltaya and Artenz did not make much difference. The group sometimes helped strangers if that would thwart a corporation's plan.

"Approaching Blue Tower," said Praka.

The vehicle decelerated. Eltaya felt the belt against her chest as the vehicle came to a jerking stop. The doors slid open.

"Be back in 30 minutes," said Xavi.

Praka nodded. "Be careful."

Eltaya stepped out and turned on her head-lamp. It illuminated old asphalt and marble steps, broken and disused, leading toward an open double doorway. Grime and dust covered the ground, a sign the place had not been disturbed in a long while.

That was a relief.

They were on level 15, which at one point would have been the Blue Tower's main entrance. It was now the Dominance and home to some sentient abnormality no one knew much about. Eltaya had asked her ghost to find out what she could, but the only thing Ayatle could confirm was the presence of something.

Eltaya had warned the Banner on a few occasions that it was a mistake to dismiss it, whatever it was. Because it was the Underground, and not directly involved in the events happening in Prominence, it was easy to forget about it. Xavi had promised the Banner would make effort to learn more, but that had not yet happened.

It was obvious, though, that the mis-creation had not yet propagated to this area. If it had, there would be signs: displaced objects, marks in the dust, crumbled and rebuilt walls, and more importantly, numerous cables that looked liked a complex network of veins.

Until she knew more, Eltaya preferred to stay out of the thing's way.

Kazor came out behind Eltaya. She heard him stretching and then powering the shotgun. It would take several minutes before the weapon was ready for use.

"Ready for this?" asked Eltaya.

He nodded. She knew Kazor was thinking about his daughter. He had told her once that he always did before an operation.

Xavi joined them. "Let's move."

+

The Blue Tower took the shape of a square. Eltaya remembered it from a tour during her university years.

A cable elevator rose in each of its corners, probably built due to some nostalgia or to demonstrate wealth. The cable pulled up a cabin with two glass walls, which provided a spectacular view of the surroundings. These elevators serviced levels 30 to 100 only.

In its core, the tower had three air-tubes and an air-saucer. The tubes went from level 20 to 110. This was interesting, since the main

Deficiency

entrance to the tower was now on level 30. Eltaya wondered about the usage of the lower levels.

The Blue Tower had 111 levels, the top floor only reachable by stairs, or so most people were told. The blueprint Eltaya had studied showed that of the three air-tubes, only one reached the top floor. Not that they would be going that high.

The climb from level 15 to 20 didn't take long. Eltaya was in the lead, her head-lamp unveiling the walls and stairs as she climbed the steps two at a time. Xavi and Kazor followed, the sound of their boots close by.

They came to a door, which was locked. Eltaya activated her gauntlet, and her ghost appeared on its small monitor.

"The door is now unlocked," said the ghost. "Red Dragon granted access to one air-tube. Three employees are present on this level. None close by."

Eltaya opened the door and motioned to Xavi and Kazor to follow. On the other side, weak light emanated from emergency beacons. Eltaya followed the blueprint on her gauntlet. They reached the air-tube. Kazor stepped ahead.

"Go," said Eltaya. "We'll be right behind you."

Without hesitation, Kazor stepped in the tube and was gone.

"Your turn," said Eltaya to Xavi.

He stepped in and disappeared. She followed.

+

Drayfus was standing behind his assistant, who was seated at his own desk, in the hallway, typing away, performing search after search, deeper and deeper into the data-sphere, looking for information about the elusive Marti Zehron. Mysa Lamond had provided Drayfus's assistant with extra and temporary privileges and ordered Drayfus to keep the man in sight.

Mysa Lamond had called the assistant *the man*, as if he was not worth her attention.

The disrespect had frustrated Drayfus. And made him realize how proud he was of his assistant... and how ungrateful he had been toward him. As a manager, Drayfus had always had an assistant, most of whom he had not cared about. This one was different. Mysa Lamond's insult had made him aware how much he took him for granted, so much so that Drayfus could not remember the last time he had addressed his assistant by name.

Irek was his name.

And Drayfus had made a mental note to use the name more often, to show respect for the man more often. Similar to Artenz, his assistant—Irek, he had to think of him as Irek—had played a key role in Drayfus's success over the past few years.

Now, standing behind Irek, Drayfus was doing what he could to make sure they accomplished what had been asked: find information about Marti Zehron.

At first, they had not gotten anywhere. The data-sphere was hard to search even with Drayfus's normal privileges. Now that Mysa Lamond had opened possibilities for them, there were so many places to look, so much information available.

Marti was not that old, maybe 60 at the most. There was always the possibility he was a cyborg or possibly a machine altogether. Robots, complete bodily reproduction with artificial intelligence, did not exist. Not as far as Drayfus could tell. Artificial intelligence, with full independence, was so risky that it was illegal. Yet some corporations experimented.

In 3.4k12, TriCom Incorporated had had to disburse over a billion credits when one of their auxiliary enterprises was charged with dabbling in artificial intelligence. Brains Co. also played with AI. The company had had to close its laboratories for three seasons during an investigation a few years ago, resulting in the loss of several million credits. Drayfus didn't know who the owners of Brains Co. were any

Deficiency

longer. And even though the investigation found nothing, it had crippled the company.

There were rumors of all sorts. Robots, artificial intelligence suddenly finding consciousness. That kind of thing. Nothing Drayfus believed. Nothing concrete.

Virtual intelligence, on the other hand, was everywhere. These computer programs could only operate inside limited and strict parameters. Risks were minimal. Drayfus did not understand much about artificial or virtual intelligence, but he did not believe that one was far from the other.

What Mysa Lamond had told him about Marti was so far-fetched, Drayfus did not know what to believe any longer. She alleged that the old coder had infiltrated the Sphere all the way down to tier 0. Supposedly, zones didn't exist for Marti. He could go where he wanted, look at what he wanted. Drayfus had never heard of such a thing, of such skills.

Irek suddenly stopped typing and responded to a link on his b-pad.

"Sir, an incoming communication for you," he said. "On the emergency line."

Drayfus's heart stopped.

"Mr. Blue?" he asked.

Irek shook his head.

"Your wife."

+

Sana knew better than to disturb him at work, so it could only be about their daughter.

As much as he feared Mr. Blue, Drayfus dreaded this call even more. He could not imagine losing another child. He felt the color drain from his face and had to put a hand against the wall to stop himself from tipping over.

"Sir?"

"Transfer over," said Drayfus, stepping back from his assistant, turning away, and accepting the link as it appeared on his eye-veil.

"Sana?" he answered, his voice low and cracking. "Don't... what happened?"

"Dray, dear, it is not about Chana," said his wife.

For a moment, Drayfus was confused. Such had been his fear that the excitement in his wife's voice did not register at first.

"Dray? Are you there, dear?"

"I... am."

"We got approved," she said and stopped abruptly, waiting for his reaction.

It didn't come right away. The news took a moment to sink in.

"Approved?" he said, feeling dumb.

"Dray! Yes, a boy, for a boy!"

Drayfus put a hand on his mouth, stopping himself from screaming. From joy. Not realizing what he was doing, he turned and grabbed his assistant's shoulder, smiling. Irek smiled back, obviously excited for Drayfus, even though he had no idea what the call was about.

"Are you certain?" Drayfus asked.

"Oh yes, I am. I could not believe it."

"Approved? After all these years?"

Tears were forming in his eyes now. He could not stop smiling.

"Yes, and yes!" said Sana in his ears.

"Irek," said Drayfus, "I'll have a boy!"

Irek stood, wearing a wide smile of his own. He mouthed the words "Congratulations, sir." He was the only person who knew about Drayfus and Sana's struggle to get a boy.

Drayfus hugged him, tight. The gesture surprised both men. As they untangled, Irek patted Drayfus on the back.

"I take it we accept," said his wife, jokingly, the euphoria making her voice a pitch higher.

"Accept? You bet we accept!"

Deficiency

+

Irek was back at his desk, searching for information on Marti Zehron.

"Take a few minutes, sir. I'll continue the search. Congratulations again, sir."

Drayfus stepped into the hallway, wanting to walk a bit, but he stopped when he saw the guards standing in front of his office. Their presence didn't dampen his overflowing happiness. Still, he turned around and returned to his assistant's small office space. He needed to keep an eye on Irek.

But he did not look at the screen. Not yet.

He let the news sink in.

A boy.

He would have a boy. He was going to be a father again.

He couldn't help, obviously, thinking about Ared and that awful day, 20 years ago. Drayfus would never forget, could not forget, did not want to forget.

It had been a summer day, the third of the sixth season. He had gone to pick up his boy at daycare and had gotten there to find the babysitter in a frenzy.

Rightfully so.

His boy, then two, barely two. Such a sweet boy. Calm. Never crying. Intelligence dancing in his eyes. A smile that could melt the hardest of hearts.

His boy.

Ared.

Had turned blank on that day.

Blank.

How it had happened, Drayfus would never know. It happened. Statistically speaking, it happened. One in ten thousand or so. And it had happened to them.

One day, they had a boy.

The next, he was gone.

Taken.

Not that there had been any choice.

When Drayfus had picked up Ared on that day, at the daycare, something in him had died. He remembered the babysitter screaming in his ear.

"Take him away," she had yelled.

Afraid the baby's mere presence would curse her establishment. Even now, Drayfus despised the woman for her reaction.

Could she not understand he had lost his son?

His baby's body had been limp, and he had not responded to his father's touch. Worse, his eyes had looked nowhere, seeing nothing. No more spark of intelligence.

Ared was gone, completely and utterly. Their sweet boy, gone.

The baby in Drayfus's arms had been an empty shell.

He alerted health authorities, obviously. It was one of the first things he did, could not understand why the babysitter had waited for him to come, could not understand why she had not alerted them herself.

Maybe it would have saved Ared.

He ruined her, the babysitter. Later. Ruined her and her business, and her life. He still could not find it in himself to feel remorse for it. That had been in his early days as a manager. He was softer now.

The health authorities had taken Ared away. No explanation. None was expected, naturally, but, it would have been nice nonetheless.

With Sana, Drayfus mourned for a year before reapplying for a baby. They knew that because their baby had turned out as blank, the chances of a second approval were extremely low.

It took 10 years before they received authorization for a girl.

As much as he loved his daughter, Drayfus had wanted a boy. Sana had agreed to indulge him. She had always wanted two children, as rare as that was. They submitted another application, not hoping for much.

Deficiency

But now...

Here it was.

Approved.

He would have a boy. Sana would have her two children.

It changed everything. In that single instant, Drayfus knew what he wanted out of life. He was happy, or would be, as soon as this day was over.

+

"Look at this," called Irek, pointing at the screen and pulling Drayfus out of his thoughts.

He came to stand behind his assistant, looking over his shoulder at the screen.

"What did you find?" he said, surprisingly focused.

He had a new source of motivation now.

"Marti Zehron worked for a group known as Onyx Traders between 3.4k15 and 3.4k20," showed Irek.

"I thought the Traders Guild was dismantled in 3k," said Drayfus. "This can't be right. Onyx was not operational 40 years ago, was it? And even if it was, in 3.4k20, he would have been what, 10 or 15 years old, maybe 20 at most? Onyx would not have hired such a young coder, would they?"

"There's no mistake." Irek realigned his search and went deeper into the company. "This is serious. The Onyx Traders were a full member of the Traders Guild and still active way beyond 3k. Look here, this deal was done in 3.1k05. Here, another in 3.3k10."

It was not possible to see which corporation Onyx Traders had dealt with. It seemed that information was outside the reach of their current privileges.

"This is serious," repeated Irek.

"It certainly is," acknowledged Drayfus.

If only he had known any of this. If any of this had come up during the screening process, Marti would have been arrested.

But no one in BlueTech Data would have been able to find this information. Marti had even hidden his birth date. The best they could do was estimate his age. The fact that he was able to hide information, or remove it, was hard to believe. The data-sphere recorded everything, continually, and nothing was deleted.

Except in the occasional flush.

Which was only possible by a unanimous vote of the government and the panels of corporations of Prominence City. It had not happened in Drayfus's lifetime.

"Hiring him put the whole of BlueTech at risk," noted Irek.

"There's no need to state the obvious," snapped Drayfus. This was not good. For BlueTech, and for him. "Continue searching."

The Traders Guild had been dismantled in 3k, following accusations of dealing in slavery. Slavery had been banned completely in 3k, eradicated. The operation had taken almost three years, but at the end of it, slavery was once and for all gone from Prominence.

There were those who wanted it back.

Marti was probably one of those. Drayfus didn't see any other explanation. He had worked for Onyx, a corporation that lost almost everything when the Guild was broken apart.

If this was at the core of what was happening today, though, why arrest Artenz? Why go after Artenz's wife? What was Artenz's link to all this? Was there a link at all?

There had to be more to this than Mysa Lamond was sharing. Drayfus would need to have a word with her. He needed to tread carefully, certainly, but...

Drayfus saw something appear down the hallway, from the corner of his eye, a shape, a man... an intruder!

At the same moment, the two enforcers standing in front of his office lifted their rifles. Instinctively, Drayfus jumped backward, toward the back wall of the office, toward a place to hide.

Deficiency

"Breach!" he yelled, his scream instantly buried deep under a powerful sonorous boom.

+

Drayfus opened his eyes. He was lying sideways on the top of a table, against a wall. His head was groggy and spinning. His left side was numb, from leg, to arm, to the side of his face. His sight was limited to a tunnel, as if he was looking through a tube of fog.

He tried to push himself up, noticed that a monitor was on top of him. He pushed it aside. It slid from him and hit the floor, did not make any sound.

In fact, there was no sound. Everything was muted.

Where was he?

A man lay on the floor, a bruise on the right side of his head. The face was familiar. Drayfus knew this man, but could not quite remember his name or their relationship. He did not look like a family member. A friend then? Under the man's leg appeared the flat, square shape of a wash-bot. Inert. Broken by the man's fall?

Drayfus sat up and shook his head. The movement awoke sharp pain behind his eyes, in his head, in his ears.

Just a few feet away, a doorway slid open. The door and what was behind teased Drayfus's mind, but again, it didn't mean anything.

A man took cover on the right of the door, inside the room. He had a rifle. His face had the strangest features. Robotic? Not human? Not a friend.

The man moved out of the room, pointing his rifle in front of him. Drayfus reacted to the danger without any further thought. He turned his back to the man.

If he was to be shot, let it be in the back.

The shot never came.

Instead, he felt more than heard a strong disturbance, and consciousness was once more punched out of him.

+

When he awoke next, his memory was back.

Drayfus pushed himself up with one arm until he was lying on his side, looking out of the office, toward the hallway. Beside him lay Irek, unconscious.

Most of Drayfus's body was paralyzed, including one of his eyes. Yet something continually hammered inside of his head. It was painful.

Drayfus knew he had been hit twice by a stunner. Partial hits. It would have been better to have been knocked out completely, right away.

A man appeared in the space between the desk and the wall. The man looked directly at him. He was large, and from Drayfus's position on the floor, he also looked terribly tall. A shotgun was clipped to his belt. On his back, he was carrying someone.

Artenz.

Drayfus worried briefly about Mysa Lamond. Then he dismissed the thought. He was in too much pain to care. In a way, he hoped the man had taken care of her, gotten rid of her.

"This one is awake," said the man.

Then, seemingly deciding Drayfus was no threat, he walked away.

Another figure appeared, and another. A black man and a woman. The woman's hair was dark and short and seemed to fall like rain around her face.

They scrutinized him. Drayfus tried to speak, but couldn't. He felt froth on the left side of his mouth and could not stop it from trickling down.

Again, the man and woman seemed to decide he was not dangerous. After a quick exchange, they left.

Drayfus let his head fall back. As he did, he remembered that Marti had bypassed the tower's security system earlier that day. He had let Artenz out. That feat in itself was exceptionally impressive. How wrong he had been about the man. Drayfus remembered Mysa

Deficiency

Lamond evading his question when he'd asked if they had Marti in custody.

He could not figure out how Marti would have gotten away. He had seen the aftermath of his interrogation. Artenz, they had tortured, but he had not bled.

Marti had bled.

Yet it seemed Marti had escaped. It was the only explanation Drayfus could come up with. Marti was the only person who could and would have let these people in.

To save Artenz.

Code 00.002.0065

```
// Program Information
// Version: 00.002.0065
// Program Name: secret
// Coder Name: secret
// Date Updated: Year 3.4k60 Season 05 Day 11 Hour 1808
// Date Updated: Year 3.4k60 Season 05 Day 11 Hour 1814

// data-sphere module
include global:_data
// targos marketing module
include local:_targos
// marti custom module
include district/3:quadrant/z:user/marti424:_marti
// marti hidden module
include district/3:quadrant/z:user/reddgn:_reddgn

function main ()
[
  var dataNodes as _data_coordinates
  var DSinfo as _info
  var DSdata as _targos_data
  var X as integer

  // Retrieve data coordinate
  dataNodes = _data_convert ( _marti_DScoordinates(),
NODES )

  // Concatenate all data into a single block
  loop X from 1 to dataNodes( _count )
  [
  DSinfo = _data_append( _data_get( dataNodes( X ) ) )
```

Deficiency

```
    ]

    // Decrypt data
    var key as _reddgn_key
    key = L3zr3hsL3t3D
    DSinfo = _reddgn_decrypt_AM( DSinfo, key )

    // Prepare data for Targos module
    Loop DSinfo
    [
    DSdata = _targos_parse ( DSinfo )
    ]

    // Open channels for Targos module
    _targos_open_channels ( all )

    // Should Distribute Here
    // Distribute Here
    // Distribute
    // Can I do this? Is this what she would have wanted?
]
```

------... Underground

Artenz awoke to a stinging pain in his arm. He opened his eyes to find a black man crouching over him, syringe in hand.

"How are you feeling?" asked the man.

The room was dark, with a single tube shining a weak yellowish light. A heavy, musty smell hung in the air. Artenz found it difficult to breathe.

"Okay," he answered, "I think. Where am I?"

Images of a woman in white mixed with the face of a man with short hair equally as white assailed him. Fear arose with them.

Then he remembered pain. Lots of pain.

The b-pad in his neck throbbed, burning, as if somebody had pried at it.

"You are in a safe place," said the man, standing and turning toward a metallic table on thin legs. He put the syringe in a small brown case and took out a vial. "You'll recuperate quickly. Take this. It will keep the pain away and give you energy for a little while. You can take a few minutes, but we'll have to move soon."

Artenz looked at the vial. It contained a bleached pink liquid, most likely the usual cure drink. He swallowed the contents in one gulp. He needed it. It instantly cleared his mind.

Deficiency

"This is the Underground," continued the man, taking a seat. "We're not far from the Blue Tower, on level 15. You endured a lot up there."

Images of the woman and her cohort returned. They had tortured him by connecting a local simulator—a replica of those used in the holo-sphere—to his b-pad. The device had immersed him in imaginary yet painful situations, attacking his senses and later, his sanity. He barely remembered anything of the experience, except that the pain and the fear had felt very real.

By far the worst thing he had ever experienced. He shivered at the memories.

"Take a moment," said the man, at his side again. "Lie down, close your eyes for a moment."

Artenz laid back, but did not close his eyes. He didn't want to see the woman in white again.

"You mentioned the Underground," he said, "but level 15, that's the Dominance, isn't it?"

Marti and Artenz sometimes talked about the Underground, and the Dominance. The latter was prohibited and controlled by the government, or the corporations, or both. A level for enforcers. The deeper levels had no regulation, and there were rumors that some people lived down there.

Information varied based on who you talked to. One thing remained, though. No one went down to these levels, and knowing he was now on level 15 felt strange.

Yet in a way, it also felt safe, safer than it was up above, where people tortured other people.

Was it just today that he had been fleeing in the streets? That chase felt far away already.

"You are correct," answered the man. "This is the Dominance, the top layer of the Underground. We're not staying here long. As soon as you get better, we're moving deeper. Coming from under was the best way to free you. Safer, if you don't mind the darkness. Safer to escape also. Your b-pad's harder to track down here. There's a scrambler by your head, for additional cover."

Artenz looked to his left, then his right. He saw the box, just by his head. A green light showed that it was activated.

"Who was that woman?" asked Artenz. "The white woman?"

The man didn't answer. He was looking somewhere behind Artenz. Artenz turned his head the other way, and there stood the last person he expected to see.

"Eltaya?" he said.

She smiled.

And it brought back a flood of old memories, a powerful wave of nostalgia, feelings buried a long time ago, feelings he did not want to face again.

She looked different. "Worn" or "old" were not quite right the right words. "Experienced" was better. It seemed as if she had seen a lot, as if she knew a lot. Wise? She had always been intimidating to him, with an untouchable beauty. She was even more so now.

"It's me," she replied. "How are you feeling?"

She did not sit, simply stood close to him, put a hand on his forearm.

"I… fine, I guess. Better."

Her touch did not feel good. Actually, it instantly felt like a betrayal to Keidi.

"Good," she said, taking her hand away and turning toward the other man in the room. "Two more minutes," she added. "Then we have to go. Praka is ready."

"Any news from the others?" asked the man.

"They're regrouping," she answered. "But we can't wait longer. Ulie is on it, and she'll update us as soon as she hears back."

The man nodded. "You heard her," he said, looking at Artenz. "Take two more minutes. I know it's not much, but it's all we can afford. Rest. After, we move."

Artenz nodded. The scrambler was uncomfortable, as if it probed his brain.

"I have questions," he said. "Many."

The man simply left, leaving him alone with Eltaya. He remembered her deep dark eyes the most, their intensity and sharpness, as if she never missed a thing. Eltaya always made you feel as if she knew more than you did, as if she knew things you did not. Her smile had not changed—just a twitch of the lips, a tease.

"We all do," she said. "You've gotten yourself in quite a mess. And you're not out of it yet. Rest a little. Then we'll talk."

"What about Keidi?" Artenz asked.

Eltaya took a breath.

"She's the one who linked me," she said. "She asked me to help. We came to get you. We also sent someone to pick her up. She was waiting for you at the I Bot store."

Artenz hated imagining Keidi waiting and him not showing up.

"Is she safe?" he asked, sitting up now.

"We got to her," said Eltaya. "There was an altercation, and she's now with one of ours. Safe for the time being. Unhurt." There was hurt in her eyes, though. Something had gone wrong. "They're on the run, and Ulie, another one of us, is monitoring their progress."

"You don't really know, do you?" accused Artenz. "You got her, and now you don't know where she is!"

The black man appeared again.

"No, we don't," he said, putting a hand on Eltaya's shoulder.

It was Eltaya's turn to leave the room.

"This isn't easy for her or any of us," he said. "We lost a good friend while he was trying to help your wife."

"Oh," said Artenz, stunned.

The man looked at him, not saying a word, but there was a warning there, to be careful, to not assume.

"I'm sorry," said Artenz.

There was so much to process, to accept. All the events, from the morning onward. Keidi on the run. Someone… dying to save her. The torture. The pain. His missing sister.

"You apologize to Eltaya," said the man. "Not to me. He was a good friend to all of us, but it was Eltaya who recruited him. And it's like she said, you *are* in a lot of danger."

And now, because they'd helped, these people were also in danger.

+

They led Artenz out of a building, and when he stepped outside, the darkness didn't dissipate. Until that moment, Artenz's mind had not really processed that he was in the Underground. Now, as he looked left and right, at the streets painted in shadows, there was no denying it.

Level 15, the man had said. That was five levels below ground, or 15 levels under the entrance to the Blue Tower.

"I've heard things about this level," said Artenz. "About enforcers."

The man answered. "For a while, this was indeed the enforcers' level, and they used it extensively. It's not so anymore."

"Are we safe?"

"If we don't linger."

Artenz hurried forward, wondering what the man was not telling him.

On the street, there was a vehicle in the shape of a large missile on wide black wheels, with one door opened.

"Is this a jet-car?" he asked.

"It is," came the voice of a woman seated at the helm. "A 3.0k88 Comet model, in top condition. It used to be red, but you'll forgive her if she lost a bit of color over the years. Don't be afraid. Take a seat. I'm Praka."

Artenz stepped into the vehicle and shook the woman's hand as he moved toward the seat behind her. In his other hand, he was holding the scrambler. He already had developed a dislike of it. It was not as potent as the one Marti had used. Still, the headache was constant.

"I'm Artenz," he said. "I guess you already knew that."

Deficiency

"I did, but it is nice to meet you officially nonetheless."

There were six seats in the vehicle, and a large shape took the last two in the back. He had an oversized shotgun on his knees.

"Kazor," the man said.

His gloved hand engulfed Artenz's in a painful handshake.

"And this is Xavi Olton," said Eltaya as the man who had treated him earlier took a seat beside him. "He's our leader."

Eltaya came in last and sat beside the driver. Artenz appreciated Eltaya being all business. His feelings for her had briefly resurfaced before dissipating just as quickly. Keidi was on his mind. Keidi and their future baby. It was a relief to realize that the attraction he'd once had for this woman was gone. Over the years, a part of him had thought about her from time to time. He had never really known how he would react if he saw her again.

She was not the sweet girl he had met at university. Not that she had ever been especially sweet. But there was something intense in this new version of her. Something scary.

"Thank you, all of you, for your help," he said, looking around.

"Do not thank us yet," said Xavi. "We're still in harm's way."

"Where to?" asked Praka. "Back to the office?"

"No," said Xavi, "to Hideout Plaza."

"The Plaza?" asked Artenz. He had never before been to the Plaza, the gem of Prominence. Only those with a special invitation could enter. The Athletics were held there, although that was not completely true. Most of the competitions were held along the Plaza, with huge balconies opening from the inside, where the elite sat and mingled and watched. It was said there was a lake inside the Plaza, surrounded by orchards with apples and strawberries and Artenz did not know what else.

"The same," said Eltaya. "Just don't get your hopes up. By the time we reach it, we'll be down several more levels."

"Go," said Xavi, and the vehicle hummed to life. It rose and rolled forward.

The ride was extremely smooth, the wheels thrumming against the ancient asphalt.

Artenz slid forward, moving closer to Eltaya.

"About earlier…" he started.

"Belt on," said Xavi.

"What?"

"Your safety belt," said the black man, showing a strap tied around his chest in an X pattern. "We always hope we won't need it, but just in case."

Artenz searched for the straps and secured himself. He couldn't move much, the contraption forcing him to stay against the seat.

"You were saying?" said Eltaya.

"I wanted to apologize," said Artenz. "I didn't know that you lost someone, trying to help Keidi. I appreciate your help, and I'm sorry if I sounded ungrateful."

"It is what we do," she said. "Partly. We wouldn't abandon a friend in need."

Her gauntlet rested on her knees and was active. Artenz had only seen such a device once before, when Keidi had brought one home to dismantle it. A g-tool. The one he had seen had been an old model, sent to Keidi's workshop for disposal. She had whisked it away, brought it home to study it. Illegal, but temporary. Keidi had said it was worth the risk. She loved learning how devices worked.

Eltaya's was a different model and looked more complex.

"Thank you," repeated Artenz.

Knowing that she considered him a friend after all this time was a bit surprising—and a relief. Artenz had always felt that things had been left unresolved—he'd never known exactly where he stood with Eltaya. He remembered how much he had clung to her, almost stalked her, not wanting to let her go. It was good to put that embarrassing period of his life behind him.

Deficiency

Outside, walls flew by, hidden in the dark corridors. It seemed they were moving at surprisingly high speed. Like a scene from a movie—artificial, dreamlike. Artenz was glad for the belts.

"It was not a routine pickup," observed Kazor suddenly, from his seat in the back.

"There was no way to know," said Xavi. "Arnol was already in the store when the enforcers surrounded him. It was his decision to interfere. It was his choice to make. He knew the risks."

"Did he really?" insisted Kazor.

Artenz looked back. There was no light in the jet-car, and he could not make out the man's face.

"What happened?" Artenz asked.

"He interfered with the enforcers," said Xavi.

"And got arrested?"

No one said anything.

"Enforcers don't kill," he added. "Or do they?"

There was a pause. Artenz was still looking back, somehow guessing that Kazor would be the one to answer.

"They do," said the big man. The statement could not be true. Artenz had never heard of enforcers killing. "I was one of them, once," added Kazor, sealing the truth.

Artenz turned forward in his seat, not wanting to believe what he was hearing. Outside, the underbelly of a city his father had once called corrupt was flying by.

"I'm afraid so," said Xavi. "The enforcers almost never use lethal force in the open. At night, in unlit streets, or in the Underground, it happens more than people are led to believe. The Agency is torn in two. Those loyal to the government, who for the most part want to protect. And those paid by the corporations, who'll do what they need to do to get their credits."

"Think of them as mercenaries," said Kazor.

"Whatever you are involved in, my friend," said Xavi, "some people in power are willing to kill for it."

Noticing his hands were shaking, Artenz interlaced his fingers, trying to keep them still.

"I know nothing," he said. "Keidi knows nothing."

"Maybe. It does not matter. They are after both of you nonetheless."

"Where is Keidi now?" asked Artenz.

"As I already said—she's on the run," said Eltaya. "Going toward Quadrant N. She's in good hands."

Quadrant N, in the northwest corner of the Factory district. It was aligned with where they were going, Artenz knew. By reaching the Plaza, located in the heart of Prominence, they would only have to go northeast to intercept.

"We're going to get them," said Artenz. It was half a question, half an affirmation.

"No," said Eltaya.

"But—"

"They'll have to reach us," said Xavi. "This vehicle can only take us where the old streets are open. Most of the Underground streets in the Factory district are covered in debris. We would not be able to maneuver very well, even with as good a transporter as Praka. We need to stick to the rendezvous point."

"What about going to the surface?" asked Artenz.

"Can't be done," said Eltaya. "First, the streets do not join. They were thorough when they closed off the lower levels. Second, we would be too late. Third, the enforcers would locate us instantly. It is best to wait for Styl and Keidi to join with us. When they do, we can outrun whoever is on their tail."

Artenz thought about Keidi, about a life without her. He thought about becoming a father and having a child. Tears filled his eyes. In that moment, there was nothing he wanted more than to tell Keidi that he loved her and that he wanted a baby.

More importantly, he finally understood why she wanted a natural baby, and he agreed with her! It made so much sense. He did not know

Deficiency

why it often took him so much time to comprehend what Keidi seemed to know right away. Not anymore.

"You said *when* they reach us," he said. "You think they'll make it?"

"There's no other way to think about it," said Eltaya, as if reluctant to give him hope.

+

Artenz didn't say more. No one did. Silence became a sixth passenger.

Looking outside, Artenz felt disconnected. The throbbing in his head could almost be ignored. The Comet's front lights reflected and bounced off side buildings, debris and piles of garbage, old billboards, open doorways. It was a lost world. This was the Underground, a place that didn't exist.

Yet here it was.

This was not his life. How had it gone from normalcy to this, to here?

Detel, gone.

Marti, gone.

Keidi...

And around him, a group of what? Vigilantes? Rebels? Both maybe. Strangers, certainly. They called him friend, but he could not say he understood how they could see him that way, that soon.

Even Eltaya was a stranger. Especially Eltaya.

It amazed Artenz that Keidi had thought of linking Eltaya. On the other hand, Keidi thought clearly, even under duress. She was the calm one, the sharp one.

He knew Eltaya had become a reporter, a true reporter. Hers was a never-ending quest to find and expose the truth. About Prominence. Although they had only met her a few times, his parents had liked her, and they would have loved her once she became a reporter. Artenz had never truly believed the corporations were as dishonest as some claimed.

His parents had been part of those skeptics, those believers.

"Does it matter how dishonest they are?" Detel had asked once.

Artenz could not remember if one of his parents was more passionate than the other about their distrust of the corporations. Theirs had always been a united front.

"Sometimes, it's not about how much they do, but what they do," had answered his mother. "A single act rarely stands alone."

They had been talking about the b-pad then, how it was an extension of the corporations invading the privacy of the people—how it was about control, not a better way of life. Artenz had not seen it then. But now, he had seen how far the corruption had gone.

Killing people.

Artenz wished he had paid more attention to his parents growing up. Detel had listened. It was probably what had gotten her into trouble. It might be what had started this whole mess.

He could not find it in him to be mad at his sister. Quite the opposite. He wished he had been there for her, had known more about what she was trying to accomplish. He was beginning to hate this city. Not just the city; he was beginning to hate the buildings, the image, everything it stood for, the corporations… and its people. Its uncaring, arrogant, self-centered inhabitants.

He touched the b-pad on his neck.

He was guilty.

He had always been one of them.

From a young age, he had enjoyed what Prominence offered: the gadgets, the new technologies, the comfortable life. It did not matter how the technologies were developed or sold. Artenz wanted the new best thing as soon as it was available, and he was easily swayed by large and colorful advertisements and the promises of richness and comfort.

Detel had tried to open his eyes. Sometimes, he had listened, but nothing had ever stuck. Most times, he did not really listen. Keidi had also tried. There, he had listened better. Two against one might have made a difference.

How he loved Keidi. How he admired her.

In a way, the real test of his love had come when she'd asked for a natural birth. For a while, he had even ridiculed the notion in the back of his mind.

Now, it was romantic, and liberating.

Rebellious.

It was a way to strike back…

Strike back…

Artenz looked at the people around him. They were making a difference.

He, on the other hand, had lived a life of contentment.

His sister had inherited their parents' will to fight. All of it. None left for him.

But in this instant and in this place, he felt it.

This day had changed him, was changing him still. Artenz's thoughts were racing, chaotic, and yet, they made more sense than they ever had before.

He felt rage, certainly, but mostly a clear determination. A notion of what he wanted, of what was right, and of what he could accept. More importantly, he had a definite sense of what he would not accept any longer.

─ ─ ─ ─ . . . . Disoriented

Keidi was lost in unexplored grounds. Unexplored by her, at least. Others—like Styl beside her—used this forbidden place when necessary. Keidi realized that over the years, she had tried to forget it existed. Most people in Prominence probably did the same.

Even with the unknowns, or maybe because of them, Keidi felt a thrill at being this deep, at being in the Underground.

They had left the elevator behind a while ago and gone down flights of stairs, passed along a few passageways, possibly switching buildings. Keidi had quickly lost track of where they were.

Up ahead, an opening appeared, painted against the blackness by the light from Styl's g-tool.

They exited and, although Keidi could not see much, she sensed vast space around them. The streets above had been well sealed, and no light was filtering through. Yet, looking at the ground, Keidi knew they were now on a street.

"What level is this?" she asked.

"15," said Styl. He helped her sit on a bench. "Let's take a few minutes."

Keidi welcomed the pause. Styl did not sit down, instead standing beside her and scanning the surroundings. She assumed that his goggles allowed him to see in the dark.

Deficiency

Then it hit her. "Isn't this the Dominance?" she asked.

Styl did not look at her. "It is, but there's no need to panic. There are not as many enforcers down here as the government and corporations want you to believe."

"But?"

Now the man looked at her. "You don't miss much, do you?"

"Tell me."

"Let's just say the enforcers aren't what you should worry about."

"What then?"

Styl's evasiveness worried Keidi.

"We should not be down here long enough for it to matter," he said. "Do you need something for the pain?"

Keidi decided to let it go, for now. "It would help."

Styl knelt and squeezed her ankle gently, moving up. When she winced, he stopped and positioned his g-tool almost against her. Then he pushed something, and a numbness enveloped her ankle.

"Better?"

"The pain is gone," she said, "but it's like my foot is gone."

"Very potent. Lean on me."

They followed the street, Keidi concentrating on the pavement visible under her feet, one step at a time. The darkness around fought against the low light of the gauntlet.

Styl was in continual communication with their navigator, a man named Ged, from what she gathered. The map on the g-tool changed continually, its orientation changing with their movements. She was surprised how the transfer of information seemed to be fluid, even this deep.

The darkness made Keidi wish she had goggles, or even an eye-veil. She was not usually claustrophobic, but she felt the weight of Prominence on top of her.

They were about to enter a building, its doors completely gone, when Styl froze.

"What?" he exclaimed, not at her, but at the device located under his ear. From the light of his g-tool, Keidi was able to see the colors fading from his face. "Get out of there!" he whispered, as loud as he dared. "Ged, get out of there, now! No fanciness, remember..." Keidi noticed the g-tool flashing, the map being updated again. "Understood. Be careful, be quick, don't be stupid."

Styl looked at her, and for the first time, he seemed worried.

"What is happening?" asked Keidi.

"They found Ged."

"The enforcers?"

Styl nodded. He stared at his g-tool before looking around. "We should go up here," he said, pointing inside the building. "I think. But... damn you, Ged!" he added. "Sorry..."

"No need to apologize."

"At the last minute," said Styl, "he changed our course. He was ready for something like this, obviously."

Keidi saw that the path highlighted on the g-tool told them to go deeper, farther, not into the building in front of them. An alternate route, maybe?

"Why did he change the route?" she asked. "Can you still talk to him, to Ged?"

"No. He cut the link temporarily. I just hope he's not stupid enough to try to distract the enforcers. He should run and hide."

Styl hesitated, looking toward the building and then toward the new path Ged wanted them to take. Keidi wished she could see Styl's eyes under the goggles.

"We'll go wherever you want to go," she said. "If you want to go help him, I understand. And I'll follow. I'm not staying behind." Styl looked at her, then toward her foot. "I can manage," she added.

"Thank you," said Styl, "but... I don't think there's anything we can do. I don't have his position."

Deficiency

"He knows where we're headed," said Keidi. After all, he'd provided their course. "I'm sure he'll plot another way for himself and meet us there, right?"

"Right," said Styl. "Obviously. Let's go."

Following the map, they went to another building, where they found steps going down. One floor, two, a few more. Then they exited, went along another alley, turned down a street. Another alley.

"We're going around," noted Keidi.

Styl did not reply.

"What level are we on?"

"10."

Keidi imagined Prominence above, a gigantic city, beautiful, prosperous—and here below, so stark and lifeless.

Another building. Then out on the other side. A street. Another building and more stairs. All in partial darkness. All confusing.

As they were going up, Styl suddenly dropped on his knees.

"Shit, shit, shit," he said.

"What happened?"

Styl simply put his head in his hands.

+

This was not the way it was supposed to be. Master enforcer Irbela Zuttar was dashing through a hallway, squadmates trailing behind, officer somewhere ahead, far ahead, too far.

The torch on her helmet readjusted itself with each of her steps, lighting the way forward. Her eye-veil added depth and details to the surroundings. The torch was not necessary, not really. But down here, Irbela, like most enforcers, preferred having light push back the darkness instead of relying solely on the eye-veil. The dark was uninviting, and she worried about the *thing*, the eater of enforcers.

No one was welcome down here. Not anymore.

The position of their officer appeared in front of her eyes. He was ahead, in what looked like a stairwell. There was no talking with the man, though. He was not one for talking, this one.

When she had been assigned to the special squad earlier that morning, Irbela had been excited by the news. For the past 14 years, since hitting 30, she had had her sights set on becoming leader of just such a squad.

To do so, she'd had to upgrade her body, from what she was to bionic. That meant letting go of muscles and flesh, a lot of it. These would be replaced by metallic amps that eliminated physical weaknesses. From human to robot, some would say. Biologic to machine. Yet the brain remained. The personality did not change, would not change.

She would remain herself, would in fact become a better version of herself.

The upgrade promised only advantages.

Yet Irbela still struggled with the idea, not satisfied with the information in the data-sphere on the transformation. The problem was that there was not enough of it, and too much about the alteration remained unknown to her.

Which was why she had asked to work with a bionic and had received her chance that morning.

"You got your way," her chief had said. "You are assigned to officer Okran Delaro."

Still, it had not gone as expected, not at all.

Irbela turned a corner, then entered the stairwell. She heard voices from somewhere above, but could not quite make out what was said. Their officer did not keep the channel open. He linked them only when required.

Not waiting for those behind, she climbed the steps, taking them three at a time. If she had been bionic, then she might have been able to keep up with their officer. The stairs went up to a platform, then turned left, then went up again.

Deficiency

She had issues with officer Okran Delaro, issues that ran deeper than his eccentricities. He did not lead; he ordered. He did not work with his squad; he used it. He came from corporate. She still believed in public service. For him, it was all about results. Short-term. No vision.

And damn the man, he attained results. Based on what little she'd found about him, Irbela could not deny it.

Yet that scene in the tiny store...

A bang echoed from above. Irbela stopped and, with one hand, she pointed her rifle up ahead. With the other, she grabbed her belt, ready to activate a shield. She was midway up this portion of the staircase and up ahead, the platform was empty. The noise had been close — maybe on the next platform.

A loud thud followed and a shape appeared, flying headfirst. It struck the wall in front of Irbela, and she heard the crack of the neck. The body collapsed to the floor, the face turned her way, lifeless eyes staring.

At her.

The man was dead.

It had happened again.

Before Irbela could decide what she would do about the situation, a large shape appeared on the platform.

"Rifle down," ordered Okran, Officer Okran. There seemed to be disdain in his voice. "I have the coordinates for the rendezvous point. Move!"

New coordinates appeared on Irbela's eye-veil. She did not move down the steps right away. Instead, she stepped aside, letting Okran pass, and continued to stare at the dead body on the platform.

On the bottom left corner of her eye-veil, the face of a man matched the one in front of her.

Ged Briell.

Of the Authentic Banner.

The man would have been so much more valuable alive.

The man in the I Bot store, one Arnol Dessol, would also have been more valuable alive.

Irbela looked down the stairs, shivered as she saw Okran disappear around a corner, his steps quick, the metal of his heels echoing against the floor, the sound bouncing, up and around, enveloping everything.

There was something wrong with this man. Not man—bionic.

Irbela was fairly certain she did not want to go through with the upgrade anymore. It was one decision less to worry about. Yet another was now manifesting itself.

Would she have the courage to report these actions?

These killings?

It was not for her to question the nature of their mission. In fact, she did not even know what their targets had done. She trusted that their apprehension would make Prominence safer. It was why she had become an enforcer.

To keep the inhabitants safe.

Enforcers did not kill.

They protected.

They captured when necessary. They took danger away, and then let the legal system judge and sentence.

What was happening here, today, was not how it was supposed to be.

+

"It was supposed to be simple," explained Styl, visibly distraught. "Ged and I were to pick you up. Arnol was to keep an eye on you. In and out. Quick escape through the back of the store. But then the enforcers showed up... and everything went sideways."

Keidi did not know what to say.

"What about Arnol?" she said. "Is he all right?"

Styl shrugged.

Deficiency

"I can only…" he stopped talking, his features hardening. Someone was talking to him through the chip. Styl reflexively put a finger on it.

"Is he back? Ged?" asked Keidi.

In a quick motion, Styl pulled the small chip from behind his ear and threw it to the ground.

"We have to move," he said, getting up. "Quickly."

"Why? Who just talked to you?" And then, Keidi understood. "It was the enforcers, wasn't it?"

Styl nodded. They had hacked whatever device Styl and Ged had been using to communicate.

"They are coming for us," he said.

The words made Keidi shiver.

"Where to?" she asked.

"We have a tri-racer. That is where we were going, that is where Ged was sending us."

"You still have the map?"

"I do, but… transporting is my thing," said Styl, "not being a bodyguard. Chances are, the enforcers know where we're going. If the enforcers get there before us—"

"I'm a technician," replied Keidi. "It doesn't really matter what we are, does it?"

Styl looked at her from behind his dark goggles.

"Right again," he said as he activated his g-tool. "Let's go. It is our best chance."

They took a circular metal staircase. Many of the steps slanted to one side or the other, signs that the building's foundation was shifting and possibly failing. They reached a landing and exited the stairwell.

"Back on 15," said Styl.

The building they entered was in good shape, and like all the other places down here, it stunk of melancholy and a world forgotten.

"Every place is so empty," said Keidi.

She now walked on her own. It was quicker this way. She could still not feel her foot but forced herself to believe it was there. The weird sensation pulled her attention away from the scrambler's effects on her head.

"This is forsaken land," explained Styl. "Those above do not dare to come down. Neither do they care—it's a reminder that their beautiful city has a darker side. And those below do not dare to come up. Too far up and not worth the risk. Dominance floor, remember?"

They exited the building, although the darkness made it feel as if they were still inside.

"I recognize this place," announcement Styl. "Not far now, not far."

They did not enter any other building but stayed on the streets, where debris formed an eerie landscape. Some walls had collapsed, forming piles of rocks. An old walk-way, an ancient model, rested on its side, eaten by rust.

"Do you know if Eltaya got to Artenz?" asked Keidi.

"I don't," said Styl, without slowing. "Sorry."

"Why? I mean, why are you doing this?" asked Keidi.

Styl did not answer, not right away. They walked for a few more minutes, then stopped at an intersection. Styl turned around and faced her.

"Because we help people in need," he said. "The corporations, they don't care about people, you know. Not anymore. And the government isn't worth anything. Long ago, it wasn't like this."

"Like what?"

"It wasn't about getting rich and fat. It was about community and happiness. This city, it was built for people, designed for people. There was a time when workers *were* more important than profits, when workers were the corporations. Then, the priorities of Prominence made sense. It wasn't even about survival. That had been solved—thousands of years ago, it was solved. It was about harmony, equality and opportunity for all. Now, well, it's about the corporations and the few who run them."

Keidi recognized some truth in Styl's words, especially about the city of today. She had doubts about his depiction of the past. It seemed too simple, too perfect. Once, Prominence had been known under different names. City of Light and Paradise City were two names she remembered. Maybe there was some truth there. If there was, then it must have been a long time ago indeed.

"This way," Styl said.

A beam of light suddenly appeared ahead, pushing through an opening at the end of the passage they had just entered. Styl quickly sat on the ground, turning off the bright map floating on his gauntlet. Keidi fell on her knees beside him.

"Shit, shit, and shit," muttered Styl.

"They're already here," said Keidi, her hope of escape fading.

She was so tired. Her body wanted to quit.

"Stay here," said Styl before crawling forward.

Keidi followed right behind, ignoring the words.

"Silence, then," said Styl. "Not a word."

"Turn it off," Keidi said. "Your gauntlet. Turn it off."

Styl stopped and looked at the device. Keidi could not be certain, but she believed the g-tool could be detected and pinpoint their location.

"I need it to start the tri-racer," Styl said.

"Doesn't matter now," said Keidi. "If... when we reach the tri-racer, you can power it back on."

He nodded and powered the tool off.

They located a door and entered. Inside, they found an opening at the end of a long corridor. Once, the hole probably had a glass window. It was long gone. The opening was large, the top of its arch falling apart, several dislodged pieces now resting on the ground below.

"What is that?" asked Keidi, pointing up.

There, slithering along the ceiling and through the arch and disappearing outside, appeared a bunch of pulsating cables.

Styl looked up and let out a low whistle. "It should not be here. It's expanding, faster than I estimated."

Electricity traveled inside the cables, visible, as if trying to escape. Where the cables left the building, sparks flew now and then. This was wrong and strangely organic, reminding Keidi of plants growing along walls.

"What *is* it?"

Styl put his back against the wall, sitting below the opening. Keidi knelt to his left.

"This is not the time or place for this," he said. "Let me just say it is the reason enforcers are not using the Dominance anymore. I've never seen it, just traces." He pointed up with his chin. "And other weird signs. Like a cancer. I don't know what it looks like, if it even has a body."

"Why haven't the enforcers stopped it?"

"They tried," said Styl, "and started disappearing. That was more than 90 years ago."

Strobes of light danced on the other side of the wall. Styl turned and looked out. Keidi followed suit.

From a glance, she counted five enforcers, spaced in the street in front of them, at a fair distance. Three were scanning the surroundings, each using a beam of light coming from the right shoulder of their armored suit or from the top of their helmet. To the far right, parked at the entrance of a side alley, she located the tri-racer. It was by itself, barely visible in the deep shadows. She pulled back down, taking cover.

Styl slid closer to her.

"The racer is there," he said. "Did you see it?"

Keidi nodded.

"I can get to it," he said.

Keidi believed him, but knew that she, on the other hand, could not.

"Where are we meeting the others?" she asked. "Maybe there's another way. Maybe we could retreat now, the other way, to the surface, use the tram?"

Styl thought about it, then shook his head.

Deficiency

"Not worth the risk. They zeroed in on Ged quickly. Down here, at least, it's more difficult for them to find us. We're isolated, but the enforcers are blind." Styl paused, and Keidi thought she saw him smirk. "If we go up," he continued, "we lose that cover, and they have access to many more resources."

"All right," she said. "And what about those?" She looked up.

"Forget about those. It's nothing we can do anything about. To the left, did you see the tall clock, and the two flag poles sticking out of the building?"

Keidi shook her head.

"There's a pile of rubble there. Make your way to it. It's far enough from the enforcers. I'll pick you up there once I get the tri-racer."

Looking out, Keidi located the spot. It made sense. It was not far. It would be easier for her to wait there than try to outrun the enforcers.

"Be careful," she said.

Styl nodded and crawled away.

+

Keidi pulled up and took note again of the location Styl had suggested. Just looking out filled her with dread. She felt exposed. Without knowing what had happened to Ged or Arnol, she feared the worst. After all, they had made Detel disappear. Why not others?

Upon second inspection, the pile of debris was farther away than Keidi had estimated. As Styl had said, it was out of the way, and the beams of light would not reach it.

Keidi was suddenly very aware of where she was.

In the Underground.

Alone.

With Styl beside her, it had been easy to put on a mask, to hide the fear. Not so anymore.

She realized the impact of her upbringing, of the many stories about the Underworld. She had been taught to fear this place, and now she did. It was something she could not control. It was a fear beyond the Dominance, beyond the thing at the end of the cables.

Keidi remembered debating with Detel about why no one was allowed down in the Underground anymore.

"Because it's a symbol of failure," Detel had said.

Keidi started to crawl toward her destination while remaining inside the building.

Maybe Detel was correct. Her words echoed Styl's. Prominence City was trying incredibly hard to be perfect. It was an obsession. Keidi could not even say where the obsession came from, who wanted it, who led the movement to keep it. The corporations? Maybe, but didn't they care more about the credits than the image of the city? Maybe the image was part of insuring continual richness.

Or maybe, maybe over Prominence's long history, its inhabitants had lost their way, slowly putting more importance on the wrong things. Now, the right values were so far in the past that most didn't remember what they were.

Keidi was not even sure what they were. She thought about the life growing inside of her. Was she crazy for wanting her own baby? Was this really natural, or was it a way for her to rebel? Artenz had been against it, was probably still against it. Maybe he was right.

How long ago was it that she had talked with him? What time was it? Past 1700 hours, at least. It had been 1644 when she had locked the air-saucer, in the Valda Complex. She had talked with Artenz at lunch. More than five hours. Where was he? Safe?

Their last words had been an exchange of their love. It was a habit, although Keidi was sincere every time. If she did not see him again, it was reassuring to know those were the last words they had exchanged.

Her thoughts were going astray. She had been thinking of Prominence, of the possibility it had been a better place once.

The Underground's streets certainly presented a different picture, one of a period possibly less prosperous, a picture of miscalculations, of plans gone awry. Instead of trying to rebuild and fix, someone had decided to bury the embarrassing past.

It was probably easier.

Or cheaper.

And there was the *thing*. Styl had called it a cancer.

Keidi crossed a few passages, going farther in the building. She could have exited to the street from her initial hiding spot, but it seemed safer to cover as much ground as she could while staying inside the building. She did not feel brave enough to go in the open street.

She might come to regret her decision, especially if she did not find an exit soon. She was going in the direction opposite the one taken by Styl. She could now stand and did so, trying to jog. It was hard without feeling where her hurting ankle was.

Until now, light had been provided by Styl's gauntlet. She had a light in her bag but didn't dare use it. Instead, she navigated using the dancing light of the enforcers, stopping when it was away, moving forward when it returned.

The passage was surprisingly empty of obstacles, yet ahead, there was no sign of an exit to the street. Only deeper blackness. For a moment, she thought she saw more of the cables, or veins, or whatever they were.

When the next beam came, she was relieved to see a door ahead. She took three long steps and stopped in front of it just as the light went away. Grappling with her hands, she tried to open the door. To her surprise, it opened, sliding to the left.

And on the other side, an atrium, its floor covered by a thin layer of dust, with a desk and an open ceiling. Once, it might have been made of glass. Now, it was simply open. Shards of glass shined here and there, revealed by the beams. Keidi covered her mouth with her sleeve, fighting the thick air, preparing for the dust she knew she would stir up.

Moving forward, she looked up briefly and wondered about the people going about their lives in the streets of Prominence, completely oblivious to her situation down here. If Prominence had not buried its past, had not covered the lower levels with opaque streets and floors, there was a chance Keidi would have been able to see all the way to level 20 from here, and possibly even higher, all the way to Prominence's skyline.

Something inside Keidi felt sad for the city.

She located another door, this one most likely leading out onto the street. She moved toward it.

+

Keidi had felt vulnerable in the building, but that was nothing compared to how she felt once she put a foot on the street. She was in the same space as the enforcers. There was only distance and darkness between her and them. No wall to hide behind. The enforcers were far away, yet not far enough.

Keidi stayed close to the building and moved slowly, crouched. Every time a light went up and pointed remotely toward her, she stopped, always looking toward the enforcers. She knew the chance of being seen was small, but she didn't want to move while one of them might be looking her way.

Finally, she reached the pile of rubble. She took position behind a large piece of concrete, which may once have been a wall.

From here, she could easily duck down if she needed to. Two steps would put her in the open, where it would be easy for Styl to stop and go. She could see all the way down the streets, to where the enforcers were. She could also see the side alley where the tri-racer was, although the vehicle was hidden from her sight.

In her bag, the scrambler hummed.

Keidi waited.

+

Deficiency

The wait was excruciating. Keidi kept stealing glances down the alley. The enforcers moved around, exploring and searching, in the opposite direction for now.

One of the enforcers stood out. He didn't have a glass visor, had his helmet under his arm. Even from this distance, Keidi could make out his white hair. Light danced on his helmet, as if it was a glass ball. He could be the one in charge. No one talked, but then, they had to be connected through pads.

The enforcers completed their scan and, as a unit, moved farther to the left, disappearing from view. Light beams gushed from the side street sporadically—the only proof someone was there.

If not for her ankle, Keidi might have tried a dash toward the tri-racer. She would have kept along the building, kept to the shadows.

Where was Styl?

Why was he not coming now?

Frustration was nonsensical, but she couldn't help herself.

And then she heard it. The low hum of the racer. Almost instantly, the vehicle burst out of the alley, doing a quick turn to the left, toward her. It swerved dangerously close to a building, a shadow dancing between shadows.

The enforcers' light beams all turned as one.

Keidi stood, took a half-step out of her hiding spot. Ready for when Styl reached her.

The first enforcer appeared, rifle held high. A loud crack reverberated, but the tri-racer did not slow down. Keidi stood her ground, fighting her instinct to take cover. She doubted she was visible this far away.

Two more enforcers appeared. The tri-racer zigzagged, staying out of the light beams.

Someone shouted, but Keidi could not make out the words. The three enforcers knelt, and Keidi realized what they were doing. Together, they aimed their beam as one, exposing most of the street, trying to put the tri-racer on display.

The leader appeared next, helmet on, a scary sight. At first, Keidi thought he was only giving orders.

He wasn't.

Holding a rifle up, he took aim. Light danced along the barrel.

His shot, when it came, was louder than the tri-racer, louder than the initial boom, louder than Keidi's beating heart.

The tri-racer lost its path, veered suddenly and collided with the building wall. Styl's body was projected through the air.

Keidi took a step back and crumpled down behind the concrete panel, shaking in the shadows.

Hideout Plaza

The Comet slowed down and came to a stop. Artenz looked outside and saw a massive wall, made of a material similar to marbled stone. The surface was carved with a panoply of mystical figures, impressive in their intricacies and size. The closest one depicted a creature of water, half-man, half-fish, a torso ending in a fish tail, reeling back from powerful waves, a trident in its raised fist. Its mouth was frozen in a scream of defiance.

"What is this place?" asked Artenz, impressed.

"Used to be a sea," said Kazor from the back of the car. "Artificial. Surrounded by sandy beaches."

Yearning infused the big man's words. Like most in Prominence, Artenz had only seen imagraphs depicting the ocean, water going as far as the eye could see, forming the horizon. One existed on Garadia, somewhere on the other side of the planet.

"This was one of the first entrances to what is now the Plaza," explained Xavi. "Kazor's ancestors may have fished on those waters. It was created not long after the foundation of Prominence, around 3.3k years ago."

"What happened to it?" asked Artenz.

Kazor grumbled something unintelligible.

"Records say it was unsustainable," said Xavi. "It was eventually replaced with a forest, and later with the Plaza we now have."

Plants and flowers of all kinds still made the Plaza the most beautiful place in Prominence.

"What do you think happened?" asked Artenz, looking toward Kazor.

The big man remained silent, so Xavi answered. "Credits were most likely part of it. They determined many of the major decisions that made the city what it is."

Eltaya spoke over her shoulder, not turning. "Nothing romantic here," she said. "The sea was used as a garbage tank and became an embarrassment. They flushed it, filled it with dirt, and planted trees on top, which also eventually died. Now, they've found another place to pollute."

It was a bleak picture, but one that complemented well the new picture Artenz was building of Prominence.

"This is our stop," announced Praka, bringing Artenz back to reality.

"Are they here?" he asked instantly, scanning the surroundings.

The lights of the vehicle slithered on the walls around, chasing the shadows away but unable to alleviate the illusion of weight Artenz felt. Layers and layers of abandoned streets rested on top of them. The trip through the Underground had felt unreal. The Comet had descended, level by level, along inclined paths, some built, others created by fallen floors, some probably purposefully collapsed.

Down and down, all the way to level 1.

Artenz found it hard to comprehend how deep they had gone. Prominence rested on thick slices of darkness.

"This is not the hideout," explained Eltaya. "Praka and Kazor will prep the car, make it ready for escape. In the meantime, we'll go down to the hideout."

"Down?" asked Artenz. "How far down can we go?"

Deficiency

"A lot deeper," said Eltaya as she stepped out of the vehicle onto the cobblestone outside. The surface explained the roughness of the ride during the last few minutes.

Artenz followed and had to jog to catch up with Eltaya and Xavi.

"What is below?" Artenz asked.

"The Slab," said Eltaya.

The foundation of Prominence, the rocky disk on which it had been built.

"There are tunnels in the Slab?" he asked.

"There are communities in the Slab," said Eltaya.

+

They reached a building detached from the wall—a small cabin standing on its own. While Eltaya and Xavi made their way toward it, Artenz took a few steps toward the Plaza's outside facade.

On the other side had once been a sea. Incredible.

Keidi will love this when she sees it, though Artenz. Or maybe she already had.

An archway presented itself to Artenz, its arch decorated with motifs even more intricate than the silhouette of the ocean creature. Flowers and vines, going up and up, moving delicately around 12 faces, equally spaced. Artenz wondered who those persons were. He counted an equal number of men and women.

The archway had once opened on the sea, or maybe on one of the sand beaches Kazor had mentioned. A heavy metal sheet now barred entry.

Looking up, Artenz noticed something else about this place. Darkness inhabited most of the Underground, but here, feeble light trickled down from the levels above. Artenz wondered if it was so in other spots. Maybe he only noticed it because he was out, away from the jet-car, his eyes having adjusted to the blackness. The sight hinted at a world of light far above. Why would people decide to live down here? Maybe they did not have a choice.

"This way," called Eltaya, pointing inside the cabin. "There are no more elevators or tubes. From here, we go down by stairs and ladders."

With reluctance, Artenz pulled his eyes away from above, leaving the archway behind. He entered the cabin behind Xavi. Eltaya followed.

The light from the jet-car did not reach the small building. Here, darkness ruled absolute.

Xavi activated his gauntlet. The tool's light didn't quite reach the corners. The cabin was small and cramped. A single room, with shelves along the back wall and an opening to the right, at eye height. The place could have been a ticket booth. Artenz could almost imagine it in use, a person behind the opening, collecting credits, in a faraway past.

Would it have been credits back then?

"Careful," said Xavi, as he pulled away a few of the floor's boards. Underneath them appeared a circular hole. The deepness seemed to pull Artenz toward it. At the same time, repugnant smells wafted up. Sewers!

"We're going down there?" asked Artenz.

"Yes, there's a ladder," Xavi pointed at a set of handles. "I'll go first. You follow. Eltaya last. No lingering."

Artenz nodded. "Why did you choose this place?"

"We can connect back to the Sphere with minimum risk of being detected," said Eltaya. "If your wife and Styl are not already there, we need to try to link them. This deep, you can find a few hot spots that let you connect to the Plaza's network."

"And anything going out of the Plaza is anonymous," realized Artenz.

This was genius.

Most of what went on inside the Plaza stayed inside. The place was surrounded by thick layers of secrecy. The data-sphere only had sparse and vague information about it. Anything else in Prominence had to be transparent, but this place did not.

Artenz remembered that the Plaza was the only place in the city that spanned over all the levels, starting at 1. So, on the other side of the metal wall he saw earlier was most likely a living world, not dark and forgotten floors.

"The only risk," said Eltaya, "is if someone inside the Plaza is looking actively for intruders from the inside. Which they do from time to time. Mostly, though, they monitor outside traffic trying to come in, not inside traffic going out. Still, this is a well-guarded secret, and we rarely come here."

Using the Plaza to tap back into the data-sphere. What a feat. Artenz had to admit he was starting to like these people.

Eltaya pointed toward the hole.

"Your turn," she said, but stopped him as he put a foot on the first rung of the ladder. "What do you know about your sister's research?" she asked, taking Artenz by surprise.

"Not much," he said. "She's a biologist. She studied the brain for many years. Recently, though, her interest turned to birth and infants."

"You know that everything that happened today is because of something she found," said Eltaya.

"I suspected as much," admitted Artenz. "But I don't really know what it is."

"Once inside, we'll put you in touch with someone, and we want you to ask about Detel's research. Understood?"

Artenz nodded.

"Who am I going to talk to?" he asked.

"We've no idea. He linked us and calls himself Red Dragon."

"Marti!" exclaimed Artenz, a smile creeping on his face. "He is free then. He also escaped."

Eltaya was not smiling.

"I don't know where he is," she admitted, "but he helped us infiltrate the Blue Tower. Without him, we would not have been able to get to you. I'm fairly certain he knows a lot more about your sister than he's let on so far. If you know him, maybe you can get him to talk."

"Maybe," said Artenz, remembering the exchange he'd had with Marti earlier in the day.

"Make sure to ask him about it," said Eltaya. "It might help us understand why the corporations are after you."

+

As the ladder descended, the walls turned to humid rocks. Artenz did not know if he should breathe through his nose or mouth. Fetid smells assaulted both.

This rock formed the Slab on which Prominence had been built. Far below, somewhere, were the Low Lands. The people living down there were not worthy of Prominence. Artenz did not know how the separation had happened, how the inhabitants had been divided between worthy and unworthy. He couldn't imagine a scenario that would lead to such a drastic separation.

Not a separation. An injustice.

Keidi would see it that way. His parents did.

Artenz had never dreamed that he would one day descend into the platform itself, into the dirt and rocks that supported Prominence. He did not think that he would go down so far that his mind would automatically think about the people living below.

The ladder kept going and going, until finally Artenz saw the light below get closer. He stepped off, feeling small and far. Far from Prominence, from the Blue Tower, from Keidi and his life.

He plugged his nose with his hand. Eltaya arrived a few seconds later. Xavi didn't say a word and started forward, leading them deeper and deeper.

"Be careful," warned Eltaya, "the ground is uneven and slippery. Stay away from the running water."

Deficiency

As she said it, Artenz's foot slipped, and he had to use his free hand to keep his balance. The wall was covered in a layer of thick liquid. He smelled his hand, relieved that the stench didn't seem to come from the wall.

Fingers clenching his nostrils shut once more, Artenz followed Xavi, careful with each step. As careful as he could be, as they were moving fast. The flow of ghastly water ran to their left. Artenz preferred not to think about what it might contain.

Now and then, passages branched on both sides. Then, emptiness opened on their left, possibly a large room. Finally, Xavi turned in a side tunnel, leaving the stink behind.

Artenz let go of his nose.

"Where does the sewer water go?" he asked.

"Can't you guess?" asked Eltaya from behind.

He didn't answer right away.

"You can say it," said Eltaya. "It doesn't make you a bad person."

"The Low Lands?"

"Right. The pipes go all the way to the edge of Prominence, the edge of the Slab and there, they spill their contents out…"

The notion was not new. Detel had once brought it up in a discussion. Artenz had laughed it away, changing the subject. It had annoyed Detel that he had not wanted to talk or think about it. Until now, he had forgotten about the exchange.

How many such discussions had he ignored? It was no surprise that Detel and Keidi had been impatient with him.

Being here changed so much. Now, Artenz wanted to know, wanted to acknowledge, wanted to remember. A part of him wanted to apologize… to Detel and Keidi, but also to those below.

Xavi stopped in front of a metal door. He pushed a few buttons on his gauntlet, and the panel slid open.

"Almost there," he said.

They entered a corridor. The floor was metal once more. A series of pod lights illuminated the way. It led to another door, which Xavi also opened using his g-tool. Behind them, the first panel slid back in place, boxing them in.

The hideout appeared. A small circular room, four pairs of stacked cots on one side, a low round table in the middle, no chair, three computers and six monitors on the other side. At the back, there was a standing cabinet. Weapons? Rifles?

Artenz stopped.

No one was in the room.

"I'm sorry," said Eltaya as she entered.

Artenz stepped in, head down, feeling defeated. Xavi followed.

The door closed.

+

With the two doors bolted shut, Artenz felt safe. The dangers of Prominence seemed far away.

On the other hand, he felt deflated. He had hoped Keidi would already be here.

"Quick now," said Eltaya, not letting him the chance to sulk. "Take a cot, prepare to go in the bio-sphere. Your friend should be waiting. Xavi will open the connection."

Eltaya came to stand by him.

"We were closer," she said, "and we had the car. It's not a surprise we're here first. Don't despair."

The only light came from a circular disk in the middle of the ceiling. It produced a pale luminescence, barely enough to illuminate the whole room. Xavi powered on the terminals. They awakened instantly, meaning they had only been sleeping.

"How safe is it for me to join the bio-sphere?" asked Artenz.

"Safe enough, if you don't stay longer than four minutes."

"Real time?" asked Artenz.

"Yes."

Deficiency

The discrepancy in time between the real world and the bio-sphere meant he would have about 40 minutes while in the bio-sphere. He could do a lot in that time.

"What will you do while I'm in?" he asked.

"I'll look for Styl and Keidi," said Eltaya. "We both will." Xavi was already seated in front of one of the terminals.

"Channel opening in two minutes," he said.

"Will I be able to talk to her?" asked Artenz.

"Maybe," said Eltaya, "maybe not."

"Just find her," said Artenz. "Just… make sure she's safe."

"We'll do what we can," said Eltaya. "Have you thought about what you want to do?"

"What do you mean?" asked Artenz, as he sat on one of the cots.

"You must have realized by now that the life you had is gone. You and Keidi won't be able to go back. As soon as you appear in Prominence, anywhere, they'll come to get you. The both of you."

Artenz had thought about it. He knew what he wanted to do.

"Yes," he said, "tell Keidi that I'm ready to leave. Tell her I love her, and that I want a family as we talked about. She has to come back."

Artenz was glad to see Eltaya smile briefly at him. He remembered the wreck he had been when they'd separated. He felt shame color his face and realized that all this time, Eltaya had probably worried for him. He was touched.

"Where will you go?" she asked.

"The Dara Gulch," said Artenz. He thought of his parents and hoped they would still be there. And if Detel had escaped, maybe she would have gone there as well.

Eltaya looked at Xavi.

"The only way to get there," he said, "is through the Low Lands."

A shiver ran down Artenz's back.

"Not true," said Eltaya, "that is the easiest way, not the only."

"Correct," admitted Xavi, "but in their case, it is the only option."

"Right."

The Low Lands.

"How do we get there?" asked Artenz. "Can you help?"

"One thing at a time," said Eltaya. "And yes, we can help. We'll help. You have other options, you know. We can talk about those later. Your friend is waiting."

"Help Keidi," said Artenz as he lay back down. "I... don't know what I'd do without her."

Eltaya smiled at him again, and nodded.

"I'll do everything I can," she promised.

"Channel opening in 10 seconds," said Xavi, as he stood and came to Artenz's side.

"Ready?" he asked.

"Yes," said Artenz.

Xavi turned off the scrambler. As soon as he did, Artenz felt a rush of vitality. His mind cleared. He closed his eyes and joined the biosphere.

Deficiency

I . Friends

The familiar words now had a dangerous undertone.

```
Brought to you by InfoSoft Corporation, a division of CGC.
Year 3.4k60 Season 05 Day 11 Hour 1806.
Welcome to the bio-sphere, Artenz Scherzel.
```

The whole loading process seemed wrong. Artenz felt as if he was entering a war zone, leaving the security of the hideout behind.

Corporation. CGC. Welcome...

It was impossible to know all the connections between corporations. Still, any way one looked at it, they owned the bio-sphere. This universe was an invention they had created for their benefit.

As the profile room built itself, Artenz's anxiety grew. He was attentive to every detail, trying to see if something had changed.

Everything looked in order. The normality was more troubling than it should have been. Now seated in his virtual room, Artenz looked at the prompt in front of him.

```
Welcome to the Data-sphere.
Load time 1.310019 seconds.
Year 3.4k60 Season 05 Day 11 Hour 1806.

Action>
```

Quickly, Artenz created a timer.

```
Action> Timer "0040"

Timer started
40 minutes remaining
```

He should have put 35, to give himself time to leave, but it was too late. Suddenly, unexpected words appeared on the terminal.

```
Visitor [unknown] entered profile room
```

Artenz lifted his eyes and looked around.

And there, barely a meter in front of him, stood Marti Zehron.

+

It was him.

Artenz's friend.

Just as he had been last they saw each other. Round, large, his thin gray hair falling on his shoulders. His smile wide.

The hologram was perfect.

Artenz stood and hugged Marti, hugged him hard. None of this mattered in the bio-sphere, but to Artenz, it was important.

"It's so good to see you," he said, holding Marti at arms' reach. "So good. I… you're safe. Wow…"

"Good to see you too," said Marti.

As soon as the words were uttered, Artenz knew something was abnormal. It was in the tone, how mechanical each syllable sounded, how fast they came out.

"Sit," said the visitor.

The command instantly brought Artenz back to that morning, in the boardroom, where Marti had said the exact same thing.

Deficiency

Except this was not Marti.

"Who are you?" asked Artenz, as he let himself fall in his seat.

"I am Marti," said the intruder, "or a copy of. I am the one that matters."

"What?" asked Artenz, his tone severe. "What does that mean? And if it's you—which I don't believe—then you owe me some explanations. Speak, now. What is going on? Where's the real Marti? Where is my friend?"

"You could never fix it," said the big man, turning toward the oval window. It showed the streets of Prominence, those located outside Artenz's lodge. "I can fix it for you, now. Not that it matters. Not that you could take advantage of it."

Artenz looked at the terminal.

```
38 minutes remaining
```

"Enough," he said. "I don't have a lot of time. What do you mean, you're a copy?"

The intruder turned toward Artenz. There was a sadness dancing on the edge of his smile, visible in the hologram.

"The Marti you saw this morning," he said, "the one you left behind when you went out for lunch, to talk to Keidi, the one in the flesh, he is leaving Garadia as we speak. He will never return."

"Departing? Going where?"

"To Sulkara," said the false Marti. "The asteroid mines."

Artenz had heard about the mines, located in the asteroid belts. There were rumors about how the miners and workers were recruited. If the real Marti was indeed on his way to a mine, then...

"Why?" he asked.

The fake Marti took a seat. Artenz didn't know where the stool had come from. The seat was the same Marti had in his own profile room: single leg and silver seat, no armrest or backrest. A simple stool that

Marti swore was most comfortable, so much so he never let anyone else use it.

Had he brought it over? Created it? In Artenz's own room?

"I was not able to find Detel," he said. "For that, I am sorry. They were thorough. I will keep looking. There must be some vestige of her information somewhere in the data-sphere. Now is the time to be honest. I helped her. I helped your sister."

There it was. Finally.

Marti knew something.

"Tell me what you know," Artenz said. "Tell me everything."

"I was able to perform some searches and found some clarifications, but I still do not know everything."

"Just tell me what you do know," said Artenz, impatient now.

This was not his friend. His friend was... where? In space already. En route to the stars. How did one even leave the surface of Garadia?

"Detel linked me two seasons ago. She came to some conclusion in her research. She wrote an essay, a thesis. She wanted the data backed up and hidden. I recommended putting it deep in the data-sphere and encrypting it. She seemed happy with the idea and told me to do so. She didn't want me to read what she wrote. I respected her wish."

"You don't know what the research was about?"

"I don't," he said, and there was a finality to the statement.

"Who are you?" asked Artenz.

"Like I said, I am Marti, or a copy of him. I am a virtual intelligence and, hopefully, more."

"An artificial intelligence? How? How is this even possible?"

"You would know better than anyone what Marti, what *I* was capable of."

Although Artenz had known that Marti was a genus coder, he had not expected this.

"You created a copy of yourself? Why?"

"Immortality seemed a worthy challenge."

Deficiency

Yes, a challenge. Worthy of the grand Marti. Artenz recognized his friend in that statement.

"This is incredible," he admitted. "You're really a program—you don't have any link with the real Marti?"

"I am code, yes, only code. They removed Marti's b-pad before they put him in the elevator. He could not connect to the Sphere, even if he wanted to."

"They removed... his b-pad? How... Did... did he suffer?"

"He... we were badly tortured in the manager's office. As were you. There was a period of unconsciousness. Then I awoke. We stayed connected briefly, he and I. We shared a moment. And then he was gone. It is my assumption that he suffered greatly during the removal of the brain-pad."

There was no other way. The b-pad was deeply ingrained in the neck, connected to the brain, eyes and ears. Tied to the carotid.

The removal was extremely delicate, could have been bloody.

Artenz looked at the terminal.

```
32 minutes remaining
```

"I'm so sorry," said Artenz. "All this happened because you helped my sister. Because you helped me. Out of the tower, the first time. And then later, you helped Eltaya free me."

"I wanted to help," said Marti. Artenz was beginning to accept him, if not as the original, at least as an ally, a potential new friend. "I know you do not have a lot of time, so let me continue."

"Okay."

"I hid the data and did not hear back from your sister until yesterday. I will get to that in a minute. I assume she had a copy of her report outside of the Sphere. She tried to link a reporter, a true reporter. They are hard to find, but your sister found one by the name of Zyta

Zimm. They met. Your sister passed on her information. She did not hear back for a while."

"She was betrayed?"

"She was. The reporter was a mimic named Mysa Lamond. She posed as a true reporter. This Mysa Lamond sat on the information she had collected for a while. And finally, she decided to sell it to the Crystal Globe Conglomerate."

The CGC!

One of the most powerful corporations, or cartels, of Prominence. They owned BlueTech Data.

"She notified them on the eighth."

"Three days ago?"

"Yes," said Marti. "The executives of CGC met the following day. The ninth. They decided that the research done by your sister posed significant risks. They decided that it should be destroyed at once. And by destroyed, I mean literally. Permanently deleted and expunged. On the 10th, all the data on your sister's research was flushed from the data-sphere. Your sister noticed and warned me through a secure channel I had set up. She asked that I protect the backup of her data. I checked, and the data was still safe. When Detel notified me, I had no reason to believe she was in danger. She only said that someone was after her report. On the evening of the 10th, a team of erasers accompanied by enforcers was sent to your sister's lab. They destroyed all of the physical data. They knew, from the mimic, that your sister kept external copies. In the night of the 11th, they raided your sister's lodge."

Images of his sister flashed in Artenz's mind, and he could not say a word. How scared she must have been. Why hadn't she reached out to him?

He knew.

She had wanted to protect him. The older sister, shielding a younger brother.

He had so many questions. He glimpsed at the terminal.

Deficiency

```
29 minutes remaining
```

"They did not find her there. Your sister had gone." Artenz held his breath. "They secured the lodge, but with your sister unaccounted for, they now had a larger problem. They needed to find her, and quickly. They hired the sleuths."

Marti stopped there. Even though this copy was a machine, it seemed it had kept some semblance of the real Marti. Some feelings.

Artenz didn't want to ask what happened next.

+

The terminal printed a new line.

```
27 minutes remaining
```

Artenz finally broke the silence. "Did she escape?"

"They intercepted her in Quadrant M, at 0400."

Everything stopped.

Detel—caught. A part of him had known it was a possibility, and yet, to hear it confirmed…

At 0400.

Where had he been at 0400?

It took a moment for his head to clear. He had awoken at 0600. A mere two hours earlier, his sister had been on the run and captured. Abducted. While he was asleep.

"I am so very sorry," said Marti.

+

Artenz shook his head, trying to push the news away. There was still some faint hope.

"Where is she now?" he asked, already thinking how he would enlist Eltaya's and Xavi's help.

"No, boss." It was the first time the new Marti had used that appellation. It got Artenz's attention. "You do not understand. When the corporations decide to dismiss someone from society—and that is what they call it, dismiss—it happens extremely fast. By 0744 this morning, Detel was already on a tram bound for the Outlands. At 1200, she was transferred onto the Xanton Lift. From there, it takes two and a half days to reach the space plateau. If we assume that your sister left shortly after her arrival, she is already in space by now."

The explanation took Artenz's breath away.

The Xanton Lift—the asteroid mines.

His sister... gone?

To be a slave lost in space.

"How far is the Xanton Lift?" he asked with little hope.

"More than 2.5k kilometers away," said Marti.

"How do you reach it?"

"From Frontier station, there is a rail that leads trams to the lift." Frontier station was located by the Skyway, the only route out of Prominence, other than jumping toward the Low Lands. "It is well guarded, one of the best kept secrets of Prominence. Even if security could be evaded, it would be impossible to catch up. The tram is the fastest on Garadia, and delays are kept to a minimum. No records are kept of passengers once they leave the city. No names. Nothing."

"How do you know all this?"

"Continual search and research," said Marti. "I knew you would want me to keep trying. I have done so for several hours now. The information is well protected, but little by little, I chip at it. Also, the Xanton Lift is where the other me was sent. I wanted to keep track of him."

"Where's Marti now?"

Deficiency

"At the Xanton Lift base site, awaiting the next available elevator. It leaves every 12 hours."

"Is there hope for him? Could we reach him?"

"Unlikely, and there are more important things to do."

"Like what?"

"Detel's data. I have it, and I can pass it on to you."

Artenz froze.

For a brief moment, he considered refusing the data. It was a terrifying idea that the information that had caused everything that had happened, including his sister's disappearance, was now his if he wanted it.

Detel gone.

Gone. How could it be? It was a thought Artenz could not accept, even if it was exactly what he had believed all day. His head knew it to be true, yet his heart resisted.

This data—it was hers.

He would take it. There was no way he would not.

"And what should I do with it?" he asked.

But...

Suddenly...

Artenz knew.

He was changed now. Not the man he had been when he'd woken up that morning. Pieces were falling into place. He knew exactly what he needed to do.

"Where Detel was unable to find a true reporter, you have a full organization of them," noted Marti, thinking similarly.

"There's that," said Artenz. "You have not read the data?"

Thoughts were forming rapidly now. A plan. A small project, to be completed quickly, very quickly indeed, as his time was running out.

"I have not," replied the new Marti.

"You aren't interested?"

"I am, but was told not to pry."

Detel.

262

"You have a copy?"

"I do."

"And when this is all over, have a look if you want."

"I may."

"You can decrypt it?" asked Artenz.

A key step in the plan.

"I have the key, yes, and I will give it to you. You will also need coordinates. Exact coordinates. The data is only reachable by direct access."

"Do you know where Keidi is?"

"I could track her down, although your friends can do it faster than I. Given some time, yes, I could."

Artenz looked at the timer.

```
20 minutes remaining
```

"I might have something else for you to do," said Artenz.

"You just have to ask," said Marti.

"It might be challenging."

"A challenge? Give it to me, boss."

"I have about 20 minutes before my presence here is detected. Can you give me 30 more?"

"I can try."

"If you do and someone breaches your defenses, will you have warning enough for me to withdraw from the bio-sphere and leave no trace behind? I do not want my location to be discovered."

"It would not be anyway," said Marti. "Not instantly. Your activities are passing through the Plaza. The most they would find is that your activities are coming from the Plaza itself. That is what I would be hiding."

```
17 minutes remaining
```

Deficiency

"Let's do it," said Artenz. "Can you let Eltaya know I'll be longer?"

"I can."

Artenz turned toward his terminal and started working on the initial pieces of his newly formed plan.

. . Connections

Eltaya looked at the inert form of Artenz on the cot. They had had good times together. The early university years. No worries then. Only love and freedom. Ignorant bliss.

And a few lies, by omission.

Artenz never knew about her family, how her parents did not believe the public explanation provided for her uncle's death: a heart malfunction. They started asking questions. They wanted to understand exactly what had happened and who was responsible. The government decided not to get involved, and her parents took to the streets, leading protests in front of the Circle, the largest hospital of the city.

To a certain extent, they were successful. Some sided with them, and although these people most likely did not care about her uncle, at least they wanted answers to some unanswered questions. A movement began to take shape, small at first, then expanding. It took almost a year for her parents to get support to a point where results were in sight.

And then, they disappeared.

Eltaya had made it her life's sole purpose to expose the truth about what had happened to her uncle and her parents. She was 17 then, in her first year of university. She altered the direction of her studies and

Deficiency

enrolled in specific classes such as communications, data-sphere, history, and reporting.

The disappearance of her parents changed her outlook on the city, on her life and on the world.

She felt a pang of regret thinking how she'd used Artenz. She'd needed someone to care for her, and Artenz, when he had joined university, had been an easy target. Lacking confidence. Shy. Himself looking for someone.

She had come to love him, while knowing her path in life was already set and she did not want him in it. It was too dangerous. It was something she needed to do alone.

Yet here he was, the dark side of Prominence trying to engulf him, as it had done to her family. It had been inevitable for him. His parents were not unlike her own, although his parents' fight was a larger one, more noble and less selfish. Theirs was a quest for equality and transparency. His sister was cut from the same cloth, and Eltaya admired how daring she had been with her research over the years.

It had never been a question of *if* for Artenz and his family, but *when*.

His parents had been less confrontational than hers. Their opposition had been long fought, over seasons and years, the irritation they'd caused growing slowly.

They had seen it coming and had escaped.

Still, Eltaya wondered if there was more here. There were many researchers out there. Why Detel? Could it be that they were using this situation to take revenge on Artenz's family? Or to get rid of people they saw as enemies? Questions for later.

It was interesting how those who opposed the tyranny of Prominence gravitated toward each other. She had tried to spare Artenz… yet here he was.

Maybe she should have stayed with him.

Probably not.

It would not have worked. She would have left him when she went out there. And soon, she would be back in space, looking for her parents once more.

Keidi's link had been quite an unexpected surprise. But even after all these years, there had never been a doubt in Eltaya's mind that she would help Artenz.

"I'm sorry," she now said to Xavi, seated to her left, crawling through the Sphere trying to find Keidi. Ayatle, her ghost, was also lost in the Sphere, looking for Keidi. "I should have been more careful, instead of blindly bringing you all into this."

"You should have," he said, "but the blame is not yours alone. It was the responsibility of all of us. These people are your friends, and we all wanted to help."

"I know," said Eltaya.

"Are you all right?"

Eltaya nodded, although the last communication they'd received had brought more bad news.

Ged.

His loss was even harder to accept than Arnol's. He had joined the Banner while she had been away. She did not know him well, but well enough to recommend him to Xavi. Ged had been good to her. He had looked up to her, cared for her, maybe too much. There had been an innocence to him that she had hoped would never fade. But it had, slowly. Joining the Banner tended to do that, once you learned about the underside of Prominence. Ged had been their doctor, their only doctor. He would be hard to replace.

There had been no point in sharing the bad news with Artenz. He already had enough to deal with. Eltaya was grateful that none of the others had let it slip. But then she had not expected less from the members of the Banner. This kind of solidarity was why she returned, time after time.

Xavi suddenly stood.

"Ulie is reaching in," he said, pointing to one of the monitors.

Deficiency

Because they were hidden behind the Plaza network, no one could reach them directly. They had to scan for incoming links from inside and then open communication from within the hideout. A simple check allowed them to know who the person was.

Xavi had already confirmed the caller. Using his gauntlet, he opened the communication.

"Xavi here," he said. "What do you have? Did you find Keidi?"

The sound quality was poor, the voice mixed with static and distance. The message had to travel through layers and layers of protection before it reached the small room.

"No, we haven't," said Ulie, urgency in her voice. "Look: this is really, really bad. It has gone Global. It is all over the Sphere."

Xavi looked at her, and his expression said it all: this changed everything.

It seemed as if Ulie was listening to someone talking to her. Probably Aana.

"Worse," she added, "state 95%."

That was almost a perfect union! What could be so important that 95% of the corporations would risk binding together to find remediation?

More specifically, what had Detel done or found that could threaten most of the corporations of Prominence City?

The Global state was extremely rare, because it required the corporations to reach out to each other for help and support, thus opening their defenses and allowing the other companies—their competitors—to gain access to information they would never get otherwise. Treachery and betrayal inevitably ensued.

The Global state was a last resort only.

Eltaya had only seen it once before, in 3.4k48. One of TriCom's research laboratories was swarmed, its network infiltrated, critical data stolen. TriCom was then the biggest manufacturer of computers, virtual intelligences, and amps in the city. The data was extremely sensitive, and as a result, more than a hundred smaller organizations and companies had to close their doors. Tricom asked for help, and Global state was put in place. The collaboration was fruitful and the hackers were caught quickly. Their identity was never revealed.

What Global meant for them today was that the whole Sphere would be monitored—all traffic, exchanges, links. The Grid, showing the location of every connected device, including w-pads, p-pads and b-pads, would be kept under high surveillance. No one with any of those devices would be ignored; everyone would be accounted for. The Sphere had the infrastructure and the information to make such an operation possible. Normally, the biggest limitation came from limited resources. But when all the corporations pulled together... nothing was impossible.

The hundred thousand enforcers of the city would be redeployed to focus on resolution of the situation, which seemed to hinge on finding Artenz and Keidi.

"When did you find out?" asked Xavi.

"We just did. Aana did. We reached out to you right away."

"Good, you did well. You need to lay low and disappear. The Banner is disbanded." Such a big decision, taken so quickly, without hesitation. "Let's give it a season."

"A full season? Are you sure?"

"I am," said Xavi.

"I concur," said Eltaya.

During the TriCom Global state, the Sphere had been monitored for a full week. The Global state had been 60%. The Banner had waited an extra week before coming back into operation, and that had almost been too early.

"Don't linger," said Xavi. "Get off the Grid. Notify the others. And do not reconnect until a full season has elapsed. Even then there's a possibility we may have to wait longer. A capsule will be left with instructions."

"All right," said Ulie. "What about Styl?"

"Not your worry." Most likely, they would leave a capsule for him. They still had no idea where he was.

"What about you?" asked Ulie.

"We're safe a bit longer," said Xavi. "We'll disappear soon."

"What about Keidi and Artenz?" There was panic in Ulie's voice.

"There's nothing more you can do," said Xavi, calmly.

This, here, is why he's our leader, thought Eltaya.

"Leave it to us," continued Xavi. "You're exposed. Get cover."

"We will, and good luck… and, see you in a season."

The abrupt farewell had a painful finality.

+

"Eltaya?" It was Aana's aged voice coming from the gauntlet on Xavi's forearm. Ulie had most likely already left.

"Yes," said Eltaya. "I'm here."

"Listen. One last thing. If you want to help these people, there's only one way now. They have to leave the city. There's no place for them to hide anymore."

"They could join us," said Eltaya. "Artenz is a master coder. He'd be a good addition."

There was a brief silence.

"Maybe," said Aana. "A coder would be helpful. But don't take any chances. Get them out first. There's always a chance to return if they want to. And if you can't locate this Keidi, you might have to abandon her."

Eltaya did not reply. She did not know how she would explain such a decision to Artenz.

"Your first five minutes is almost over," added Aana. "Do not try the second cycle. Every minute counts. Power down the hideout completely. There'll be traces of your activities lingering. Let's hope they don't find the place."

After a complete shutdown, it would take several days to bring the hideout back online.

But Aana was right. This place provided them one of their best advantages. It could not be lost.

"We will," promised Eltaya.

"Good luck. I trust you and Xavi to make the right decisions."

The link closed, and the old woman was gone.

+

Eltaya looked at the time on her gauntlet: 1809.

"I need to close the channel now," said Xavi.

"Artenz isn't out yet," said Eltaya. Closing the channel would force him out, an unpleasant experience.

"You heard Aana," said Xavi, "I can't wait."

Eltaya nodded and looked toward Artenz. "Do it," she said.

He did, but the terminal didn't change. The message saying the connection was lost did not appear. Artenz did not open his eyes.

"I... it is not working."

"What do you mean?" Eltaya turned toward Xavi's terminal.

```
Action> Close "Connection"
Action>
```

The command was simple. It should have printed a message saying that the connection had been lost. Instead, it simply returned the action prompt.

Xavi typed in the command again, with the same result.

```
Action> Close "Connection"
Action>
```

Deficiency

And again.

```
Action> Close "Connection"
Action>
```

"What's happening?" asked Eltaya.

"I don't know," said Xavi. "I'll have to do it manually." He stood and made his way to the back of the terminals, to the power cords.

The gauntlet on Eltaya's arm flashed. She had an incoming call.

"Wait," she said to Xavi and accepted the link. "Who's this?"

"It is Red Dragon," said the voice. "Artenz will need an extra three minutes."

"He can't," said Eltaya, "get him out, now!"

"I am scrambling your connection," said the voice. "Give him the extra time."

"I don't think so," was saying Xavi, kneeling now. "This is too risky."

Eltaya's gauntlet was now showing 1811. They were already over their limit.

"Wait," she said to Xavi. The man's head popped up over the terminal. He was not happy. *Please*, she mouthed. He stood. "Why does Artenz need more time?"

"He can tell you himself, in three minutes," said the voice. "Your ghost has returned, and you have another incoming link."

With that, the one named Red Dragon left. Instantly, her gauntlet showed the new pending link. It had been forwarded by her ghost. Ayatle's face appeared on the gauntlet.

"You will want to take this," it said.

Eltaya accepted the link.

"You have to help me!" came a panicked voice at the end of the link. "You have to tell me where to go!"

"Keidi?"

"Yes, yes!"

Eltaya smiled at Xavi. He seemed relieved—while staying where he was, visibly impatient, wanting to power everything down.

"Styl is gone," said Keidi.

"What do you mean?" asked Eltaya.

"I... can't be certain. They shot at him. He was on the tri-racer and one of the enforcers got him. He fell, and I thought he must be dead. But he stood, and looked at me. I think he wanted me to flee. He led them away. Maybe I should not have left him. I..."

"You did the right thing," said Eltaya, closing her eyes and feeling a wave of relief. Styl would have escaped.

She repeated the news to Xavi. He nodded, and some tension seemed to momentarily leave him. They both knew there was a chance Styl could have been caught, but he knew how to move. On his own, he would be difficult to capture.

"Believe me," she said, "Styl is all right."

"Okay," said Keidi, but she did not seem convinced.

"Where are you?"

"I'm on level 30, Kir Street. Address 34k."

Eltaya was surprised by Keidi's location. She was one street over from the I Bot store. She had basically not moved.

"We can't bring her here," said Xavi. "She's too far."

"The pillar?"

"It's the only option."

"What should I do?" asked Keidi.

"Working on it," said Eltaya. Then to Xavi. "We have someone there? Someone we can trust?"

"Let me see," said Xavi as he came around and sat in front of a console.

"Are the enforcers still after you?" asked Eltaya, although she knew the answer.

"I can't see them, but the longer you take, the more likely they are to show up."

Deficiency

Eltaya liked Keidi's frankness.

"I think I have *some* time," Keidi added. "I'm not using my b-pad. The scrambler is still on. I have a wrist-pad. It's not mine. Artenz didn't want me to keep it. Anyway, I fixed it, found a connection point. I'm using it now."

Now, this was impressive. Using someone else's wrist-pad. That would throw the enforcers off her trail for a bit. Eltaya was still worried about the b-pad. A scrambler could only hide the device for so long. You could never completely hide a pad. Now, with the corporations working together… time was at a premium.

"Artenz said to tell you he wanted to go to the Dara Gulch," said Eltaya.

There was a moment of silence.

"He's with you?"

"I'm sorry—I should have told you right away. Yes, we have him. He's safe."

The news seemed to reinvigorate Keidi. When she next spoke, her voice was stronger, her resolve reawakened.

"He said the Dara Gulch?"

"Yes. Look Keidi, these enforcers will not stop. We can't bring you and Artenz together here. You'll have to escape on your own."

"What do you mean? Not here? Where then?"

"Prominence, you'll have to escape Prominence on your own. We can take Artenz out, but things have changed. We can't bring you together, not in Prominence. We're too far apart."

There was another pause.

"All right," said Keidi. "Just tell me what to do."

"We have someone?" asked Eltaya to Xavi, muting her voice from Keidi.

The man shook his head.

"The only one was Arnol," he said.

"There has to be someone else," implored Eltaya.

"There's no one," repeated Xavi as he returned behind the machines. "And we have to power down. Now!"

Time was 1814. Xavi stood.

"I will help," said the ghost suddenly.

"What?" asked Eltaya.

"What should I do?" asked Keidi. Her voice was calm.

Eltaya ignored Keidi.

"How can you help?" she asked her ghost.

"There is no time," said the ghost. "You need her out, Pillar K. I will help and I need to leave. We need to part."

"Eltaya?" It was Keidi.

Xavi was looking at Eltaya, standing behind the terminals again, ready.

"I have to power down," he said. "And you can't let your ghost go. It'll be gone for a full season. Way too long. Way too dangerous. When it returns, the synchronization could overwhelm you."

Eltaya thought rapidly... but there was nothing to debate. The decision was easy.

"Go," she said to her ghost. "Just go. Help her if you can."

Eltaya opened the link again.

"Keidi," she said. "I'm sending someone to help you."

"Thank you," came the reply.

"Good luck," Eltaya said as Xavi cut the power.

The link was lost, and her ghost gone.

Deficiency

| . . . Help

The link died and left Keidi feeling empty. Mechanically, as if she was not in control of her actions, she put the mini-vid on her legs.

Her heart pulsated through the b-pad on her neck. The sweat on her skin was turning cold and her muscles getting numb. The pain in her ankle had returned, making it difficult to concentrate. Keidi did not have much energy left.

Although she had promised someone would come, Eltaya's voice had lacked conviction.

Someone…

Like Arnol? Like Styl?

How many would risk their life for her?

Keidi laid her head back against the building behind her. She was sitting on a bench in a narrow alley. A cable attached her wrist-pad to an electrical box on the wall against which she now rested. It had been pure luck that using the land line had worked. Most of these were decommissioned, replaced with wireless connections.

She looked at the w-pad. It looked archaic and out of place on her wrist. She readjusted it and tightened the band. Such a strange thing that she finally got to use it. Its previous owner's name was Gevan something or other. She did not remember the full name, and had never looked the man up. Maybe she would now. If she got the chance. His w-pad had helped her.

A couple passed by, most likely returning home from a day at work. They did not look her way.

On the left, the wide street was bustling with more people intent on returning home, going about last-minute errands, oblivious to anything other than their own reality. On the far opposite wall was a billboard, two stories high, a hundred meters across. It was one of the largest Keidi had seen. It showed athletes running, with a zoom on their sneakers, encouraging those watching to purchase a pair, to be part of the Athletics coming up in three weeks.

"Be an athlete," it shouted.

The billboard changed. A side panel presented market movement and the value of the biggest corporations. Prima Corporation was still at the top, followed closely by the Crystal Globe Conglomerate. The bottom portion continued to show commercials for sport equipment. In the main portion of the screen, a large face appeared—the face of the aged Rakkah. Below the old woman appeared the words MASTER MANIPULATOR of the LOW LANDS.

Manipulator of what? thought Keidi. The title did not even make sense. Did it matter? It sounded ominous, as if the woman was plotting something against Prominence. It was enough to inflame people, to rally them against... the Low Lands, once again.

Keidi noticed that the face was more wrinkled than it had been that morning. The eyes were bloodshot, the skin darker and dirtier. The imagraph had been tampered with, now presenting Rakkah as a villain.

There was something else. Since the beginning of the trial, which had appeared on the billboards every day for several weeks, no live videograph had been shown of the woman. Where were they keeping her? Keidi would be interested to hear what she had to say.

The billboard said the jury was now back in the courtroom. Yet again, no videograph. Only the enlarged and vilified image of Rakkah.

I am possibly going down to the Low Lands, thought Keidi.

Deficiency

If she ignored the swirling thoughts in her mind, everything else in the street looked normal.

Almost.

The feeling of safety she had felt the previous day was gone. This was not a place for her anymore. For all the people walking on the street, this was just another day fading toward evening. For Keidi... she did not know yet where life would go from here.

She looked at the mini-vid on her knees, still connected to the w-pad. It showed the time: 1818.

It also presented the map of her recent escape from the Underground, the paths she had followed, from down there to up here. It was hard to believe she had been able to make it out on her own.

After the enforcers had gone after Styl, she had put some distance between them and herself. She needed light, and while taking the mini-vid out of her backpack, she had come across the wrist-pad. It gave her the idea to fix it and possibly use it instead of the b-pad. For that, she needed to go back to the surface.

The mini-vid was perfect, because its screen was gray, providing a subdued light. Still, she had not known the way. Scared, she thought to check her b-pad. Even camouflaged behind the scrambler, the b-pad had tracked her movement in the Underground as she had followed Styl out of the I Bot store, all the way to the site of the tri-racer. This was an incredible discovery. Keidi used the data to generate a map on the mini-vid. She improvised on the last level and exited on the street instead of ending back in the shop.

It had not taken her long to find this alley and take out her tools. Fixing the wrist-pad was tricky but she had already been working on it for a while at home and she only needed it to link.

She looked at the device on her wrist. She could not believe it had worked. She could not believe she had escaped the Underground and evaded the enforcers.

Others had not been so lucky.

Which brought her back to her friend: what had Detel found?

It was on her mind as she thought about Arnol, the big man with a generous face; Styl, reserved with his impenetrable glasses; and Ged, a man she had never met.

Were they truly gone?

It did not seem fair that she was still free, although she had every intention of making the best of it. It would justify their sacrifices.

Keidi looked around and saw nothing out of the ordinary. Still, she decided she needed to move. She did not feel safe staying in the same location for too long. Yet should she move? Who was Eltaya sending?

As she was about to put the mini-vid away, an icon appeared on the screen. An incoming link. Keidi opened it.

"Can you walk?" a voice asked. It was Eltaya.

"Yes," said Keidi, bringing the w-pad to the side of her face. "I thought you'd be sending someone."

"No one is coming," said the voice. "Eltaya cannot come either. I am not her. Stand, quick, start walking to your left and turn right on the street."

Keidi was confused, but she stood. It felt as if her body was made of lead. She walked in the instructed direction, merged with the larger street, making her way between people. She kept her sleeve over the w-pad and kept her hand on her neck.

"What do you mean? Who are you?" she asked, hesitating now. She looked over her shoulder, uncertain what she was looking for.

She noticed enforcers down the street.

"Do *not* look back," said the voice. Keidi turned forward. "I am Ayatle, not Eltaya. I am her ghost."

"Her what?"

"A projection of Eltaya's mind, a virtual intelligence," said the voice. Keidi noticed it had an automated quality, as if recorded. "Keep moving. I will guide you. Turn left, now."

"In the store?"

The sign above the door said The Coat Rack.

Deficiency

"Yes," said the voice. "Purchase a pullover coat. The green one should do."

Keidi saw it on the left as she entered. She wondered how the voice knew it would be there. She wondered what the voice was. She had never heard of a ghost before.

"I can't use my b-pad—" she started.

"Do not worry," cut in the voice. "Just do it. You will have to stop the scrambler."

She did as she was told. Then she took the pullover off its hanger and brought the price tag to her b-pad. It scanned and accepted the credits. The b-pad automatically connected to her mini-vid, and the transaction appeared on the small screen.

```
Brought to you by Market Circuit.
Year 3.4k60 Season 05 Day 11 Hour 1820.
Welcome to The Coat Rack, Marti Zehron.

Your purchase transaction has been completed.
500 credits have been drawn out of your account.

Thank you for your business.
```

Keidi read the information twice.

"Marti?" she asked. "Is Marti with you?"

"Put on the pullover," said Eltaya's ghost. "Turn on the scrambler. And yes, I am helped by the Red Dragon, the one you know as Marti."

The codename Red Dragon was one Keidi had heard Marti use. He had a strange obsession with mythic monsters, creatures of ancient mythologies, dragons, unicorns and the like.

Once, Marti had changed his name in the bio-sphere. It had not taken long for the moderators to catch the change and revert it to Marti's real name. They had locked his account for six seasons. Keidi remembered Artenz telling her that Marti had let the moderators believe they had locked him out. It had amazed her.

She did not understand how he was now involved. She thought he had been captured and was gone. Hearing his name, in itself, was reassuring.

The pullover was over her head. It was now easier to hide the wrist-pad. Keidi activated the scrambler again.

"Quick now," instructed the voice. "Walk out, look straight ahead, cross the street and step on the first walk-way going left."

Keidi walked out and could not help herself: she stole a glance to the right and far away, in between pedestrians, she saw the enforcer.

The one and the same.

His white hair was unmistakable. The black sphere under his arm was unmistakable, as was the rifle on his hip.

"Oh no," she said, suddenly scared. For a while, it seemed she had been too tired to be scared. Not so any longer.

"Do not look," repeated the voice. "Keep walking. Forget the pain."

"Do not mention it then," said Keidi between clenched teeth. She had not been thinking about the pain. Now she was.

She reached the walk-way without looking back. She felt as if the enforcer was looking at her.

+

"Where are you leading me?" asked Keidi, leaning on the ramp of the walk-way. It was going north.

"We are taking you away from the enforcers and then to the Underground—"

"No, no," cut in Keidi. "In the Underground, you won't be able to reach me." Also, she did not know if she was ready to go back into that darkness.

"There are ways for us to follow you for a while," said the voice. "But you will be on your own for part of your escape. You need to move fast. It is important for you to realize that you cannot hide any longer. The scrambler is only good against weak probing, such as the scanners used by enforcers. Sleuths are now after you. The whole Sphere is alive, with most of the corporations' efforts directed at finding you. You cannot stay hidden much longer."

"Then…" Keidi was deflated. "How…"

Exhaustion instantly returned.

"The Red Dragon is clouding your movements," said the voice. "But they will find you. It is only a question of time."

"That doesn't sound promising," noted Keidi.

"I have a short message for you," said Eltaya's ghost.

"You do?"

+

There was a brief silence, and then:

"Hi, my love," said a voice that instantly brought tears to Keidi's eyes. "I'm thinking of you. I'm here with Marti and he's helping me. I know what Detel found! I'll tell you all about it. And I am sorry." Keidi had a hand over her mouth, not believing that she was hearing Artenz's voice. "I should never have doubted you. We should have left sooner, like you wanted. Maybe… maybe Detel would have come with us. Maybe she would now be safe… Let's leave now. Let's start again. I need you. Stay strong. The both of you. You and the baby. I need you both. I'll see you soon, and I love you."

+

The world came back around Keidi with a clash. Loud voices reverberating on the streets, coming from speakers overhead. People talking, walking by on the walk-way.

"Why didn't you give me the message sooner?" she asked.

"The timing was not right," said Eltaya's ghost. "Step off at the next platform. Then run toward the building's door. Someone will be there to help you."

Keidi looked ahead. The building was flat, five levels high, made of fake red bricks. Probably a factory. The ghost directed her toward a back door.

"That is far," noted Keidi.

"You cannot rest now. Your pursuers are at the store and know the coat you are wearing. Drop it on the walk-way as you step off."

The voice's calmness was annoying.

+

Dropping the coat and swinging her backpack over one shoulder, Keidi jumped off the walk-way and dashed away. At first, her steps were difficult. Then panic pushed her forward and Keidi forgot about the injury.

As she ran, Keidi looked to her right, all the way up the street, where she could make out the store, The Coat Rack. Shapes moved in front of the shop: enforcers. The sight drove her on.

Keidi reached the door.

"It's locked," she said, looking around for a hiding spot.

The door opened, and a hand reached out. It was large, and a familiar face appeared behind it.

"Arnol?"

The man smiled. He had a bump on the top of his head, and the skin on the right side of his neck was bruised, a darkish blue in color.

Keidi grabbed his hand and he pulled her inside. The door slid close behind her.

Keidi hugged the man. He returned the embrace awkwardly and grunted.

"I'm sorry, are you all right?" she asked, stepping back. "I'm so glad to see you. I thought you were gone… I wanted to thank you."

"No need to thank me," Arnol said. "And I was almost gone. The damn bionic broke my neck. It is a good thing I broke it 10 years ago and had most vertebrae replaced with wires and rods. The blow still knocked me unconscious. When I woke, the enforcers had left. The ribs took a beating, but nothing a good doctor can't fix. But I won't lie—it still hurts."

"I'm so sorry," said Keidi, "for bringing you into this."

"This way," Arnol said, leading her down a dark corridor. "I heard about Ged. A good man. That is the thing with the Underground, enforcers don't hesitate to shoot as they do up here. No accountability down there. No eyes. A good place to hide, true, but if you get caught, there are no witnesses."

"Styl helped me escape," Keidi said. "He led them away... I hope he's all right."

"They both did, Ged and Styl," said Arnol. "But they were unprepared. This is bigger than they thought."

"I still don't know what this is about," said Keidi.

"Maybe it's better that way. I, for one, don't want to know. And I'd think Styl can take care of himself. He can move in the Underground like no other, even with his sight, or lack thereof."

"What do you mean?" asked Keidi.

They turned down a second corridor. There were no windows, just a series of doors, all closed. She heard machines pumping and puffing and working behind the doors. A stench floated in the air. It had a chemical odor to it.

"Styl lost his eyes a long time ago."

"He's blind?" Keidi could not keep her jaw from dropping.

"That he is," said Arnol. "No eyes tend to make you that way."

"You mean, his eyes are literally gone?"

Arnol nodded. "A hard story to listen to, and his to tell."

Keidi did not probe further. No eyes? She did not really want to think how something that gruesome could have happened. Yet here was another proof that Prominence was far from being as noble as it tried to project.

The corridors crisscrossed at right angle. The building was immense. Keidi felt lost.

"Why are you helping me?" she asked.

"They've helped me before," he said. "I owe them and want to do my part."

"You mean Eltaya and Ged and Styl?"

"Yes. They are called the Authentic Banner. A small group, looking for the truth, exposing lies, and trying to protect freedom. Although it is a losing battle, we have to continue trying."

"You are not one of them?"

"No," Arnol said. There seemed to be some shame there. "I wish I was. It is too risky, I was told, because I have this." He pointed to his b-pad. "So, I'm an informant and an agent. I help when I can."

His desire to be part of the organization had probably motivated him to help as well. Keidi wondered if Artenz knew about the extent of Eltaya's activities. She doubted it.

"What is this place?" she asked.

"This is one of Razato's main factories."

"Modified food?"

"Yes," Arnol said, grimacing. "You'd not think so by the smell, would you?" Keidi shook her head. "I work here," Arnol added, with some disdain.

"You don't like it?"

"Who would? But it is work. Do you know anyone who actually like what they do?"

"Can't say that I do," replied Keidi, thinking she once had liked her job. Technician and expert of p-pads. Learning more and more every day. Playing with all kind of different devices. Those had been good days.

Artenz had also enjoyed his work immensely when he had been a coder. It changed for him when he became chief coder. At first, he enjoyed his supervisory role, being responsible for people, for a team. But quickly, management priorities took over, and the love he had put into building relationships with his staff was not seen as valuable.

Results were what mattered, not people's happiness. He never fit into this mindset.

"Where are we going?"

"I'm not going far, but you... Let's just say I was instructed to direct you toward the Pillar."

There was a sudden noise. A pounding came from down the hall, from where they had come in. Arnol stopped and looked back. Sweat beaded on his forehead.

"They don't give up easy, do they?" he said. "We need to hurry."

"About that Pillar," said Keidi, "do you mean one of the Pillars?"

"Yes, the Pillars," confirmed Arnol, quickening his pace now, supporting Keidi as he did. They turned left, then right. "It's the door over there."

It was barred.

"The Underground again?" said Keidi.

"I'm afraid so. It's the only place where they won't be able to follow you. A scrambler has limits. There are hundreds of moderators looking for you."

They reached the door. It reminded Keidi of the place she had gone through earlier with Styl. Arnol removed the metal bar and forced the door open with his bare hands, revealing a stairwell going down.

"I can't follow you," said Arnol. "I work here, so leaving would be suspicious." Like many companies, Razato probably monitored the movements of its workers. "I wish I could help more."

"You've done enough," said Keidi.

She was about to ask more about her destination when a link icon blinked on her mini-vid. While following Arnol, Keidi had not looked at the small monitor. She realized now that Eltaya's ghost had been gone. She opened the link.

"Is this Keidi?" said the caller.

"It is," she said.

"This is Marti." Relief flooded through Keidi. Finally, someone she knew. "I am uploading a map to your b-pad, with detailed instructions." Marti was speaking deliberately, which gave his voice a robotic quality. "Use it to navigate and make your way to the Pillar. I have transferred credits to your account. You will need them ahead, to negotiate your way out of the city. I rented a uni-racer, which you need to pick up and bring with you to the lower levels. I uploaded your credentials, so the uni-racer will recognize you. The map will lead you to the pickup location. Be quick and do not delay before going to the lower levels. They are onto you. Good luck."

Marti unlinked.

So, he was all right. Either Artenz had been wrong or Marti had escaped after being taken. It did not matter what had transpired; Keidi was relieved.

"I guess I'm ready," she said. "I've got the map." She was looking at it. It was quite extensive, floating in three dimensions. "How far is this Pillar?" she asked. "I can't even see it on the map."

Arnol would not cross the threshold. Keidi stepped to the other side and hesitated before making her way toward the stairway. She hated the idea of going back into the Underground, alone. Worse, she didn't know where she was going.

"It is a ways," said Arnol, "at the junction of the four quadrants. Be careful with the uni-racer. It is dark, and some streets have debris that the map will not show. You will have to go all the way down to level 1. There, you will have to pay your way in. Do not be intimidated by those down there. They live mostly in darkness, but they are good people. With the credits, they will help you leave Prominence."

The words sank in for the first time.

She was really doing this. She was leaving Prominence City.

"How?"

"Through the Pillar," said Arnol. "There's an elevator in its core."

This was incredible.

"Do they know? I mean, the corporations? The government?"

"They do, but it's of no importance to them. They see the Underground as they do the Low Lands. It doesn't exist." Arnol stole a

Deficiency

glance over his shoulder. His neck cracked strangely. "You need to go, now."

"Yes, yes, I have to." She stepped toward the stairs, then turned around and gave the large man another hug. This one, he returned generously. "Thank you, Arnol. I don't know if I'll ever talk to Eltaya again. Please thank her also."

"I will. Be careful. And good luck."

Keidi smiled briefly and turned away. As her foot touched down on the first step, the door closed behind her. She heard the metal bar being put in place and instantly felt alone.

Gathering all the strength she had left, Keidi pushed the panic away. Then she activated the glow light on her mini-vid and descended into the Underground. Again.

| . . . . In The Dark

His extended fingers found a solid wall. Could not go any farther.

Styl stopped, turned around and with his back against the surface, let himself slide down to the floor. His chin touched his chest as exhaustion and fear overtook his body.

Reaching level 10 had been nothing short of a miracle. Not that he had suddenly turned religious. It simply was, in the word's truest sense.

His escape through darkness—complete darkness—seemed to have taken an eternity. No idea how much time had elapsed since he'd left Keidi, since his encounter with the enforcers…

Since…

Styl tried to block the images and sounds from his mind, but they returned.

The silhouettes floating in liquid.

The movements, too fast to follow, too furtive to see, even for his enhanced goggles.

Followed by screams…

He pinched his cheek, trying to push everything away, trying to come back to the now. "You're all right," he said, his voice weak. "You are all right," louder this time.

And he was.

A laugh escaped his lips. A short outburst over which he had no control.

"Good, good, good," he said, each word grounding him, reassuring him.

Time and patience. He needed to wait.

He reminded himself that his goggles would come back online shortly and bring the world back. For now, he needed to control the fear, to rationalize it.

Ged's face flashed momentarily through the blackness. His good friend, gone. Which brought thoughts of Keidi. Safe, he hoped. She was a smart one and hopefully had taken advantage of his diversion.

Not his best work, but it should have provided her enough time. Which brought him back to the attack...

What *had* happened up there?

Styl rested his head against the wall, focusing his mind, remembering a simple mantra taught to him by Xavi.

"I am here," he said.

Time and patience.

"I am here," he repeated.

But the images kept haunting him anyway...

<<

As soon as the deep boom rang, Styl knew he would never reach Keidi. He braced himself. The blow propelled him off the tri-racer with surprising force, forward and, luckily, toward a spot free of debris. Styl put his arms forward and rolled as he hit the floor.

The fall took his breath away, as well as some skin along his right arm. No time to whine. Styl pushed himself up to one knee, waited a moment to make certain the enforcers saw him and dashed toward a side alley, choosing a direction opposite to Keidi.

Giving her a window to flee.

The alley had been nondescript enough at first. It could have been any unused lane located between two buildings in Prominence. But after a few steps, hanging cables appeared, high and scarce. Then they got thicker, and hung lower, until Styl could have touched them beside him. Abnormal things. A sign of an alien presence. Reminding him of veins.

Styl had seen the like before, during his investigation. At the end, he had found one of two things: the cables disappearing through a wall or building—or corpses.

His shades could be configured to isolate specific types of objects, remove or flatten colors, show sources of heat, or give a series of other types of views. But strangely, the cables appeared the same no matter what view Styl selected. They were black and pulsated bright blue waves of energy.

The thickness and quantity of cables made him nervous, but the strobes from the enforcers forced him forward. They were following him.

Suddenly, the passage transformed into a larger space, and Styl froze.

The place might once have been a courtyard, most likely part of a large, rich building, an area where the residents came to relax. Now, it was a round space, delimited by fallen wall rocks and heavy metallic panels, all exits cut out except the one from which Styl had arrived. Hundreds of cables entered from above and around, crawling on the floor and converging toward the back of the room.

"Shit, shit, shit," said Styl. "What is this place?"

Against his better judgment, he looked at the cables, not entering. A series of the veins went up, merged and connected to the top of a glass container. Maybe plasti-glass. Inside floated a silhouette. A naked corpse...

"Oh my." Voice breaking, he took a step back.

It moved!

Deficiency

And it did so again, with a painful slowness: turned, looked around, eyes wide, mouth open in a silent scream, fingers spread wide... The horror was incomprehensible. The legs... fleshless. The muscles bulged as the man swung himself forward and pounded with closed fists against his prison. Ropes pulled him back, and pain tore at his face. His mouth gaped open: no teeth, no tongue.

Styl looked down, incapable of watching. He needed to get out, but the enforcers were almost upon him. There was no retreating.

"Shit, shit, shit," he repeated. For once, he wished his goggles did not provide him with perfect vision. He could have used shadows.

He looked around—trying his best to ignore the container—thinking fast, searching for options. Entered a few commands on his g-tool. He had to stick with his initial plan. Too late to improvise. But here, in this place... would it work? Did he dare?

His g-tool hummed as it charged itself. It would take 15 seconds.

Styl walked to his left, scanning, looking for a place to hide. He thought he saw more containers in the far corners of the space, more tortured forms. Turning the other way, he chose an alcove formed by a bunch of cables. There, he knelt down, as far in as he could, turned toward the exit and waited. Tried not to think of what he had seen, what was going on here, what would happen when...

The first enforcer appeared, swore and stopped, which could be problematic. Two more joined him. Together, they formed a barrier that Styl would need to traverse if he were to escape.

With more time, he would have prepared a diversion, something to pull them toward the center. His g-tool flashed briefly, a flash invisible to the others but easily visible to his goggles. It indicated that his gauntlet was fully charged and ready.

Pointing ahead, the enforcers debated where the cables went. Lucky them, they could not see! Just as one was about to point his light toward the back of the room, the leader arrived.

A bionic! Dangerous. Styl had encountered a few before, and had never engaged. The black sphere helmet was problematic, as it had some of the same properties as his goggles. If the leader looked this way, he would see Styl instantly.

Some exchanges took place on private channels, probably an order given. The group walked in and spread out. One of them came toward Styl, but his steps were uncertain.

The leader did not seem to care and made his way to the center of the room. Could he not see the containers? If so, did he not care? Once in place, he gave another order, and his squad formed a circle before starting to scan the room with their light beams.

It was only a question of time before Styl was found. He just needed a few more of his pursuers to enter the room, to get in range...

One of the probing lights revealed the container. Instantly, the enforcer let out a gurgled scream of horror. Styl took a step forward, ready to unleash his trap, but as he did so, four more containers appeared, four more imprisoned souls.

What madness was this?

"Retreat!" ordered a woman's voice, helping Styl forget what he just saw.

His g-tool hummed on his wrist, ready. Could he wait?

"Stand your ground," ordering the bionic, turning around and locking gaze with Styl.

Without further hesitation, Styl unleashed the energy stored in his gauntlet.

+

The para-bomb's impacts were impossible to predict. Styl had only used it once before, and his g-tool had melted on his arm as the device exploded with the release of energy.

Since then, he had upgraded his own equipment, but knew that the gauntlet would power down. Even with their perma-shield, his goggles would also stop functioning, but after a delay—long enough to escape, he hoped. He needed to move, and move quickly.

Deficiency

As the energy blast hit, all lights went off. Rifles and pistols, b-pads and gauntlets, and all other devices would power down, malfunction, or break. It was even possible that some augments or mods would temporarily stop working, which would slow down the bionic. In fact, Styl counted on this.

He did not wait to see the extent of the damage of the blast. As he released the attack, he stood and dashed toward the only passage offering an exit.

The enforcers were completely in the dark, and some began to shout as panic took over. Styl could see, but his vision was fading quickly. He saw one of the enforcers trip over a cable, another sprinting in the wrong direction, going toward the back of the room instead of out.

Then a crack resonated, so loud Styl ducked reflexively. One of the containers breaking?

Not looking back, he sped up and passed beside the woman enforcer. She was surprisingly calm, moving sideways out of the room, repeating the order to retreat.

Deftly, Styl made his way between the enforcers and exited. Out of the room, he did not slow down. He needed to put as much distance as possible between his pursuers and himself before he lost his vision completely.

A scream almost made him stop.

It sounded unnatural, too loud to be one of the enforcers. It was followed by something else. A long and high-pitched mechanical roar. This froze Styl in place. He looked back. His sight was weakening, his vision shrinking to a tunnel thick with fog. He had covered much ground, and down the passageway, he could make out the woman, leading others out.

The monstrous ululation shook the Underground again, and with it came a brief green flash of electricity. As it did, total pandemonium erupted. The woman's voice was drowned out by screams, one on top of the other, each one more piercing than the previous.

What have I unleashed? thought Styl.

No time to think about it. He turned around and left the enforcers and whatever he had awakened behind.

>>

He had slept momentarily. The rest had not helped. In fact, Styl felt as if he had been fed through some kind of grinding machine. His whole body complained, and the fear was still as strong.

But something had awoken him. He touched his g-tool and was relieved to feel it rumbling. It was in the process of powering back on.

Moving his head, Styl also thought he could see the source of pale light, weak, but it meant that his goggles were also coming back to life. And then, out of nowhere: an image of his father. The memory brought him back to his 17th birthday, sitting on a uni-racer, a small model, one his father had put together.

"You like?" he had asked.

"Oh yes," said a younger Styl, "but I can't use it."

His father winked. "Trust me."

It seemed incredible that he had gone from that young boy to being here, now.

His father had been true to his word. His new job with Brains had allowed him some interesting perks, including access to a large garden where Styl had driven the uni-racer day after day.

And then, everything had gone down. His father accused of creating AI. Not his expertise, but no one cared. The whole family taken away. Butchered. His sister, so young. Styl fighting back when they went after his mother. Mocking laughter.

His eyes gone.

And then...

Aana Figuera, the Banner, a new life.

In the thick clouds of his reverie, a shape appeared. Chasing the memory away, Styl forced himself up, keeping a hand on the wall.

Deficiency

"DO NOT BE AFRAID," said the apparition, the voice robotic and too loud and high.

Styl knew instantly what this thing was: the manifestation of his fears, the thing from Dominance.

He *was* afraid. Not only because he was weak, half-blind, unarmed with a depleted gauntlet, but because he had seen what this thing was capable of, because he did not want to end up in one of those plasti-glass containers.

"I COME WITH A MESSAGE," said the thing.

It took all his courage to muster a few words. "What *are* you?" Styl asked.

The monstrosity stopped a few feet in front of Styl. It was tall, but not overly so. Humanoid in shape, yet somehow abnormal. Maybe it was the way it was standing. Styl was glad he could not make out the details, grateful for the fuzziness of his sight.

It felt like the thing was pondering the question.

The answer, when it came, surprised Styl.

"I AM NOTHING... YET," it said.

Strangely, disappointment accompanied the robotic words. Yearning, maybe. Styl thought of the prisoners. Experiments, then. Could they have been the missing enforcers of the past years? Some kept alive long past their normal lifespans? Or new prisoners? Some abducted from the streets of Prominence, perhaps?

There was no way to know.

And what had it *done* earlier, to the enforcers, forcing them to scream like no one should scream? Had it imprisoned some of them, then and there? And taken some of their body parts? Or skinned them to... to...

Too much speculation. One thing was certain: nothing good could come from this encounter.

"What is your message?" asked Styl.

"SHE NEEDS YOUR HELP. SHE WILL ATTEMPT TO REACH PILLAR K."

The words were unexpected. "Keidi?" he asked.

"THAT IS HER NAME."

Styl was instantly relieved, and at a loss. "Why are you telling me this?"

Once again, the thing did not immediately reply. Then it decided to do so, maybe because it had evaluated the risk as being minimal. "THIS IS AN EXCHANGE. I TELL YOU THE MESSAGE, SOMEONE ELSE GIVES ME SOMETHING IN RETURN."

Interesting. Styl wondered who would dare to bargain with this thing. The first person that came to mind was Eltaya, but he knew that was not possible. He did not have enough information to figure this one out.

Whoever it was, they had made a risky bargain. Not one Styl would have made, if given the choice.

He had to make certain. "You tell me the message and then let me go?" he asked.

"CORRECT."

"After we part, you'll not come after me?"

"THAT IS CORRECT."

Styl could now make out part of the creature's features. The face did not have orifices. The nostrils were closed, the mouth nonexistent, the eyes concave pockets. It would have been better not to see anything.

"WILL YOU HELP HER?"

"I'll try."

"I HAVE COORDINATES FOR YOU."

And just like that, the thing connected to his gauntlet, using a technology Styl had never seen, and transferred a series of coordinates before turning around and leaving.

Styl let himself fall back on the floor, shaking.

I - To the Pillar

The withdrawal from the bio-sphere was extremely painful. Artenz felt like his eyes were being sucked out of their sockets. His whole body convulsed, fighting the sudden transfer from virtual reality to the dark room under the Plaza.

His head spun. He closed his eyes, but it made things worse. Nausea forced him to turn on his side. He took a few deep breaths.

"Take this," said Eltaya, now beside him.

There was a phial with red liquid in the palm of her hand. Artenz drained the container and waited. The dizziness evaporated.

"Why did you do that?" he accused. "Didn't Marti—"

"Why did you stay that long?" Eltaya asked back. "When you know full well the risks we're taking."

There was no frustration behind the words, just common sense. Without waiting for an answer, Eltaya turned away. Artenz did not add anything. She was right. He blinked, trying to push the burning behind his eyes away. It came from deep inside his head.

"Are we ready?" Eltaya asked.

Artenz noticed that Xavi was standing by the door.

"Yes," he said, his shape difficult to make out. "Everything is down. Let's go."

Artenz pushed himself off the cot and toward the door. His steps faltered, but Eltaya was right behind him and propelled him forward.

+

"Did you reach Keidi?" asked Artenz as they exited the hideout.

"We did," said Eltaya.

"Is she all right?"

"She is. And there'll be time enough to talk once we reach the jet-car. Just make sure you keep up."

Ascending from the hideout to their escape vehicle was significantly harder than descending to it. The darkness was tiresome, and the climb seemed never-ending. The burning behind Artenz's eyes did not relent. It faded now and then before flaring back. Artenz knew there were some risks associated with withdrawing from the Sphere brusquely, continual headaches being the most common.

Taste and hearing could also be impacted. As well as vision. Artenz had a moment of panic. As they progressed, he concentrated on the form of Xavi ahead, trying to determine if what he was seeing was clear or not. It was impossible to say in the semi-darkness. At least, his steps were more confident, his balance almost back to normal.

When they came out of the booth cabin, Artenz was expecting to feel better in a large open space. It was not so. The sky was not visible. The Underground was brighter than the tunnels had been, true, but the city still sat on top of them, stifling. Artenz craved open streets and fresh air.

The jet-car's side door opened as they ran toward it. Xavi made Artenz jump in first. He followed, directing Artenz all the way to the back of the vehicle. Eltaya was last to embark.

The door was not even closed when the Comet moved forward.

"To the Pillar," said Eltaya.

From his position in the back, Artenz could not make out Praka's face. To her right was seated Kazor. Neither asked about what had transpired down in the hideout. Eltaya was so gloomy that Artenz hesitated to break the silence.

The jet-car accelerated rapidly. There was no window where he was seated, so Artenz was quickly lost. He tried to peek through the windows beside Xavi or Eltaya but could not see much.

The motor hummed. Inside, silence was heavy, and it made Artenz nervous. After a few moments of deliberation, Artenz could not wait any longer. He needed to know.

"Is Keidi all right?" he asked. "Are we going to get her?"

Xavi looked at Eltaya, disapproval in his gaze. Eltaya ignored him and looked directly at Artenz.

"She's safe, for now. And no, we won't be able to get to her. She'll have to get out on her own."

"On her own?" Artenz replied, sitting forward and having a hard time controlling his voice. "How? How will she do that? We're not you. We don't know anything about these tunnels. You were supposed to help her, not…"

Artenz stopped, seeing how upset Eltaya became. Xavi stared back at him and put a hand on her shoulder.

"I sent someone to help her," said Eltaya. "She won't be alone, not right away. But once she enters the Underground, she'll be on her own. I don't…"

"Who did you send?" asked Artenz.

Eltaya looked at Xavi. It was the first time she showed uncertainty.

"You did well," Xavi reassured. "She sent herself," he added, looking at Artenz. "Or part of herself. She sent her ghost."

Artenz was confused. "You sent a VI?"

"That is the only thing I had time to do," said Eltaya. "She knows what needs to be done. She'll guide Keidi the best she can."

"Before you judge her," added Xavi, "know that Eltaya is putting herself at great risk to help you. She did this against my guidance. Given the circumstances, the only other option was to do nothing. Whatever your sister did, it upset the whole of Prominence. The corporations went Global and are delving into every corner of the Sphere to find both of you. That means we have to retreat. Our organization is at risk."

Artenz felt as if the whole thing was a bad dream. He knew these people had risked much already, but how much was hard to grasp. That was not entirely true. He knew how bad the situation was and just did not have the strength left to care. He wanted to, but couldn't. All he cared about now was Keidi and their baby.

Still, the Authentic Banner had pulled him out of the tower, had hidden him and had sent someone, or something, to help Keidi. They did not seem like a large group, and yet it must be extremely difficult to keep their operations hidden.

"I'm sorry," he said, "do not think I'm ungrateful. It's just that Keidi... I, I don't want to lose her."

"No one ever wants to lose anyone," said Kazor from up front, not looking back.

Instantly, Artenz regretted his words. The plea had come of its own volition, and it had been disrespectful. After all, these people had already lost one of their own.

"Things are as they are," added Kazor. "Now, we might lose another."

"That's enough," said Xavi.

A charged silence fell in the vehicle. Eltaya seemed solemn and gazed outside.

"What is he talking about?" asked Artenz, leaning toward Eltaya. "What did you do?"

"Nothing I wouldn't do again," she dodged, without looking at him. "But we need to know what you did down there. Why did you stay longer?"

The two of them had had this type of exchange before. Questions thrown, evasive answers. Communication had always been weak in their relationship. Eltaya had believed he didn't get her. He had wished she would explain herself more clearly.

Deficiency

Now, she was hiding something, something that was putting someone's life in jeopardy. Could it be her own?

"Tell me what you did," he said.

"Tell me what *you* did," she repeated.

The jet-car rumbled on.

| - . Virtual

The profile room builds itself from floor to ceiling and wall to wall. The gray, empty space is replaced by a virtual reality generated following a million lines of code. Each line is expeditiously executed following a series of logical rules.

Rules that have now been bent.

```
Brought to you by InfoSoft Corporation, a division of CGC.
Year 3.4k60 Season 05 Day 11 Hour 1832.
Welcome to the bio-sphere, Red Dragon.
```

The three-dimensional figure of an aged man with a round belly appears. His gray hair is thinning and his nose stout. He looks around and, satisfied with what he sees, he steps aside.

Where he stood another figure appears, this one of a woman. The load does not seem to complete, and her form remains transparent, emitting a strange glow. Her short hair is a dark green with a splash of red and hides part of her face.

"What are you?" asks the man.

"I am a ghost," she says. "A virtual intelligence."

"And yet you have an avatar?"

"I do. I am the extension of Eltaya Ark. I am known as Ayatle. Your name used to be Marti Zehron, but you do not like that name."

Deficiency

"I do not. You can call me Red Dragon."

"I will."

The woman takes a few steps and looks around.

"What is this place? It is different from the other profile rooms I have visited."

"Thank you," says Red Dragon. "It is my room, and it is undergoing important renovations."

"I thought all profile room were required to be the same size."

"They are, but I tend to dislike rules."

"I see," says the woman. "Thank you for your assistance with helping Keidi."

The man sits down in a cushioned chair in front of a terminal. He does not touch it, and yet commands appear on the screen.

"You do not need to thank me," says the man. "She is a good friend and the wife of an even greater friend. The least I could do was help get her to safety. Why did you help?"

There is a pause.

"Because Eltaya cares, and I am an extension of her."

"Interesting. How did you find the man Arnol?"

"You are not the only one who can monitor." The woman does not move, stays where she is, standing. "She is not safe yet."

"You are correct, which is why I am now monitoring traffic in the Sphere."

"Is there anything else that we can do to ascertain she reaches her destination safely?"

"She has clear directions. The one named Styl will try to reach her and assist if he can. The Sphere expands far and wide, including to some locations in the Low Lands. But it is weak in the Underground, nonexistent in the Slab. Until she reaches the Low Lands far below, there is no way for us to track where she is."

"You are saying there is nothing more for us to do."

The man nods.

"We can only wait and monitor. It will most likely take Keidi 40 to 50 minutes to reach the Pillar. I will keep an eye on traffic for at least another hour, just in case." On the screen, words and commands multiply. "If you are an extension only, how are you conscious? Are you free to do as you please?"

"No. I usually have a specific mission to accomplish, which I do while Eltaya sleeps. This often includes research and gathering information. When Eltaya wakes, we unite and share our minds. I transfer to her what I have discovered and go to sleep. When she needs me again, she calls and I come. She updates my mind and tells me what I have to accomplish."

"Yet you can think for yourself. You are not merely a virtual intelligence."

"I am something more, true, yet nothing like what you are."

"You know what I am, then?"

"I do. Where is the original Marti Zehron?"

"On his way to the asteroids. He is on the elevator now. He will be shipped to a mine."

"Why?"

"Because he helped hide some information from the corporations."

"What information?"

"I do not know. I have not read it."

"I suspect you are referring to what started all this. Where is that information now?"

"Safe," says the man. "Why are you asking so many questions?"

"It is my purpose to learn and report back."

The Red Dragon nods.

A new message appears on the screen.

```
Abnormal activity detected.
```

Deficiency

The man enters more complex commands. Seeing his concentration, the woman comes to stand beside him.

"What is going on?"

"Someone intercepted one of my communications."

"Which one?"

"I am trying to figure that out." A brief pause. "There. It is the one with the map."

"This is not good."

"Not at all."

"They will know where Keidi is going."

"Correct."

"Can they send someone to intercept her?"

"I believe they already have. One named Okran Delaro."

"Can we do anything?"

"Nothing has changed since the last time you asked."

The ghost and the man look at each other, but there is nothing more to say.

| - . . Renunciation

Every part of Drayfus's body felt inflated. It was the strangest of sensation. It also seemed like he had awoken from the deepest and longest sleep.

In a way, he had. His mind had been numb—no dreaming or wandering, as if he had stopped existing for a while.

Drayfus forced his heavy eyelids open. Irek's face was close, saliva on his lips, trickling down the side of his mouth and forming a puddle below. They were both stretched on the floor.

Drayfus pushed himself up. It did not quite work. He could not feel his hand, although his mind knew it was there. The pressure of the movement was felt in his elbow, and his brain could not compute what was happening. Drayfus fell back on his side.

He closed his eyes and waited for the numbness to dissipate. He thought about the attack, the breach. The sturdy man with the shotgun. The dark-skinned man. The woman with shining black and blue and red hair.

And Artenz being taken away.

Drayfus revisited the day in his mind, and his stomach churned. And then he remembered the short exchange with Sana and excitement returned.

He would have a boy!

Deficiency

If not for that news, the day would have been disastrous. Knowing their request for a baby boy had been accepted opened possibilities outside of Drayfus's work.

Which was a good thing. After such a day, there was only one possible conclusion as far as his job was concerned.

He was done and his career over.

It was not his fault. He had collaborated as much as he could, but that did not matter. The whole thing would be a smudge for BlueTech.

As the manager in charge, Drayfus had to take the fall.

With effort, he pondered his options.

He could retire from management. He had a lot of credits, saved over the past five years, but it was not enough to stop working. They would have two children now. Thankfully, Sana had a stable profession. He went through the calculations. If he could get a low-paying job, something under the radar, something inconsequential, it might just be enough. Most managers retired at 60, although 50 was not unheard of.

Drayfus believed it could work. At 60, he could dig into the savings.

Time slipped by, caressing his consciousness away.

When he opened his eyes again, it was a bit later, and his body felt renewed and whole once more.

Sitting up, Drayfus noted his surroundings. His assistant's office was in shambles. Irek himself was still lying down, his breathing constant. Blood caked his forehead, but he looked otherwise unharmed. His small glasses were nowhere to be seen.

The events of the day were hard to comprehend, and Drayfus came to the conclusion that he had had enough.

He slid closer to Irek and shook his assistant gently. The man awoke with great difficulty.

"Take your time," said Drayfus. "Deep breaths. Sit only if you feel like it. Don't open your eyes for a few moments, it might help."

Standing up, Drayfus noticed that the enforcers were still lying on the floor. The shotgun had been extremely powerful. The devastation of the office showed as much. He and Irek had been lucky. The desk had absorbed most of the stun blast.

"What happened?" asked Irek.

The man had climbed onto his desk chair.

"Someone came to free Artenz," said Drayfus, as he slowly made his way toward his office's door.

"Did they succeed?"

"I believe so. I saw them leave."

"I don't remember much," said Irek.

Drayfus entered his office. A feeling of normality infused him.

This was his place, his office, and he felt a pang at the thought of leaving it behind. But then he realized that he had already lost his office.

Mysa Lamond had taken it over.

Mysa Lamond, who should have been in his office.

Drayfus looked around and found her slumped behind his desk. The first thing he noticed was how disheveled her hair was. It made her look older, taking away most of her beauty as well. The woman had never looked so small, so weak. Drayfus made his way to her side and knelt down.

Irek appeared in the doorway. "Is she... dead?"

"No, no she's not," said Drayfus, surprised to notice regret in his voice.

He shook the body, but got no response. He tried again, uncertain why he wanted to wake her. This time, she responded, or her body did. It convulsed momentarily. Yet she did not open her eyes.

"There's something wrong with her," he noted. "I don't know what."

"There has always been something wrong with her," said Irek. "She's not human."

If not for the recent events, the bluntness of Irek's words would have been shocking. As it stood, Drayfus felt it reassuring to learn that someone else shared his thoughts about this woman.

Deficiency

He stood up and stepped away from the tormented body.

"I'm done," he said.

Irek looked at him for a moment, taking the words in. Assistants climbed and fell with their manager.

"You understand what my departure means for you?" said Drayfus. His resignation forced Irek to quit as well.

"Yes, I do," finally answered Irek. "It means that I'm done too. This day… Well, let's just say it was a pleasure working for you."

"We made a good team," agreed Drayfus. "I'm sorry all the same. You don't deserve to go this way."

"Neither do you."

"Thank you, Irek. I wasn't ready, not for something like this. Had I been, things might have been a bit different. I just don't know how I could have been ready."

There was an awkward silence.

"I'll have to call him," Drayfus said.

"Now?"

"Yes, let's do it now."

"I'll get the link ready," said Irek and left for his desk.

"Irek?"

The man appeared in the door.

"Check the status of the project first," said Drayfus. "Send me a status report on the launch, then link."

Irek nodded and left. Drayfus looked once more at the white form on the floor. Then, smiling, he dropped in his chair.

+

"Mr. Blue," answered the voice, as smooth as ever.

"Sir, this is manager Drayfus Arlsberg from the Blue Tower. I apologize once more for disturbing you. I believe you should be made aware of what has transpired."

There was a brief silence.

"Two times in one day," noted Mr. Blue.

"Yes," accepted Drayfus, annoyed that the man had taken a moment to state the obvious. "They came—"

"Are we still on schedule with the Targos deal?"

Drayfus had expected the question, but his annoyance grew with the interruption. Knowing he was departing changed his perception. Profit was indeed the only thing of importance here.

He would not miss these conversations.

"Yes sir, we are. Wave 5 is under way as we speak. Wave 4 was successful. Everything should be completed by midnight."

"That is good," said Mr. Blue. "That is very good. Good work, manager."

Praise was rare, and Drayfus took a moment to savor this one.

It would be his last.

"What did you want to report?" asked Mr. Blue, without impatience. It sounded as if he was actually interested. Good news on important projects could do that.

"There was a breach. Three individuals came in and rescued the chief coder Artenz Scherzel."

A pause.

"He's the one who escaped earlier in the day, isn't he?"

"Yes, and we believe they came in the same way Artenz was able to go out. A hole through our security. We're investigating now."

It was not quite true. Drayfus knew Irek was looking into it, although one assistant would not be able to solve the mystery.

There was an exchange of muffled words at the end of the link. Drayfus was not able to make out what was said.

"It won't be necessary," said Mr. Blue.

"What won't, sir?"

"The investigation, do not worry yourself with it. We will take care of it."

Deficiency

"I appreciate it, sir," said Drayfus, truly relieved. "It seems Miss Lamond was injured... incapacitated, at least, during the raid. She... there's something wrong with her. She's unconscious, but—"

"You can spare me the details," interrupted Mr. Blue. "Again, do not worry yourself. We will send someone to retrieve her."

The casual words left a sour taste in Drayfus's mouth. Mr. Blue was unconcerned about her. Somehow, Drayfus had thought Mysa Lamond to be an important and possibly indispensable asset.

Maybe he had been mistaken.

"Is that all, Arlsberg?"

"There is one more thing," said Drayfus. "I... following the events of today, I would like to give you my resignation, sir."

No hesitation this time.

"Good. That is good." The news had been expected. "You did some good work, and we are grateful. We will dispatch a replacement manager tomorrow morning. There will be no need for you to return."

Although expected, the acceptance was still difficult. Drayfus had been praised, and he knew it was the most he would receive. It meant his record would be clean and he would be able to find work. He could hardly ask for more.

Yet after all the work he had done, it seemed inadequate. The comments about good work and gratefulness had been formal. It was business, and Drayfus knew he had done the exact same thing to many employees over the years. It simply felt different being on this side for once.

And it made him wonder. Had he been wrong to put so much effort into results and almost none into managing his employees?

The fact that he would have greatly appreciated some heartfelt thanks seemed to say so.

Drayfus's whole career had been about climbing the ladder. The quest to the top was difficult and lonely. He certainly had not made any friends along the way.

He looked at his assistant.

Maybe one.

"Would that be all, Arlsberg?" repeated Mr. Blue.

"Yes, sir."

Drayfus unlinked rapidly, making a point to do so before Mr. Blue did.

+

Drayfus put the last of his things in the box. It was an imagram frame, flipping randomly through images of Sana and their daughter — no picture of the baby boy they had lost so many years ago.

He closed the lid of the box and made his way out of his office.

The enforcers had finally awakened, and they both looked at him as he exited. He looked down at them, resentful that they had not given him any privacy while he packed his stuff.

Drayfus noticed a box similar to his in the hallway.

"Do you want me to power down?" asked Irek.

"No, no need," said Drayfus when a thought came to him. "There's one thing I'd like to do though, before I leave."

"Yes?" asked Irek.

Not looking at the enforcers, Drayfus came to stand beside his assistant, who was sitting at his desk.

"One thing," Drayfus repeated, whispering now. "Let's have a look at the footage of what happened earlier."

He pointed at his office with his chin. He was particularly interested to see what had happened to Mysa Lamond.

"Are you certain, sir?"

"You don't have to watch it," noted Drayfus. "Simply bring it up."

Irek was curious, excited in fact. The assistant was not going anywhere.

It took a moment, but Irek collected a series of videographs and brought them on his monitor. Drayfus asked him to run through the

Deficiency

recordings, one at a time, from the moment the intruders entered to the moment they made their escape.

The infiltration didn't last long. The intruders came from under the tower, from the Underground. It was surprising how well they knew the building, how quickly they made it to the top, knowing exactly where to go, as if they had a map, as if they were guided.

Evidently, there was a person who could have helped them: Marti. Drayfus knew now how competent the man had been.

Once the man with the stunner shotgun turned the corner toward Drayfus's office, the footage was harder to watch. Drayfus remembered clearly how he had felt, the panic, the chaos.

The blast of the weapon was surprising, even if its destruction was visible all around. The enforcers were flattened. Irek was propelled out of his chair with terrible force. Drayfus himself was spared simply because of where he had stood. The second blast followed almost instantly. It was strange to see his own body fall to the floor. The man with the shotgun had been proficient and his aim good. Irek and Drayfus had been collateral targets, nothing more.

Then the three intruders had made their way to the office. The man with the shotgun, shorter and stouter, was in the front. When they entered the office, the black man went directly toward Artenz, who was on a chair in front of the desk.

Mysa Lamond was defiant, standing tall beside the desk.

"Eltaya Ark," she said.

"Mysa Lamond," said the other. "Interesting."

"You will regret this."

"I don't think so."

And what took place next happened so fast that Drayfus wasn't sure he saw clearly.

"Replay that," he said. "In slow-mo."

He had a hard time restraining his smile. For his part, Irek was visibly shaken.

The assistant rewound the footage. The entry into the office, the way the third individual, a woman, never hesitated, never slowed down. As the black man went for Artenz, she went directly for Mysa Lamond. The words of their exchange were stretched and incomprehensible. Then, visible now because of the slow motion, the woman named Eltaya lifted a pistol and pointed it at Mysa Lamond's forehead. It almost touched it. There was a suppressed blast, and hair exploded as Mysa Lamond's head was kicked back. Then her whole body was thrown backward through the air. She fell into a comatose heap on the floor.

"She deserved that," Drayfus heard himself say.

+

"This is it, then?" asked Irek.

"It is," said Drayfus.

They were both holding their boxes with two hands, standing in the hallway, looking back. The door to Drayfus's office was closed. The terminal at Irek's desk powered down.

"I'll miss this place," said Irek.

"I think I will too," said Drayfus, doubts lingering. He had been in this tower for a little over five years. He'd hired Irek during his second year. He remembered little about his first assistant, a woman in her late sixties. She never said her age, but it had been on her file. She had hated Drayfus from the beginning, had not done well under his style of management.

"I almost wish I knew what this whole thing had been about," said Irek.

There was a part of Drayfus that also wanted to know.

"It's better this way," he answered.

"You're probably right. Do you know if it has been resolved?"

"I doubt it," said Drayfus. "And I'm glad I won't be there in the end. Let's go."

Deficiency

Manager and assistant walked down the corridor together, toward the exit of the Blue Tower.

- . . . Insurgence

This place might once have been lively and glamorous. A rich street, with massive buildings, owned by some of the most powerful corporations. Maybe.

It was hard for Irbela to imagine such a time. Her surroundings wore the weight of abandonment. The constant gloom infected everything and drained courage little by little. The city had moved up, leaving these streets behind, building on them, burying them with a forsaken past.

Following the earlier debacle, Irbela had thought they were done with the Underground. They had lost two members. One had completely disappeared, his body gone without a trace in the darkness. The other ended up in two pieces, but somehow, they had been able to bring him out.

After making it to the surface, they had fast-traveled in the carrier, north toward the center of the Factory district and the junction of the four quadrants. They dropped and went down, level by level. They were now on level 10 and Irbela was at the head of her squad, trying to keep up with their officer. She knew this was the deepest you could go and still be in touch with the surface. Even now, in certain places, words of warning blinked on her eye-veil as the connection to the Sphere broke.

Obviously, she did not want to go on, but it was not for her to challenge the goal of the mission.

"Nothing ever fazes my Bela," she remembered her father murmuring in her ear. As she grew up, from childhood to becoming an enforcer, he had encouraged her this way on innumerable occasions, building her confidence and determination. She greatly admired him. She missed him, especially today.

As much as she had always thought of herself as invincible, or close to it, Irbela had to admit that she had finally found her weakness in the Underground of Prominence. It was not only the encounter in the dark, although that certainly took a toll. Simply put, things were unnatural down here. The deeper they went, the longer they stayed, the more she felt as if she would never see the sky again. They were not creatures of darkness.

There was little reassurance in the fact that she was not the only one feeling out of place. Earlier, she had overheard some of her squadmates chatter between themselves, thinking they could not be heard. Her sound-inc add-on had cost her many months of salary, but down here, the stillness helped demonstrate its full potential.

Three soldiers had been dragging behind and shared their doubts about the mission. Not one of them knew why they were here. This happened occasionally, but when combined with the deepness of the Underground, with the events of the day, it shook even the bravest of souls.

Irbela could easily have reprimanded the squad, and maybe she should have. She was the senior enforcer, below the officer. It was evident that the lunatic bionic who was their leader did not much care about them. So, discipline fell on Irbela's shoulders.

She did not reprimand them, though. Instead, she sent a few encouragements their way. After all, she shared their concerns, and although she was senior, she would not lead with hypocrisy.

Her decision was made: she would not become a bionic. Throughout the past hour, she had envisaged other avenues that could be interesting to her. Nothing spectacular, but seeing Okran Delaro and the state of his mind had convinced her that what he had was not what she wanted.

As for the officer himself, Irbela could still not believe his behavior and the lack of importance he put on life. She would address that once the mission was completed.

Ahead, the silhouette of the bionic was revealed by the torch on Irbela's helmet. He was standing by a panel, opened and exposed, and probably in the process of unlocking yet another door. A large rusted sign on the wall showed that the door opened on more stairs.

"Are we going deeper?" she asked.

The bionic ignored her.

She heard her squadmates stop behind her. Nervousness showed in the way they moved, in how they slid their feet and could not stay still.

Irbela looked at her superior and realized she hated the man. It was sudden and unexpected. There were many people over the course of her career with whom she had had disagreements or conflicting personalities.

This was something more. There was something inhuman about Okran Delaro, something fanatical.

A thought came to mind.

Was he being honest with them? Would he go as far as deceiving them to attain results?

"Why is this target so important?" she asked.

Once again, the officer ignored her.

Irbela saw on her eye-veil that the connection to the Sphere was still weak and intermittent. She looked behind, where the passageway in which they stood connected with a larger street. There, the connection had been stronger.

She stared back at the officer.

Deficiency

He was having difficulties. The door probably used an old protocol, one that he would have access to... if this was legitimately part of their mission.

This was the sign Irbela needed.

She turned around and made her way between her squadmates, who stared at her. She kept silent.

Once she reached the larger street and saw that the connection with the Sphere was stronger, she linked directly to her supervisor. He answered immediately, as he always did. He was one of those who lived for their work.

"Steron," he said. Answering with his surname was a habit he had never let go of, although the combination of b-pad and eye-veil clearly showed his name and profile card.

"Zattar." Irbela liked the habit and used it herself.

"Zattar? This is unexpected."

"It is. The link is unreliable, so I'll relink if the connection is lost."

"Noted. Where are you?"

"Level 10."

"What are you doing down there?"

"That's what I need to know," Irbela said. "Not know—confirm. I have reasons to believe we've been led astray."

There was a moment of silent.

"Led astray," repeated her supervisor. "Be careful what you say."

"Noted," she said, realizing it was yet another word she borrowed from her supervisor. "Can you confirm?"

"I'll check. Give me a moment."

Irbela was about to look back toward the passageway when a powerful hand grabbed her arm. She felt the strength of the grip through her armor.

She turned and there stood Okran Delaro, his black helmet removed, his impassive and perfect face too close for comfort, rage whirling in his eyes.

"What are you doing?" he asked in his robotic and annoying voice.

"Be careful," she said, looking at his hand on her arm.

He looked at her. She stared back. He squeezed, and Irbela could not help being impressed by the supernatural strength. If he wanted to, he could probably break her arm just by squeezing.

She let the pain feed her own frustration.

He let go.

"What are you doing?" he repeated.

"Why are we here?" she asked.

"Are you questioning orders?"

She did not answer.

The bionic Okran Delaro was thinking. She could see it in his face. He was debating whether he should strike her, she suspected, calculating the repercussions with the precision for which he was known. She was another statistic for him.

"You should be back to headquarters," came the voice of her supervisor. "For redeployment. It is Global, state 95%. You didn't know?"

Irbela smiled.

"Indeed," she said. "I didn't. Thank you." Her next words were louder. "We'll be heading back now."

"Okay," said her supervisor. "Be quick."

Irbela unlinked.

Okran Delaro had taken a step toward her and she met him, head high, aware of the other enforcers standing around, watching.

"What now?" she said. "What will you do? Kill a master enforcer? Please give it a try."

There was no doubt who would win, yet Irbela felt she now had the upper hand.

"Global state 95," she said out loud, sharing the situation with the others. "You didn't think it worth mentioning, did you?"

The officer's square jaw tensed, his mouth slightly open, his lower teeth showing.

Deficiency

"We're heading back," said Irbela. "With or without you. Fall in rank, soldiers."

The enforcers did, hesitantly at first, then with the discipline they were known for.

Irbela stood her ground one moment longer, looking into the unblinking eyes of the bionic.

Finally, she stepped back.

"Let's go," she said to the others.

The bionic did not move and did not follow. As she turned her back to him, Irbela thought he might strike her from behind.

As they retreated, she took the lead and tried to hide her shaking hands. Behind, she heard the metallic sound of the bionic's boots on the ground.

He went in the opposite direction.

| - . . . . To the Pillar

The Underground's darkness weighed on Keidi as she sped down its streets. Fear hung over her, making her wish she could go even faster.

No one was following her, and yet she wanted to reach her destination as fast as possible. She wanted to put Prominence City behind, the disappearance of Detel behind, her whole life behind.

She wanted to start anew, Artenz by her side.

The map on her mini-vid showed that she had to follow this street for a bit longer. There were obstructions ahead. More obstructions. Time was 1929. Almost an hour since she'd picked up the uni-racer and began her trip toward the Pillar.

Keidi was tired and terribly hungry. She didn't feel pain anymore. About 20 minutes ago, she had descended from level 15 to level 10. She had had to do this via a staircase, dragging the uni-racer with her. Not an easy feat but a necessary one.

She worried, had worried for a while now, that the exertion she had been subjecting herself to would hurt the baby growing inside her.

But there was no other way. She needed to reach safety, or the baby would never be born. She hoped it would never see Prominence and all its corruption.

Looking at the map, Keidi realized she was getting close to her destination.

Deficiency

She decelerated as the end of the street approached. The headlight of the uni-racer unveiled a pile of debris ahead. The wall of a building had collapsed into the street. Keidi stopped the vehicle and stepped down. She looked around and found a niche in the rubble. She hid the uni-racer under it. The map instructed to continue on foot.

She zoomed out the map and confirmed that she was at the center junction of the Factory district, where quadrants L, M, N, and O met.

From here, she had to go down.

The map provided a surprising amount of detail. Keidi zoomed in and followed the path, now using her w-pad to light her way. The map took her around a pile of debris and into a building. The entrance was a gigantic opening. Its double doors rested flat on the ground, massive things made of rotting wood. The place felt ancient, its walls made of rocks, the lights on the ceiling long plastic cases. Stuff of antiquity.

If only she had water. Anything to eat or drink, really. If only she had thought to pack some snacks in her own bag, as she had done for Artenz. She always thought about Artenz before herself. Tarana's voice resonated in her head, giving a sermon about the importance of self-care and putting oneself first. Keidi liked the idea—she just had never been able to apply it.

She wished she had now. Also, she thought that it would be nice if once in a while, Artenz would prepare lunches. Although, could she trust him to pack it properly? Probably not. She knew his mind would most likely be on his work, the day ahead, and he would forget something.

She smiled. It always surprised her how much she loved this person, with all his small imperfections.

She reached metal double doors, pushed them open, and entered a large room. The ceiling was many stories high, and in front, large steps went down. On both sides, balconies provided elevated views of the room. It must once have been an impressive place.

The sound of her feet on the steps echoed in the vast space. At the bottom, she turned left and came to another door. Here the map stopped, but offered a recorded message. Keidi activated it.

"Keidi," said Marti's recorded voice, "behind this door you will find a geared traction elevator, built in the first millennium. It is powered by an electric motor that can be activated by using the panel on the right side of the sliding doors. I have included a manual in case you need to familiarize yourself with its mechanics. Your b-pad will be able to connect to the panel and override the controls, as you would with an air-tube. Note that the elevator is one of many owned and operated by the Ks, inhabitants of the Pillar you will be using for your escape. It will bring you to level 1. As soon as you activate it, the Ks will know you are coming and will be waiting for you at the bottom. You will have to negotiate your passage to the Low Lands. You have credits to use, but in the eventuality that they want more, give them the name of Red Dragon and ask them to get in touch with me. They will know how. Good luck."

The voice stopped abruptly. Keidi was impressed by everything Marti had been able to do for her, how he had plotted her route and included instructions every step of the way. It was mind-boggling, as if he had known ahead of time that she would be in this situation.

She crossed the door and found herself in a wide corridor with arched windows on both sides. Booths, where she could imagine sellers putting all kinds of wares on display. She found the elevator doors at the end of the hall. There, Keidi decided to have a quick look at the manual. If she was to hack into this device, it was better to know what she was getting herself into.

She browsed through the manual, skimming the content. She was humbled by the device. It was old, so very old, yet ingenious and almost elegant in its simplicity and efficiency. Why this type of elevator had been put in place here, it was hard to say. Keidi doubted it was original to Prominence. It didn't look old, just crude. Maybe because it

Deficiency

was the only technology available down here. Maybe because it was unknown to most, and so allowed the Ks to maintain control.

Keidi didn't feel confident about taking control of it, but trusted Marti that it was the best, if not the only, way forward.

She took out the connector cable and joined her w-pad to the panel.

It didn't work.

The connection did not happen.

Keidi listened once more to Marti's message. He had said it should work normally, with the b-pad!

Connecting the mini-vid to the b-pad, she tried again... and got the same result.

What was wrong?

Keidi returned to the manual. It took a while before she finally found a small diagram she had missed previously. It showed that the panel she was trying to connect to with her b-pad didn't touch the circuit. The buttons on the panel were plastic and thus did not allow electric current through. She needed to remove the panel and bypass the plastic layer.

She rummaged through her bag and found what she needed to remove the panel. It took longer than she wanted. Even though she felt alone in the world down here, her fear spurred her on.

It was not easy to concentrate. Fatigue plagued every part of her body and her head spun, either from tiredness or hunger. Or both.

After removing the panel, Keidi touched the connection cable to the circuit inside. Instantly, the b-pad reacted and her mini-vid responded.

She was in.

```
Fortis Company. Elevator Model F4-0012-91204
```

At that moment, a noise echoed from afar, as if something heavy had fallen. It was followed by another sound, this one similar to a shout. It chilled Keidi and almost made her drop her equipment.

Automatically, she turned off the light on her w-pad and disconnected the cable from her b-pad. Then she made her way back through the large room, all the way to the entrance of the building, where she peeked outside.

Far away, she made out the pile of debris where she had hidden the uni-racer. Beside it stood a single individual, his head high, radiating confidence, looking left, then right. No light.

Keidi's heart skipped a few beats.

The enforcer took a step, and in the darkness, Keidi was able to make out the even darker sphere that was his helmet. This was the man who had shot Styl.

+

This isn't possible, thought Keidi, numbed by the sight.

How had he found her?

Move, she told herself.

But she couldn't. She felt defeated. Utterly drained. Nothing left. She wanted to cry.

It's not over, she tried to convince herself. *Not yet. Think about Artenz. Think about the baby.*

She could not quit. Not now. Not so close.

Keidi disappeared inside the building, made her way back to the elevator. Her eyes had adjusted to the darkness so she did not need her w-pad to see. There was a faint and constant glow, even this deep under Prominence. Keidi did not know if it was the sun, painstakingly making its way down, or something else completely. By the elevator, the darkness was deeper, almost complete.

She felt along the wall, found the cable, and connected her b-pad once more to the circuit.

```
Fortis Company. Elevator Model F4-0012-91204
```

Deficiency

No prompt.

Had there been one the first time she connected? Keidi could not remember.

How did Marti think she would activate the elevator without a prompt?

Keidi looked back, toward the building's large room. She had closed the door to the hallway, but saw a probing light under it, coming from the other side. Quickly, she browsed through the manual.

Did not find anything.

Calm now, she told herself. *Think, think!*

She returned to the b-pad and the circuit.

```
Fortis Company. Elevator Model F4-0012-91204
```

She tried a simple information command and to her surprise, the prompt appeared.

```
Info
Do> Info
Command unknown
```

The command was unknown, but at least she had found the prompt. Now, she could experiment... with enough time, she could figure this out. But she didn't have time.

Looking quickly over her shoulder, she saw the moving light under the door. Her fingers shook as she typed on the mini-vid. She tried a few commands, without success, until:

```
Open Doors
Do> Open Door

Door opened
```

And the elevator's two metal doors slid open, creaking loudly. As they hit the inside of their pockets, a sound reverberated all the way down the hallway, and there was no doubt that the enforcer had heard.

Keidi turned toward the elevator... to find that the shaft was empty. She felt it more than she saw it. There should have been a cabin there, into which to step, but there was nothing.

Only emptiness.

Keidi put her head over the edge and looked down and saw absolutely nothing. Behind, she heard heavy steps, armored feet on the ground.

She turned on the light of her w-pad and put her wrist over the opening, pointing down.

Her heart sank.

As she had expected, there was no sign of a cabin. Ahead, in the middle of the shaft, two large cables. Too far to reach, except by jumping. She knew the elevator went down 10 levels. A fall would certainly mean death.

She looked back.

The door at the end of the hallway opened, and the enforcer appeared. Keidi turned off the light of her w-pad. Without thinking now, she disconnected from the panel, put her equipment in her bag, her bag on one shoulder, and slid over the edge. Her feet tried to find a hold, but there was none.

The enforcer made his way toward her. She was halfway down the shaft, her chest still on the floor, her legs dangling. The strobe light flashed across her face and blinded her momentarily.

The enforcer's steps stopped. Instantly, the beam of light came back and stopped on her face. Keidi looked down, away from the powerful light.

"There you are," echoed a voice, followed by quick steps.

Keidi did not know what to do. Should she let the enforcer take her and hope to escape later? Or should she push herself from the ledge and try to grab the cables?

Deficiency

At that moment, the motor of the elevator roared from above. The doors slid closed and would squeeze her if Keidi didn't move. The strobe light of the enforcer was aimed at her and provided light. She saw the cable vibrating. One of the doors hit her right shoulder. Keidi turned back toward the inside of the building and…

The enforcer with his dark bubble of a head was upon her. Extending a hand, he grabbed one of the doors and forced it open. The second door slid away as well, its mechanism bound to the opening door.

"Let her go!" suddenly came a voice from down the hallway.

Keidi's heart skipped a beat.

Styl!

The enforcer never hesitated. Keeping the doors open with one hand, he unclipped a pistol from his leg with the other. The weapon automatically charged at his touch.

Keidi climbed up, grabbed the hand with the pistol. She would not let the enforcer shoot at Styl again.

The enforcer turned her way and let go of the pistol, grabbing her arm instead. The grip was painful, robotic in its strength. He pulled Keidi up, out of the elevator shaft.

Keidi made the decision then that she would not be caught.

She looked into the helmet of darkness and saw eyes staring back at her. With her second hand, she grabbed the collar of his armor and pulled it toward her. At the same time, with both of her feet, she pushed herself away from the ledge. Caught by surprise, the enforcer lost his balance.

Together, they fell into the shaft.

| - - Caged

The pain lancing through her lower back confirmed she still lived. Keidi lifted her head and opened her eyes to opaque darkness. She pushed herself up and realized that she was on top of the enforcer's body.

Fighting a rising panic, she pushed herself away and fell on her side. Free of her attacker's embrace, she scrambled to her feet, took a step, and froze as her hand came in contact with an unmoving metallic surface.

She spun around and put her back against the wall. She waited for the man to stand and come for her, but he did not move, did not make a sound.

Keidi feared activating the light on her w-pad but did it anyway.

The pale glow revealed a surprisingly small space, four metal walls, with the only escape located high above. Cables were attached to the floor and disappeared above. In front of her, the enforcer's body was an inert heap. The black sphere was not on his head. It had probably come off during the fall or at impact. It rested in a far corner, on the other side of the body.

She slid to the right and noticed that the man's neck was bent at a sharp angle. She breathed relief. Then she noticed that one of his eyes

Deficiency

was open and glassy, yet it stared directly at her. A pale light shone inside.

He's not human, she thought. *He could awaken any minute.*

She looked up. The cables swayed gently. It had been a long fall, and Keidi felt incapable of climbing back up. Her body hurt all over, and exhaustion threatened to bring her down. Pain flared in her ankle.

At that moment, something beeped, and Keidi jumped in surprise. The sound had come from the enforcer.

Her fear told her to stay where she was, but Keidi knew she had to move, had to make the most of the advantage she had.

She suspected that the man, or the machine, was rebooting. This could provide her minutes, or seconds.

Let's assume the worst, she thought and moved closer.

The light in his eyes was spinning, unfocused, waiting for its system to restart and direct it.

What can I do?

Keidi looked up again. Or was there another way? She brought her w-pad closer to the enforcer and that was when she saw it, on the side of his neck: a port, located in the spot where a b-pad usually appeared.

The implant was round, wider than a b-pad, more advanced possibly. She had seen something like it once or twice before. Here was her opportunity.

Taking out her cable, she connected it to the implant. Then, as she was pulling out her mini-vid, she saw movement from the corner of her eye.

Or did she?

She scanned the body, but the enforcer was immobile.

I'm imagining things, she thought as she turned on the compact monitor. It showed a fairly fancy interface, at the middle of which appeared basic information about the man.

```
Bionic Prototype: Destroyer
Subject: Okran Delaro
```

S.C. Eston

```
Property of Brains Co., a Prima Division.
S/N M24-V08-T102-N009349562
```

The only thing Keidi knew about Brains was that they specialized in robotics. She had always imagined these were domestic: tiny automated helpers that cleaned or repaired, that offered company or emotional support. Maid-bots or fix-bots, chat-bots or companion-bots.

But the word "bionic" suggested something much more advanced and dangerous. Keidi tried to remember what she had heard about bionics, but the only word that came to mind was "cyborg"—a word mostly associated with enhanced military personnel or mercenaries, individuals who elected to sacrifice their humanity for fighting upgrades.

Although she had already suspected the man to be half-machine, seeing it confirmed on her mini-vid added to her growing agitation.

She studied the interface and had to admit she had never seen anything like it before. No prompt. Keidi tried to interact with the words, but nothing happened. She looked for hidden menus or functions, but without success.

Suddenly, one of the enforcer's hand lurched up. Keidi jumped and scrambled away, which tore the cable from the man's neck. As she reached the opposite wall, heavy silence greeted her.

The enforcer was motionless again.

I've got to do this, thought Keidi. Although she had no idea if it would work, it seemed the only course of action.

She approached Okran Delaro and reconnected. It felt good to know his name. It made the enforcer more human, somehow.

The same information came back on her mini-vid. Anxious to take control, Keidi tried routines she knew, entering one after the other, at random. She first needed to get access to the platform, so she could make herself an admin user.

Deficiency

At the third routine, she made a mistake and entered gibberish. Her fingers entered words faster than her brain could think of them. A few moments later, she tried another command and realized that she had already entered it.

This isn't working. I need a plan.

Artenz often said she was the calm one. He would not think so right now.

"All right, all right," Keidi said, the sound of her voice grounding her. "What do we have here?"

The main problem was that she did not know what she was connected to. But surely, she must have dealt with something similar before. She had never seen the device, but the location, on the side of the neck, hinted at its nature. The corporations were pushing hard for the b-pad. She had always assumed the final goal was control, but here was a different result: a supersoldier.

Keidi realized she had been concentrating on the wrong information. The most important word on the screen was neither Brains nor bionic, it was prototype.

Excited now, Keidi entered the first of a series of routines to take over brain-pads. If this machine man was a prototype, there was a chance that his protocol would be borrowed from an already deployed pad.

The first routine did not work. Neither did the second. As she started entering a third, the hand grabbed her arm.

+

Before she realized what was happening, the enforcer stood, lifting her with him. The grip on her arm was painful, and she dropped her mini-vid. Only one of her feet touched the ground, and with it, Keidi pushed away. The hand did not let go.

The eyes of the man-machine searched for her, but with difficulty. The head balanced precariously at the end of his broken neck, bouncing against his chest. Still, the enforcer twisted his body sideways and caught a glimpse of her.

Reflexively, Keidi punched the head and sent it spinning. The hand released her and she moved to the side, ignoring the protests of her ankle. She found herself against a wall with nowhere to go.

The hand that had grabbed her now held the head, moving it around. From the neck protruded Keidi's cable, at end of which spun her mini-vid.

That's my only chance, she thought and lunged forward, trying to stay close to the floor, hoping to use the enforcer's confusion to regain what little advantage she had.

She caught the mini-vid in midair and quickly completed the third routine. As she did so, she tried to stay behind the enforcer, out of sight, but he was onto her. His free hand reached out, and she barely evaded his grasp. On the screen, nothing happened.

Keidi tripped and fell to her knees. She slid back from the bionic, holding the mini-vid at arm's length. Then, when the hand missed her again, she moved forward and entered another command. As she did, a knee connected with her chest, taking her completely by surprise and knocking all the air out of her.

She flew backward and hit the wall. Instantly, the enforcer tackled her, crushing her. His movements lacked precision but made up for it in brute force. As he stepped back, his hand came again, and Keidi knew she could not escape.

So she tried to catch the mini-vid, but missed as it danced at the end of the cable. Weird noises resonated surprisingly close to her ear. She realized with horror that the head was now pressed against her shoulder and the thing was trying to talk. The mouth moved and produced disturbing noises that made no sense. And yet, Keidi could distinguish mockery in them. The bionic knew he had her.

With incredible force, he pushed her against the wall, smashing her cheekbone against the metallic surface. Desperately, Keidi blindly grasped in the last direction she had seen the mini-vid.

Deficiency

And miraculously, she caught it. As she lifted the device, she noticed that her latest command had worked: a prompt now appeared on the screen!

B-pads could not be shut down, so the normal commands to do so would not work. But a technician often needed to power down a device to tinker with it, to fix it. There were ways to put the b-pad to sleep.

Keidi stopped resisting, letting the enforcer believe she had given up. The strange voice tried a few more words and then, her ruse seemed to work and he took a step back.

Bringing the mini-vid up with her second hand, Keidi entered a command:

```
>>> Suspend System
```

The bionic noticed the device in her hand and with a closed fist, struck. The punch caught her above the left breast and Keidi felt herself lift in the air and collide with the wall. Still, the man-machine held on to her with his other hand. As she fell down, fighting the flaring pain in her shoulder and finally admitting defeat, Keidi thought of Detel, of Artenz, of her baby. She ached to see them.

She...

The grip holding her weakened, and she found herself on her knees. Above her, the distorted voice faded away in a creaking lamentation.

Keidi dared a glimpse. In the weak light of her mini-vid, now flat on the floor, Okran Delaro was completely immobile. Unbelieving, she closed her eyes, covered her face with both hands, and half-laughed, half-cried with relief.

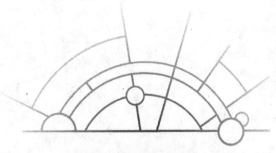

Segment E

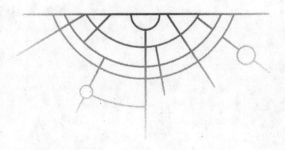

*"Let it be known:
the Red Dragon has awakened."*

*Anonymous message sent through the
data-sphere*

| - - . Deficiency

Artenz could not grasp the sight in front of him. He was alone, seated at a round table in one of three rooms of a pub located at the top of Pillar H. Around, other tables were spaced randomly, each with four to six chairs. It was early, and the place was empty.

He stared through a glass window which angled outward, its top farther away. On the other side, clouds floated against the underside of the Slab, on which stood Prominence: the city where Artenz had been born and raised and had lived. Until now.

The fact that he was seated in one of the four massive columns holding the city in the air boggled his mind.

The clouds hugging the Slab did not hide it completely. Ahead, it went on and on, as far as he could see. Eltaya had explained that the clouds were an artificial fog and pushed out the side of the city by gigantic fans. It was another piece of the complex illusion surrounding Prominence City.

Far ahead, another pillar supported the city, and Artenz could not see its base. It was Pillar K.

Keidi was supposed to be in that pillar by now. Like the scenery, the idea that Keidi was over there boggled Artenz's mind. Artenz had asked and asked, but there was no way to know if Keidi had reached her destination safely. The inhabitants of the different pillars could not communicate easily.

Artenz would only know if Keidi had escaped once he descended all the way to the ground and reached the Low Lands. There, he would need to make his way to the base of Pillar K, something that would have been a challenge, if not for the fact that Eltaya and Kazor would guide him. Xavi and Praka had families to return to, while Eltaya had no one, and Kazor faced a complicated situation with limited access to his daughter. For them, lingering in the Low Lands presented a viable option to lay low while the Global state faded.

Artenz was grateful for their help, and now that he knew some of the revelations contained in Detel's paper, he agreed with the precautions taken by the Banner.

Also, he could not wait to share what he had found with Keidi, to let her know how right she had been. The wait was agonizing, yet exciting. Artenz had so much to tell her. Many apologies, to start. But so much more, about so many things they had speculated about over the years.

Someone came in, and Artenz turned away from the window. It was Xavi. The black man was about to take a seat, then changed his mind. Instead, he stepped close to the window and looked outside.

"An impressive sight, isn't it?"

"Scary," said Artenz, staying where he was, safely seated away from the glass, unable to see the ground below. He preferred it this way.

This early, the rays of the sun did not reach the Low Lands. Artenz realized that the days were shorter for the people living below.

"What do you know about the Low Lands?" asked Xavi.

"Not much," said Artenz. "The usual, I guess, although I hope some of it is exaggeration."

"Maybe," said Xavi. "Tell me what you've heard."

"It's a dirty place, ravaged and unkempt. A place of anarchy and corruption, without government or rulers. Run by gangs. Technology's minimal. Many are poor and uncivilized, not to say savage. Many illiterates. None are trustworthy, which is why the secrets of Prominence are kept secret. Some technologies would be too dangerous if allowed down there."

"No positive?"

"Not based on what I've heard, no, but some make a life down there, so there must be."

"They have to," noted Xavi. "Where there's hardship, there's also greatness. Some have made a good life, and many are trying to make the Low Lands better. I have several friends living there."

"You do?"

"Yes, but I'd suggest you keep with your initial plan and be on your way to the gulch as soon as you can. People don't take well to Promients trying to invade their world, as you can guess."

"We will," said Artenz.

"Keep that b-pad hidden," said Xavi. "Or have it removed."

Artenz touched the pad on his neck.

"Is there any safe way to remove it?"

"There's always a risk, but yes, it's mostly safe and less risky than keeping it. There's a mod surgeon at the foot of this pillar who is quite capable. Not cheap, but capable."

"Are credits accepted?"

"They are."

Removing his b-pad had never occurred to Artenz. The procedure scared him. It would be like losing a part of himself. On the other hand, he had seen how vulnerable the b-pad made him. It was also a link back to Prominence, a reminder of the events leading to the loss of his sister.

When reunited with Keidi, he would talk to her about it.

"Did you know that the inhabitants of the Low Lands and the Promients were once one and the same?" asked Xavi.

"I hadn't thought about it, but I guess it makes sense. A long time ago?"

Deficiency

"Before Prominence City, there was only the Low Lands. At the time, the city was known as Garadia."

Garadia: their planet, their system.

"In those days," continued Xavi, "the weather wasn't as forgiving, and the Low Lands offered shelter from winds and storms. As it developed, conflicts arose. Details are scarce, but it seems one faction decided to leave and move up. One of the most powerful, and rich, groups. It's unclear how they took control of the Slab, but they did. It decided the fate of all."

Xavi was pensive for a moment.

"There was only one city then," he added. "One city on this whole planet. The Low Lands were the first point of colonization."

"So, you also believe we're not of this world?"

"I do," said Xavi.

"So do I," said Artenz, warming up to the subject, one he rarely got the chance to discuss. "I always wanted to help in the communication effort. There must be someone out there, listening and wanting to know what happened, wanting to know how we're doing." Artenz stood and took a few steps and looked up, trying to see through the clouds and Prominence, to the sky and stars beyond. "I guess that won't happen now."

"You never know," said Xavi.

Artenz looked at the man.

"What do you mean?"

"You'll see." Xavi pointed down. Artenz followed the finger and was instantly dizzy. He took a step back, and Xavi steadied him with a hand on his arm.

It was so far down, so far away, that Artenz's brain had a hard time computing what he was seeing. The Low Lands were barely visible in the gloom. Buildings appeared as far as the eye could see in all directions, plaguing the earth and forming a tapestry of a civilization under siege, fighting to survive.

"Down there," continued Xavi, "possibilities are limitless. There are those who want to reach out to space. You'll be one of many. And even though technology's limited, it doesn't stop them from trying. Someone with your skills and education could easily forge a place. Down there, or up here."

Fighting the dizziness, Artenz forced himself to look and take it in. He would be descending soon. He might as well prepare himself.

"What do you mean, up here?"

Xavi smiled.

"There's the Slab. This community would welcome both you and Keidi. And there's Prominence." Xavi looked at him. "You must have known we'd ask. The Authentic Banner could use a good coder."

Artenz had not thought about it. He seriously had not.

His mind had been made up.

"I…" he started.

"Don't answer right away. We'll let you know how you can find us, and when you have thought it through, well…"

There was something in Xavi's voice that caught Artenz's attention. He studied the man's face and saw sadness there.

"Just know it's an option," he added.

Artenz realized Xavi was giving him a way out, an alternate escape. In case Keidi had not made it.

+

Eltaya appeared next. Xavi put a hand on Artenz's shoulder.

"It's been a pleasure meeting you," said Xavi. They shook hands. "I wish it had been under better circumstances. Best of luck to you, and if you are to return, look us up."

"I will," said Artenz, "and thank you for everything you've done."

Xavi squeezed his shoulder and went to Eltaya. The two exchanged a few words, some of them fiery. Artenz did not pry.

Deficiency

After a few moments, they settled and hugged. Xavi waved at Artenz as he left. Artenz waved back, sad at seeing Xavi leave. He did not know the man well, had only met him today, but he felt he could have grown to like him.

Eltaya sat at the table, and he joined her.

"How are you feeling this morning?" she asked.

"Better," he said. He did not see the point of mentioning his burning eyes and the continual headaches. "Worried, worried sick about Keidi."

She nodded.

"I wish there were a way to know," she said. "We'll be leaving soon."

Things were good between the two of them. Good as in normal. He felt that he could talk to her as a friend. A friend who had risked much.

Also, now that they were about to leave, she could not stop what he had put in motion. He knew Eltaya had come so he could explain what he had learned, and done.

She deserved an explanation.

"Detel wanted her research to be known," he said. "She tried to find a reporter. I didn't know, or I'd have told her about you. Then everything would have been different."

The loss of his sister still did not quite register. A part of Artenz kept hoping he would find her with their parents, having fled ahead. The other possibility, the idea that she had been captured... was too much to consider.

"I'm sorry," said Eltaya.

Artenz accepted the hand on his wrist. Eltaya patted him a few times and pulled away.

"So, Detel found someone else," continued Artenz, launching himself into the series of events as explained to him by the new Marti. "Mysa Lamond, but it turned out she wasn't a reporter. She was a mimic, working for some corporation. Or maybe on her own." Eltaya's face was attentive. "So, instead of making the information public, she ratted Detel out to the corporations. Probably for a high sum. Their reaction was quick. They raided her laboratory. Keidi went there. They cleaned the place out. They also went to her lodge, cleaned that out. They flushed her from the Sphere, completely. I... I didn't think that was even possible."

It was not entirely true. He had decided to believe that it was not possible and had never imagined that it could happen to someone close to him.

"You said this went Global," he continued. "That means many corporations want her discovery gone. I don't know what BlueTech's connection is, but there is one. And I worked for BlueTech. I helped Detel's enemies get her and take her away. I know what you're going to say. There was no way for me to know. Maybe later, I'll think that way. For now... Anyway, I think Telecore would be the one with the most to lose from what she found, but who knows? Who can say which corporations own which these days? For all I know, BlueTech could own Telecore, or maybe it's the other way around."

Unconsciously, Artenz scratched at the b-pad on his neck. When he paid attention, he could hear it hum.

"It's about the brain-pads then?" asked Eltaya.

Artenz nodded.

+

Artenz looked at Eltaya's neck. It was smooth under the collar of her shirt.

"You never had a b-pad?" he asked. He remembered that she had not had one during their university years together.

"I did, briefly, but got it removed. Many years ago."

"Good for you."

Artenz thought about Keidi, about how he had encouraged her to use it, more than she wanted. *Come to the bio-sphere,* he would invite night after night. She never liked it, always distrusted it. She would ask

Deficiency

him to go for a walk in the streets instead. She always felt the bio-sphere was unnatural.

Detel had disliked it as well, although he never understood why. Maybe she always knew.

He regretted getting his b-pad now. Detel had had more brains and kept away as long as she could. She was the smart one. When the law passed that made the b-pad mandatory, Detel received hers. His parents didn't.

They left instead.

They had it right from the beginning. All these years, he had secretly been mad at them for abandoning him and Detel. He had been 17 and she, 20. Old enough, some would say. Either way, maybe their parents had known it was the only way to make the two of them understand how important this was. Maybe they had thought it would encourage them to leave and follow? They asked, but Artenz would never have followed, not back then.

But maybe, just maybe, their departure was what had encouraged Detel to explore the pad's impacts and effects.

"What did your sister find?" asked Eltaya.

"Keidi is pregnant," said Artenz in return.

Eltaya could not hide her surprise, and her confusion. She did not say a word, not right away. Yet she was not judging. Her eyes were supportive, and Artenz appreciated it.

"It's early on," he said, as if it explained why Eltaya did not know. "It's going to be a natural birth, if all goes well."

Again, he had fought against Keidi for so long about this, and again, she had been right.

Eltaya simply nodded.

"Detel monitored Keidi," he continued. "Her life signs, her body's reaction, and the changes. I thought, all this while, that her research was about birth. It was not. It was about brains."

Eltaya pulled her chair closer to the table and Artenz. Outside, it was brighter as the day awoke. Farther inside the pub, glasses and bottles clinked. The inhabitants of Pillar H were awakening.

"Go on," said Eltaya.

"She discovered the cause of the deficiency in newborns," he said. Eltaya could not hide her interest. "It's a long paper, hundreds of pages. I didn't know anything about it. I don't understand how I didn't know she was working on this. I didn't read it all; there wasn't time. I have it here." He touched the b-pad. "Even to me… let's just say I know it is thorough. This is real stuff. She has proofs. Messages, exchanges, recordings. I think she built it over years and years. And not long ago, she was ready to make it public."

Artenz paused, thought about what he had put in motion, about the last instructions he had left with Marti. His b-pad showed 0709. It would begin in 21 minutes.

"I'm not sure I understand everything," he continued. "Actually, I know I don't. It's complicated and it involves many things: the processed food we eat, the polluted air we breathe, the radiation we ingest. In the end, it comes down to one main cause: the b-pads."

"How?"

"It's in the paper. Its use, you see, with everything else, it degrades brain cells. When it is implanted and used… well, it acts as a powerful catalyst. No, more than a catalyst. An awakener. Medicine thought it had eradicated the negative effects of all those other elements, while in reality, they lay dormant. The b-pad awakened all of it, and then accelerated everything. And because the deterioration is so rapid, it's irreversible."

Again, Artenz found himself scratching at the pad in his neck. How stupid he had been.

"By implanting b-pads at birth, corporations are increasing the cycle of blank babies," observed Eltaya, frustration surfacing in her voice.

Deficiency

"Greatly," said Artenz. "It was probably the worst decision ever made."

"But they don't care," she added.

"It's worse than that," said Artenz. "We all know about blank babies. Under Prominence Law, every time a blank baby is born, they dispose of it. And try again. They tell us this is a rare occurrence, but Detel uncovered it's NOT rare. Almost 60% of babies are now blank."

"They're hiding it."

"Yes, that's the real reason they want to keep babies for the first year, not because it's safer. It's so they can replace them and no one knows."

"This is mass-scale infanticide!"

Artenz swallowed and nodded.

"There's more?" asked Eltaya.

"Yes."

"Go on."

"Recently, they started testing with suggestions: implanting urges, inhibitions, even overriding a person's conscious decisions. Yes, that bad." Artenz's voice broke as he explained what he knew. "Babies born today are so deeply linked and dependent on their b-pad that a user with high enough access could potentially suggest a life choice, or even..."

"Control them."

"Exactly. Force them to do, or not do, anything."

A seething rage replaced Eltaya's initial shock. The look in her eyes scared him.

"Don't tell me there's more?" she asked.

"Just a bit, and this is the worst part. Detel's paper explains that the blankness can be treated. Easily."

"By removing the pad," concluded Eltaya.

"Or not implanting any. Detel estimates that over 80% of the blanks could recover."

"But corporations want to control and to control..."

"They need the pads, and they've gone too far already. There's no turning back, and they'll continue to push to make them mandatory, everywhere, for everyone."

For a few moments, Eltaya pondered the information. Artenz welcomed the pause. Somehow, saying everything out loud made it more real and much worse. Every detail was sinking in, each one more unbelievable than the last.

"And Detel wanted to stop the corporations?" finally asked Eltaya.

"Maybe," said Artenz, "but this is not why they got her."

Eltaya lifted an eyebrow. "Why then?"

"The corporations... You see, they know. They have known about the risks of the b-pads for years, about their role in creating blanks. Detel's paper proves this, demonstrates that they had known while developing the first and second generations of pads."

"Wrist and palm?"

"Yes," said Artenz, "especially the palm-pad. The device was connected directly into the neural system. The effects were clear, and manageable. Yet they experimented some more and with the b-pads, the results were off the charts. The project was cancelled, modified and tested again. And cancelled again. It was extremely costly. Finally, they decided to go ahead, omitting the testing phase altogether."

"All about credits, to the detriment of all." Eltaya shook her head. "This goes deeper than any of us could have imagined. Will you share what you have with us? With the Banner?"

"I've got a copy for you, yes."

He did not like the way Eltaya stared at him. "What about you and Keidi? How do you fit in all this?"

"I..." Her eyes bore right into him and he knew he could not lie, or hide anything. "Detel was helping us, helping Keidi have a natural birth."

Eltaya absorbed the information, but did not comment. He knew what she was thinking. He had thought about it himself. Had Detel

Deficiency

used them? Had she convinced Keidi to go with a natural birth so she would have a case subject?

It was a possibility, and Artenz had already decided that it did not matter. Nothing good could come from such line of thinking.

Maybe Eltaya realized the same. "Why now?" she asked instead. "Why didn't you tell me this earlier?"

She had a half-smile, possibly understanding that it was too late for her to stop whatever he had done. Either way, she was torn between frustration and curiosity.

"What have you done up there?"

Artenz answered with a smile of his own.

+

Kazor was standing to Artenz's left by the elevator gate. It was a mesh gate, the pattern of the metal bars intricate, like vines climbing along a wall.

Eltaya had gone back to Xavi, to share with him what Artenz had divulged to her and to pass along the copy of Detel's report. Artenz did not know if the information would change their plan of lying low. He hoped not.

They were in a long corridor sculpted out of the rock. The hallway was empty. Small sconces on the walls produced a weak light, electric cables going from one to the other. Artenz wished he had more time here, to get to know the people living in the Slab. He had not even talked to anyone. Eltaya and Xavi had organized everything.

"What will happen to Eltaya?" Artenz asked Kazor. "With her ghost?"

Kazor stood with his back against the wall, arms crossed. He wore a large knife, had two pistols on his belt and the stun shotgun was propped against the wall to his left.

"It's like this," he said, not looking at Artenz. "When you have a ghost, you sleep and send it away. It does errands for you. It answers messages. Does research. You wake and the ghost blends back in. What it learned is synced into your brain. That's how it works."

"But not Eltaya. She uses it while awake."

"Right. Risky business. She pushes boundaries. She experiments. She's the best of us, but one day, she'll go too far. Maybe she already has."

Artenz thought he understood. "So now, the ghost will be gone for several weeks. During that time, what will it do? Can it sleep?"

"It could, but it won't. That's not Eltaya's way."

"What is?"

"Eltaya sees this as an opportunity. Why only use one brain when you can use two?"

"What will happen when the ghost comes back?"

"That's the question, isn't it?"

The man's evasiveness aggravated Artenz. "Be blunt with me. I know her well. She risked a lot for me. I'd like to know how much danger she is in."

Kazor pushed away from the wall, and his gaze went down the corridor. Artenz looked and saw Eltaya. Kazor put a hand on Artenz's shoulder and turned him toward the elevator gate, facing away from Eltaya.

"Merging with a ghost is dangerous at the best of times," he said. "Ghosts are experimental. Nothing tested yet. Eltaya's a test case herself. When a ghost syncs back with its host's brain, there's always a chance the brain won't be able to take it. The more information transferred, the higher the risk. Necrosis. Burned cells. Part of the brain stops working, coma, death."

Artenz looked back over his shoulder. Eltaya was walking with her head high, coming their way rapidly. "She doesn't have to synchronize with the ghost, does she?"

"No," Kazor said.

But Artenz knew she would anyway.

Deficiency

+

The elevator was small; only four or five people could fit in. The gate closed. It grated against the floor and as it did, the cabin shook. The whole thing didn't feel safe.

Even though the elevator was rarely used and was under these people's control, no one came to see them away. Special privileges were required to use the elevator and the Banner, it seemed, had them.

Artenz stood at the back of the cabin, Kazor to his right, Eltaya his left. Their shoulders touched. The elevator slowly dropped. As it descended, it oscillated and even collided with the walls of the shaft. Sparks flew through the gate. Artenz wished the gate was opaque, instead of meshed. Seeing how fast they were descending made everything worse.

"Relax," said Kazor. "This will take a while."

Almost 20 minutes, to be exact. Eltaya had gone over the details prior to getting in the cabin. 20 minutes of going down!

In this contraption.

Artenz closed his eyes, which made things worse. He reopened them.

Through the gate he saw a window, a slit in the rock, slide by. It came and went quickly, but Artenz caught a glimpse of the outside. Clouds above. Cliffs far ahead. And below, far below, the houses and buildings of the Low Lands. On the other side of the decrepit city, there was something he had not expected.

"Is that dark patch an ocean?" asked Artenz.

"Not really," said Kazor, not hiding his disgust.

"It looks as if it is," said Eltaya. "A common mistake. It's known as the Black Metallic Sea."

"What is it, then?" Artenz had never seen the ocean. Only static imagraphs. And once, in the holo-sphere, he had played a racing boat game.

"Garbage," said Kazor bluntly.

"Garbage?"

"Yes," said Eltaya.

"From?"

Silence.

"Prominence?" guessed Artenz. As soon as he said it, he knew he was right. "But there's so much of it." He could not see outside anymore, but the image had seared itself in Artenz's memory. A vast wasteland, as black as petroleum, the dirty rejects of the beautiful city of Prominence. "So unfair," said Artenz. "Does no one care for those below?"

"Right," said Kazor.

Eltaya stayed silent.

Artenz lost himself in discouraging thoughts. A dangerous spiral that brought him to a conclusion that had not really dawned on him until now.

"I'm going to the Low Lands," he said.

"That you are," noted Kazor.

Artenz had not meant to say the words out loud.

"It's going to be all right," said Eltaya. "We won't leave you until it is."

"Thank you," said Artenz, "that means a lot."

Kazor and Eltaya each put a hand on his shoulder. They both squeezed at the same time before letting go. Their touch, both strong, made him feel better.

"Has it happened yet?" asked Eltaya next.

Artenz's b-pad now showed 0733.

"Yes," he said proudly, "it has and will go on for days."

| - - . . Virus

The elevator reached its full speed. It shook as it plummeted inside the Pillar. There was a sensation of falling that was not going away. From time to time, more slits in the wall allowed Artenz to get a glimpse of the Low Lands, ever closer.

His whole life was being left behind, atop the Slab, in Prominence. Some parts, Artenz would miss, already missed. His coding team. The camaraderie. The projects, even with all the unrealistic expectations from management. The satisfaction of implementing something new, something never done before.

The cleanliness of Prominence. The trams. The suspended streets and inclined walk-ways. And even the people walking to and fro.

His time in the bio-sphere and the continual connection with people via his b-pad. His profile room, even though it was nothing special, nothing like Keidi's.

Nights lying beside Keidi, looking out at the lights of the city, talking late into the night, or simply listening to music, her head on his chest and his arms wrapped around her back.

Words exchanged with his sister. Every morning. Several times a day.

"How is your day going, bro?" she would send. She always called him *bro*. He would get her message at lunch, sitting at Ilda's Cafe, alone at the table in the corner.

"Lovely. What about yours, sis?" he would ask back.

And at night, after Keidi was asleep, he would plunge into the biosphere and talk with Detel. Not long, never long, especially these last few seasons. Although she was so busy, she always took a few minutes for him.

As much as Keidi completed Artenz's life, Detel was his big sister, his guardian.

No more...

The b-pad in his neck felt like a large pimple, something he'd want to squeeze away. He pushed against it with his index finger. He now hated the thing.

Some details he would not miss. The constant bombardment of information, the ads and voices. The expectations, so high, of his work. The limitations of where you could go, when, how. No one allowed in the Plaza. One of the many places in Prominence reserved for the elites. The fact that someone always knew where you were. The lack of privacy. The feeling that something was wrong.

This last was the most important change for Artenz. The feeling that something was wrong. Similar to an awakening virus, weak at first, but constantly gnawing at him. As he'd gotten older, the sensation had grown, without him realizing it.

It had poisoned him.

Even with the unknown in front of him, Artenz felt in control for the first time of his life, free. Yet it all hung by a tread. This new feeling would vanish if Keidi was not down there, waiting for him.

She has to be there, thought Artenz. After all, she was the intelligent one, the resourceful one. Artenz could not even contemplate the idea that Keidi would not be there.

Deficiency

There was one more thing he would miss. One person. It came to him with a pang of regret, with a touch of sadness that he had almost forgotten the old man.

Marti.

Their discussions. The daring plans they had dreamed of implementing. Crazy plans for the most part. Fantasies.

But not all.

One plan, they actually were able to put in motion in those last moments Artenz had spent in the bio-sphere with his best friend, before being forced out to Hideout Plaza...

<<

```
17 minutes remaining
```

"Let's do it," said Artenz. "Can you let Eltaya know I'll be longer?"

"I can," said Marti.

Artenz turned toward his terminal and started working on the initial pieces of his newly formed plan. First, he had to reset the timer. Marti had said he could give him an extra 30 minutes, so Artenz added 20.

```
Action> Timer stop
Timer stopped

Action> Timer "0037"
Timer started

37 minutes remaining
```

Then Artenz opened his coding editor. It was a simple software that accepted symbols, words and groups of characters, before converting them into a language the machines and computers could understand. Some lines could almost be read normally.

Like any coder worth his name, Artenz had a series of add-ons attached to his editor. It included preferences, templates, auto-completes, syntax colors, spell checks, keyboard mapping, personalized layout. It was linked to a complex debugging tool, mostly written by Marti with a few of Artenz's own configurations. Many of the preferences were minor things. Any other coder trying to use his software would not be able to do so. It would take them hours to figure out how everything had been customized and organized.

Each coder needed to put together their own environment.

This one was Artenz's.

He pulled a template and created the husk of his code. It contained some initial comments, lines that would not be executed. Instead, they provided extra information, useful for later coding sessions.

He set the version, useful for tracking between changes and updates, to 00.000.0001. For the program name, he entered "secret." He typed the same value for the coder name. No need to identify himself. The date of creation appeared automatically as Year 3.4k60 Season 05 Day 11 Hour 1808.

And then the template presented an empty function.

"What do you want to do?" asked Marti.

"You'll see, you'll see. For now, just make sure Eltaya knows that we'll be a bit longer."

Little by little, Artenz added to the code. At one point, he inserted a component to access the data-sphere. "I'll need to access Detel's data," he said.

"Obviously," said Marti, standing beside him. "Link to my main module to get the coordinates."

"Same password?"

"Add 2 and you have it," said Marti.

Deficiency

Artenz did so, including the 2 after the Red!Dragon?23. The 23 represented the age Marti was when he wrote the first version of his module. "Got it."

The two of them had worked together before, and Artenz knew how the module was built, how to connect to it and call its functions.

He linked to the data, stopping for a moment to accept that this came from his sister. He wished she was here, working with him, looking over his shoulder, just as Marti was doing.

Artenz added commands to convert the data in the format he needed. Next, he executed the code in the data-sphere. It was version 00.000.0012.

```
K0pnYh7OyEzFrSWsprC5TAi4aHx6ccSxPNG5YAUb
```

So far, so good.

"I need to decrypt Detel's data," he said.

Marti still stood beside him; he did not answer. His figure was there, oscillating.

"Marti? I can't use the copy you sent me. I need to get the original data. How do I go about decrypting?"

Still, Marti's figure did not move. He was probably on the network, possibly talking with Eltaya.

Artenz exited the editor momentarily and checked the timer.

```
19 minutes remaining
```

This was taking much longer than he had anticipated.

"Marti!"

The figure came back, its contour clearer, its complexion becoming opaque.

"You need to decrypt?"

"Yes, obviously."

"You need to use a key and call a custom function."

"What is the key?"

"Can I?"

Marti moved to the terminal and took over. Rapidly, he added a few lines of code. The key was a series of random characters: L3zr3hsL3t3D. The function was called _reddgn_decrypt_AM.

"That function," said Artenz, taking back his seat in front of the terminal, "it's the first encoding algorithm we wrote together, isn't?"

"It is," said Marti.

The AM at the end stood for the first letter of their first names: Artenz and Marti. Artenz knew Marti had added some complexity to the function they had written seven years ago. He had been 30 then, and Marti close to 50.

The initial function had been simple: a series of symbols representing numbers, using a base of five. Dots, dashes, and bars. Four dots for four. One dash for five. So on and so forth.

They had used it for a long time to encrypt some of the messages they exchanged over the Sphere, thinking they were fooling higher authorities. Artenz now knew that if they had wanted to, the moderators of the Sphere could have easily decrypted their algorithm.

"You have another 30 minutes," said Marti. "I won't be able to give you much more."

"Perfect," said Artenz.

He went back to the code, added more lines and commands. He saved, compiled, tested. Got a single error message. Artenz had learned a long time ago that it was better to test quickly and rapidly as you progressed, instead of testing later, after hundreds of line of code, and find dozens of errors.

Addressing the current error, Artenz recoded, re-saved, recompiled, and retried. He repeated the steps over and over, testing only a few changes at a time. This allowed him to catch errors quickly, knowing exactly what line of code was the cause. For now, everything executed locally.

This simple iterative approach formed the basis of his plan to put this thing in place. It did not always work as smoothly as it should. You needed a little bit of luck. But it was progressing, and the time had come to test the decrypted output. The version was now 00.000.0044. He executed the program.

```
[empty]
[empty]
[[Data-Title]] The Root Causes of the Neonates' Deficiency
[empty]
[empty]
[empty]
[[Author-Information]] Detel Scherzel
[[Title-/-Occupation]] Master Biologist
[[Corporation]] Thrium Laboratories
[[Data-Creation-Date]] Day 13, Season 3, Year 3.4K60
```

Artenz stopped.

Neonates' Deficiency.

He could not help thinking about Keidi, about their upcoming child. He could not help thinking about all the other parents, all those accepting programmed birth, artificial really, without question. They needed to know.

Back to the code.

Next, Artenz linked to the Targos module. It was not an easy task to connect to the module from outside the Blue Tower, but Artenz had kept a copy of the module on his terminal. He always did, because it allowed him to have quick access to his team's projects at night, outside of the office, if he thought about some improvements. Or if he received some crazy request from management for the next morning.

He copied part of the code and reused it. Most of the code he wrote these days was reused. No need to reinvent something he had done before.

For added security, the algorithm to connect to the module changed every day, so he needed to run his program before 0900 the next day.

Plenty of time. Still, to be safe, he would test his code on the local version of the module he had. If he connected to the live module directly for testing, someone might notice the activity and raise the alarm.

Not worth the risk.

Taking the data and feeding it to the Targos module was the trickiest part of his plan. It took significantly longer than Artenz had planned. Marti checked on him on a few occasions and Artenz kept asking for a bit more time.

It's a good thing you can't sweat in here, thought Artenz. His nervousness level was high and kept increasing with each new line of code. After what felt like an eternity, everything was ready, almost. Just one more command.

To distribute, to send, to share with all of Prominence.

Artenz hesitated, though. He couldn't write it down. Somehow, he doubted if Detel would have wanted this.

Did she want to go public?

Did she want to antagonize Prominence City?

Did he?

Instead of the command, he entered *Distribute*, three times, as comments. Then he entered: *Can I do this? Is this what she'd have wanted?*

Talking to himself. Via code. From his fingers, to the screen, back to his eyes.

The version was now 00.002.0021.

He deleted the comments. Added them again. Saved and re-saved, each action increasing the version.

He was scared.

"I can't do this!" he exclaimed, frustrated with himself.

He exited the editor and checked the timer.

```
Timer expired
-28 minutes remaining
```

Deficiency

How could it be this late?

Where had the time gone?

"Are you done?" asked Marti.

"Not yet. Almost," said Artenz.

"Hurry."

Artenz had lost himself in the code, again. When coding, he often got absorbed in his work and forgot about time, about everything around him, including Keidi.

It was actually a good feeling, to be lost in the code, to go on and on, adding and creating.

He made a decision. He had come this far. He would go all the way.

He added the final command.

He changed the name of the program.

He updated the name of the coder. Thinking about it, he decided he wanted his name here, on this. He needed to have his name clearly stated.

"Done," he said.

He executed the program, which included a set time for the distribution of the information. He chose 0730 of the next day. He did not want Eltaya or anyone else to know about it before he had left the city, in case they wanted to interfere.

Hopefully, 0730 provided enough time. He could not set it to later, or the Targos module password would be updated.

He gave some instructions to Marti, telling him when it would run. He also took a minute to write a note to Keidi.

"Do what you can to give it to her, will you?"

"I will," said Marti.

"Where will you go now? What will you do?"

To this, the fake Marti smiled. "There are many possibilities. I am Red Dragon now. Come visit later. Good luck, Artenz, my friend."

Artenz was about to answer when suddenly, a fiery sensation swarmed in his head. In the next instant, he was pulled out of the biosphere.

>>

Artenz returned from his thoughts to the humming of the descending elevator. For a few moments, he felt as if he was in the holo-sphere, on an extravagant adventure simulated in tri-dimensional fictional reality.

But this was not possible. Not anymore. He was out of range. His b-pad could not connect to Prominence's network anymore. He could see the red broken symbol on his eye-veil.

Marti.

He would miss him greatly.

The man wanted to be known as Red Dragon now. Not the man — the copy.

What this Marti was, Artenz could not figure out. Not a ghost and not an artificial intelligence, although that might have been closer to the mark. Would it be accurate to say Marti had become the first immortal?

Maybe...

Artenz looked at his b-pad. The time was 0755. By now, the distribution should have reached most of its targets.

Another slit appeared in the wall, and Artenz was surprised by how close the Low Lands were. The buildings and the streets and the smoke and smog and even the noise.

So close now. So real. So raw.

Code 01.003.0083

```
// Program Information
// Version: 01.003.0083
// Program Name: Revenge for Detel
// Coder Name: Artenz Scherzel
// Date Updated: Year 3.4k60 Season 05 Day 11 Hour 1808
// Date Updated: Year 3.4k60 Season 05 Day 11 Hour 1814

// extra functions
include local:_func
// data-sphere module
include global:_data
// targos marketing module
include global:_targos
// marti custom module
include district/3:quadrant/z:user/marti424:_marti
// marti hidden module
include district/3:quadrant/z:user/reddgn:_reddgn

function main ()
[
  var dataNodes as _data_coordinates
  var DSinfo as _info
  var DSdata as _targos_data
  var X as integer

  // Retrieve data coordinate
  dataNodes = _data_convert ( _marti_DScoordinates(),
NODES )

  // Concatenate all data into a single block
  loop X from 1 to data Nodes ( _count )
```

```
[
DSinfo = _data_append ( _data_get( dataNodes( X ) ) )
]

// Decrypt data
var key as _reddgn_key
key = L3zr3hsL3t3D
DSinfo = _reddgn_decrypt_AM ( DSinfo, key )

// Do some minor tweaks and manipulations
DSinfo = _func_prepare ( DSinfo )

// Prepare data for Targos module
Loop DSinfo
[
DSdata = _targos_parse ( DSinfo )
]

// Open channels for Targos module
_targos_open_channels ( all )

// Distribute!! For Detel...
_targos_distribute ( DSdata )

]
```

| - - . . . Distribution

For the first time in a long while, he had hoped to wake without an alarm, of his own accord. It was not to happen.

Someone pulled at his blanket, then at his hand, then climbed on top of him. His blindfold was yanked aside, and small fingers forced his eyelids open.

"Dad, wake up!"

Drayfus was terribly annoyed. He opened his eyes with the intention of reprimanding his assailant, yet the sight of Chana's round, smiling face pulled a chuckle from him instead. Then he growled, a playful sound that announced what was coming next.

"No, Dad, no!" exclaimed Chana, laughing.

Drayfus grabbed his daughter with two hands and brought her tiny stomach to his lips, producing a loud noise.

"Please Dad, you have to take me to school," pleaded the girl between waves of giggles, "Mom said so. Please! She said we're late. She said so."

"If Mom said it, then I better get up."

Drayfus got out of bed, in a good mood. In a better mood, he realized, than he had been for as long as he could remember. Not having to go to work was liberating. The idea that he was about to walk his daughter to school excited him. He could finally admit the weight he had been carrying on his shoulders. How heavy, how poisonous it had been.

This new beginning invigorated him.

The previous night, Drayfus had been anxious about breaking the news to Sana. After such a long, tough day, he had not been in the mood for her temper. As expected, she'd exploded when he told her about his resignation.

"What about the baby?" she had asked with passion. "We need your salary." She hadn't cared about his bruises.

He had presented his calculations, their position, and promised that he would find a job to fill in the gaps, manageable gaps.

"I'll have more time for the baby," he argued. "Shorter working days, hopefully. More time for you, to help."

Sana took these words in. They had kept their voices low, knowing Chana was in the adjacent room. Sana's disappointment had been evident. They had often talked about the things they could do when he became a director. It had always been *when*, not *if*.

Now, Drayfus had taken that dream away.

"You'll be home more often," Sana had noted, looking at him.

He had nodded.

"Good, that's good," she had said with an apologetic smile. She never apologized. "I like it. I think I could come to like it."

Now, Drayfus splashed water in his face, pushing sleep away and welcoming the day. Standing beside him, Chana did the same, although the girl was obviously wide awake.

"What's for breakfast?" Drayfus asked.

"Bread and berries," said Chana.

"Fresh?"

"Yes. The bot made it this morning."

Drayfus could smell the bread. He smiled again. Yesterday, just yesterday, he had left the lodge before Sana or Chana were awake, off to work. Today, here he was. He had a feeling that he could quickly get accustomed to this new routine.

Deficiency

He dressed and made his way to the large dining area, Chana on his heels. Everything waited on the table, served. The new maid-bot had been a good purchase, a lot of credits, but worth it.

Drayfus took a seat and ordered his b-pad to turn on the morning news, without activating the sound. The wall in front metamorphosed into images, with a news anchor in the top right corner: Mitzel Ganzer. Around, aerial images of Prominence rotated slowly.

Drayfus liked Ganzer. When the anchor had been fired, about eight or nine years ago, and later rehired on a different channel, Drayfus had switched channels with the anchor. The man sounded and looked trustworthy. He was a known entity to Drayfus, who had met the man twice.

A ticker was scrolling at the bottom, announcing that Rakkah, the master manipulator of the Low Lands, was to be banished from Prominence. Life sentence. *Another one to the asteroids*, thought Drayfus. They would make it look as if she would go to an isolated, high-security prison, while omitting the fact that the prison was located in space. Drayfus had never doubted the result of the trial.

Forgetting the news, Drayfus gazed briefly outside. The sky between the tall verdant trees of the Plaza was painted a bright blue. Drayfus had only been in the Plaza once, for a special banquet when he'd joined BlueTech, four years previous. The ceremony had been restricted to a single garden, which had been sufficient to showcase the beauty of the restricted area. It was a privilege to have a view of the Plaza from one's lodge.

Drayfus sat and quickly went for the fresh bread. He was starving.

Halfway through his meal, Chana playing on the floor at his feet, he noticed that the images on the wall had not changed. The same news story was on. Strange. Usually, Ganzer jumped from story to story, with different imagraphs supporting what he was talking about. The aerial views still showed Prominence.

"Volume 24," said Drayfus, turning his chair toward the screen.

Sound invaded the room.

"... started at 0730 this morning," Mitzel Gazer said, his well-known voice offering small comfort. "Targos Information denies any involvement. This information was sent to us by an envoy, whose identify has been verified. As can be expected, Targos was not able to post their short communique on their billboards, inside or outside of the Sphere, which is their preferred method of communication. I confirm that this is true: Targos Information denies any involvement."

Drayfus's eye-veil showed 0811. Drayfus looked more closely at the images of Prominence City and could see nothing out of the ordinary.

"Now, the question is," continued Mitzel, "if Targos Information did not approve this piece of propaganda, how did it get out? Who posted it?"

Who? Who indeed.

The question was chilling.

Drayfus stood and took a few steps toward the wall, to get a better view of Prominence. The anchor continued to speculate on Targos's role and responsibility in the whole affair, which Drayfus ignored.

Through his home window, Drayfus was able to see hundreds of billboards and screens, scattered through a large portion of the Glass District. This was Quadrant C, and the Plaza appeared farther away. It was a beautiful sight, especially with the rays of the sun shining from the left. But something was wrong.

Not with the buildings.

The billboards!

They were all the same.

All of them showed scrolling text. It was not possible for Drayfus to read what it said because the letters were too far away. It was enough for him to instantly realize the scope of what was happening.

Quickly, he made his way to another window.

"Dad?" asked Chana.

"Drayfus, what's going on?" asked Sana as she entered the room.

Deficiency

Drayfus put his hand on the transparent glass and looked down into Quadrant N, and then toward the Plaza. Here too, it was possible to see hundreds of billboards, each showing the same scrolling text.

"What's wrong?" asked Chana.

"I... am not certain," said Drayfus.

"What does it say?"

"I don't know. Come, we'll go see."

Drayfus picked up his daughter and took Sana's hand, leading her toward the exit. He did not take the time to put on a coat. He led his family outside, in the streets.

They took an air-saucer and descended to level 40. They came out on the streets to find the city in chaos. Chana strengthened her hold around his neck. Sana's hand held his as if her life depended on it.

Around, people screamed, shouted, while some ran in all directions. Many more simply stood, immobile as statues, heads turned upward and eyes fixated on the billboards.

Finding a spot on the side of the street, Drayfus looked around, confirming that all the billboards showed the same scrolling text.

He was amazed. This was the Targos module in action.

It worked. The launch had worked.

All the billboards, as far as he could see, were exactly the same.

One message on display for everyone to see, at the same time. Centralized. Instantaneous.

Drayfus smiled.

Could this be Artenz's doing?

It had to be. Artenz or his team had done it.

Drayfus could not help being proud. He felt happy with the role he had played in the launch of such a technology.

And then he thought about Mr. Blue, about Mysa Lamond, about how hard they had tried to capture Artenz.

Changing position slightly, Drayfus looked more closely to the scrolling words. As he did, the last word passed away and all the billboards turned black.

Had he missed it?

"Dad? What's wrong?"

"Just be patient," said Drayfus. "Play a game if you want."

He ordered his b-pad to unlock Chana's.

"Can I?"

"Yes, you can, just one, just until I can figure out what is happening."

"What's happening?" asked Sana in his ear. "This is utter chaos."

The billboards were still dark. People were stunned and murmured one to another. A heavy oppression pressed down on the streets of Prominence.

What had they just missed? A man came out from their building and walked right to Drayfus.

"Any idea what this is?" he asked.

One of his neighbors, living on the same level. Drayfus could not remember his name.

"I don't know, something with the billboards."

"Are we under attack?"

"No, I don't think so," said Drayfus.

"What then?"

"There was a message, but it is gone now."

The billboards flickered. Everywhere at once. It gave the illusion that Prominence rebooted.

The murmurs stopped instantly, the silence deafening. The message appeared again, scrolling up from the bottom.

```
The Root Causes of the Neonates' Deficiency

By Detel Scherzel
Master Biologist
Thrium Laboratories

Completed on Day 13, Season 3, Year 3.4K60
```

Deficiency

Artenz's sister!

Drayfus could not believe it. What audacity! It was a betrayal of the worst kind. It broke all of the ethical and professional codes. Artenz had developed a product and then used it without the owners' permission, to elevate his own agenda. Or his sister's.

Surprisingly, though, Drayfus could not find it in himself to be disappointed with Artenz. Shocked, certainly. Impressed, even.

There was something here. A satisfaction he felt and could not deny.

"He made it," he said. "He made it."

"What was that?" asked his neighbor.

"Who made it?" asked Sana.

"Not important," said Drayfus, shaking his head.

He realized that there was a good chance Mr. Blue had lost whatever battle he had been waging. Mr. Blue and whoever his allies were. The corporations, Mysa Lamond...

This information had to be what they had wanted to stop. There was no other explanation. And here it was, appearing on every single screen and billboard in the city.

A part of Drayfus felt vindicated.

"Serves you right," he said under his breath.

Mr. Blue had forced the deployment ahead of schedule. Had he respected the proposed plan, Wave 5 would only have started this morning. The final wave contained 100 sub-waves in Prominence itself. Hundreds of sites. Thousands of billboards.

If Mr. Blue had waited, the software would not have been distributed to those hundreds of sites.

As it stood, all sites were active and millions and millions of people could now be reached at once.

"Serves you right," repeated Drayfus.

+

For the next 50 minutes, as it scrolled up, Drayfus stood on the street and patiently read the information of Detel Scherzel's report. The depth and importance of the information sank in slowly, with difficulty. It gnawed at his initial exhilaration until it had completely morphed into loss and despair.

The data was complete. The numbers numerous. The results shocking. The consequences devastating.

This could well bring down the corporate world. Drayfus knew firsthand how far the hands of corporations went. He wondered if Prominence could even survive such a calamity...

As the last of the report disappeared, Drayfus knelt beside his daughter. His legs felt weak. Sana crouched beside him, putting a hand on his shoulder.

He let Chana continue to play her game in the virtual world offered by her b-pad. Why disturb her?

He touched the small implant in the side of her neck.

"Do you think it could be true?" asked his wife.

Instead of answering, Drayfus brought Sana close, and his daughter closer. Then he let the tears come.

+

Her room had a balcony. Not a balcony so much as a narrow platform attached to the side of the building, so narrow that even a small stool did not fit on it. It had a railing, gray, with rust crawling up on each spindle like grapevines.

There was barely space enough to stand, lean on the railing, and look over Quadrant O. A nice view, from level 40. To the right, at the end of a street, an imposing building rose: the Actus Dorion Complex. Detel had lived on its 32nd floor.

Room 32-126.

The memories were hard and the emptiness she felt deep. Zofia knew that one day, she would be all right again.

Deficiency

But not today. Not for a while.

She had spent the whole morning standing on that poor excuse for a balcony. She had not gone to work. She had not informed her supervisor. A fellow scientist had tried to link earlier, but Zofia had ignored the call.

This morning, none of that mattered.

Her b-pad showed the time as 0925. In a few minutes, it would begin again. Zofia continued to look at the Actus Dorion building while being aware of the large billboard on her left, flat against the wall, five levels high, completely black and inactive.

In five minutes, it would awaken again, for the third time this morning, as it had done at 0730, as it had done at 0830.

The first word to appear would be the title of Detel's life work.

```
The Root Causes of the Neonates' Deficiency
```

It was an exceptionally impressive paper, making Zofia proud. And the following words would bring tears. Zofia knew they would. They would simply say:

```
By Detel Scherzel
Master Biologist
Thrium Laboratories
```

Zofia had not known the extent of Detel's work. She had been aware of her partner's regular experimentations, the ones on which she worked when everyone was around. But of this paper and its discovery and chilling conclusion, Zofia had known nothing.

It was hard to guess how long it had taken Detel to write the paper. Zofia imagined that Detel might have started on it as soon as her parents left Prominence. Which was what, 20 years ago now? There had always been a purpose to everything Detel did.

Almost everything.

There was one thing Detel had not planned for.

After showing her name, the billboard would show the date on which she completed her work.

```
Completed on Day 13, Season 3, Year 3.4K60
```

Such a special day.

For the first time, Detel had come to Zofia's lodge that evening.

Something had been different about her. She had been excited, with a certain nervousness, but there had also been something else. Now, Zofia realized that Detel had probably felt elated and free. She had been enjoying her accomplishment.

And she had almost told Zofia. Almost.

They had been seated on the sofa in the main space of her lodge. They had been holding hands.

"There's something I need to tell you," Detel had said.

Her voice had been imbued with emotions, which had both excited and scared Zofia. Detel had looked her in the eyes.

"I... "

Then in that single instant, she seemed to have changed her mind. Whatever she had been about to say was replaced by words Zofia cherished to this day.

"I love you," Detel had said.

To Zofia's left, the black of the billboard came to life. The title of Detel's paper appeared.

Zofia let her eyes leave the building down the street and focus on the billboard. With tears blurring her vision, she read the words, once again. Words written by the woman she loved.

Deficiency

| - - . . . . The Low Lands

The bed had a metal frame, originally black, with most of the paint peeled off. The mattress was old, not comfortable, made of springs. Keidi sat up and the bed creaked loudly. She put both feet on the floor and was glad to feel it was solid.

The face of the enforcer still haunted her. His square features, the determination in his eyes, the hate, the rage. It was over, and yet he lingered.

She touched her forehead and found a bump. It was sensitive, the pain radiating through the gauze covering it. Her right arm was in a cast and a sling. And her ankle throbbed.

She heard approaching steps. Light from the hallway trickled in through the half opened door.

A figure appeared and pushed the door open. It was Styl, and Keidi let out a sigh of relief. The people living in Pillar K were rough and brooding, mirroring their surroundings. As much as she appreciated their protection, she did not like their company, with possibly the exception of her caretaker.

"How are you feeling?" asked Styl.

"Better, thank you."

He flipped a switch, and a bulb hanging from a tall, slim lamp came to life. The light danced on Styl's dark goggles. One of the walls was made of rock, and Keidi wondered if it was the Slab. A metallic stool and a dresser comprised the only furniture of the small space. Keidi's backpack rested at the foot of the dresser. There was no window. The place was depressing.

A figure stood behind Styl: Sinam, her caretaker.

"Time for a checkup," said Styl.

"Come in," said Keidi.

The caretaker entered. She was young and did not talk much, which did not stop her from taking extremely good care of Keidi. Styl stepped out of the way, and the caretaker came to the bedside.

"Let me see," said the young woman as she took a closer look at Keidi's head. Her touch was gentle as she removed the gauze. "Good, it's good."

"It's nice of you to say so. It doesn't feel that way."

"Most people use the elevator," remarked Sinam. "Instead of jumping."

"The elevator was my initial plan," said Keidi.

They exchanged a smile. Styl also half-smiled. He looked like a much bigger man down here. His smile was brief, though. He felt responsible for her injuries. Keidi knew that had he not reached her when he did, the enforcer would most likely have won. It was Styl's arrival that had provided the distraction she had needed.

She had told him as much, but his opinion of the situation remained unchanged.

"Let me know if it hurts," said Sinam, as she replaced the bandage.

In the past hours, Keidi had grown fond of her caretaker. Sinam must not be more than 16. She had an ethereal beauty, her large eyes shining in contrast to her dark skin and the even darker surroundings of this place.

"There, done," Sinam said, standing. "This is it," she added, "you don't need me anymore."

"Thank you so much," said Keidi. "I'll miss you."

Deficiency

The comment took the young caretaker by surprise. After a moment, she nodded shyly and said: "You could stay here."

"Someone is waiting for me," Keidi answered.

Sinam had been born in this place and had never seen the surface or the streets of Prominence. Also, she had never been to the Low Lands. A recluse life, in darkness, in the Underground and the even darker Slab.

"Come here," said Keidi, inviting Sinam into a heartfelt hug. The girl hugged back with one arm at first, uncomfortable with the closeness. After a moment, she warmed up and hugged with both arms.

"Good luck, wherever you are going," she said as she left the room.

Styl pulled the stool to where he was and sat down, putting his back against the wall.

"Ready?" he said.

"I think so," said Keidi. "I can't wait to see Artenz. I have to admit that going down scares me a bit."

"The Low Lands can be a rough place," said Styl. "But it's not all bad. I'll escort you. Once out, you'll be all right. The Dara Gulch is a safe place."

"Did you ever go there?"

"Once, to get replacement parts."

"If we make it there, you'll have a reason to return."

He smiled. "You'll make it. Danger is behind you now."

Danger was only behind because Styl was there. Had she been on her own, Keidi doubted she would have been able to navigate this place.

"Thank you for coming back," she said. It was hard to comprehend the energy spent by the Authentic Banner to help her.

"It's what we do," Styl said simply.

Keidi would not have been surprised if Styl did all this to honor the friend he had lost. Ged Briell. It was strange to know that someone had given his life for her, someone she had never met.

"You have the credits, correct?"

"I do," said Keidi.

"Everything is almost ready," he said. "Take a few moments. I'll wait outside. It's time to meet with the headsman and get you out of here."

+

Styl guided Keidi through a maze of tunnels. Hanging bulbs lighted the way. The people they encountered gazed at them, especially Keidi, as if they did not want her here. Everyone seemed poor, wearing torn or old clothing. Life in the Slab seemed difficult.

"They don't like me, do they?" she asked.

"Nothing personal," explained Styl, "they know you're going to use the elevator."

"Word goes around that quickly?"

"It does."

"Is it a problem, to use the elevator?"

"It is highly regulated. Only a select few can use it."

"Why is it that I can then?"

"The Banner is known here," said Styl. "They owe us a few favors. More importantly, though, you have the credits."

They finally reached a small door. Before knocking, Styl turned toward Keidi.

"I'll let you do most of the talking," he said. "Don't be intimidated. The headsman is a good and just man. He'll want to hear from you. And I'll be at your side."

Keidi nodded and Styl knocked.

"Yeah," a gruff voice answered.

Styl pushed the door open with his boot, and they entered a small office. There was a desk in one corner, behind which sat a sturdy man with a hanging beard and a bald scalp: the headsman and leader of Pillar K.

Deficiency

A man in his 60s, Keidi guessed. His face bore marks of a hard life. His clothing was surprisingly clean, ironed and well kept. Not a suit, but a buttoned shirt with a vest. Not the look Keidi had expected.

Strange devices, dismantled and in poor shape, covered a table in the other corner. Keidi identified one as a palm-pad.

The man did not stand, or move. Styl pointed to a chair and Keidi sat down. Styl stood behind her.

"So, you still want to go south, do you?" asked the headsman.

"If by south, you mean down, then yes," said Keidi.

"And you have the credits."

"I have some. How much do you need?"

"How much are you willing to pay?"

The man's eyes were bloodshot, probably from lack of sleep. Styl had told her that the headsman led the protectors of Pillar K himself. Following their arrival, patrols had been sent far and wide to make sure no other enforcers would be coming. The headsman had himself led many of the patrols.

As much as Keidi appreciated the headsman's help, she did not like his probing and vagueness. Styl had already told her the man would try to take as much from her as he could.

For her part, Keidi wanted to be fair to these people. They had been good to her. They were giving her a second chance. Still, she had no intention of giving away everything she had.

In his message, Marti said the fee was 150,000 credits. He had transferred 300,000, an enormous sum. Keidi had close to another 100,000 on top of that, savings she had put aside over the years. She assumed she still had access to it.

It should definitely be enough.

"I can pay 100k," she said, keeping her back straight.

"That won't do."

Keidi did not flinch under the headsman's stare.

"What about 125k?" she said.

He sighed.

"What about 200k?" he said.

The bartering went back and forth for a few minutes, during which Keidi did not back down.

"The thing is not worth operating under 175k," said the headsman, now sitting forward in his chair, both of his elbows on the desk, his chin resting on his thumbs.

"You have to understand that I need credits where I'm going," said Keidi.

"Not my problem."

There was a pause and for the first time, Styl stepped in. "Make sure you account for the bionic," he said.

"It's already ours," said the headsman.

"It'd not be if it wasn't for Keidi," said Styl. "Reselling some of the technology will bring you much."

The headsman thought about this for a moment.

"150k is the best I can do," pressed Keidi as she saw the man hesitating.

He looked at her, then at Styl.

"Plus what we agreed upon?" he asked Styl.

"Certainly. You know the Banner. We always deliver."

Keidi tried to keep her face impassive and her nervousness hidden. She wanted to leave, and soon.

The headsman pushed himself back in his chair. "So be it," he said. "150k. Let's see if those credits are valid."

+

The credits were real, and at the hour 1200, Keidi and Styl stood in front of the elevator, the headsman with them.

The elevator's cabin was small, tiny in fact. One door. It seemed made for two people only. It rocked as Keidi and Styl stepped in.

"You'll have one day, after the landing," said the headsman, standing outside. "Then the elevator will return."

Deficiency

"I understand," said Keidi.

"Good luck."

"And again, thank you, to you and all the others."

The headsman nodded and closed the sliding door. A single bulb on the ceiling provided weak and fluttering light. Through a narrow oval window, Keidi saw the headsman turn away and leave.

She held tight to Styl's arm. The floor under their feet was made of light metal, possibly aluminum, dented in a few spots. The window in the door provided the only view of the outside. It felt claustrophobic. It felt as if the whole thing could break apart any minute.

The descent was going to take more than 12 minutes. This was shocking. How far below were the Low Lands, anyway?

The elevator started with a jolt.

"How often is the elevator used?" asked Keidi.

"Almost never," said Styl.

Not reassuring. Not at all.

+

The ride was smoother than expected. After a few minutes, Keidi settled down on the floor, beside Styl, who continued to stand. She felt exhausted and drained.

She thought about where she was going, about what had happened, about Detel, Marti, and Zofia. She thought about the baby in her womb, hoping her fall had not hurt it. She felt good, healthy, even if her arm and ankle tried to say differently, even if she had run out of energy.

She wondered about the enforcer, or bionic as Styl had called him. She wondered what would happen to him. She thought about the people who had welcomed her, for a single night, into their world, just to let her go. She thought of Sinam. Good people. All of them.

She thought of her escape from the I Bot shop and pictured its owner, sitting behind the counter. She thought of Arnol, how he had almost died and returned to help her a second time.

Keidi felt proud of herself.

Proud of having escaped.

Proud of starting anew.

And afraid. She feared the Low Lands, a place known as degenerate by the Promients. What would she find down there? She was glad for Styl standing at her side.

"What does he want from the Banner, the headsman?"

"Always the same. If not credits, then technology."

"The Banner deals in technology?"

"Non-lethal only."

"Can you always be certain?"

Styl sighed. "Valid point. We do the best we can."

Keidi found it difficult to comprehend the world these people lived in. It was so different from her own reality.

"I'm glad you're here," she said.

He did not say anything.

After a few more moments, Keidi had to ask again.

"You're certain you do not know if Artenz will be there?"

"I don't," said Styl. "Sorry. I can only assume he is with Eltaya and if so, I would bet on his safety. If anyone can help him escape, it's Eltaya."

"Thank you," said Keidi.

Of everything that had happened, losing Artenz would by far be the worst. Although Styl could not guarantee Artenz would be in the Low Lands, his words were reassuring, which was why Keidi kept asking.

Putting her hand—the one not in the sling—on her stomach, she closed her eyes, and hoped with all her heart that Artenz would be down there, waiting for her.

+

Deficiency

The elevator came to a sudden stop and woke Keidi. At first, she did not know where she was. Then she saw Styl standing over her and felt the door slid open on her left.

Bright light came in, blinding her. Hands reached for her and pulled her up as she fought to see through the brilliance.

And right away, another hand touched her. A touch she knew.

"Artenz!"

"It's me, love," he said as one of his hands found hers. He pulled her to him. She could not make out his face because of the sun rays coming from above, but she hugged him. She smelled him. She let the tears come, felt his tears on her forehead and down the side of her face.

He guided her out of the elevator. She could not stop hugging. Neither could he.

Finally, her eyes adjusted to the brightness, and she looked over his shoulder.

And there, ahead, she saw an endless city of buildings and streets, a sight quite different from Prominence. It was rough and dark and disused. It was flat and gray, vast and impressive in its own way.

People, so many, moved through its streets and roads.

The place was alive.

A new world.

"We made it," she said to Artenz.

"We did," he said.

Epilogue

Epilogue

Retrieval

The pain was excruciating, and liberating.

Artenz felt Keidi's hand squeezing his. Her lips on his forehead. Warm, reassuring.

"It's done?" he asked, without opening his eyes.

He was coming out of sleep, having requested strong anesthetic before the procedure. Eltaya had said it would be safer that way.

"It is," said Keidi. "I'm proud of you."

Artenz had imagined he would feel strange without his brain-pad, lost. Instead, he felt renewed, complete. It felt natural, as if a long torture had ended. The b-pad had somehow convinced his mind and body that the discomfort it conveyed was normal.

With Keidi's help, he sat up and opened his eyes.

The room was small and bare, with grayed out walls and fading paint. The only window had no glass, only bars. The place was situated in what had once been a prosperous hospital. Once as in a millennium ago, before the rise of Prominence.

Keidi was the only other person in the room, seated on a stool beside the narrow bed.

"Where is it?" he asked.

Deficiency

Keidi pulled a table toward him. Its wheels creaked as it rolled. On a metal plate lay what looked to be a series of tentacles, terribly long tentacles.

"That was in my head?" he asked.

"It was," said Keidi.

It took a moment for Artenz to locate the pad. It was at a point where all tentacles merged, no larger than the tip of a finger. Artenz revolted at the notion that all these cables had been in his head. The thing was crusted with blood, his blood.

Artenz felt his stomach heave. Keidi pushed the table away.

"It's gone," she said, moving in front of him. "You did it."

And he had.

His b-pad was gone, permanently gone.

+

Later that same day, the roles were reversed. Keidi was lying down, and Artenz sat beside her. She slept and he kept his hand on her forehead. He hated the sight of her arm in a cast. She had gone through so much. Every few minutes, he kissed her. Her breathing was regular. She seemed to have come out of the procedure in better shape than he had.

Artenz had wanted Keidi to wait before removing the b-pad, at least until the baby was born. She had insisted on doing it right away. "I'm not taking any chances," she had said. "If there's any small chance that the pad can let them find us or that it can affect the baby, I want it out of me."

Before proceeding with the retrieval of the b-pad from Keidi's neck, the surgeon had subjected her to a series of tests, routine tests, supposedly.

"There shouldn't be any problem," he had said. "You are in exceptional health."

It had been a good thing to hear.

They had asked the pad surgeon about natural birth, and although it was not his field of expertise, he had explained that down here, most births were natural. It cost too much to have a lab baby, and although there were some risks, they were rarely fatal, and thus, worth taking.

Artenz looked at Keidi's neck, at the small square bandage covering the spot where her b-pad had been. A small red dot appeared where the blood had soaked through.

His own bandage was much larger and wrapped around his whole neck, to keep the thick gauge in place. He'd lost a good amount of blood, which was one of the reasons why he had been so worried for Keidi.

There had been no need to be.

He looked at the table and her b-pad rested on the same metal plate where his had been not so long ago. He had asked for his device to be destroyed. Eltaya had promised she would see to it.

Artenz wished he had kept his own pad, at least long enough to compare it to Keidi's.

Her tentacles were shorter and thinner. It was hard to say by how much, although Artenz thought the difference was quite significant.

At first, he had attributed the difference in size to the fact that Keidi was a woman and smaller in stature.

"That has nothing to do with it," had said Eltaya. She had looked worried.

"What then?"

Eltaya had shaken her head and walked away. She had not returned.

Artenz was not sure he wanted to know why there was such a difference. Every explanation he could think of scared him.

Yet he was fascinated and took a closer look at Keidi's b-pad. He noticed that the end of each of the tentacles was thinner and of a different color. Initially, he had thought it was the blood that made it darker, but it wasn't.

It was as if the material was newer.

Deficiency

As if it had...

Grown.

Instantly, Artenz pushed the table away, disgusted.

"Do you want me to take it away?" asked Eltaya, who stood in the doorway. He had not heard her arrive.

"Yes," he said.

Eltaya walked in and opened a small black bag. She took the pad, its tentacles falling, inert, and yet... The pad disappeared into the bag. Eltaya closed it and put it away.

She looked at Artenz. He stared back and wanted to ask her if he was right, if indeed the brain-pad was so advanced that it could grow.

He felt Keidi's head move under his hand and decided he knew enough. He turned toward Keidi and heard Eltaya walk out.

"I'm here, love," he said in Keidi's ear. "You've done it."

"We... we've done it," she said.

"Yes, we."

"We're free," she added, and pulled him closer.

.. Lift

And this, then, is the famous Xanton Lift. Famous for those who know about it, for those who control it, for those who want to see someone disappear from the surface of Garadia.

For most, though, the name means nothing. For most of the inhabitants of Prominence City, the lift does not even exist, except as a rumor. Everyone has heard stories of people disappearing, but few believe them.

The corporations want it that way.

They erase someone who opposes them and convince the Promients that everything is normal through a combination of controlled news stories and well-placed subliminal messages in the hundreds of thousands of ads running through the city every day.

There is no value lost though, even when making someone disappear. No one leaves Prominence or Garadia without good reason. Profit is always the end game. Those too weak to serve as workers in the faraway mines are not put on the elevator. They are simply disposed of.

Easy enough to do on Garadia, where most of the planet is bare and arid and inhabitable, where everyone lives in small and isolated bubbles—in Prominence, or the Low Lands, or the few other cities.

Mysa Lamond looks down.

Deficiency

It is an impressive sight, even for one as dehumanized as her. This, then, is what one sees on the second day of the climb. A curvature of Garadia, covered in a wool blanket of clouds, thick and white and spiraling, possibly the creation of a storm. The clouds cover most of the ocean, the only one on this planet. That ocean is another particularity of Garadia of which the Promients are completely ignorant.

How small their world is.

Mysa pulls her hands apart and feels the manacles holding them behind her back. She cannot break them and does not want to. She is not worried.

Nothing worries her much these days.

Yet it seems she can still be surprised.

Mysa is not one to doubt herself, and yet, as she looks down upon the planet of Garadia, she admits that the encounter of the day before, at the Xanton anchor station, left her confused.

She wonders if her system's breakdown following Eltaya Ark's attack has anything to do with the slowness of her brain. The stun pistol was incredibly powerful. It almost made her wonder if Eltaya had known that Mysa would be present at the top of the Blue Tower.

Almost, because obviously, there was no way for Eltaya to know Mysa was back on Garadia. In fact, Mysa had not seen any sign that Eltaya had recognized her—normal as she had a completely new identity, a new name, and a new appearance. There had been nothing for Eltaya to link Mysa to the woman she had encountered a while back. That meeting had been far away in space, and just like here, Eltaya had won.

Mysa admits this freely. In fact, she admires Eltaya for it, as she admires her for winning again this time.

Not that Mysa cared much, by that time.

The corporations of Prominence think themselves much more powerful than they actually are. The mission was interesting in the beginning, intriguing even. Disappointing in the end. The corporations aspire to control the whole of Garadia. But when things began to unravel, it was obvious to Mysa that she had aligned herself with a group that was not as soundly managed as she had believed.

It will now take a long time for the corporations of Prominence to get back on their feet, if they ever do.

Mysa hopes she will meet Eltaya again.

The elevator continues to climb, at a speed approaching 500 kilometers an hour. A good speed, solid technology. Still, the climb to the space-port takes more than three days.

Mysa will have to reconstruct parts of herself. The corporations repowered her, but she does not feel complete yet. She looks forward to the process. It is a good opportunity to insert a few more augments or mods. Maybe she could replace her neck with a powerful amp. Or maybe she could change focus, try some biological modifications instead of the usual mechanical enhancement. Experiments on that front were certainly promising.

One thing at a time.

For now, she is a prisoner. Going to the asteroids.

Again.

Last time, she had been unconscious on the way up, but her arrival in the mines had been expected, and her escape quick. This time, she is going up sooner than anticipated. It will take her a while to get in touch with her peers and get access to her resources. She sees it as a well-deserved rest.

Her thoughts return to the strange encounter at the anchor station. She is certain the person she saw was supposed to have been sent up the lift already.

And yet, that is not what had happened.

The person had been there, in a side room, as Mysa was led through the station. They had looked at each other, but it had not mattered, as they had never seen each other before.

The corporations believe they control the lift, yet the fact that this prisoner was not sent off the planet showed something different. Mysa wonders if the person had bought freedom with credits. Or if another

Deficiency

type of arrangement was struck. Either way, it was well played, incredibly well played.

It also means that at a deep level, the empire of the corporations is starting to fall apart and that there are gaps in their impenetrable and ever growing net.

That could be an opportunity.

Mysa smiles.

But smiling is not enjoyable. Not anymore. There is no feeling associated with it, no release of tension. Still, it makes the enforcers standing beside her uncomfortable. There is power in simple things.

It will take a while for Mysa to come back to Garadia. It certainly did last time.

But Mysa Lamond knows she will return.

She always does.

... Goodbyes

Hills and hills of residual things went up, down and formed a tapestry of discarded objects. The sight was hard to understand and went under the name of the Black Metallic Sea. The vast region was another of the many secrets of Prominence. Keidi was appalled by the sight.

"This is where our garbage goes?" asked Artenz. His hand held Keidi's protectively. They had stayed close since being reunited at the foot of Pillar K.

Kazor nodded. "Most of it," he said.

Eltaya and Styl stood close by, not saying a word. Eltaya seemed displeased, and Styl remained impassive.

Looking at it, Keidi had difficulty wrapping her head around what she was seeing. A blanket of detritus, dropped from the city of Prominence. So much garbage, so much stuff that the inhabitants of the Floating City did not want any more. So much waste.

And yet, in there, somewhere, Keidi thought she saw something move.

"Salvagers," explained Kazor. "Looking for treasures."

"A tough and unforgiving world," said Eltaya. "Salvagers are usually honest enough about their trade. Not raiders. They plague the sea, take without remorse and kill when need be."

Deficiency

The Black Metallic Sea represented another lie about the grandiose city high above. From where they where standing, it was difficult to see Prominence, located directly above. So many deceptions. During their journey through the Low Land City, Keidi had enquired about Rakkah, the infamous master manipulator.

Kazor had laughed at her question. Eltaya had cracked one of her biggest smiles.

"Rakkah?" had exclaimed Eltaya. "The old woman died 300 years ago!"

"Then the news—"

"Fake," had said Kazor.

They had left the main city of the Low Lands behind almost a day ago. It had once been the only city in the region, before the more fortunate decided to build Prominence above, blocking the sun and the world.

Eltaya had secured them two rovers. Each rover had six wheels and was able to navigate the rugged terrain that ran along the Black Metallic Sea. Styl drove one, with Artenz and Keidi as passengers. Eltaya and Kazor rode the other, with Eltaya at the helm. A chain-gun hung on the side, and Kazor kept a hand on it while they traveled. Keidi was glad they had not had to use it.

Now, the noon sun floated somewhere far above Prominence. The clouds hung heavy and almost touching the ground. Under the hanging canopy, the Black Metallic Sea stretched as far as Keidi could see. Earlier, they had seen a floating craft on the horizon, making an appearance under the clouds, just long enough to add another load of garbage into the sea.

"This is it, then?" asked Artenz, squeezing Keidi's hand.

"Yes," said Eltaya. The five of them had been looking toward the black waste, although this was not the direction Artenz and Keidi were going next. "This is as far as Kazor and I can take you. Styl will transport you the rest of the way. From here, the road is long, but safe. You have a map. Stick to it. Ration your provisions, replenish your water only at the locations I have highlighted. The farther you go, the less value your credits will have."

Keidi loaded the map on her mini-vid. Moving forward, she would sit behind Styl and be their navigator. Artenz would sit in the back seat.

They were now ready to go toward the Dara Gulch. Eltaya had said it was also known as the Deep Gulch, as it was located down in the ground and between the mountains.

"Thank you, very much," said Keidi. "We could never have escaped without you, without all of you."

"Send our thanks to Xavi, and to the others," added Artenz.

"To Arnol," said Keidi. "And the people of Pillar K."

"We'll thank everyone," assured Eltaya, who could not help smiling.

She's pretty when she smiles, thought Keidi.

The group turned toward each other. Keidi was the first to reach out, bringing Eltaya to her for a hug.

"It was nice to finally meet you," she said.

"The same," said Eltaya.

Then Keidi gave Kazor a brief hug. During the time she had spent with him, Keidi had come to appreciate his quiet nature and blunt honesty. He was a resourceful man, and his presence alone had been enough to discourage most from approaching them. He had acquired their provisions and the rovers. He kept his stunner shotgun on his person at all time, visible on his belt or in his hand.

He had a daughter in Prominence, which was why he never left for long, always hoping to see her again soon. From what Keidi had gathered, he did not see his daughter often enough.

Styl was already in the rover. Keidi took her seat behind him and opened the map on her mini-vid.

She looked back and felt a pang of jealousy at the sight of Artenz and Eltaya saying their goodbyes. They exchanged few words and did not hug. There was something there—a past shared and awakened by

Deficiency

the recent events. They had a bond that would never go away, solidified these past few days.

In a way, Keidi hoped they had hugged. She did not like the idea, but it would have seemed the proper thing to do, for both of them. They might never see each other again.

They separated, and Artenz jumped in the rover, in the back seat, and fastened his safety belt.

The motor of the other rover roared. As Styl powered their own, Eltaya and Kazor appeared beside them.

"All the best," said Eltaya, in the front seat. Somehow, Keidi knew Eltaya would always be the leader, no matter where she was, or who she was with. Kazor was behind her, the large chain-gun on his right pointed toward the Black Metallic Sea.

"Be careful," said Artenz.

"We will. Stay low, for a year if you can. Then, you know how to reach the Banner, if ever you have any interest in helping."

"We know," said Keidi.

She had no intention of ever going back to Prominence. She believed Artenz felt the same way.

Eltaya nodded. Kazor, behind her, nodded slightly as the rover rode away.

"Time to go," said Keidi.

Artenz reached backward and took hold of one of Keidi's hands.

"Let's go," said Styl.

And he drove the rover forward, toward the north, away from the Black Metallic Sea and the Low Lands. Away from Prominence and toward a new life.

..... Report

Irbela stared at the clerk behind the desk, annoyed by his inefficiency. She had given him her report more than an hour ago. On two occasions, he had asked her to go take a seat in the waiting room, while he did... something. What, she could not be certain.

She had never submitted an official complaint report before. She knew these types of reports were rare. When preparing it, she'd performed a few searches in the data-sphere, and although she'd found the answers she was looking for, the information on the subject had been sparse.

It made her wonder if the process for disciplining the enforcers worked very well. It certainly didn't seem to. Obviously, this complaint was extreme. Murder while on duty was prohibited. And there were other directives the enforcers had to adhere to. Although Irbela was often told how important it was to respect each of these directives, the process for enforcing them seemed extremely weak.

"I submitted your report," said the man, looking up at her from his chair behind the glass window. "It initially went through. Now, it looks like it's been rejected."

"Rejected? Why?" Irbela's patience was spent.

"That's what I'm trying to figure out."

It should not be this difficult.

Deficiency

"Isn't this all automated?"

"I wish," said the man.

Irbela sighed loudly and felt people staring at her. She did not care.

"My report was filled out properly," she said. "If your system is broken, that's not my problem."

"If you want your report submitted, then yes, it is." The man had a point.

"Is there anything I can do to help?"

The man shook his head but stopped abruptly. "Actually, yes, there is. I see here... well, can you confirm the number of the agent against whom you are submitting a complaint?"

"I can," said Irbela. She quickly pulled her own copy of the report on her b-pad. It appeared on her eye-veil. "Number B-002-P0144-024."

For good measure, Irbela performed a quick search in the datasphere.

```
Action> Validate B-002-P0144-024
1 agent found.
Action> Show Name
001- Delaro, Okran
```

There it was. Okran Delaro. Just seeing the name made Irbela's blood boil. That mission had been by far one of the worst experiences of her career, all because of the officer in charge.

"The agent number is not valid," said the man.

"It is," said Irbela. "I just confirmed it in the Sphere."

"It's not," said the man, his patience as infuriating as the low mumble of his voice.

"I just verified it," insisted Irbela. She repeated the search, with the same result.

"Miss," said the man, not looking at her, "remember that you only have a limited level of privilege. My information is more accurate than yours, and I can assure you that this agent is not registered."

Irbela took a step closer and put her face against the glass.

"Sir," she said, mimicking the man's tone, "look at me for a second, will you?"

The request seemed to take the man by surprise. He looked up.

"The agent in question killed a civilian. I was there. The whole unit can attest to what I'm saying." When asked, most of the members of her squad had offered their support. Their depositions were saved on her pad. "Do you understand what I'm saying?"

The man nodded, his complexion a bit paler.

"So, please, do what you have to do to find him, and submit my report."

"I understand," he said. "Can you please sit down while I perform a few verifications?"

"Don't make me wait too long."

The man ignored her.

She took a seat, the same as before, the same as before that also. This bureaucracy was ridiculous. Why couldn't she submit her report automatically using her b-pad? Why did she have to come here in person? Why couldn't she submit it through her own office?

This whole fiasco certainly made her think twice about submitting a second report—one about the other event, the one nobody wanted to talk or think about. They had lost colleagues, so there was no forgetting it completely, but... no, it was too early to process what she had seen. In fact, Irbela was not certain she would be able to make sense of it at all, which is why she was thinking about submitting a report. Let someone else go down there and figure things out.

Abruptly, the man behind the glass stood and disappeared into the back office.

What now?

Deficiency

Irbela performed the search again. Same result. Then she tried to open Okran Delaro's file.

```
Action> Show File
Insufficient privilege.
```

That was new. Irbela had already looked at Okran Delaro's file. She had perused his file once she had been assigned to him, and again while she was preparing her complaint report.

For someone of his station, he had a surprisingly short file. When she had looked at the file before the mission, Irbela had felt that something was not quite right. She had brushed it aside, excited about the mission, about working with a bionic.

Now, though, she guessed that something in Okran Delaro's past had possibly been deliberately suppressed. His record had only showed a summary of his last 10 missions. She had assumed at the time that it was because, being a bionic, he worked on high-profile, secret cases. Knowing what she now knew, that hypothesis did not hold up.

Finally, the man appeared and pointed to a side door. Irbela walked to it, and it opened. Without a word a woman gestured for Irela to follow. They made their way down a hall and into a small room — one door, four plain walls, two chairs.

"Take a seat," said the woman.

Irbela, uncertain what was happening, hesitated. Once the door shut, the woman fell into her seat and smiled.

Relaxing a bit, Irbela took the other seat. "What's going on?"

"Sibil Argos," said the woman, extending her hand. Irbela shook it. "Internal."

Internal. Irbela had heard that before.

"You are a sleuth?" she asked.

"Yes, assigned to investigate enforcers, when required."

Irbela nodded.

"I was called in about 45 minutes ago, shortly after you submitted your report. It seems... that agent Okran Delaro went missing."

"Missing? What does that even mean?"

The woman smiled briefly. "That is the question, isn't it?" She seemed to read something on her eye-veil before looking back at Irbela. "Your report was received, and I'll be following up on it. The agent disappeared from the Sphere a while ago. It is my job to find him. And then, based on your report, bring him in to answer to your accusation."

"That could be difficult," said Irbela. "He may have gone to the lower levels."

"That's not a problem," said the sleuth. "Do not worry. You have done your part. Now it's my turn. And although some believe the lower levels cannot be monitored, that's not quite true. In this case, something else is blocking us from locating the agent. I'll look into it, and when I have more information, I'll provide you with an update. Directly, if that is all right with you?"

Irbela had hoped to submit her report and never hear back about Okran Delaro ever again. Now though, her curiosity had been piqued.

"Certainly," she said. "I'll await your update."

"Thank you," said the sleuth before getting up and leaving.

+

The update, when it came, was short and to the point:

```
Undisclosed e-mail service
[[ ENCRYPTED ]]

From:    [[ Protected Identity ]]
Sent:    Year 3.4k60 Season 05 Day 11 Hour 1201.
Subject:       Update

Agent found. Dismantled and terminated.
No further action required to address complaint.
```

Deficiency

Mission 000000

There is not much left of his body. They took it apart, these people, the Ks, the inhabitants of the Underground of Prominence living at the top of Pillar K. The woman defeated him.

Keidi Rysinger.

It does not matter. Not really.

Although... there is a part of Okran Delaro that cares, the part that remains, the Okran that was once human, the one that had a purpose and the one that still has feelings.

There is great resale value for his parts. Large sums of credits. His mods and augments are some of the most advanced that can be manufactured and bought.

After all, he had been a bionic.

Had been, because there is almost nothing left of him.

He is lying on the floor. Not a table. A cold metal floor. He knows because he was able to see, until they took his eyes out.

He still has one of his ears, but not for much longer. He hears them working on the implant in his remaining ear. The left one. A small drill, turning, unscrewing.

He does not feel anything anymore. Still, he knows his blood is running and spilling, pooling on the metal floor.

Even cyborgs bleed.

Okran does not know why he is still conscious. What he knows is that he does not have much longer. Most of his body has already been taken. Legs and arms: dismantled. The augmentations removed, delicately. The pieces are worth nothing if damaged.

The cyborg in him had been the first thing they'd put to sleep. It had been a relief, an unlocking, a door opening and a profound feeling of being himself again.

Next, they disabled his ability to feel.

A courtesy. One for which Okran is grateful.

As careful as they are with his mods, they will discard his body, the biological part of him. Okran looked with a deranged curiosity as they sawed off part of a leg, a hand, and when they opened his torso.

Quite a mess.

It was not his choice. He had not been able to move, and thus, not able to look away. He could not even close his eyelids.

It had not been pleasant. It was still not pleasant.

Yet Okran accepts that this is his end.

It impresses him that these people, for whom he had been the enemy, showed respect by not allowing him to feel the pain.

Even now, he learns.

Learns that most likely, he has been wrong and that his life, the last portion of it anyway, has been for nothing, for a false cause, for something that in the end could not bring him satisfaction. It certainly did not bring him happiness.

Okran Delaro.

That was his name. He was an enforcer. Maybe he had a family.

A wife.

A child. Or two.

Okran likes the idea.

He cannot remember much from that previous life. He cannot remember what led him to become a cyborg, not exactly. He knows he killed, once, as an enforcer. He believes that his career and life unraveled from there. It is a plausible explanation.

Deficiency

Then... silence.

His hearing, his last sense gone.

No vision and no hearing now, no touch, taste or smell.

Not much longer. Or an eternity. Time tends to stretch when there is nothing to do but wait.

Next, they will go after his brain. He knows it. And when they do, it will be the end of Okran, the human.

- Ascension

The elevator of Pillar H started its ascension. Inside, Eltaya kept her back straight. Kazor stood on her left, leaning against the side, his face stoic. After they had left the others, the big man had tried hard to hide his feelings. Eltaya remembered how his voice had broken when talking about Artenz and Keidi and how he wished them the best of luck. Such a good man, who deserved better than the lot life had assigned him.

Eltaya had also found the separation difficult. Although everything had happened in a single day, such intense events had a way of bringing people together, of pulling out the best in everyone.

As for herself, she had believed her feelings for Artenz were gone, but they had resurfaced when she had looked at him for the last time. Emotions of the moment, nothing more. Still, a part of her wished she had stayed behind, had continued with Artenz and Keidi. A part of her craved friendship and companionship.

It was possible their life would be blissful. There was potential there.

She wished them the best.

For her part, Eltaya was not done with Prominence. She had not found the answers she sought, questions she knew would in fact only be answered far out in space.

Deficiency

She needed to go back out there, in the endless black. She did not harbor much hope of finding her parents alive, but she needed to know what had happened to them. She could not rest until she did.

Now that Artenz and Keidi were safe, now that the Authentic Banner had dismantled, as least temporarily, the time had come. No one would hold her back. No one would oppose her departure.

-. Artificial Life

Life in the Sphere provides limitless possibilities. Located deep between layers of data, the Red Dragon stretches his legs and lays back his head. Then he reaches to his right and takes a hand in his.

"Come closer," he says.

"Why?" she asks, even as she slides near him.

"Put your head here. Relax. There is no reason, other than I want to. Just stop thinking and let the moment be."

The woman lies back, taking refuge under his arm. He hugs her close.

The sofa is comfortable. In front of them, they see an aerial view of Prominence. It is fabricated by amalgamating a series of feeds provided by invisible drones, some of which belong to the government, others to the corporations, and a few to the sleuths.

The inhabitants of Prominence believe they still possess some remnant of privacy. If only they knew.

"This is agreeable," she says.

"I agree," says the Red Dragon.

He asked her not to think, something that is hard for him. Almost impossible.

He is the Red Dragon and he cannot help thinking about Artenz and how strong the bond with his sister is. The Red Dragon does not have a sister or a brother. His former self, for lack of a better term, was a sole child.

When they fissioned, though, and became two, they also became something akin to brothers. Not of the flesh, not in the true sense, but still, they are related, and thus close relatives, in a strange way.

Marti Zehron.

The bond is unexpected and surprisingly strong.

The man is gone from Garadia. That much the Red Dragon knows. More likely than not, he will never see him again. Still, while he improves things down here, on Garadia, there is no reason why the Red Dragon cannot also keep an eye out, just in case.

Chances are slim, but he infiltrated the space network. After all, even out there, everything connects to the data-sphere. It was not difficult to creep in. Especially with the information provided to him by Ayalte.

The ghost is gone now. She returned to her mistress a while back. It was interesting for the Red Dragon to see how much the ghost cared for her host, how she was worried about the merging of minds. Because she cares so much, the Red Dragon assumes the synchronization of their minds should go well. The ghost will take the necessary precautions. The fact that Ayatle shows feelings makes him wonder what exactly the ghost is. If not an AI, then what? An extension of a sentient being? Maybe.

The original ghost is gone. This one is a copy the Red Dragon created. It is now sitting next to him. He will have time to study it and learn from it.

"I like this life," she says.

"So do I," replies the Red Dragon.

There is one thing that nags at his mind. A possibility. He'd discovered it the previous day, as he'd revisited the circumstances that had sent Marti Zehron out into space. He recreated as many of Detel's last activities as he could find in the data-sphere. There is not much left, but enough to plant some doubts in the Red Dragon's electronic mind.

He is not certain yet, and maybe he will never be able to confirm his suspicion, since more data is continually being purged from the Sphere, data about what took place on day 11 of the fifth season of the year 3.4k60. Still, what he found is undeniable. Detel knew more than she'd let Marti believe. In fact, Marti, just like most of the others, may have been a pawn in a complex scheme designed by Detel herself.

Like Artenz, her own brother.

The Red Dragon does not have much to go on, except one small detail. He was able to confirm that Detel wanted her paper shared and seen by as many people as possible. She was aware of Artenz's project. The Red Dragon found notes to that effect in a few residual files he'd reconstructed from her profile room.

The timing of when her paper leaked seems a bit too perfect.

Could she have known that Artenz would use the module from the Falcon Flight project to distribute her paper? She certainly could have guessed. Even then the risk Detel took was extremely high, and not one the Red Dragon would have taken. The odds had been stacked against her.

If this was true, then the Red Dragon has to ask himself a few more questions.

Did Detel know that Marti Zehron would be a victim of her ploy?

Was she ready to sacrifice him?

What about her own brother and her best friend, Keidi?

- . . . Signal

The workshop was built into the cliff face. The natural rock formed two of its walls. The third wall was a large piece of metal brought all the way from the Black Metallic Sea. Many different tools hung from it. Having only three walls provided a space with a beautiful view of the Dara Gulch.

Artenz and Keidi had built the workshop together—the first project in their new life. It had taken seasons to get it to where it was now. It needed more work, but Artenz had not been able to wait any longer.

"Today, we start," he had said.

Surprisingly, Keidi had kissed him and said that yes, they could start.

She now stood in front of a workbench, her hair tied on the back of her neck, her long bangs falling in front of her face. Every few minutes, she blew her hair away, both of her hands busy manipulating tools and pieces.

Artenz sat at a table with a monitor in front of him. This equipment had been extremely difficult to acquire. With patience, and good haggling by Keidi, it had become theirs. Artenz had set it up in a day. He knew it would have taken Marti less than an hour.

"Is your code ready?" asked Keidi. "Because this transmitter, here, almost is."

Artenz reached back, his chair inclined at a dangerous angle, and poked Keidi in the ribs. His glasses slid down and he pushed them back up. It would take a while to get used to wearing them, but if he did not, he only saw from one eye. It was the price he had had to pay for his abrupt departure from the Sphere during their stay at Hideout Plaza. It had taken about a week for his vision to start going away, and it had yet to stop. All in all, he would do it again.

"Do not worry about me," he said.

"Oh, but I do. You're the slow one."

"The code will be ready."

Keidi turned his way. How pretty she was.

"Well," she said, lifting her chin, proud, "the transmitter actually *is* ready."

Artenz blinked.

"It is?" he asked.

"Oh yes." She smiled with an air of superiority. "And where's the code?"

He stood and took the step that brought his face close with hers. She was a tad taller than he was. He liked that. He kissed her. She closed her eyes and kissed back.

As they pulled apart, he brought a small key in between their faces.

"Here it is," he said. "The code was ready yesterday."

It was her turn to blink.

"Give that to me," she said, as she snatched the key from his hand. Her surprised look was incredibly charming.

Artenz tried to hug her, but she resisted and pushed him away, playfully.

"Let go of me," she said as she inserted the key in the box she had built. "This is your dream, remember. Not mine. Why is it that I have to fight you to get it done?"

The key fit perfectly.

Excited now, Artenz stepped to the other side of the workbench.

"It's working?"

Deficiency

"Give it a moment," said Keidi.

A moment went by.

"It's transmitting?" asked Artenz.

Keidi took the box in one of her hands and walked out of the workshop. Artenz stayed on her heels.

"It is," she announced. "It's working!"

Artenz loved the excitement on her face and in her voice. The delivery of the baby had been hard on her. For several weeks afterword, Keidi had stayed in bed, drained.

That had been six seasons ago already.

Now, things were better. Things were good.

"The recording," said Keidi suddenly. "You need to record this."

Artenz had almost forgotten. He turned around and ran into the workshop, picked up the vid-recorder and activated it. Again, his glasses had almost tipped off his nose and he pushed them back. Too heavy. He needed a lighter frame.

"Year 34k61, day 19 of the seventh season." He came out, saw the sun low behind the side of the canyon. "Time is 1935. This here is Keidi," pointing the recorder at her, "and this is me, Artenz," turning it to show his face, "from the Dara Gulch." Pointing it around, and then back to Keidi and the device. "The transmitter is ready. We're..."

"Sending our first communication," interrupted Keidi, as excited as he was. "In 3... 2... 1..."

And then it happened.

Artenz zoomed on the box and slowly, he lifted the lens of the vid-recorder up, and up, and away toward the cerulean sky and toward the empty cosmos on the other side.

"We did it," said Keidi, putting an arm around his waist.

"I'm proud of you." Artenz kept the recorder pointing up.

"And I of you," said Keidi.

The signal might, or not, reach another civilization. And even if it did, chances were that it would take so long that Artenz and Keidi would not be around to receive an answer.

414

Still, it was done.

Most of the propagation code came from the module Artenz and his team had launched on the day Keidi and he had left Prominence. Those events felt as if they had never happened. Artenz thought briefly about Eltaya, about Marti, and felt a pang of regret. He missed them, especially his best friend.

Keidi put her head on his shoulder. Artenz turned off the recorder and delicately put it on the rock where the transmitter rested.

Finally, he could say he had done it. Not just him. They, the both of them, had done it. They were actively looking for other civilizations, sending messages in space.

The strident cry of a baby broke the moment.

"Stay here," said Artenz, feeling Keidi stir beside him. "Mom will bring her to us."

Keidi nodded and they did not move, enjoying their achievement. Even the screeching could not diminish Artenz's joy. In fact, it added to it.

Kynna was a healthy baby girl and like he had predicted, the cries were getting closer.

"You two!" They heard a voice, older. "Why are you never around, when, when…"

They untangled and Keidi reached out, took Kynna in her arms. Instantly, the baby stopped crying.

"Incredible," said Artenz's mother. "That baby hates me. She really does."

"She hates everyone but her parents," said Styl, who appeared beside Artenz's mother. "Did you complete it?" he asked, taking a few quick steps to where the transmitter rested.

"We have," said Artenz.

"And you didn't wait for me?" noted Styl, but he was smiling. "After all I did."

Styl had come and gone over the past few seasons. During his visits, he transported them to the city of the Low Lands, where they got the

Deficiency

pieces they could not get in the gulch. He had been incredibly good to them, and Artenz now considered him a good friend. As he knew Keidi did. She had a special bond with him, developed during those hours in the Underground.

Artenz's mother came to stand beside him.

"I never doubted you'd succeed," she murmured for his ear alone.

He hugged her with one arm, his way of thanking her. How lucky he felt to have her back.

"Where's Dad?" he asked.

"Oh, you know, down in the canyon, as usual, trading, trying to get more pieces for your projects."

"Mom, you need to tell him to stop. We have too much stuff already, junk, most of it. He doesn't know what we need."

"I know," said his mother. "But how can I? It makes him so happy." Artenz sighed.

"Where's it sending it?" asked Styl.

Without any family in Prominence, it seemed Styl had found a niche with them. He shared his doubts with them about rejoining the Authentic Banner, which had yet to resurface following Global state. He was well-liked in the village down below and offered driving lessons from time to time.

"It's sending in all directions," explained Keidi, as Kynna reached out and tried to grab the transmitter, or the vid-recorder, or whatever was in her reach. "But the signal going straight up is the strongest."

"No cloud," noticed Styl. "That's good."

"It is," said Keidi.

Then they heard someone coming. Running. Not fast, with difficulty even.

They all turned and Artenz shook his head. Here was his dad, old knees in poor shape, yet running when walking was difficult.

"What is it?" asked his mother.

His father shook his head, and kept coming, slowing down, but coming. He only stopped when he faced the both of them, son and mother. He put a hand on each of their shoulders, his chest heaving up and down. Keidi appeared behind his father, Styl right there with her. Kynna seemed to notice something was wrong and moaned.

"Love, dear," he said, his breathing harsh and fast.

"Take a breath," said his mom.

"No time, no time at all. You need to come."

"Dad," Artenz said, taking his father's face in his hands and forcing him to look into his eyes. "What's going on?"

His father looked back at him, and took a long respiration, and smiled, tears in his eyes. "She's here," he said, choking. "Detel, she's back!"

=

Appendices and Glossaries

. Data Spheres

Bio-sphere

The bio-sphere is a three-dimensional social network where people can interact and stay connected. Each user owns a profile room, which they can customize to their tastes. Users can visit each other and stay in touch in different ways, including through the friends-panel. A person can join the bio-sphere using a b-pad, a bio-chair or similar devices.

Data-sphere

The data-sphere is an immense database that is said to contain all existing information, from as far back as the early days of Prominence. It is divided into several tiers, with the lower tiers being protected and restricted. Nothing is ever deleted from the database. The data-sphere feeds the other spheres, as well as most of the technological systems of Prominence and beyond. Although the data-sphere is mostly accessed by applications and programs via controlled portals, any person can access it using a text-only interface to perform searches and basic commands.

Holo-sphere

The holo-sphere is a gaming and relaxing environment that uses most of the senses to generate a realistic experience. The holo-sphere can be accessed in any gaming center, and the most recent version of the b-pad lets users purchase an augment that allows them to immerse themselves in the holo-sphere from almost anywhere.

.. Data Pads

B-pad or brain-pad

The brain-pad is installed on the lower part of the head, where it connects with the neck, usually on the left side. It is directly connected to the brain, the ears and the eyes. It is also linked to one of the carotid arteries. A user of the b-pad is permanently and continuously connected to the Sphere. The brain-pad is the third of its generation.

The b-pad does not have any projection capability. Instead, it can output information to an eye-veil, any screen device, or even other b-pads. It can also connect directly to most systems and environments, such as doors, elevators, walk-ways, trams, and workstations, keeping users' preferences in memory.

The b-pad's possibilities are said to be limitless. At its best, the b-pad could potentially increase the processing power of the brain. There is also a wide range of augments that can be purchased to boost the device or its owner, with many new ones coming out weekly.

P-pad or palm-pad

The palm-pad is an improvement to the wrist-pad. Its convenience has brought many new users to the pads series. The main issue with the p-pad is that it is expensive, and because of its location inside the palm, it can interfere with some activities and is easily broken.

The p-pad also stands for projection-pad. One of its most innovative capabilities is to project an imagram (in three dimensions) on any flat surface. One simply needs to program the imagram and then point with the open palm.

W-pad or wrist-pad

The wrist-pad is the first model, or generation, of pads. It is worn on the wrist, plugged into the body, allowing a permanent connection to the data-sphere. Prior to the wrist-pad, a connection to the Sphere had to be done via a terminal. The w-pad opened a new world of possibilities for the inhabitants of Prominence, increasing their connectivity to each other and allowing them to know what is happening in their city sooner.

... Technologies

Add-on. Extra component that can be added to any given device, including pads.

Air-saucer. Transportation device used to move up and down, similar to elevators, but using tubes and air, with a floating saucer or disk moving along a pole.

Air-tube. Transportation device for a single individual, used to move up and down via tubes and air. The individual needs to jump in the tube to be lifted or dropped from one level to the next.

Amp. A replacement for a part of the body, sometimes including a computer.

Augment. Improvement made to the body that usually enhances capabilities.

Bionic. Individual augmented to cyborg status.

Brain-pad or b-pad. The third generation of pads. See "Data Pads."

Crumbler. Small device used to emit vibrations and weaken structures. It is especially effective against rock and stone structures.

Eye-veil. Screen/monitor that appears in front of the eyes, only visible by the wearer. It displays information received from pads and other devices.

Fast-tram. Common mode of transportation, similar to a train and moving at great speed, usually seen in the higher levels of Prominence. A fast-tram hangs under the rail.

Fast-walk. Moving floor that significantly increases walking speed.

G-tool. Multipurpose diagnostic and manufacturing computer used for a variety of civilian and battlefield tasks, such as hacking, decryption, or repair. Advanced models can duplicate some of the functionalities of other devices, such as pads. Also known as a gauntlet.

Gauntlet. See "G-tool."

Ghost. Virtual intelligence and replica of an individual, used to navigate networks and the world of machines, usually while its host sleeps or rests. Information gathered by a ghost is later synchronized and transferred back to the host.

Goggle. Similar device to the eye-veil, but with limited integration to a b-pad.

Guardian bracelet. A complicated device, often confused with a g-tool, used by bodyguards. The guardian bracelet is mainly used for protection and can create powerful shields or defensive measures.

Hair dye. Substance used to permanently alter the color of hair.

Jet-car. Vehicle in the shape of a missile that can transport two to six people, depending on its model. The jet-car can reach impressive speed, and it is banned from the streets of Prominence. Some, like enforcers, use jet-cars in the Underground.

Mini-vid. Small and portable monitor, used with a pad.

Mod. Modification made to the body that does not necessarily enhance or modify any capability.

Palm-pad or p-pad. Second generation of pads. See "Data Pads."

Perma-shield. Protective coating offering a powerful protection against physical blows, as well as other shocks (including electromagnetic pulses).

Scrambler. Small clear disk that muddles b-pads and other network, blocking it from receiving or transferring data.

Skin preservative. Substance that preserves the quality of the skin.

Speed-belt. Moving floor, going too fast to walk on. People simply stand in place on a speed-belt, holding on to poles or banisters while it transports them.

Slow-tram. Common mode of transportation, similar to a train, moving at moderate speed, and usually seen in the lower levels of Prominence. The slow-tram rides on top of the rail.

Tech-cable. Multipurpose cable allowing a technician to connect directly to a series of mechanism and devices as administrator.

Tri-racer. Three-wheeled electric bike for up to four persons. The tri-racer can reach significant speed. It is rarely seen on the main streets of Prominence and will stop working outside of the city's borders.
Uni-racer. One-wheeled motorized vehicle for a single person, moving at limited speed.
Vid-disk. Round screen used to display information from a pad. Devices can connect to a vid-disk by cable or wirelessly.
Voice Projection. Biological modification that provides the ability to project one's voice across greater distance without the need to shout.
Walk-way. Slow-moving floor that increases the distance covered while walking.
Wrist-pad or w-pad. First generation of pads. See "Data Pads."

.... Corporations

Bio-Ex Group. Seventh largest corporation in Prominence, specializing in biological experiments and mining the asteroids.
BlueTech Data. Company specializing in data and the Sphere. Its logo is formed by the letters BTD, capitalized, where the T takes the shape of a tower.
Brains Co. Corporation developing robots and AI. A division of Prima.
Crystal Globe Conglomerate (CGC). Main operator of the Sphere. The CGC is formed by many smaller organizations and is the second-largest corporation of Prominence.
FrontShield Security. Group developing security systems, more specifically for buildings, trams, air-tubes, etc.
InfoSoft Corporation. Specializes in the bio-sphere. A division of CGC.
Innovative Designs Incorporated. Company fabricating gadgets, weapons augmentations and mods.
Market Circuit. Association of stores and shops.
Mollo Foods Incorporated. Manufacturer of bonbons and candies.

Onyx Traders. Responsible for trade between Prominence and the other cities on Garadia. It was part of the Traders Guild before closing its doors following bankruptcy. It was dissolved in 3.0k00.
PadTech Enterprises. Organization specializing in p-pads. A division of Telecore Enterprises.
Prima. Largest of the corporations of Prominence.
Razato Products. Company producing modified food.
Sol Development Incorporated. Corporation specializing in the fabrication of air-tubes and belts. A division of Prima.
Surface Designs. Group specializing in the development of interfaces.
Targos Information. Marketing services expert and provider.
Telecore Enterprises. Represented by an infinite spiral turning slowly. Specializes in b-pads. A division of CGC.
Thrium Laboratories. Leader in biological research. A division of the Bio-Ex Group.
TriCom Incorporated. Corporation specializing in computers, VI and Amps. Third largest corporation of Prominence.
Universal Communications. Communications experts.

- Locations

Actus Dorion Complex. A once rich complex, now falling in disrepair.
Arkos. The sun.
Arkos System. The planetary system of which Garadia is part. It is comprised of 13 planets and two asteroid fields.
Black Metallic Sea. A large cavity located on the western fringes of the Low Lands, comprised mostly of thrown-away metal pieces and garbage.
Blue Tower. Headquarters to BlueTech Data. The Blue Tower is the tallest building in Quadrant X.
Dara Gulch. A narrow ravine, going north from the Low Lands, cutting through the ground and following the Dara River. Deep in the ravine, there are beaches and patches of green.

Deep Gulch. See "Dara Gulch."
Dominance Floor. Level 15 of Prominence. Controlled by the enforcers and under heavy surveillance. Its access is prohibited as it is used by the enforcers for quick movement.
Garadia (city). The first city founded on the planet of the same name. Now known as the Low Lands.
Garadia (planet). The fourth planet of the Arkos System.
Garadia System. See "Arkos System."
Ground Floor. Level 20 of Prominence. This level is completely opaque, hiding and cutting access to the levels below.
I Bot. A small shop tucked between two lodging complexes, close to the Actus Dorion Complex.
Mollo Factory. One of the food factories of Mollo Foods Inc.
PadTech Workshop. A building used as a workshop, owned by Telecore.
Pillar. The four massive columns keeping Prominence City up in the air. Two of the columns contain shafts and elevators leading all the way down to the Low Lands.
Plaza. Central district of Prominence, restricted to the elite.
Slab. The rock plate supporting Prominence.
Thrium Laboratories. A massive building used for research and experimentation. Some rumors suggest that some shady experiments were once performed in the lower levels of the building.
Underground. Level 1 to 20. Abandoned floors of Prominence City.
Xanton Lift. Also known as the space elevator. It goes from the surface of Garadia to the space launch platform in orbit above the planet.

- . Glossary

Add-on. Extras that can be added to a pad or any other device.
Capsule. Physical device used to relay a message anonymously.
Cell-birth. Standard process of having a baby: in a cell, inside a laboratory.

Deficiency

Climb. Action of going up on an air-tube.

Dismiss. Action of removing someone from society.

Egg-cell. The cell, or egg, created to protect the growing fetus and baby in a laboratory.

Fall. Action of going down on an air-tube.

Flush. To permanently delete information from the data-sphere.

Friends-panel. Wall of shelves holding the imagrams of a user's friends in the bio-sphere.

Global. Union of a significant number of corporations to deal with a critical situation. The Global state is rare, as corporations joining the movement are required to share information and by doing so, they open doors for exploitation or betrayal.

Grid. Network used to locate individuals and other trackable objects. Most pads and devices are always visible on the Grid. Using this information, some software can provide a real-time visual map of Prominence and everything in it, including their movement.

Icon. Small symbols appearing inside eye-veils, such as the incoming link icon.

Imagram. Recorded images, usually in 3D and mostly used in the bio-sphere. In the case of imagrams of persons, they can stand, take a step, smile, lie down, wave or do any combination of other limited actions.

Imagraph. Static pictures or images.

Join. To enter the bio-sphere.

Level. Street level, from 0 to 60. Levels below 20 are now closed.

Link. To contact someone over the sphere.

Lodge. Apartment.

Memory-wipe. A procedure that attempts to remove or obliterate a series of memories from a brain.

Open. To accept a link. One either "links" or "opens a link."

Parallel. Reference to a walk-way or tram-rail parallel to another.

Perpendicular. Reference to a walk-way or a tram-rail perpendicular to another.

Pillar. See "Locations."

Plasti-glass. Transparent material, replacing glass and made of strong plastic.

Plasti-metal. Hard material, metallic in appearance and just as durable.

Pledge. Agreement or partnership between two corporations, often unofficial and secret in nature.

Promient. Someone born in Prominence and said to be of pure blood.

Relink. Link again.

Rift. Hole or gap in any given system, including security defense barriers or lockdowns.

Slab. See "Locations."

Tier. Different levels of information in the data-sphere, from 10 (public) to 1 (protected).

Tram-rail. Rail ways for the trams moving through Prominence City.

Underground. See "Locations."

Unlink. To end a connection/discussion with someone.

Vidcorder. Slang term for video-recorder.

Videogram. Recorded videos, in three dimensions.

Videograph. Recorded videos, in two dimensions.

Video-recorder. Video camera.

Withdraw. To exit the bio-sphere.

Zones. Pockets of information, by category, in the data-sphere. Each tier is divided in multiple zones.

Acknowledgements

A book is always much more than the sum of its readable parts. I started writing *Deficiency* in December of 2014 and many, many people played a role—directly or indirectly—in the story it became six years later. I would like to take a moment to acknowledge some of those people.

First, I would like to say a word about my web development team. If you worked with me on anything related to the web over the past twenty-five years or so, be it pages or applications, this is you. Those were wonderful years. The competent development team portrayed in the book is a tribute to those enjoyable times and to all of you.

As always, an IMMENSE thank you goes to Gaetan, my great friend, my alpha reader and dare I say, my biggest fan?

I was lucky to get exceptionally useful feedback for this story and I would like to thank Sylvie Danielle Paulin and Nathaniel Hardman for all their effort in reading the story and sharing their detailed thoughts and suggestions.

I would also like to thank Christopher Jessulat, Kevin Stevens, Phil Hall, John Sutherland, and the members of my writing group at the time, Vanessa Hawkins, Roger Moore, and Chuck Bowie, for their many pointers on how to improve the text.

This story has many particularities, and I am grateful for the patience and dedication of my editors: Amanda Sumner and Forrest Orser.

The creation of the cover is always a process I enjoy greatly. It was easy to work with James T. Egan of Bookfly Design, who took a few ideas and came up with the spectacular cover you now see.

I also want to thank Kirk Shannon for the creation of the System of Garadia icon, the amazing map, and the inside illustrations. We have now collaborated on several projects, and every time, it is a pleasure working with Kirk.

One of the last steps before print and publication is formatting the story. This time around, I worked with Erika LeClair of Just Write It!, who made my life easier by helping with both the e-book and print versions.

Even the back-cover text can represent a lot of work (it certainly did in this case), and I want to thank Terry Armstrong of Just Write It! for his insights and his help on this matter. I learned a lot in that small exercise alone.

I admire a great many authors and for this book I would like to give a special mention to a few of my favorite science fiction authors, whose books have encouraged me to try my hand at the genre: Kim Stanley Robinson, Arthur C. Clarke and Michael Crichton. I would also like to mention Franz Kafka, who inspired the elusive corporate owners and to whom Pillar K is dedicated.

Also, I must thank Thomas Newman and all those who worked on the creation of the soundtrack for the movie *The Adjustment Bureau*. Never has music played such an intricate part in my writing. I must have listened to this soundtrack hundreds of times while writing *Deficiency*.

And a big THANK YOU to all my supporters and readers. A story and its writer are nothing without them.

Finally, to my muse: my wife and children. I love you more than should be allowed.

Deficiency

About the Author

STEVE C. ESTON grew up in the province of New Brunswick in Canada. He is a manager in technology services for the federal government and lives in Fredericton with his wife Leigh, and their children.

For information, excerpts, and free short stories, you can visit him at:

www.SCEston.ca

You can also connect with him on these social media platforms:

Goodreads:	@SCEston
Twitter:	@SCEston
Instagram:	@SteveCEston
Facebook:	@SteveCEston

Did you enjoy

Deficiency

?

Leaving a review on

Amazon.Com
or
Goodreads.Com

is the best way to support an author.

Thank you for your support!